BLUE WALLS FALLING DOWN

PRAISE FOR THE WORK OF JOSHUA HREN

"A rare bird...not just a brilliant novel but, in the truest sense, a divine comedy."
— THE LOS ANGELES REVIEW OF BOOKS review of *Infinite Regress*

"We few, we happy few, who follow the world of Catholic fiction like it's a major league championship, welcome a new frontrunner."
— Australia's CATHOLIC WEEKLY review of *Infinite Regress*

"The mending words of Joshua Hren tickle our word-shaped fancy and testify to truths eternal."
— R.R. RENO, editor of *First Things*

"What an intense read! The novel keeps asking the reader, 'How do you live if you're going to die?' *Infinite Regress* faces the evils and tragedies of our current cultural moment with prophetic eyes."
— JESSICA HOOTEN WILSON

"[The story's] violent eruption recalls O'Connor in the way it turns the funereal into a dreadful, and wholly unsentimental, flash of celebratory joy, detonated by surprise for both character and reader. [This Our Exile is] rooted, also in the cornucopian vitality of a Balzac (memorably referenced in one story) or a Joyce. A whole European cultural tradition is refracted in these unmistakably American pages. In short, there is something for everyone in this engrossing, diverting, and nourishing book."
— THE UNIVERSITY BOOKMAN review of *This Our Exile*

"Hren has a deep moral imagination, but these stories are not mere morality tales. *This Our Exile* is full of contradictions — or, rather, paradoxes...the paradoxes in *This Our Exile* come together to show the reader that exile, the grit of life, is not counterpoint to salvation, but part and parcel to it."
— FIRST THINGS review of *This Our Exile*

"...the novel's most canny feature: penetratingly funny satires of the shallowness of contemporary American life. It surpasses C. S. Lewis's *The Screwtape Letters* in its originality, cunning, speed, and penetration into the mystery of evil."
— THE UNIVERSITY BOOKMAN review of *Infinite Regress*

"...a stunning combination of alliterative verse and a Joycean stream of consciousness reminiscent of *Ulysses*."
— AMERICA MAGAZINE review of *In the Wine Press*

BLUE WALLS
FALLING DOWN

A Novel

JOSHUA HREN

Angelico Press

First published in the USA
by Angelico Press 2024
Copyright © Joshua Hren 2024

For information, address:
Angelico Press, Ltd.
169 Monitor St.
Brooklyn, NY 11222
www.angelicopress.com

ppr 979-8-89280-032-7
cloth 979-8-89280-033-4

Many thanks to the New York Bar Association for the sample legal
document of which my own fictionalized document is in part derivative.

Grateful acknowledgement is made to the following,
excerpts of which appear throughout the novel:

Miles Davis, *Kind of Blue*

H.D., *The Walls Do Not Fall*

Bob Dylan, "Love Minus Zero/No Limit"

Frantz Fanon, *The Wretched of the Earth*,
translated by Constance Farrington

Plato, *The Symposium*, Benjamin Jowett translation

The Cure, "10:15 Saturday Night"

Nirvana, "Smells Like Teen Spirit"

Shakespeare, *Henry IV Part 2*

"Ninna Nanna," Italian folk song
translated by Andrew Frisardi

T.S. Eliot, *Four Quartets*

"Joshua Fit the Battle of Jericho,"
African American Spiritual

Cover Painting:
"Gypsy Woman with Baby," by Amedeo Modigliani
Book and cover design by Michael Schrauzer

For Vin and Vince,
these finite words —
low frequencies —
these *cris de coeur*

The direct deed is the most meaningful reflection.
                    — Bill Evans, from the liner notes
                         of Miles Davis's *Kind of Blue*

It's always night, or we wouldn't need light.
                    — Thelonious Monk

          there, as here, ruin opens
          the tomb, the temple; enter,
          there as here, there are no doors:

          the shrine lies open to the sky,
          the rain falls, here, there
          sand drifts; eternity endures:

          ruin everywhere, yet as the fallen roof
          leaves the sealed room
          open to the air,

          so, through our desolation,
          thoughts stir, inspiration stalks us
          through gloom:
                    — H. D., *The Walls Do Not Fall*

PART I

. . .

My love she speaks like silence,
Without ideals or violence,
She doesn't have to say she's faithful,
Yet she's true, like ice, like fire.
People carry roses,
Make promises by the hours,
My love she laughs like the flowers,
Valentines can't buy her.
— Bob Dylan,
"Love Minus Zero/No Limit"

STARTLED, STELLA LIFTED HER MOUTH FROM THE poorly-tined knot of home-made noodles, face blotched with sauce like a baby's, like the child she might never have, ever, as the years when cycles begin again in blood were almost gone, and the pain, the pain every time she bought a pack of pads, shaking her head at the monies she would save when the fertile flow of blood finally stopped. Looking at the wall where the off white paint peeled away to reveal a cloudy blue, she could sense her chances petering out as she picked up a napkin stitched with her name and a constellation she had never seen in the real night sky because Nonna had invented the little black stars that circled the elaborate S. She felt bad as she wiped the stain of sauce from her nose, an offense against the orderly pattern, and Nonna rapped the magazine again, this time on the temple, lightly, playfully, but Stella was dabbing a fleck of red pepper from the corner of her eye, a blight of blood on Nonna's white napkin. A petal of rose between the stellar geometries.

She stared at the scroll as Nonna unfurled it — black and white with tiny print — and fixed on a picture of a young girl, nervous, chalking an answer on a used blackboard, a canvas of question and answer gone gray, squinting to see if she could read the equation, solve it too, check the answer, adopting the girl's hard questions as her own, leaving uneaten the outer circle of angel hair noodles she never could order at restaurants anymore because trying to chew them with proper politeness led, without question, to public choking, standing up silent before total strangers and asking, wordless, for somebody's Heimlich, like a student called to the front of the class to give an answer she cannot figure.

Here — all familiar — she'd been slurping rudely at a Sunday dinner around the circular table that typically also seated Mom and Dad, but they were out (on their anniversary!) visiting her brother

3

at St. Joseph's Hospital, the old wing on Center Street. A stranger, lately, to the Tęsknota family, "the kid who's been denied what kindness? what want? washed up overdosed on opioids, my son, a statistic, a statistic, my son." Her father's face had been fallen, as if frightened, of what "my God!" he might do to Jacob — kiss him or kill him — as he pushed out the door, left it swinging on the shrill hinges instead of slamming the ancient thing shut, letting the chill into Nonna's stone walls. As Stella had coaxed the groaning screen closed she'd seen her mother's hand lift a little in something like a wave from the passenger seat.

Nonna handed Stella a cerulean napkin, intoned an "*asperges me*" under her breath, then seized the occasion of intimacy to curve the magazine into a telescope and — though you could get her to spit in her own hand if you mentioned the psychic's shop on Bherstr Boulevard — peered into the untold tense: "Stella, I have a fortune to tell you. In this Year of Our Lord — oh *mea culpa*, what year we are?" — "Two thousand eighteen?" "Ah, *ingannato*, you think I don't know. *Stellina, tesorina mia*, I schooled you, a test. Good omen: you passed. Now here's your forecast. You can pay me later. It's vague enough to fit anyone. In the words of my Nonna forever ago: 'Forever the power apparent in lots'!" Stella shook her head, smiled, shut her eyes, felt the burn of garlic when she rubbed them, wet the napkin and soothed, repeatedly, on the rough cloth corner, her stinging — *what if I'm blind?* — orbs of sight. "Nonna please, you're killing me. I'm dying of suspense. I want my money's worth." "*Ordinary Woman Does the Extraordinary!*" Nonna pulled the cylindrical magazine away, in slow motion, from her socket and watched it split in two in her hands — "Bad binding, all's now made cheap! Not a bad omen, no superstition!" — crossed the curling halves of the fortune scope over the wooden bowl that contained a little day-old half crust from the past. "My future," Nonna said, shaking her head in distracted disappointment. "My future, however, is baking bread." The faint blue circle around Nonna's eye swelled like a bruise when she failed to find sleep. "No, *di' di no, di' di no* to self-pity." She intoned with all the solemnity of a sacrament: "I do declare before God and man, and before this young lady who

4

says she's getting old in this Year of Our Lord whose number she knows but I, forgive me, have forgotten already, that this is the year, so fated, in which the scroll here laid out shall be fulfilled: *Ordinary Woman Does the Extraordinary!*"

And then she unfurled the future through a feature on St. Cabrini's school, a success story in South Chicago, which seemed like a sign because her mother's whole side shared the name of the American saint. "The name of a saint, but all the spice of an Italian princess got mixed into Nonna and nobody else," her mother had said, always nervous, a little cold, looking older than her years in the last several, ever since Stella's brother started to disappear, then reappear, in repetition, her mother legally as Polish as cabbage rolls and cucumber salad, the kvass fermented in the basement dark and then bloomed into a biting ginger that overpowered the cherry flavor, the bitter brightness sending shivering synapses running laps through your brain's backwoods, or the famous borscht Dad cooked on low flame even through the night all Christmas week, the steam like a life breath rising from the red broth, the breathtaking purple of slow-simmered beets — staining the napkins when you wiped your lips clean — nature's lipstick, which made her look lush like the spaghetti sauce now spread thinly as Nonna's old rouge on her almost forty-year-old face. She laughed when Nonna held her palm out and said "You think the future's cheap? A penny for your fate, please, *tesorina mia*. You know the laborer deserves her keep!"

Stella searched her pockets but came up empty. She pressed her hand against Nonna's palm, tried not to cry when she ran her finger through a dried red furrow and felt there the lifetime of loss. "You need some aloe! How doesn't that hurt constantly?"

"Don't you dare pity me. I'm happy. If you want to feel bad then make yourself helpful. We'll pick some aloe from the plant on that pane. None of this bottle kind with alcohol in it — stings like hell instead of being a salve."

Standing at the sink without the stool that used to be there, Stella could barely reach the half dead plant. She broke a triangle off a still-living tip and the snap left her scared. A thief of life.

5

Shaking her head, trying to smile, she took from the cupboard the blue plastic cup that was hers — not her brother's or cousins', in childhood — and filled what felt like a thimble to the brim, so small compared to her too-tall mug brimmed with a constant pour of tea, taking a sip of the lukewarm water. As she tossed the empty cup into the sink she saw, reflected in the dirty dish water, whatever was left of a woman who has spent the better part of a decade doing time in a stasis Nonna had called paralysis. She sat back down with the thieved aloe, shoved a bitten nail through the tough green skin, revealing, slowly, the translucent center.

"No. Now. We'll get to that later. I'm not in pain like you like to pretend. But if you're in the business of loving you can do the dishes, too, really, if you've any pulse of a heart left in you." She shook her head, hitting her replaced hip on the brown chair arm as she lowered herself next to Stella. "But first I'm so stuck on this crossword I'm afraid — don't tell me if so — my mind's gone. Look here. Look. Look. Found BLUE. Found WALLS. Found FALLING. Found DOWN. But the words don't add up. The meaning is missing."

Stella squinted, scrutinized the puzzle, but her eyes wandered to the girl at the chalkboard, glossy sad eyes trying to smile, trying to figure the missing meaning.

. . .

After another quiet month making bouquets for Miss Beat's, the staple florist shop on Silva St., after wandering evenings like an apparition in the squared circles of Milwaukee's Bay View blocks, she applied to be certified over the summer and passed the psychological test (said the doctor, off the record) with the equivalent, if our minds could be graded, of a C+. The whole ordeal of qualifying revealed how desperate they were for teachers and how hard she had to suppress that sense of superfluity through an awkward interview where she sipped from Styrofoam and bit a white wedge and swallowed it quick rather than spit the mistake out as refuse, and the principal, knees nervous, complimented her "clear love of learning, a love that will easily become infectious for students

6

who haven't been taught to love," tried to suppress the sense that her wrist was wearing a Dead on Arrival diagnosis when she stood there on the first day of school and feigned the seasoned face of an elder, nearly forty thank God thirty-nine, a few more years to find a man to make the baby she had meant to make with Blake before he disappeared, before she stood here nearly forty feeling like a fifth-grader being graded on a speech she'd forgotten to memorize until she wiped from her eyes the need to somehow apologize for sins of every generation that had conspired — across the centuries, across the continents — to fate her students to such fraught lives, such freighted, impossibly weighted heads that hung from spines like heavy grapes, low hanging through the school day's seven hours, begging to be taken for granted.

"They tell me," she told them, "that you don't know how to read. That you can't do math beyond basic addition. I don't believe it and neither should you: as if your futures were already arrested to a mean *moira*, an irreversible fate." As she said this and scratched out an equation with chalk that whitened her fingers the color of sheep fleece, and when she called Paulo to the front of the class to solve it and show his proofs, too, a cinematic loop played against her eyelids: a series of lynched ghosts hung low, blew, from an over-determined tree not of life and neither of knowledge but of — she turned away and blinked — certain death. Paulo, who shielded his steps as he took them, shadowed his scrawling with a free hand, proved her wrong at the board: 3.33 was precisely the answer.

· · ·

Jackie Vettrano had told Stella the first year was always the worst — "it sifts the serious souls from amateurs" — so she stayed for a second to prove them wrong. Midway through, though, in early January, when the frequency of her useless demerits had decreased to perhaps one per week, P. C. came to the school to mend the psyches of students she had learned how to tolerate but, she told Jackie, "not really care for. It's too hard to care when you're hated so much. You know?" Jackie had sniffled and shook her head no. "No, to be frank, I don't."

7

She stayed away from his office for months, shy and stupid and sure to disappoint until, in March, on a strange balmy day when the sudden flowers spoke of fertility, like one of the teenagers she was hired to teach, Stella had passed the principal's office late one night after a grading frenzy and, seeing no light on, had looked both ways before taking out a permanent marker and crossing out the Not on the sticker that said *Self-Care is Not Selfish*. Foolish — she shook her head — both what she did and what she removed. Surrounded always by teenage troubles, had she absorbed, by osmosis, their vandal pettiness? But then she saw the sign, dark blue and hand-written with a strange calligraphic care, posted to the psychologist's quarters: Mr. Peter Clavier, Master of Science in Counseling. His name was little, but the title was so small she had to strain to read it. Analyze the analyzer. Once they had advanced such a science: that the way you scrawled said such and such and such and such about your psyche. Graphology: textbook graphs of your soul's own shape. Lacking an audience, she laughed at her joke, let out an exhale that whistled too loudly, and unwrapped a concave blue menthol drop, surrogate for the cigarettes she had quit last year but never ceased to crave. Although she had heard the principal pronounce the name each Tuesday and Friday for weeks, at once and only now did she find in his name a familiar resonance, and she stood up taller, straightening her hair on the threshold of fame. She had meant to come into courage enough to knock each day since they announced his arrival.

She had first heard P. C. on public radio, before a surge of syncopated jazz and after the host lavished him with praise: he had abandoned his quick-comet trajectory with Color Consciousness, an outfit that fought optimistic "color-blindness," and disappeared for the better part of a year. His articles on South Chicago funerals and the failed collective bargaining in the final days of Chicago's steel industry had been recognized at the highest levels as possessing a disarming sincerity sewn through the lost preoccupations of old-school labor that — he explained to the interviewer, who asked him to describe his youthful aspirations — "aimed to recover that old conjunction of material conditions and concerns of the

8

spirit, home ownership, and decent wages that had for decades been not so much outsourced as eclipsed by the new cosmologies of the digital sky and the *de facto* globalism that our elite treat us like idiots for calling into impious question. I got — I mean, my whole reason for getting into this —"

"The movement?"

"Well, if you like, but, I'd rather mean the work I'm doing, day after day, which is all I can speak to or answer for, actually . . . the whole reason I got into counseling is frankly that I was getting suicidal after attending too many funerals — my uncles, my cousins, my childhood friends — can't tell you how many lost to overdose or accidents, gunshots or prison stabbings — and, don't know why but it seemed the only way up was down, the only way through this surplus of death was not to turn away but attend, look unflinchingly at the dead faces and the faces of their families as they made sense of the senseless."

When the public radio reporter (her name was Charmaine, or was it Charm?) had asked him to define the "new cosmology," he'd smiled through the microphone — you could hear the curt, censored laugh — and said "Excuse the bluntness, miss. Don't take me for smoking a Phillies Blunt laced with weed and maybe crack. But almost everything that your show stands for."

"And this was after you quit playing jazz?" She pivoted quickly to that hidden year when he disappeared into New Orleans slums to serve the victims of Hurricane Corrina.

His voice was smooth, like a slow-paddled boat over once-troubled waters now calm, almost lazily stretching out the oars — unneeded because the current would carry him, but dipping one in to stir the waters nonetheless — *"And I'd been writing for The Bullet for bout a year at that point and mainly my beat was covering homicides and involuntary manslaughter, which turned into funerals and what this terrible tapestry of caskets revealed about our community's acclimation to Death, the sick acceptance through apotheosis —"*

"— by which you mean?"

"the specter of religion, but the string of children's not-inevitable deaths, not willed or fated but so obviously preventable, this got to me, made me,

9

as my uncle says, twitchy, and so I'd switched toward the end to chasing the ghost of industry instead — "

"Because what was it about the deaths that you discovered — "

"I can't, it'd take a whole hour, but the crux was that people'd started to look forward to the weekly funeral, as a ritual, as a means of catharsis for all kinds of chaos that was threatening to drive them crazy. Beside the basic fact that most of the latter being killings of women and little girls, I remember, I knew I'd been in the trenches too long when I first got this sick kick out of the fact that most of the slaughtered were not men at all, but what really proved I was past due to duck out of that line of work was the repeated dream I had — mind you, at this point I couldn't even keep up with covering the murders, more than one per day, though sometimes I'd step into one funeral parlor, pay my respects, flash the press badge to show the parents that, I don't know, someone gave a damn and was watching what was happening, like God but more human, more helpless, but at least here, as witness to their suffering, because, as one of the mothers had moaned, mid-eulogy, at a funeral that lasted five hours, God's closed his eyes, done turned away in the fullness a time, even He can't take what we're seeing, so I don't know how we expected to. Round that time the dreams started, and my palms would stay clammy for the whole next day, check, no fever, check again, no fever, chew on an aspirin, no difference — like something, some deep dread, could find no other way out and was demanding a fair trial in my dreams and in my bloodstream because — fair enough — I was ignoring the heart and the cost of the killings because after the first dozen it was either harden or panic, pull over to the side of the road, when, you know, you're supposed to be on the beat. I mean the heat of Chicago summers sans air-conditioner, in a car whose radiator you gotta water every morning if you wanna keep it moving. And too many times I was sidelined there, sitting in the idling car with a face numb, forcing myself to breathe, feeling — how else can I put it? — funerary. Started seeing a psychiatrist and popping some prescribed pills, and something about feeling halfway fixed by him, by the medicine, seeing how real the materiality of our minds is, the way a cocktail of chemicals really can, fairly quickly, repair what in other ages would have remained broken 'til the grave or at best healed over the course of decades — well, that amazed me, lit under my lazy ass like the blue flames under mamma's tea kettle, got me starting the night-school Masters in Counseling, but none of that stopped this repeated dream which swung down on my sleeping body at three a.m. every single night for nine months straight: I walk into the back of the church, see my Uncle Cedric muttering something I can't make out, but he's muttering it matter of fact and his eyes keep lifting up to me to answer a question he keeps posing until he drops his head and stops looking to me, bent over a closed casket, and whatever he's mumbling is picked up by the women — all women — who are gathered closest to the podium and the closed casket . . . and then my mama stands on top of a pew and turns around so all can see and hear and starts berating herself for what she should have done for her son, how she hated the idea of teaching him how to wield a gun but she would have done better had she bit the bullet and half the congregation says Amen! and the other half say Get Behind Me, Satan! But she's shaking her head and her body's convulsing, closing in on itself like a crocus, her blouse not black even but purple like a flower and she castigates Nobody else but myself for all the little negligences, the missed dinners and midnight visitors, until one by one others chime in to rebuke her and volunteer their own faults, all the things they could have done but didn't for the woman's dead son and I'm just leaning on the banister in the back and feeling happier than I've ever felt to hear the praises of the dead boy gone who was me, greedy, gluttonous really, feeding on their pampering admissions like a starved, big-bellied, third-world orphan, like hoping they never stop this madness but marathon the chain of confessions until morning, all these affirmations like adornments I'm pocketing to pull out later and the dream remains always the same with me walking out before they finish praising me because I know it cannot go on forever but if I leave while they still going strong it'll feel kind of like an endlessness preserved, perpetual, like after I'm gone they'll always be going on and somewhere — no matter that everywhere else no one cares — there's a circle of people concentrated on someone who could die and not be noticed by the millions whose gazes are understandably else-where, and so I woke up every morning hocked up on happiness, I mean ridiculously giddy, and not because in the dream I was dead but now — lo and behold — life, no, not that, not so fast: because I was siphoning the benefits of my own f-ing funeral without having to pass away, because instead of meeting Rhadamanthus or Minos or St. Peter I woke into the same lifetime, as if this life were what's eternal, never-ending, an infinite process or regress or what you will, and without willing we're all thrown down to die and live and live and die in an endless regress, a helix swirl, like a loose screw with a sharp edge, see?

[Silence. Silence. "Hold. Peter. Hold, no, please I apologize, hold the commercial, Maxwell, please."]

"But then by the time the workday started and I was driving from crime scene to parlor to crime scene to parlor like a maze rat, repeat, or later haunting the abandoned factories and plants that had given the city its solidity, its towers and streets, to say nothing of the significance of steel shaped by so many local works, giving millions of Chicagoans something to eat — well the dream, the damn dream, something so unreal, a profusion of illusions that seized my sleep, this weirdly discolored the work I was doing, so that the funerals started to seem like these chances for everybody to vomit, to get it all out with an excuse, for free (except it cost, its price tag was a life, an f-ing life, like, like, my uncle's God — just think just think of what it cost the families, all those families), to say the shit both good and bad they wouldn't couldn't whatever say otherwise — no I won't say couldn't, 'cause what's not possible if you push past the pain — but wouldn't make another way to, because this was easiest, a cloak of tragedy, a way to be excused and praised . . . but this kind of cynicism made me sick, and I knew I needed a new line of work and I'd saved enough from the pieces I'd published in the past year, some big glossies and a half dozen in The Chimes — and stepped back from the funeral beat, which had slowed to a trickle when I shifted to factories but which I could not shake 'cause a fascination with what I witnessed — the kiss of bliss and death — had become an addiction, an obsession until I quit, cold, failed to fulfill the story I told my editor I'd cover, I let the sixteen-year-old who'd died in the passenger seat of a Buick stolen by her boyfriend who was fifteen and was going fifty down a side street, let them work out their own salvation, denied them the dignity of my megaphone — so to speak — and that night, I swear that very night, the dream visited one final time, albeit with a . . . twist.

"At this point the thing had become elaborate, people paid to buy tickets to the funeral, and they seized the rare and precious chance to wail without being told to shush, to let it all out without having to blush, but my Uncle spies the scalpers at the entrance, hawking tickets for a month's worth of rent, people throwing down dough like it's nothing, hurrying up to wait in line, and he raises his hands like a regular maestro and orchestrates this perfect silence, a totally awesome, impossible sound. When he hangs his head to pray, palms out, the podium falls flat horizontal, looks straight up like a wooden casket, and everybody who was standing in line walks into it and disappears out of sight. And then he puts his hands in his pockets, but not because he's searching for something, more like he's stepping back, restraining himself, almost, like, and his lips are clamped, unmoving, no noise, but it's clear that he's praying, until — get ready — the child I was rises from the casket with the same unremarkable taking-it-all-for-granted demeanor of a boy who's just had a sound night of sleep, and he walks down the aisle straight towards me and holds out his hand and says 'Always wanted to meet you dad, to meet the man behind the fad, the greatest practical joke ever played: pretending that you didn't exist, or pretending that I didn't exist, depending on which way you look at it, but meanwhile you're alive and well, sure, sure, bad cholesterol, blood pressure medication, but all in all alive, which meant that I had to be you, old man, to play dad to myself, dad. You mad? Get mad, because I — my fault, this message is meant for . . . I mean, sure you can do the bloodwork, you can prove the genes we wear is the same, but you, Sir, who sired me, you didn't even bother to fight, to wage a custody war to keep me, no, no, father, no, no, you're not no father, you're farther from a father than some anonymous ignoramus who, without knowing it, on a weeknight impregnates and exits without calling — or knowing — her name!' Now tell me, Charmaine, if you were handed that ticket what would you do for the rest of your life? For me it was a lifetime pass through the thicket of consciousness, not an eschewing of the Color I'd been fighting for, but a new thesis that material things like wages and whatnot was not the core trouble that was killing, too quick for comfort, my people."

Stella had been spellbound by P. C.'s voice when he launched into an imitation of the kinds of folks that he found in the submerged streets of New Orleans he was almost absorbed by, disappeared behind, someone else's voice: "'Listening to water levels rising and the ocean's tongue lashing against the bay windows, cans of paint clanking and spilling white all over and pickled jars breaking while your eight-year-old

("*Idiot! Stop it! Idiot!*") *is running in circles around them and screaming* OWWWW *oh God he's bleeding, barefoot, where are the new shoes I just bought him, he's hopping on one leg beyond your arm's reach because all your concentration is needed to balance the baby you thought you were too old to have, not that, I mean, some women even have them at forty-five, my auntie had one at forty-eight (he couldn't talk, the kid she bore), but after your, by your I mean my, my first husband died of diabetes — I know this sounds like a . . . pity party, but, heh, that's what I pay you for!? Damned if I could afford your services, sir, without the aid of . . . Anyhow, but it's as damn straight true as the ocean is blue, sugar, sheeat — okay, it wasn't exactly the disease but Mister's own negligence, nodding off without insulin, and then all that, enough for four lifetimes, and you have to start over again, all it took to make a home with your second husband, and ain't no way to wring the old one from the flood, not that you'd want to take up residence there, where your first husband died because his foot was so swollen he couldn't get down the stairs in time,'* I mean this is the sort of story I'd hear, day after day, year after year, down there, and I mean once you start listening and trying to sort out some semblance of sense from these, these *stuck lives*, I mean, paralyzed lives whose truth is tied to so many lies, tied in double and triple knots, it's hard to ever imagine stopping because walking away feels like a kind of . . . no, not guilt, but like this weird thing that doesn't make you guilty but also is kind of criminal, I mean, if you happened, by chance or whatever arrangement, to *not* have been through all of that, then what does it mean to be answerable for what you now know? But then on the other hand there's a kind of . . . I guess you could put it like that, Savior-complex, but it's much more complex because the whole time I was down there I knew, more than before and after, how inadequate I was to the task, how much I *wasn't* a savior, a fixer, just like when I was at the end of my days as a jazz musician and I realized my talent lay more with mixing others' instruments than blowing on my own damn horn, but I do think it's not wrong to say we need more young people to train in psychology because, look around without the aid of a stiff drink: the world's not getting any more sane on its own — though" — and his exhale was three pages long — "whether the legions of therapists are equipped to heal the madness is not clear to me."

P. C. came to St. Cabrini pro bono every Tuesday and Friday, sat for hours in the makeshift nurse's room, a refurbished janitor's closet and what had last year been the anteroom of the principal's office until Mr. Atkins took a leave of absence. After days of redundant announcements, nasal invitations wrapped in loud-speaker crackle, predictable slogans that cajoled students to stop on in and spill their troubles to the counselor during study hall ("everybody hurts sometimes"), his clientele tally could be counted on one hand.

"You may not even know that you're struggling," said the principal, an interim substitute hired in an emergency when Mr. Atkins took a mental health leave of absence. Miss Halves' appearance had rankled faculty, inciting several mid-semester resignations. The exiting teachers, who had met in the basement and banded together in a fit of discontent, said they "would rather go back to corporate newsletters . . . flipping burgers . . . nursing-home laundry . . . than work for a real live walking bitch," and an evening session of muttered complaints grew hotter when Patrice Snow from Second Grade B said if they wanted to be taken seriously they would have to assemble a substantial list of real and consequential damage done. Her advice won no standing ovation but incited a shouting match between two other opponents who gestured toward the supposedly obvious: the irritations of Miss Halves' appearance would coincide, in the official narrative, only by accident with their mass exit, because after they lashed Miss Halves with accusations not a one was willing to file formal complaints. To keep their careers, they planned to cite vague personal issues, defensible quests for self-fulfillment without telling Miss Halves to her face how capacious she was at sieving morale, because who could secure a new position without the former boss's recommendation? No one would reiterate Snow's allegation, which the shouting match had failed to garble so that every tallied head at the meeting had heard the verifiable gossip from the sore throat of Second Grade B (strep was circulating through her class, but she had tested negative, she said): "Yes, I get it, Atkins left without notice, but why replace him with someone whose only educational experience consists of 'Wellness Seminars' held in her Highland Park home? Why? I'll tell you why. She's the chairman of the board's sister-in-law — sister-in-law, I said, I didn't say out loud the chairman's lover."

Even the least conspiratorial conceded that Miss Halves had appeared in St. Cabrini's like an alien from an alternate reality. As she stood in front of the rusted-out white radiator Atkins had recovered from the foreclosed steel factory, her tan glowed a radiant, ripened mango that could not be acquired in the Sloan Street manicure — the booth next to Psychic Mama and across the street from the heroin house kitty-corner to St. Cabrini. Her sun-charged skin boasted frequent escapes to private islands whose never-heard names bespoke utopia or maybe, for a day trip, a Florida shoreline that for most, here, was as other-worldly as Eden's ancient, well-guarded garden.

"Shit I bet she got that tan from the angel's fiery sword," said Bee, and Stella recollected the cardboard Bible her Nonna read on repeat from the time she was two until her fourth birthday, at which point her girl self had held up her hand and said with an eye roll she'd learned from her brother, "Nonna, I'm not little no more," to which her Nonna, twitching and tsking and pinching Stella's cheek, said "Not 'not no more' anymore," and smiled, slipping the cardboard Bible beneath her bottom and pulling out a mildewed Missal and reading from the Latin without explanation. Stella shot back to Bee, directly: "Bee, please, we're not little no more." No one seemed to know what she meant: their eyes, as ever, said O *Stella*. She did not really begrudge the lady the others tarred and feathered with such naked pleasure (no one even placed a fig leaf over the defamations). Not that the lampoons were mostly lies. What lawyer could charge them with calumny for claims so clichéd, so ready-made: Mrs. Halves was astute, aware of the human resource of her cuteness, shaped by catalogue-cutting-edge fashion that asserted not only all thirty of her years but also, as if time could be sprayed still via fixative, the first shy bloom of faintly erotic adolescence. Sipping mochas from an ergonomic chair ordered with what donor's dollars, and sprinkling obligatory self-care cautions over every meeting and all-school assembly, she was spurned by everyone except for Stella, who saw in her a funhouse mirror that threw back a warped but familiar incompetence.

"Sometimes it takes someone else to show us how badly we are really doing. An outside eye," Miss Halves counseled through a hand-held microphone, standing atop the cafeteria stairs from which she made announcements to children lost in chocolate milk cartons.

Stella stepped away, disgusted with her own tongue, which tasted like the bitter apple of cider vinegar she took for migraines.

. . .

Circling back to her selfish crisscross — still there three days later — gripping the brown bag she had reused for a week, noting only now the rotten apple stain that must have been from last Friday and covering it quickly with her widening hand, she rushed away from P. C.'s closed door, then tiptoed in the opposite direction toward Catherine Vettrano's office, rehearsing the various registers she might take — an abstract question about classroom discipline or uncensored confession of her utter incompetence: "In situations where most of the students bring no books, no paper, no pencils, and not even an eraser, what is the disciplinary best practice, since you can't send your whole class to the principal? Not every day, anyway." Or: "Jackie" (no one knew why, but Catherine went by Jackie), "I'm not one for ugly self-berating. That kind of, what's the word?"—"Excoriation?"—"Yes, I knew you'd know, strikes me as almost always"—"Disingenuous?"—"Yes!" And then Jackie would deliver the pleasing consequence, which meant that they could talk calmly and at length about her mishaps as if there were, in fact, a way, still, to be a good teacher.

Stella could hear the pleasing remedy, a safeguard against the yearling's despair: "If you're going to last in this line of work, you can have no truck with that harsh cover for the hard work that needs to be done with patience and without self-indulgence, like the way you'd take a kit of delicate swabs and brushes to cleanse a rare painting, softly, so as to bring out the brightness, treading with such care, as if you could ruin the picture if you pushed too hard at any pass."

17

Stella lifted her feet by bending at the knee and letting her legs down in a demi-plié, the way she did in grade school — she smiled — before her parents pulled her out when the performances scattered like satellites across states and even across the ocean. Too serious for a ten-year-old. An amateur, she scuffed her toes at Jackie's threshold.

Jackie gripped her armrests and jumped. Her chair rolled into the desk.

"I'm sorry, I mean. I meant to not trouble you. Tried to be quiet because —"

"How would that help? A silence, I mean, some kind of stealth?" Jackie always incorporated your words into her replies. Her canvas shoes were dilapidated. She wore an oversize collared T-shirt that said St. Cabrini in black against the red. Her bulldog eyes were circled by a sadness that did not dim their hazel glow; her mouth chewed the customary gum taken from confiscated packs (she made it a boast, her endless supply, smacked her chaw in front of the classes, said "Every infraction works in my favor." At one of the assemblies an eighth-grader formed a megaphone with cupped fingers and cried "Like the cops did with my brothers' weed," to which Jackie (Mrs. Vettrano) pulled out a lighter and a package of gum shaped in cigarette cylinders and lit one on fire before she waved it out, but the smoke set off a series of sprinklers that dampened the wonder bread and bags of a hundred children, who complained to their parents, who complained to the principal, who again assumed a podium at lunch and said to the dry and gathered children: "If you rain on my parade again I'll assign a long-division problem that if you don't solve by the end of detention you'll be scrubbing the floor with the fabled toothbrush which — I'm pleased to say — we have plenty of after that charity visit from the dental office."

Later in the classroom, when the same eighth-grader mumbled loudly about her "bad breath," Mrs. Vettrano, a husky lady, walked the boy in front of the room and had him recite from a piece of paper the entire poem of "Ozymandias."

It was during this recitation that Peter had walked in on his lunch break, as the boy declaimed with a fervor he had only

18

attained after Jackie had put him through seven iterations, each of which, she complained, had been "said without passion, like you're reading a laundry list." Now the boy forced verve from skinny rib edges as the class, stunned into quiet, at last heard him:

> My name is Ozymandias, King of Kings;
> Look on my Works, ye Mighty, and despair!
> Nothing beside remains. Round the decay
> Of that colossal Wreck, boundless and bare
> The lone and level sands stretch far away.

Peter looked on, arms akimbo, hungry to take a crook or umbrella and remove the boy from the cruel comedy, but at the moment the delinquent said the Round the decay Jackie saw Clavier — though she'd not known his name — nodding his head to a round of applause.

This time, after Stella confided the latest rearrangements of chaos in what she called the war zone of the classroom, Jackie said "I'm sorry, but I think in spite of my brashness you'd do well to listen to me. I've seen it all, have seen hundreds come and go, and I think at year's end you'd better stop teaching here. I say this without condemnation. I say it for the sake of our children, because some who come here simply can't handle them, and to pretend that you can when you can't could harm them — and you. Each passing week you'll inch closer to a nervous breakdown. Stella I don't think you should take this personally. If I tried to be a nuclear physicist the earth would be decimated by now. One thing I've been wondering for a while now is why are you not married? You may not be a good teacher but I can readily see you with children."

"Multiple?"

Jackie had closed her eyes. "I can see you."

"See because that's exactly what I've concluded. One child only. I could do that. I could give myself totally to one but not many. It's the being pulled in thirty directions at once that overwhelms."

"Any man would be fortunate to have you."

"I don't need to you say the sugary thing."

"Are you accusing me of being a liar?" she opened her eyes with

19

a bulldog smile, the fierce, fixed wrinkles gave her smile harsh angles hedged by hanging flesh.

"I was nearly married not long ago. It's — not something I want to speak to. Everybody's always asking 'Why aren't you married? You'd make such a good mother.' All I wanted to be was that. Didn't want to do anything. But what I wanted disappeared. Died."

"Forever? I can't — won't try to draw you out. But for all my sins I've seen a lot. What if what you wanted did not die but is only playing dead?"

When Stella nodded *yes* she felt the ache of untruth pulling like sprained muscles. The abstraction of her broken engagement felt like a strange, surreal surgery where the one she knew, the one who had fled, had become easy geometries — a man-made shape you could summon like a ball at recess, upon request. But she could not say aloud his name or start to explain the ordeal, either, not least because she did not know herself where he had disappeared to or whether he was in fact alive, though there was no reason to suppose he'd become a corpse.

Jackie's thumb had a rubber thimble that kept it clean as she corrected papers and helped her flip through the massive pile (she taught all sections of composition that all the other teachers feared or refused) and the washed-out yellow coloration startled Stella, who saw herself reciting "Ozymandias" in an eternity of after-school detentions, and she backed away with a small curtsey that made her feel small, but Jackie received the silent farewell with a warming smile bereft of condescension, a smile purged of all cynical disappointment, a smile that said, before Jackie said it, "God bless you."

Stella left Jackie wiping sweat from her palms onto the ankles of her pants, lifting her legs awkwardly to leave all evidence of anxiety somewhere no one would look or see. Go home. All the way. Milwaukee. But first she needed a drink from the fountain which sprayed and surged an arc against her forehead when she leaned low to cool her face. Slightly dizzy, she had to stay close. No going all the way home. She walked in circles, bereft of direction, returned to the long administrative hallway, passed the only bathroom that way, and thereby lost the easiest excuse as to why she was here and not somewhere else, in the faculty kitchen, where people went, in the case she went clammy again and reversed, a pathetic tactic that felt so familiar since the broken engagement, as if she were acting out, on repeat, Blake's devotion and cryptic departure, that she could almost call it her signature move. She did not want to do that again — the man, the promise, his easy exit. She could not bear a second time the disappointment, the cannon-shot hopes and inevitable decline. But she could not root out what she knew she could do: the baby, *her* baby, she would pay all the pain to pour herself out in that direction, that devotion, for the rest of her life.

But first she needed to find her bearings. There was no way she would turn around now, no playing chicken with the traffic of students who were itching for recess and passing her fast as she ducked from their pressure, jutted quickly into the wide and perpendicular hallway that ended at the principal's office. She could — how would her father put it? — tender her resignation. She made as if to traipse down this hallway with a cooked-up excuse that seemed officious enough (a stack of signed waivers due to the principal, though under her arm now the pulp was softened by sweat — oh shit — after Jackie's judgment).

Across from the principal's well-locked office, which could be occupied though she decided it was vacant, she saw P. C.'s door propped partially open, tiptoed to the threshold and stood there, breathing, listening, hearing an impassioned muttering that at first seemed madness before she realized he was reading aloud:

". . . create a feeling that is extremely uncomfortable, called cognitive dissonance. And because it is so important to protect the core belief, they will rationalize, ignore, and even deny anything that doesn't fit in with the core belief."

She knocked hard, once.

"What the — ?" he said, rising. "I'm sorry, you startled me, that hallway magnifies the slightest footstep, how did you —"

"I didn't want to disturb you," she said. She had come because she felt awful for him, had imagined him there the night before while she finished the last of the bagged lettuce. Felt awful for him and wanted to see if he lived up to the voice she had heard. But he must be making money elsewhere if he could waste every Tuesday and Friday's lucrative hours waiting for kids who never arrived.

"How's business?" she asked, surprised by her own tack. The washed-out blue walls had water streaks that stretched like veins from the ceiling to the floor.

"Freeloaders take for granted what they're given," he laughed back, his eyes lingering on hers, as if watching for a hint. An outside competition of subwoofers shook the window glass until Peter walked there and, laughing in the sun, held the pane until the rattling ceased.

"The kids, my kids, what they really need, I say, from experience, is a strong hand," she grew dizzied by her own exhilarating dare.

He pretended to jot something down, then made real marks on his pad as he said, "You're making my theses too easy to test. The repressions of the oppressor should be harder to tease into the light of day."

"It's been a long one. Week. This whole position, I mean. Has been hard. I'm in over my head most days. A war zone. You know, I'm sure, from dealing with the kids."

"Things have gone well with the ones who came. Surprisingly so. Usually the resistance is a frozen sea no foreign explorer could hope to crack. He'll die before what's under the ice begins to bubble up." He continued to stare into the sun — a dare? or a hothouse flower desperate for photosynthesis?

"Does Lake Michigan freeze over in Chicago?"

"Huhm? Why, you're not from here, then. It can, yes."

"Born and raised in a place called West Allis. 'White trash' section of Milwaukee county. But you're saying that the axe can't break the ice. Or can, but — is it because the profession is a dull blade, or the ice's freeze is just that far beyond us? What? Superhuman? Bodes badly for your profession. I heard you, a couple times, but one in particular, spreading doubts about the strength of your tactics, science, what have you."

"I got at once much more and much less," he said, pursing his lips into sphinxlike puzzlement.

In a smudged picture tacked up behind Peter, a yellow-armed sun with short arms gripped an umbrella and made a toothy grin as a downpour of rain or a maelstrom of asteroids smacked against the sheath and ricocheted away into the finger-painted ether.

"A student made that for me. Maria. You know Mar —"

"Much more and much less." Here she gestured toward the door sign which he was swinging closed behind her, asking with his eyes *do you mind?* and she shook her head — *no, please do* — as she asked, "A *Master of Science in Counseling* — does it leave you cynical, with a hip pose of a higher degree that teaches you really how little you know?" Something about his stance — his jaw? — drew the banter out of her. "I kid. A joke." (His jaw had hardened through the slight upward curves that surrounded his lips like parentheses, that lifted his mouth, lent it levity against the chiseled gravity of his face.) "Mr. P. C. I knew you from before you came, a number of interviews you gave that really moved me, helped me make sense of why I'm here. Didn't know you. Sorry. Knew *of* you. Or — well, I felt I knew you from the things you said. They made so much sense it was like I really did know you, I guess. The session about abandoning your former career — I admit I forgot what you did before — to serve the victims of the Hurricane, when so many had been abandoned."

"It takes an abandoned one to see the abandoned. But seeing isn't the same as really serving. I mean I'm in no place to posture as a savior, I —"

But he could not, would not finish and she knew she should not say "Say more."

"The host," she teased him, "lavished you with praise. And here you're saying you couldn't fix somebody even if you were given a lifetime of trying?"

"I think if you gave me a lifetime I might be able to mend somebody's mind real well." The vent blew a gust that flapped a fold of dead paint whetted by a watermark; like scalp flesh after brain surgery — the procedure Nonna refused to undergo — the piece fell back to hide the crack. "I swear. I've seen healings and fixings you can't fathom. I still can't. Tah. The trouble? All sessions,

23

except for those who can fund a decade's worth, end up being fits and starts. Duct tape, band-aid, what have you."

"You don't believe what you're saying. I mean," she bit her thumb, "excuse me. But that's a talking point."

Peter bent and tucked in the lace of a shoe that looked well-waxed but well lived in. "I like you." He looked out of microscope eyes, near-sighted and nebulous, but their fascination as exercised on her felt good.

"I'm, I'm sorry, I just: I guess I was hoping things were otherwise. Because I think I've got my own problems. I don't need saving or absolution even. Though I'm sure I need both — my Nonna would say. And surely she's right, but I — I'm not ready. I — I'm not. Do you talk with students only, or do you take old ladies?"

"Forgive me, but you don't look a day over eighty."

Stella pulled at her slightly gray-streaked braid of shimmering, buoyant, dark red hair, twirled it under her chin like a girl, sad eyes she knew well from too many mirrors — always when she saw herself she was shocked by the dour pockets around her pupils, but then, always, at once, her lips would lift. The faint freckles she so hated in youth would brighten like a meteor shower that shone with some unspeakable sorrow whose depth scared even her and many away from looking again, or ever, into the playful, peaceable eyes that leapt like children if finally noticed under the jump-rope arcs of her eyebrows. An incongruous face at odds with itself.

"I'm forty. Almost forty-one. Not, actually, for a while, but I feel it." Too soon. "I'm — Stella," here she reached out her hand, retracted it to wipe the sudden sweat, and gripped just the end of his fingers with her thumb. "Can you see someone who's not a student? Shoot. That didn't — I don't mean *see* in that way, but, like, uhck, what am saying, tongue-tied, looking for, not saying what the hell is it called — therapy."

The second her misstep put even a toe tip into anything sexual he drew back, and the muscles of his face went rigid like some rehearsal for rigor mortis.

"You feel bad for me and want to make sure I don't lose my chops?"

In the spirit of honesty that was making her drunk she nodded, "Something like that, I guess."

"I don't blame the kids for staying away. You know how many cases of sexual abuse were reported in Chicago just this last year, school teachers hooking up with students. Violating them?" He rose and paced over to the window, resting his hand on the radiator only to reel when he found it still hot. "Here I am believing in Spring and they're reminding me we're still hunkering through winter. But to the point — more cases of corruption than I care to share. And you think grade schoolers and high schoolers keep it all discreet? So, distrust of adults is like a rite of passage — something you do to show you're not a baby anymore. It's like a brag of maturation, distrust. We call it affective disorders. A bad-way rash of 'em, ma'am."

"God," she said.

The window latch had been poorly attached, and when the window blew open he rose to close it, though they both breathed deep and sighed aloud at the fresh air that filled the room faster than he could move. He let one last blasting gust wake him up before he clamped the clasp down with easy strength.

"I was destined to be a pastor. But my uncle's prophecy backfired. Got the God strain injected the wrong way." Stella finicked with her fingers. "Long story. God. I don't mean to be old hat, here," Peter said, tapping on a table with a pencil that looked lovingly chewed and dull, "and I'm a sucker for songs that hit the high hat with a crazed kind of syncopation, but God appears to be spectating more than intervening. Maybe on intravenous. Life support."

In the several seconds when she closed her eyes Stella saw Nonna in a strange sterile room, IV stuck in her arm, faded red carnation pajamas barely covering her breast as she struggled to rise and stepped, with a struggle, to the hospital's high rise, rectangular window, a narrow aperture of blinding light, and shook her head at what she saw below, but the indulgent pity worked into her face had been replaced with a blinded fury though Stella could not see what she saw.

"Okay," she shot out, unsure what to say.

25

"So," his voice switched, deepening into a mellow note that was soothing and distant at once. Soothing *because* distant? She felt her palm and found it dry.

"Sign this waiver and we're set. Sit down. Please," he said, motioning her to a plain chair whose upholstery had abandoned any pretense of class. The foam spilled out of a tear in the seat, but as she sunk into its softness she smiled, seeing at the same time that his own chair was fit for a short fourth grader. He looked ridiculous hulked at the edge, hands folded over his knees, nowhere to put his long legs so he leaned all the way forward toward her.

She scratched half-legible answers as fast as she could until the form was full and underwrote her gibberish with a signature that waved and swelled with grace.

"Have you received therapy before?" he asked.

"I cut out the talk and went straight for the chemicals. My regular doctor wrote the prescription."

"So you've not seen a psychologist, then?"

"I'm looking at one right now, I suppose."

"Looks like I'm going to be all disappointment. You guess wrong: I'm no more than a *master* of the science. But please, what kind of medicine did you take? Or do you take it, still, now?"

"Vomitus Psychosis. Twenty-five milligrams daily."

"I like to laugh but I can't help you if you —"

"Rationalize and ignore to protect my core belief, keep it in place at all costs even if it kills me."

"At another school this girl came in every day for a session. But she never said what was bothering her. Clear as day she'd been abused, all the signs, nothing missing, but she always talked about how amazing her dad was, how her friends were jealous of his affection for her."

"Okay, you're right. I have this harsh streak, cruelty that hands out jokes like candy, to keep who happy I have no idea. The medicine made me functional, very, very functional. F— that word, though, I'm sorry, but *function*."

"Rage Achilles. Against the machine."

She thought to tell him of her thesis on *Antigone* but censored

26

what he'd surely see as leisurely theatrics. Her whole life felt suddenly unjustified and she could not thumb her sleeve bead back through the shrunken buttonhole.

"Why so many of us are half mad. My guess is it's something like — among other mutations — we're all living under nuclear skies and a million other accruing horrors that, whatever we do to make them normal, ends up bending our nerves to no end — what a boyfriend's brother of mine called 'crossed wires of the mind.' And I guess the theory I just spouted and passed as my own may have been partially his too."

"I'm not an intellectual-property policeman."

"Right. Follow me. Forgive me. At the time, my boyfriend. I mean — we almost got married, but he flaked out. Through the meds, I was . . . made disturbingly functional. I was working as a florist at the time, and I finished all my orders in half the time it usually took."

"Time," Peter said, and Stella looked up at the clock whose second hand spun without a tick, face without guile. "What time was it? In your life, then. I'm trying to follow where you been versus are."

"I worked at the florist from, hmm, ages twenty-six 'til thirty-eight. When he left me."

"Two years ago, then — or almost?"

"Two years ago, then," she repeated. "Almost." A discovery. "I can't believe it wasn't farther back. So much has happened in so short a while."

Something about how the crow's feet alighted at the sleepy corner of his eyes made her feel foolish, as if her flaws were luxuries and her hardships those of a child acclimated to delicate cuisine choking on a half-burnt back-burner dish. "I — mmm, like a spoiled child." Her tone stayed steady but she avoided his face. "The problem was nothing original, I'm sure. None of the lows were abysses any more, not even, really, remarkable valleys. But everything I did was like a blunted knife. Dull as hell. And I stopped feeling bad when I did something wrong."

"Maybe you felt badly beyond what you needed to."

27

"Needed to according to whom? Who dictates the criteria here? That's what's kept me away from the couch. Whose criteria are you using to determine if I'm sane or long gone crazy and what depths do you have to kill to make a person *functional*?"

She stared down a stack of blue books, left over from another era, hand-written essays that ribboned through her mind like a rare score of medieval chant illuminated by an obsessive monk. In college almost all their classes ended with a blue-book exam. The one time she tried that trick here, half of the class walked out (one dangled from the first-floor window, and, while perfectly safe, had to be rescued by a bronze-faced firefighter who seemed not at all irritated, but relishing, rather, this break from the real infernos they tied to put out — temperatures that rivaled hell).

"Seems to me," her tongue finally let loose, "to give a close-to-home example, that most schools have as their end goal *functional incompetence*, that these so-called 'schools' are mainly training grounds for low-level functionaries."

"And why would that be a shock or great revelation? Isn't that what the world they are going into demands, in the main, that they be? Isn't the greatest market demand one for, precisely, unthinking *functionaries*? But, wait, I see what you're up to. Let's not wipe out into some other hell's ditch here. The easiest way to stay trapped in our own flaws is to point out those of others that make us forget the worst of what's inside us. Now, have you been steady on the meds?"

"Me and the meds don't go steady. More like an on-again-off-again love affair."

"Why not try a more moderate dose, that is, if you stopped taking the medicine, which it sounds as though you did — when was this?"

"Two years ago after a decade of dullness. I went back on and off and on. Whatever. You don't know me, Mr. Clavier. I can't do a damn thing by halves, partially, without coming out worse. Flowers, for instance."

"Flowers?"

"How familiar are you with flowers?"

"Hmm," and here he leaned back but the chair creaked as if about to crack. He went slack, long legs dangling down. "I didn't see many until I was a teenager, but when my mom married her second husband our table had a bouquet every Friday. Very, very pretty, but florist industry's a racket, right?"

"Once a florist always a florist."

"Until you realized it was a racket?" he pleaded, hitting his forehead with the heel of his palm.

The clamped-down chaos at the edge of her eyes could only be called fury.

"I'm sorry, I. I'm sorry, ma'am. You seemed to appreciate a good joke."

"Stella. And yes, I appreciate a *good* joke. But florist racket isn't a funny one. Tired, cliché. And besides, whatever you say, flowers in my home city of Milwaukee mid-winter are worth whatever the going price-gouge is. And don't tell me I'm speaking from privilege. I made for most of my adult life a little more than a thousand per month."

That she wasn't the only one who'd said something regrettable was a sudden source of solace.

"Right, I saw from the paper."

She perked up. "What paper? The *Tribune?*"

"Aw, the *Chicago Tribune*. Don't make me get nostalgic. Have I got stories to tell you! (I lived, for a time, in the Tribune building.) But no, not in the paper. Which is, I assure you, nothing but what my uncle would call a blessing from God. I know your history from the form you filled out, this here," he waved it like an authoritative flag. "Stella. Nickname: Star. Now I sound like a grade-school kid."

"Your workplace tends to rub off on you. You'd better get out fast if you don't want to find yourself acting a fool like I'm likely to do. Do you ever take time to just be still, to simply *exist* outside of your work, without even a snag or worry or preoccupation dragging you down?"

"A human being can't simply *be*. We — forgive me, I was ruined by my schooling — are always both being and becoming."

29

"You know what I mean."

"No actually not. Words either mean something true, something intelligible, or nothing at all."

"So much for metaphors."

"You know what I mean! We go into the meaning of a metaphor knowing it isn't a literal thing. There's clarity, there, in the mystery."

"Your mastery of digression is . . . what can I call it?"

"An object lesson."

"So you can't, and have never been able to be, to lean towards *being* outside of your work."

"My work *was* a kind of, not meditation or prayer. No. But, maybe, a kind of . . . contemplation. Before the war zone. Peace — but deceptive, or at least subject to an awful decay."

"Peace," said Peter, forging his fingers into a funny hippie sign. "Give me, for clarity's sake if not God's, a good definition."

"Chamomile and hydrangeas arranged around a dozen spray roses. On certain days — what a co-worker called my 'epileptic fits' — a few of these could take me half the morning. My boss at first complained and warned I could be let go if things didn't quicken. A sweet old woman, Louise, a riot. But the harder I tried to finish fast the longer the arrangements took, rotating and coiling and — it's enough, I know, to make you recoil. Already a racket and add thrown-away time, yes, I agree, crazy. Don't get me started on dusty millers and carnations! Heaven. But the symmetry came out scary-level perfect, and the accents and offsets left customers open-mouthed. I know it sounds silly, but it made me so happy to see them so happy over something so small. But when I tried to make an arrangement on meds, they came out fine and totally blasé."

"I see."

"And the meds were for —"

"Anxiety. Sorry — it's with me, still. See: I interrupt you to set things straight, to play what my boyfriend, well, former fiancé —"

"Boyfriend still?" His question came out damp with disappointment.

"No. Sorry. I swear I didn't regress back from husband to fiancé to boyfriend. Blake. My former fiancé who left me — another story, we'll get to someday — called me 'the maestro of the madness.'"

"In my line of work that's about as good as it gets!"

"Millions suffer from anxiety disorders. Is it true or helpful to call it madness?"

"At least you offer a choice between the two?"

"Helpful or true?"

"Can't the truth be helpful?"

"Are you crazy? Can be, sure, but maybe most of the time it's — likely to induce something I'd like to call madness, in little doses or big, depending."

"Oh I see what you're saying."

"Yes. Most times we live like whatever is 'helpful' — whatever that means — is the truest thing to do. And so, thank you, very much, for asking a question that doesn't constrain me into a manufactured answer. It's true. That millions suffer from anxiety disorder doesn't mean the millions are not mad."

"..." Peter flipped the dog-eared, marked-up book he had been reading aloud when she arrived. Wretched was all she could make out of the title, because his fingers crossed the rest like jail bars.

"You agree with me, but your professional strictures prevent you from stating your agreement openly, understandable. If your license were revoked, you couldn't legally take the axe to attack the abominable snowman . . . I mean, that ice-mold that keeps the truth frozen inside us." At this he blinked and leaned back and cracked his neck. She hedged: "I'm sorry. I'm not usually so cynical."

"I tend to bring out folks' best sides, Stella."

"I didn't think I moved here with crazy expectations, didn't pack in my luggage some grand Helper costume that would fix how . . . fucked up these students' lives are. My best friend came from a broken home, and I saw the split between school and family, the way her father and mother's awful tangle spoiled almost everything her best teachers gave her. Like leaving school with a fresh bouquet and then watching it all wilt when you walk in the front door. But I also didn't think I'd sink so fast, or so low. Like not sleeping because I worry about my kids. Students. Justine, yesterday, for example, was quiet and she sat the whole day with her hands in her back pockets even though the bend of her elbows looked painful sitting like that so I asked and she said every morning she walks past a sick crew of dudes who show up no matter how many times she changes her route and they always put their hands in her pockets —"

"I trust you reported it to the principal's office."

"Oh yes, I did, but I've done it before and — what can be done if it's happening again?"

"Isn't that life? Acting as if you can eliminate pains that can't be cooked out of our condition? Spending decades and centuries seeking justice even if it only lasts for a year and is undermined or undone into oblivion far faster than you can fathom without feeling like nothing's worth it . . . but that's only when you forget those decades, those years, those hours when it wasn't so hard to be good in this world, for someone at least, even if not for you."

"I like you," she said, reaching over his shoulder, her breast brushing against his cheek, her fingers confiscating the consent form and ripping it in two, then halving the half and so on until she tossed the contract up in confetti that fell like amateur snowflakes made by some demiurge while God was on life support, rough-edged specks that descended slow and fell to the floor, though more than a handful caught in the halo afro he wore so well.

"You can tell me, now, that you don't, that it's over before it begins. But something is humming in my heart, right now, and I can't not take the risk."

Peter bit at the tip of his pencil and slipped the thin golden wand into the weathered, well-read copy of The Wretched of the Earth.

"I'll be by your place to pick you up. Your address, you mind jotting it here? Waiting outside around — shall we say nine?"

She left then rushed down the hall and turned, tiptoed back and listened at the door crack, tying her shoe as he fell back into the book:

"We have seen that this same violence, though kept very much on the surface all through the colonial period, yet turns in the void." He recited it softly, without rancor, almost like a lover

32

practicing aloud a letter he had not the courage to send. "We have also seen that it is canalized by the emotional outlets of dance and possession by spirits; we have seen how it is exhausted in fratricidal combats. Now the problem is to lay hold of this violence which is changing direction. When formerly it was appeased by myths and exercised its talents in finding fresh ways of committing mass suicide, now new conditions will make possible a completely new line of action."

· · ·

Stella got lost in The Wretched of the Earth, not checked out from the public library since September of 2001 . . . *a string of philosophico-political dissertations on the themes of the rights of peoples to self-determination, the rights of man to freedom from hunger and human dignity, and the unceasing affirmation of the principle: "One man, one vote." The national political parties never lay stress upon the necessity of a trial of armed strength, for the good reason that their objective is not the radical overthrowing of the system. Pacifists and legalists, they are in fact partisans of order, the new order — but to the colonialist bourgeoisie they put bluntly enough the demand which to them is the main one: "Give us more power." On the specific question of violence, the elite are ambiguous. They are violent in their words and reformist in their attitudes . . .* Her father had taken a vague interest in politics and her mother declared no commitments at all, but in these rare, mood-lit leisure hours on her little sapphire couch, flipping through pages with absorbed abandon, Stella felt her sympathies explode, unexpectedly, like Molotov cocktails set off in a quiet place — strange sympathies that blew her heart up.

She took one break to check the calendar, to count each scarlet x since her cycle started, each x a star missing its other points — they were getting erratic, irregular, scary — the marks on the calendar chiseled each one harder, and as she counted with the dead fountain pen the days again, again, again, the tip tore through the year and cut into the cold, concrete wall. Give us less power. Liberate me, please, from me, please, free me from me. By violence, yes, by labor and child, liberate me from the too many ways my mind can wander, my steps can falter. Demand my attention in one direction. I'll pay it, I promise. I'll pay attention.

She stopped, startled. Who was she pleading with? She went back to the book but the words now lost their startling power.

At quarter after nine she checked the time and descended to meet him, pulling her V-neck blue blouse down as she did, coated in cool sweat before she reached the outer door.

Peter Clavier wore his favorite suspenders — a bright striped red crisscross pulled tight around a bleached, starched shirt — his belly hanging slightly over his belt, his Malcolm X glasses just barely too small to properly latch around his ears, cheap plastic lenses mirroring the blared halogens that hovered over them like searchlight security converted into a colorful key — purples and blues up and down the street — a leftover Christmas decoration the neighborhood council had approved and now it was early March without a single light replaced.

"I'm sorry, so sorry, I'm late."

"Grading?"

"Getting schooled," she said, and smiled.

She looked across the street where a bent-over woman pushed a stroller with twins, resting her chin on the back handles and letting her arms hang straight down. *That* was the pain she really wanted. Not this trying to fix Chicago.

"Anyhow no harm. No time lost. It's always possible to try and do some thinking."

She did not cite a line or ask him a question though the lesson scared and thrilled her too.

"You cold? You're shivering."

She found his eyes and gave them hers. "I'm actually nervous because I want you to like me but I know I know nothing of what you know."

"I like the truth," he said, "very much."

The street trash was so profuse Peter couldn't avoid stepping on a wrapper or a bottle with every passing foot but he kicked a way clean and she followed him she did not know where. His gray eyes warmed by red, burst veins running every which way went big and

34

burned with frankness over shiny, bony cheek lines dark against an albino glow that was almost, she caught her breath, otherwordly, stretched from years blowing trombone — blowing hard blowing long again and again, "in my uncle's band — he was a preacher and jazz man," — blowing against the crowds' constant combustion, their inclination to scatter apart into departing particles, trying to breathe them back together, call the skilled feet back to the dance floor, and he blew everything that he knew into those notes, "it nearly killed me, like, when I was finished, I fell over and they took me in once to test for drugs and couldn't believe it when I came out with clean blood. But it would have been a good way to go. Dying at the end of song. Let's walk, shall we? I've a place in mind."

Before walking he produced — from where? — a big bouquet that was suffocated by a sheath of hard plastic. The streetlamps threw little yellow suns onto the translucent wrap, blinding her from seeing the colors, but from the hints that she'd unwittingly picked up on he had fetched a standard day-old dozen roses from a gas-station shelf. She grinned, sympathetic — no one could send flowers that would wow her — but kept the automatic crawl of criticisms quiet from even her heart.

"Oh thank you," she said, and meant it.

She kept pace — he walked fast — and stole glimpses of his shifted look. Rounded blonde hair framed his head like a theater curtain, suspended, something that could never come down, and the yellow lashes made his widened eyes look like weathered copper, like the statues back home Nonna pointed out as Stella drove her, "faster, chauffeur," from specialist's office to pharmacy to the closest bar where she could quickly "soak my nerves a little." One of the bar counters was vert-de-Grèce blue. "The Statue of Liberty is that color," said Nonna. "Hope mixed with what my father — a navy sailor, the best of fathers — called the sea's endless expansiveness. But green also means young and dumb. The color of this country, maybe. Nah. Forget it. Ellis Island, you've never been? I'll take you there before I die." Nonna threw out these promises like a child tossing pennies into a pond, whispering wishes with the sugared energy of the unjaded. They'd never travelled to the Statue of

Liberty, and soon Nonna's bones would be pale and lightless under a copper crucifix destined to turn *vert-de-Grèce* in time.

Nonna, wrapped in a leopard skin shawl too small for her, winked at the lawyers biting down on their salmon-olive sandwiches at the other end of the bar. Pinching Stella's cheek, she said, "But this one's righteous, almost blameless in her evil generation. Any boy would be a flat-mallet idiot who had the chance to marry her and messed it up." Her dyed orange mane radiated from her head like the scribbled halos Stella oversaw when the St. Cabrini art teacher called in sick and then never came back. But the boys were all fools and her grandmother the grandest of them all, because at almost-forty-one Stella was no closer to marriage than she had been at eleven following Felix Perez around the playground, shy but doting as he pretended that she wasn't more than a passing shadow. Further from vows than sixth grade, flirting with being further from God than Nonna's absentee husband, a legendary drinker Stella never met but whose alcoholic abuses never stopped Nonna from sipping a Bloody Mary at half past noon.

As they made their way to Charon's Kitchen, P. C. straightened his feet into a mock-stern march. She started with a double-take, but she couldn't keep from joining his goosesteps. He had started the step when they passed a policeman whom he saluted, violently, asking, "And what do you say, official sir, shall we bring the National Guard into our city to keep us from killing one another?" Feigning a nonchalance that flared out his nostrils, the officer reached down to pick up a package of emptied condoms crushed at the edge of a sewer grate. When he tried to shove it into the trash can he couldn't do so even with force.

"I'm sorry," Peter said to Stella as they double-timed it past the cop, "I get carried away, only in this case, I've tried to keep it, only in these cases."

"What cases?"

"I can't tell you. Legally."

"That sounds scary."

"Great. Now I come off as a criminal. As if I didn't from being born into this skin. Off white. White but not white. Half-n-half.

36

Make a commitment. Be part of your people or deny them outright. Am I right?"

She knew the statistics he went on to offer about profiling and policing — some of the things she had successfully ignored or played into inconsequence for every year of her life until last.

She sneaked a look at the flowers. That they were kept alive artificially, pumped with chemicals in their water, was nothing out of the ordinary, but this bouquet was as if already dead with its decay covered, painted over with some sort of coating that stalled with its glistening, thickened shellac the difficult truth of pre-packaged death.

They passed a woman wrapped in gray wool whose white hair was braided beautifully and whose eyes exclaimed that kind of unknowing that belongs only to the blind. Stella leaned toward the bent-down woman and handed the roses to her outstretched fingers — chapped but ending in faux nails that gripped in their tiffany blue claw the flowers she smelled with a solemn smile. The smell, as if feigned by a splash of perfume, was as of fresh picked shoots, and the woman inhaled with all she had and sunk back into her bed of newspapers like a piece of meat at an old school butcher's, left there for the night dogs to pick at.

"Why'd you give what I gave you away? You can't do that. Go get it back, now. She won't notice a damn."

She crossed Damon Street though the orange hand warned her with increasingly frequent blinks as a recorded voice said at violent volume "WAIT!" The violence set the spine bones at the base of her neck singing with the tremulous threat of a migraine.

From the other side of the intersection — Peter was planted in a cross-armed protest — she shouted back: "You either gave them to me or you didn't. If they're mine I suppose I can do what I want with them. And I'm not sure tomorrow I'll want to remember my night with you if you don't shape up. Tell me why you were so off with that officer." Her breath came out gray against the dark tarp sky. Her every exhale joined the wispy clouds that barely blocked the moon's fulsome light.

"Maybe I can't for professional reasons. Maybe I mostly counsel kids, but maybe the city of Chicago is desperate for therapists at this delicate juncture in our nation's history when no one knows what'll come of the — I mean we're just on the cusp — this is crazy, like, a pandemic of proportions that we can't make sense of, bringing on or following up a civil war's worth of tensions. People are reporting anxiety and suicidality at a crazy spiked rate that should shake us all awake. Maybe I pitched my card in the hat of counselors available to work with cops doing long shifts at a time when their whole — kind — is being called into question. And maybe, just maybe, I met with an officer who's the spitting image of the one we just passed, and he's out of gas bad but can't turn down the double pay, even though the beat's making him *pay* in the form of fists raised against his wife and his five-year-old son every time they even twitch with opposition to something he demands, and he demands — and now maybe I'm in violation of the entire code of ethics of my profession and I ought to be dropped down that grate right there to spend the end of my days in a dungeon: but these police, what we expect of them, what we make them into and then demand they won't become. Or else, what we demand they become, machines able to switch on and off. *Unthinking functionaries.* Living automatons straight out of the movies. This man, he cannot be contradicted for a second, loses his cool and leaves them all bruised, and then lines them up later that night to lecture the family about how if you should speak or leak a single word you're off my payroll, you're out of my house. And maybe he told me that this all started when he stopped beating the misdemeanor dudes he'd catch and take out all his shit on — for years, for his whole *career*, he done that, and only just stopped when the nation went loud after noticing the obvious loss of law and order."

The entrance to Charon's Kitchen was lit with two flaming torches that the Chicago wind flattened and flicked and wrestled down into back-burner nubs but always they returned, the orange pillars, and never did their fiery edges dare to lick you as you passed. The space inside seemed doubly dim. All shades and fuzzy outlines. Before they were even seated, he said "Now you go first."

She could see no seats but, blinking, could make out disparate circular tables set apart in solitudes, each as if existing at infinite distance from the next, an unalloyed darkness between them, while the tables themselves — she blinked again — were faintly warmed by mellow red globes that spun like many models of Mars, suspended from the ceiling like science projects.

"Go where? Pick a seat?"

"No, wait for the waitress, but I want to hear your story."

The waitress, brushing aside her ringlets, waved familiarly at Peter — was there something flirtatious in the flick of her wrist? — and she walked them around to a potbelly stove, bronze as an Abraham Lincoln penny freshly minted by the federal reserve. The defunct stove had been converted, not beyond recognition, into a makeshift jukebox.

The waitress, who was clearing the ovular table spread with three heaping leftover plates, clattering and clinking and scrubbing with abandon, was clearly pregnant, held her waist in pain, paused to breathe before pushing hard the heel of her hand against the remaining stains. Stella wanted to steal it from her. That kind of devotion. The job did not matter. The child. The circles she made with the rag not fruitless but bringing the baby into being. That kind of devotion she could do, she knew it.

As they sat he kicked the table and salt slid toward her and spilled into her lap, the fancy Tiffany blouse her grandmother sent her when she first arrived at St. Cabrini's (when her mother, upset at her absence, refused to answer calls for a year). Feeling his pockets, Peter did not notice. He sighed as she brushed the salt to the floor but then, on second thought, let it sink into her skin, which she kissed to taste.

"I don't carry spare change," he said, eyeing the waitress — her shoulders or her waist, the place where a baby bumped from oblivion and swelled into the crowded room — or maybe the juke-box, not the waitress at all but the music player's shapely selection which shone out through a deep purple light. "It's strange. That's not a brag — I make a social worker's salary, counselor, remember, not psychiatrist — not a brag but a mourning, because they got Kind of Blue on the juke box here, and I'd like to treat you to a couple hours of 'Stella by Starlight' on repeat."

She shook her purse and heard the clang of coins she always carried for the L-train, never having gotten around to buying the tickets beforehand in bulk although, she knew, that would save her money.

"Done with the days when I made many, many more dimes working for the movement. At what cost I can't yet say. Still mulling, studying from afar, trying to find where I stand on everything. Re-reading *Wretched* from a different planet. Reading as a kind of purgation. Passages I'd staked my life on crossed out. Apologies for politics as war by any means. Some of this still really *gets* me. I mean, I get it. I admire some of the *diagnosis* happening here, but it's not foolproof and I don't take directions anymore from books like this. Not to say I know where to go next. '*Deciding to embody history in his own person, he surges into the forbidden quarters.*' What I cleave to is the case studies of colonized psyches, a wretchedness deeper than earth can bear. At once they interpreted and interrupted my nightmares and woke me to see the meaning of the dream: 'The first thing which the native learns is to stay in his place, and not to go beyond certain limits. This is why the dreams of the native are always of muscular prowess; his dreams are of action and of aggression. I dream I am jumping, swimming, running, climbing.' I know that stuckness and the flights it authors. How to get those flights down to earth — from psyche to body?

"What I do know is *this*: it's not a way to be forever, though some would see such as the ultimate virtue: standing back from all the action and commenting from armchairs about the limits of commitments. Gods above almost freed of their bodies, condemning any compromise as unconscionable. It's not enough to draw the art of the possible on a pad of paper, see, in the privacy of your own quarters. To *be* the truth you recognize, it seems to me sideline chattering ain't enough. Precious feelings of guilt ain't doin' it. Precious pleasures of victimhood ain't gone bring young bodies back from the dead. You have to surge into forbidden quarters."

She tossed a Washington onto the table, watched it wobble and collapse.

"I really only got into the movement 'cause I was tired as hell of my cousins getting killed, 'cause I couldn't attend one more uncle's funeral, one more friend's memorial service." The lines were practiced but the globes of his eyes were covered, suddenly, with water. "Forget it for now. Another time."

When she held out the coins he pulled out a checkbook and said, "Can I make out the equivalent right now? I'd rather not go into debt right away to a lady I already owe something unpayable — you look lovely, rather, you're lovely tonight."

She laughed and threw coins down on the table — seven quarters spinning and catching whatever they could of the faint kitchen light.

"You can only say that because you can't even see me," she said, but it came out like a plea for a compliment. She wanted to ask him but withheld her wonder: Words we say and can't retract all day, mistakes of minuscule consequence, but where do they go, the worthless ones, the coined alchemical worthless words?

Washington's profile spun a spastic aura of scintillating light, like a cat's eyes when readying for the pounce. She steadied the salt and he said "Oh my, did I do that, I'm so sorry, I —"

And she held up her palm like the walk-sign warning that she had earlier defied. He started to defy hers but thought better — bit his cheek and chewed ostentatiously like her little brother when he was a boy with his Big League Chew gum, practicing imaginary pitches at the dinner table until her Dad gave the eye. "My Nonna says if salt loses its flavor it's no better than dust on the floor."

"Christ," he said, and her shoulders tensed even though she had lost the muscle of faith — had only a frayed nerve of it left. "I'm sorry, again. I — and by the way, I'm not going to pretend my way into your good graces, lovely as you are, but I also want you to know I respect you, there's something about you — I mean I'm already ready to be, I don't know, to concede happily."

"Careful," she said. "Careful."

"Of course blackmail is never off the table. I could report your beloved Nonna for plagiarism of the highest degree. That bit about salt losing its flavor, it was Christ, not Nonna."

41

"Oh I know that. But for me the two are so intertwined I can't quite keep them separated."

"Seems like a bad idea to me."

"That's fine. With my faith as weak as it is I can hardly claim to believe in God but when I believe I believe in a God who is madly in love with analogy."

"Oh that, I guess I'm a — by blood — iconoclast. Runs in the family, though my mama dragged that New Orleans Catholic all the way to South Chicago."

Stella wiped clean her lip and jutted her chin at him, signaling the sweet tea flecks of sugar that had stuck there like a crust of ocean salt left on the shore at low tide.

Peter said, "Well, let's move from one forbidden topic — religion — to another, just to test the temperature of the waters between the two shining seas. Now I'm of two minds. George Washington makes me uneasy. Owned slaves but freed them in his will. Emancipate but only after the ease needed to be a great man carried him on its back like a mule. Oh yes, he enjoyed the moral nuances of heartache at the awful thought of selling slaves separately so that families would be chopped and parted like butcher's meat. That luxury of pain in a delicate but slack conscience. But — and so when I use his face to purchase a few rounds of a black man's music — alright, okay, so Miles had a white pianist, but, forgive me, you get where I'm going? When I use his face to make that music play, should I be disgraced by the use of such presidential power or relieved that I've rid us of these dizzying faces — one, two threefourfivesixseven, oh man! Infinite Washingtons. How should I square that sum?"

"I can't tell," she said, "if you're joking. The *way* you say it's meant for laughter but *what* you say is vexed and serious."

"Who are you?" he asked.

"What do you mean?"

"I mean there're certain things we're not supposed to say. But you don't seem confined by those boundaries."

"They, I, they *hound* me like crazy, but somehow I can't — settle — for safety that comes in the form of a straitjacket."

"Shit! You *are* my kind of woman." She pressed her sternum and felt with her pinky the blouse seam. Forty felt close to losing fertility. Sometimes she was sure she was past her time but then the blood would come again. "Now tell me," he started in earnest, then stopped. "Wait, one second"— he rose, his long legs radiating energy as he ducked under the low ceiling that housed the bronzed potbelly jukebox. Closing his eyes, he dropped the coins in the slot that split the gargoyle mouth, beneath the snout of the ironwork stove, and pressed a code that seemed perfectly familiar, which set the speakers above them crackling, then the ivory keys unfurled like tiptoes trying the waters before they ran down the ascending pier and dove into the frigid liquid and swam, frenzied, as much to keep warm as to get to the other side, where they entered a lighthouse with a wood-crackling fireplace which she snuggled up close to as he came back and asked, "Are you? I mean, who —"

As the syncopation propelled the saxophone, she spoke louder than she liked to in order to be heard over the bluesy croon that massaged her back. For the first time in months she went slack, but the relaxation made her feel nervous. She sipped water, sipped more, and smiled into his full moon eyes, which, when lidded, matched the crescent of her mouth. She told him her life had been extraordinarily ordinary, how before she'd worked as a florist for ten years she took five years to finish two university degrees — she'd double-majored in math and ancient literature — with two theses, on Euclid and Greek tragedy. The exposition was a neat outline, a suddenly nervous and uptight narration over a first course of sweet tea that she sipped in pretense because sugar made her sick — and he saw this and asked the waitress for a bitter cup, to the sound of Stella's "Coming right up!" She spoke longer than intended of Nonna — who, you just had to meet her, and spelled, poorly, with apologies, with what Nonna's best friend Mary called "palaver," a dumbed-down rendering of the damned debacle with Blake, volunteering unconvincing upswings at the ends of parts irredeemably sad.

When they finished the steam-shrouded jambalaya and ate two packs of oyster crackers, cracking them open as if one could house a pearl, after three rounds of bitter and sweet drinks and a detour to the bathrooms, he asked if she needed to be leaving, and she said "I thought we were only now starting, darling"—and the dare was insane but she made it anyway and couldn't press delete, and the tea seemed liquored but was possessed of no poison.

He raised his hand—more a fist, tilted back with two fingers up, nothing like the peace sign he had mocked earlier—and asked the waitress for a comfortable table that could be conveniently occupied for a couple of hours. The waitress obliged. Soon they were sitting, on the same side, all alone at an unused zinc counter that stretched in front of the defunct juke box in cushioned bar chairs with backs that let customers tip back and be caught, spun the same as carnival fun.

"So, you're slumming it?" he smiled. His voice was sharp, like the question was a test more than a curious line of inquiry.

"Pretty fancy lighting for a slum. Apartment's got heat and running water. Relative."

She bent her right elbow at an awkward angle and pulled at the long chandelier earring that threw back the room's blue illumination like a single working headlight in a downpour. The room was too dark. She leaned against the wall and adjusted the bulbs, feeding the currents all their watts could take. When the room's faces found her tampering there without an explanation, she pretended to be searching for something on the floor.

He joined her, generously, pointing at nothing—which she promptly picked up. Reversing the dial of the dimmer switch, she restored the reassuring darkness, strangely calmed, herself, by its return. Too many conversations came back out of tune, rising and converging in polite competition to remain private and yet be heard. Stella laughed.

"I mean," he pursued, elevating his thickened eyebrows in playful arcs, "unless you plan to take up residence here permanently. How many teachers I've seen flee after the first year. Not that I—I mean, it's *hard*, practically happy dumb mule-like, to keep coming back after you see how little you can really do in spite of spending yourself so . . . Meaning I'm sympathetic, but it also makes for a problem that's *systemic*. You think the merry-go-round of teachers helps these kids whose nights and days are devoid of anything looking like stability?"

"I know the drill. I'm not cut out. I'm points and lines and Antigone and Creon — a tragedy waiting to happen to my kids. This'll be my last year, actually." Actually she had not decided until now.

"Wait — where you going?"

"I'll let you know."

Go, she told herself. *Leave now,* and she repeated this command as he continued his critiques. But she could not put one foot in front of the other.

"My admiration for you just grew. Must be hard to let go of that image you had of yourself when you entered the classroom." A bottle popped behind the counter. Glass crashed across the floor. She missed what he said except "the work we need is maybe not so much *be the change you want to see* but figure out who you are, first. I hate to cite Gandhi, too much a cliché, but if I recall the man took his time in deep self-scrutiny before he decided he was fit for the work he set out to do. My Uncle Cedric was fond of saying the same in another way, a better, more beautiful: 'And whosoever doth not bear his cross, and come after me, cannot be my disciple. For which of you, intending to build a tower, sitteth not down first, and counteth the cost, whether he have *sufficient* to finish it? Lest haply, after he hath laid the foundation, and is not able to finish it, all that behold it begin to mock him, Saying, This man began to build, and was not able to finish.'"

Before his compliment her headache had flashed back, the headache that had peaked as the children shouted and ran at recess. As she pictured those little bodies — launching a half-flattened kickball over the fence to a chorus of cheers and shrieks, bulletproof glass circling the perimeter, disrupting the illusion of openness and ease given by the chain-link fence — a blood rush drowned out the migraine's flicker. She found his eyes and fixed hers there.

He winced for a breath, his furrow assuming the angular bent her headaches gave her eyebrows, startled by the boldness of a glare she gave to him unknowingly. After she nodded to his "You okay?" he

45

resorted, now, to memorized statistics spouted like precious verses that could crack open the meaning of life, cited the names of peer-reviewed articles she should really — no, she needed — to read.

"Four thousand homicides in my city of Chicago. Any hypotheses on how many of that number have a darker skin color? Vast majority not motivated by money. Mayor's nonsense about poverty. Take the *spirit* of oppression out of the equation. The soul of it."

"The psyche, in the ancient sense," she dared.

"I do declare you are my kind of woman! The shtick of how all of this is talked about makes me sick. Ain't gonna work: wrestlings with the history we've shared are either dismissed as *resentment politics* or cheap blame for crimes committed centuries past. It's not — I could lend you a book, what's its name? — all about white indentured servants, human cargo. But if oppression isn't essentially bound to color, we can't — c'mon — act colorblind either . . ."

Her father had used some of the same questions and figures he cited during their last hard conversation.

"You're not a child," Dad had said. "Stella."

"I'm *not a* child. Maybe you missed that because I got stuck in stasis for over a decade. I'm more than halfway to a natural death. Do you happen to know who I am, I wonder."

" . . ."

"Hello?"

"I thought you hung up."

"You ought to hang your head, Dad." She had never dared to be so bold and regretted what she said for days before she sent him a short letter that said *I'm sorry. I meant what I said but I said it badly.*

Dad had been calling nearly daily to be sure she was alive, was weekly mailing her printouts of jobs for which she'd be suited, highlighting the salaries with a dry green marker (and yes they easily surpassed her current wages), *Love you Stella* underlined and signed in his illegible, gentle hand.

When P. C. fell into his arguments he set off a tingle in her spine — she saw him bent like the linebackers who ran perpetually across the TV screen of her childhood Sundays and holidays — and again she was scared and excited by such intensity:

46

"What *Wretched* taught me was exploitation — the rationalized excuse to harm a fellow human is not *essentially* a matter of race. Follow me. It *can be, has been*, fixed on color in a way that makes a people so subject that they can't shake the dominance for centuries. But any number of nameless nobodies can become the source of leisure for their rulers. Sub-minimum wage *plus* the spirit of oppression." She wanted him to define that spirit but followed, running behind, his arguments, which shattered, again and again, her known lines. When any of the statistics he could conjure were not without good-faith counterpoints — his mind was a switchback dialectic that made him argue aloud with himself — she took it all in like the gravy cooked down with a patient simmer that filled and spilled over her mashed potatoes. She yearned to learn all he had to tell, to know him long enough to test the ideas. She felt bad for him when he started to sound lifeless — long day, I'd better end it — and groped for talking points dragged up from up polls. But once he finished the statistics, she saw, it was as if he was cleansed like the mythical Roman who visited his vomitorium daily and left feeling shipshape. He sat up straight and made, with his fingers, the timeout symbol and then stayed silent, rubbing his cheeks with a cramped fist. "Since I first heard it said, 'History's what hurts,' made an indelible impression on me. But now that line seems overdetermined. History's not a nightmare nor a sweet dream. There's another choice: the insomniac who's never caught off guard at the midnight hour.

"We could claim we're so different we're past all but sympathies. But on a low level, where the caricatures don't obscure — you and me are the same. Don't get me wrong." She certainly had. She steeled her nerves and then let her shoulders down. "More, we're the same as everybody like us. Indistinguishable one from another, if you look at the pattern from far enough away (which, God, both clarifies and obscures). Not happy with that state of things. This state. Not happy staying unknown." No. Ridiculous: her hermit soul. But the gesture was sweet and even cute in its clumsy grasping after common ground. "A gnawing need to be looked at by many — a hundred, a thousand, ten thousand? For me it was . . . millions. Millions. Look at that *greed* in my soul. You think I'm just a victim, think again."

Her eyes, finding his, narrowed, as if his admission dwarfed their significance.

If she stared at him long enough she could surprise him, sate his appetite with one pair of eyes. Would he see her, then? And could she cease to care if, in fact, he failed to see her, then? And if he helped her make a child — what then? That mind, bringing whatever was worth it from her mind. The music of his voice. That mouth's curves. His. His mind. Not reasons, really? Not things she could say, aloud, to explain to Mom and Dad. Not a reason, right, but she loved the angle of repose that went from his mouth edge to the tip of his nose. The perfect line. Madness. The haste of her thoughts made her blush.

"Now I, I'm the first to confess that I was the worst of all. Never underestimate the human being's capacity for pandering to celebrity, even of the small-pond variety. Cleaving to a Name's aura. But, mind you, behind that Name! A tangle of pettiness, pomposity, self-importance. I've met others along the way who got this crazy, inimitable knack at tilting a half-truth this way or that to approximate a pleasing *yes* or eke, just barely, a frightened *no*, while also saying — without saying — f— off. While also signaling, with a flat, amused smile, 'Man, I got thoughts that would give you a heart attack, but I recognize that reality, for you, is drip-fed in meted-out increments that will never accrue or increase in frequency to the point of insomnia, let alone indigestion.'"

Stella stopped, bowed, and gave him her best flat and amused smile.

"Isn't that just manners? I mean, without them, without some measure of —"

"Dissimulation —"

"Consideration that all can't be said at once — we're not God, we can neither say it nor take it."

Peter pulled out a piece of gum and, gnashing the white strip between his teeth, awkwardly turned to her and offered her one of the thin aluminum columns. It felt warm in her fingers and she

48

pocketed the silver just as it reflected a condescending gleam, an inanimate wink. She waited for him to speak, but he censored himself with an agitated stubbornness. Streetlights wore short golden skirts, sharp angles that tried to hide the rounded wombs she could see swelling. She wanted the light to reach down farther. To cover the whole long pole legs. She who was ready to follow him through the doorsill of his bedroom. She was not her Nonna's child anymore.

"Maybe. Manners. Never thought of it that way." Then, as if recovering from local anesthesia, he recovered his former tack. "But if manners may be *more* than the lubrication that whets power's wheels, they certainly are *mostly* used to hustle and climb. The self-made slave can't help facing this truth from time to time, but it's easier to keep pandering than to leave into the long empty hallway that leads away from the Big Party." He was looking straight ahead down the long empty hallway but she, following him, could not see it. "Because it took so long — so much of your life . . . at least for me, how hard it could be to walk away from the Big Party? You see?"

"Please," she said. "I want to. Please."

"Man I could *confess* to you, something there is about you. Thank you, Stella." Flattery a flat-out impossibility. The wet globes of his eyes. Her face burned as her lips lightly parted, her tongue barely touching her teeth. Her cycle's clock throbbing louder and louder. She wanted to. Please. I want you.

"I used to fix like a desperate homing device — dressing desperation in the fineries of confidence — on whoever, with power, showed the slightest sympathy to some *cause célèbre* I cared for. It's a *fact* most everyone's familiar with, at least everyone who's climbed his way back from a future of mass, anonymous, grass-covered graves and arrived where he started ready to make a splash, bent on leaving a mark — meaning something more than that nightmare version of his future where all he is is a nameless nobody. Refusing to see that future come to be, he throws himself — abandoned — into the ambition. And with each climbed rung of the ladder he can point to his merits even though it's the case that what makes a man is less his mind or merits or money than the second sense. 'Cause if your orbit, your wheel, has run, for a time, close to the top, you know your ascent is totally dependent on a second sense — a subtle antenna — that can identify who has the sovereignty, the exact kind of sway you need to be lifted off your pleading knees, someone who can find some common ground you can cling to, who can make your dependence feel like an alliance, who can justify a pound of self-interest with a few pennies' worth of alms. So after all that lackeying, a decade of banal pandering and daily flattering in so many minor gestures, you forget that you're doing what would have once shamed you, and all the humiliations you have to swallow and all the conscience pricks you have to thimble: you think you itching to leave when you wake up and find *yourself* the naked emperor at the center? I been at the *center* of that Party — the honored guest, hands held by ladies who smiled and nodded and had no idea that my politics, then, would have them stripped of power and of wealth, have them scrubbing the basement bathroom like the maids they hire twice a week with a husband's big checks. Standing at the center so long I forgot what it felt like to be banished to the margins. Where people not only introduce you to others with a 'Surely you've heard of,' this constant buzz of sycophantic frequencies and under it, all the while, the low-level pleasure of half the room's on-looking eyes watching and waiting for your wit, your attention, some indulging in that strange pleasure of standing there longer the more you ignore them, never making eye contact exactly, they may even put a paw on your shoulder, but maybe they just know you see them there waiting in the periphery, waiting like little boys in the wings, desperate for the spare change of your conversation. And you can't help being disgusted, frankly, by the temperature of their desperation. Sigh. Doing the little boys a service by leavin' 'em standin' there. Shit.

"But, take it from one who knows, you stand at that center of attention for so long and you start watching what you say. Simple self-censorship, but it spreads through the bloodstream until every synapse in that widely praised brain is chained to some consciousness of how you'll come off, and who could misinterpret or twist this claim or straightforward contention. And so — for me — it was

50

necessary, finally, to leave that Party and walk the long hallway that leads to what feels by comparison like the faded half-lit ghost world of utter insignificance. How easy it was to have opinions formed for me, comparatively, ready-made by a servile self-censor saving me from hard-won thought. And same for the fawning ones. Took my every opinion piece for inspired opinion, sage. Shit. It's hard for both parties to part from the Party, to walk away in opposite directions down the two long hallways that lead to Loneliness."

"My Nonna, when young, met Dorothy Day once. You know her book *The Long Loneliness*."

"Heard of it. Haven't read it."

"How she puts the problem of the climb. 'Everybody wants a revolution, but nobody wants to do the dishes.'"

"Damn that's it. And for me counseling, *being* with kids"— he loved them, then, the kids, he loved them — "was, as you put it, *doing the dishes*. And man how — how can I put it — *saving* it was to get things done. To get away from the grand ideas eked out daily in countless articles mixed with mingling too many evenings with so-called admirers who flattered a mirage. Marjorie, who I met at a police brutality rally, was the one of the arrangers who maybe knew my mind. Who maybe heard what I argued and knew the hurt and hope of my heart. Wanted to make me a leader in no time. But her boss Curtis — the head of the movement — undercut half what she did when she stopped sleeping with him. Damn. Please don't repeat that. I'm lost — you got me, arrested, I mean I don't mean to blame you. But to thank you, again, for hearing me out. It means, I mean, *everything*.

"What I meant to say is long after you leave the Big Party you bring the heartstrings with you, there, outside, away from it all. You can't walk away from the hurts. Maybe they even get roused more there, outside, away from it all."

"I mean," she said, switching her tone from that of one who could collude to one who is criticizing while fearing the consequences — "I've seen that, sometimes, in you."

When she said it the brevity of their acquaintance lengthened like a prismatic optical illusion. They might have been dating for years. As if. "The bitterness. Like, I mean, I know the words you say aren't the whole story. Who am I to know, I mean to notice, but I, I, I felt like I *knew*, I saw when you talked about your former champions, enemies now, rivals, all that, your words were steeped in"—she bit her lip—"it felt like—bile."

"Oh, here we go," his chest heaved out farther than the breath he took in could explain. "The secret. Shhhh," he exhaled, smiling through a cringe and then falling silent until the flush that colored his face faded. "You hit the switch. You have the secret." His lips lifted away from his teeth and his tongue, poised in anger, pressed against an incisor. He looked at a passing wall of glass and then back to her eyes with a bold stare that dared her to keep her own open. "When you reach the end of that empty hall and you escape through the exit into ghostly insignificance, *that's when the resentment starts to roil*, replaying all your past glories, the things you should have said, would have, now, with the wisdom of a nobody, and so there I was serving your students, so generous, pro bono, but all the while I'm stewing with jealousy for the man I used to be, becoming a fan of, of . . . Myself."

Here, when he cleared the final hidden hurdle of truth, gave her a harsh, hurt look. As if she had made a fool of him and he'd slipped on the too-waxed floor of Charon's that reflected a garish glare between them. Peter never—sober or after several nightcaps, but especially when he ran for alderman and slid into a spastic cocaine spell for a week—never ever brought this hint up again.

His eyes rested on the rouge circles beneath her eyes, watched them darken with the blush of blood. She showed the tips of her teeth through lips that trembled, slightly, muscles held tight, picking up the napkin she'd put down on the circular tabletop and setting it back down again. He stood and said, "Excuse me for a moment," and disappeared down another nook than the one where the bathroom signs pointed.

A blue stain had spread in the napkin's corner—a sweated-out fingerprint that bled the marks of the day's grading. Jackie's obvious thimble-full of wisdom. Looking down, she found blue all over her hand. How had she not noticed something so obvious?

She thought she saw Peter across the room, faded like a shade against the thick background.

Her father had never subjected her to such probationary tactics as the classroom now schooled her in daily. Old-fashioned, he could maybe not fathom that a female might have sturdy enough feet to stand on. Whereas her brother had felt dad's every impatience, he spared her from the forced discomfort, the necessary correlative of high expectations — a favor she had come to resent. Even sitting, even unmoving, the short stilettos of her thrift store heels hurt. She should have worn the sensible pumps. The soles stung until she shook the shoes off and bared her feet under the table.

The pump of adrenaline was starting to empty. Too many nights with too little sleep. Tired and ready for bedtime by now, like Nonna who turned in no later than ten, because the schooldays were yellowing the whites of her eyes and shooting them through with little burst veins. Between classes — having quieted the caco-phonic students by putting a young man in a headlock (not too puny and not a weightlifter, needing to show her muscle without risking the embarrassment of being outwrestled) — she'd taken to ducking under a desk like her mother did during fallout drills, but instead of fearful subconscious twitches she napped without dreams. No conceptions of mushroom-cloud nightmares — the total anni-hilation of her existence — dreams she had had after Blake broke the engagement, a sick longing that for weeks became a tactic: the promise of suicide kept in the back pocket, ready to explode the pain away whenever the hurts of her heart returned. Coming to Cabrini's had cured her wholly. It seemed that every week one of her students was on suicide watch — a protractor slashed against a wrist, a waistband hung from a bathroom ceiling. The sweet act of annihilation, the O of oblivion, was robbed of its romance.

He stayed gone. She strained her neck but refused to stand and look stupid. Sitting in the dark, absent Peter, she now found opened like never before the possibility of letting it out, of feeling her lungs move from strained, starved, to heaving with satisfying sobs — no stifling, no shortcuts, no short shrifts of the soul. She felt the pressure behind her eyes spill onto her blouse and at the blurred edges of her vision appeared her desk, the pretty mint tiles of Cabrini's floor.

That morning she had come to the classroom prepared, had let her eyes dampen in little stingy pathetic trickles a whole box of borrowed tissues, perking the blurred mascara lines in the projector's blurry glass before braving the high-traffic hallway that wound around to the faculty lounge, and snatching her brown bag lunch from the refrigerator, she'd retreated before Jordan Ellison could ask questions. He always offered, with searching eyes, a cup of lukewarm coffee, freshly brewed, and because she had twice said yes, and had taken the watery mixture down the hall and dumped it into the drinking fountain's drain, he did not stop asking no matter the odds. Not to mention she always said "Not today, thank you," which could without wild projections be taken to mean that tomorrow would come and his offer would again be received, he believed, and she wanted to be him, Jordan Ellison, without guile. But leaving without making eye contact, brown bag under her arm like contraband, she knew — the mess of mascara on her face an unforgiving accusation reflected from the microwave mirror: slutty, cheap, can't keep it together. She was feeding prefabricated gossip to the teachers who would gather there in seventh hour. Yet that mattered less than making it to the bell, to the next scheduled class — a new chemistry that could replace the last — mouthing easy division lessons as they tapped forbidden phones beneath the desk or gave her — always a boy named Eduardo, one of whose eyebrows was erased by a scar and a tall girl Talik who stayed after class and sat there penciling extra-credit equations — sympathetic smiles, learned from . . . where, she wondered — then chided herself for such a silly fantasy: as if none of them had their own Nonnas who had seen it all and could take it all, the world's pain absorbed in their skin and still they could stand and cook dinner every evening, soothe the weary and salve the wounded as if they were not wounded and weary too. Stella, watching Talik after class, took cheap certitude in the chalked outlines of clear answers broadcast against the well-washed but whited-out blackboard.

"Stella by Starlight" still played on a loop underwritten by a deep pocket of George Washingtons as she leaned on elbows bent at sharp angles. He wasn't coming back. She'd hurt him with something, unknowingly, she'd said.

But the flow of self-pity stopped when she heard his exhale, whispered a warming wind in her ear, sent Stella's shoulder against his fresh-shaved face. Sitting back down he leaned consciously close. She breathed him in as he backed away and, assuming his chair, asked "We'd best call it a night, I'd bet, with all the both of us will face tomorrow." Clove and cinnamon with a charcoal edge. The smooth soap wrung from Nonna's wrinkled hands. Sweet scent from the same source? She flicked a dab of shaving cream from his face, feeling chin stubble he had missed. He laughed. "My old boss'd Curtis'd appreciate the scrag. *Look street, look smart,* he said. *If this works, if you fit, if . . . we'll let you lead the march . . . If I can stand the gaze of millions.* To which I frankly said 'As if.'"

As if.

He laughed so hard he spit out coffee and she did too just to keep him company, anything to keep the pendulum of conversation swinging like a cast iron chandelier from power outage to one thousand watts, stay awake, no joke, electric this chemistry *ignotas animum dimittit in artes, ignosce mihi,* me he, how can I be half in bed already when my heart is repeating his name with each beat, say anything to stall departure, *naturamque nouat,* play the suicide card if you need to, no you *are* crazy and not just sleepy hotel or my room or his or he'll stand up, fumbling around for socks, like he's standing, fumbling, saying niceties, now, and say so politely *It was a pleasure to meet you, I'd best get going as tomorrow's an early morning, a painful case who's been shuffled around what I call the Carousel of Counselors (just as much if not more turnover in my line of work than yours, see?) and if all the king's horses and all the king's men couldn't put this client together again — I hate that way of talking, 'client,' by the way — a disgusting thing to say, as if . . . but then I am charging him for services rendered, right, not like I'm laying down my life free of cost for all the world's insulted and injured.*

Out of her mind he said, "Anyway, Stella, I got to go before I, because I . . . it's hard to be so quickly at ease with you, see, and I'm, I'm a lonely man, okay. Millions of us, sure, nothing original there, but I've been with Marjorie for a while now, not married and we're basically over but I want to be plain with you: she's a mean lady, okay, but brilliant, and I loved her like crazy. Really don't now, not just saying that. Really glad now that it's over, don't feel awkward. But it's hard to trust the stirrings, the motives. When you spent so many years counting on a person to always just be there, in the living room, at the end of the day, even when you're a walking dead man, fair or foul (and it was mostly foul), you can't help longing for the abstract of what's been taken away. Okay. I need to stay careful on several levels . . . I can't pretend on no sleep I'd stand a chance, not that I'm saying — I mean I could keep you up all night talking if you let me and I don't want you to, because you have duties too, doings, tomorrow, don't you? I won't walk you home 'cause I don't trust myself, but I'd pay the cab fare, please?"

"No thank you."

"You sure? Please."

"No thank you." Maybe he would walk her home anyway.

"Alright. Can't force it. But, you," he bit his bent thumb and look at her with the stupid mandibular drop of an unguarded child — "*a real pleasure, the pleasure's all mine*," and on that platitude he exited stage left, pretended to tip the hat he didn't have and disappeared out that damn door for what she was sure was forever.

· · ·

They paid a week's worth of awkward aversions, bypassing tactics achieved with the aid of chaotic hallways filled with schoolchildren. But before long both devised a way of wandering the cracked sidewalk that abutted the school in such a way that an accidental run-in — "Fancy seeing you here!" — was inevitable, they made sure to discover that their intended directions happened to take the same Southbound trajectory, so they shared a bus ride toward her apartment, then a brief, brisk walk down Pullman, where sidewalk construction demanded a detour.

56

Peter walked against oncoming traffic, right shoulder out, calm eyes daring the flying cars down, holding his left hand behind him as if, were he hit, flesh and bone could protect her against the insane screech of impacting steel.

And then when she caught up with him, breathless, he ducked into a nameless bar — or maybe they had entered through the back exit. The place was shoulder-to-bared-shoulder crowded. She smelled the classic dive admixture of sweet cologne and fresh sweat and followed him into a hidden back room that seemed familiar and she was filled with fear that this was where he took his women, on rotation, before he beckoned them to bed. The walls were sand-textured peach — flat with stipples of dust — painted with generous circles of rouge. Strange. She unbuttoned the tip of her blouse, blaming *it's hot in here* which it was — bad ventilation despite a rackety fan that rumbled and hacked and clacked so loud that they had to shout sometimes to be heard, and it thrilled her to shout out elations in public but have no one else here hear it, but what if she came off as drunk or delirious instead? so she buttoned back up and straightened her back against the chair's skeletal cross rail and splat and her own bones still barely covered by flesh flashed with pain that did not let her forget the anorexic stretch of years, who cares she unbuttoned the blouse again at the top so it was only Nonna's golden, azure-lined cross around the neck and her outfit showed none of what she'd once called fat. So *done with that,* she couldn't believe she'd ever succumbed to the never ending contest of slimming, how she'd gone from mocking such first-world problems to finding herself unable to consume, in conspicuous resistance so restless to beat out the skinniest rivals, for there was always a figure more sticklike than yours, and the tines of her fork harpooned what he'd ordered, a bubble of bacon and something so simple as chewing was good, God, he said "Good? I'm not a betting man, but this hood food I bet is the best you've had lately."

"Or ever," she said, leaving out the sob story because then she'd be a victim for him or he'd think she conceived of herself as such and the very thought struck her as so atrocious that she accidentally looked angrily at him. They occupied the cornermost spot in a place he called — as a nickname? — Cabrini's Collard Greens, a restaurant she'd never seen on Pullman St., brownstone wedged as by a jackhammer drill between the chiseled limestone of an abandoned theater and an abandoned apartment complex marked for demolition whose thin apertures looked out on the neighborhood like an astigmatic, cross-eyed angel from Nonna's cardboard children's Bible, the Book of Revelation penned by a prisoner but those illustrations like hallucinations — four with six wings completely covered with faraway piercing filigree eyes, sparkling like sequins and here, too, in Chicago after dusk, each apartment an identical eye and almost all lit golden still. She'd passed the aperture angels daily and never noticed Cabrini's Collard Greens. She could see through the ticket window into the kitchen, was watching the cook's doings while nodding to Peter who leaned into complaints about Marjorie again — de facto second in command of the movement — who was pushing him to run for alderman in the ninth ward. "Not a chance," he said, "shew," cocking his head back, all confidence. "Shoe don't fit."

Tired and tending toward confusion, she could not figure the extent of his involvement with the movement he had purportedly abandoned, and because she should have been paying attention she did not dare ask for clarification: one elder cook wearing a meticulous hairnet and washing his hands with scrupulous compulsion but when he'd tapped the last bean from the can and lathered the legumes with lard that sizzled fast, he'd pick out a bean from the big iron skillet and chew without a kink of qualms, even when she locked eyes with him once he winked, licked his lips, and went back to work, not pleased yet by the level of lard.

P. C. leaned across a lanky table that tipped like a scale that's been falsely weighted and looked at the check and said "Damn, they charged us for three plates of hash, and it's only two, two of us — what?" But she said "don't ask for a refund, now, wait: when she comes back we'll ask for another. We can split it, slow, so I can hear where you came from. I want to know," and as she asked she was at once alert as if she'd swallowed an amphetamine.

58

"Heard you tell some on that radio show, but I'd rather have it from the horse's mouth."

"I was born on the first of '81. March was the month when the Mayor of Chicago moved next door, well meant for sure but a fast failure, three weeks she lasted on Sedgwick Street, couldn't quite take it in the saint's hell's gate, thousands of units in seventy some buildings, Cabrini Green, named after —"

"Saint Frances Cabrini," she finished.

"How'd you know?" but then backtracked, like a walk that simply circles the block but returns home with recovered eyes. "Stupid me. You work for the school! My God, I'm slipping. The first —"

"First American Rome canonized — Sister, virgin, my Nonna's maiden name."

"Mother Cabrini. Not mother of ghettos that grew vertical for a century straight. First cropped up in Little Sicily, spotlight her doings after her death, they named my neighborhood for the Old Country folks" —

— "because Cabrini took foundlings from the Italians —"

"With her hands, her outstretched humerus, it's funny, her arm bone preserved in the city to this dying day."

"You're kidding me. We should go see her humerus. How did I not know?"

"I got suspicious — 'superstitious' — once when my Uncle said stay away from Catholics."

"I like you. You got a good sense of humor."

"But no one gives a damn about Cabrini's humerus. It was Mayor Jane Byrne got the real Cabrini spotlight, National TV every night for three weeks, what they now call 'building awareness,' which what the hell, is this a yoga class? We weren't aware what awareness of our building would bring besides 'Thanks be to God I don't live there!' from the screen-soaked gazes of millions. And my mama always said it was hard for her to come and go from doctors' appointments with a colicky newborn when security at Cabrini got thick as thieves and the rear entryway of her apartment was sealed with a welding fury that'd please old what's his name —"

"Hephaestus," she said, "the god of blacksmiths —"

59

"Crazy, what's the frequency we've found? Damn. Yes, that's him, Hephaestus."

When she finished his sentences she flushed like a card hand — a red-of-hearts victory she fanned her face with — her fevered mouth watering for more.

"But the thing was, when the mayor moved out the gangs used the welded rear as a fortress and others mimicked the seal as a tactic which was, my mamma always said, the only thing the high-heeled publicity stunt did to our neighborhood: seal us further into our vertical ghetto. But I wonder if it was that bad. Jane Byrne and her awkward rallies. Can't see condemnable ambition in a lady my uncle'd call 'without guile.'"

"Jesus."

"Don't swear."

"Just dinging you for your plagiarism. Again."

"Guilty, baby, but this time without guile! Life was something awful for us. Maybe everyone wanted a home run and all the mayor had was a bunt, bodyguarded by trenchcoated moustached men. Man, you might ask what else she should do? You can't win, right? I sometimes shake my head at these harsh thoughts in our time that condemn everyone whitelike, like rough cloth that could scrub burnt food from the bottom of a kettle, I mean that's the problem with harsh and hate — what does it do to you, versus what does it do to the one who's got you grinding your teeth in the bathroom mirror, look at me enemy you don't even know me, my brother Amos with his busted sandals watched her reaching up to clasp the black railings, *beneath us,* he said, *I was in awe between the black railings, at the royalty or whatever you call her,* but Amos went on and left us, a company man now, though then he was wagging that day, already an achiever, catching her attention — her mayor-mama's blown kiss — where the black kids all leaned all in a line behind rows of cast steel, smiling to touch the blousy saint, I'm sorry, I mean, I know she meant well and maybe we should've all been grateful who lived in that hell, yet mama never framed the Mayor's face but she did get hooked on Sister Cabrini —"

"You're kidding me."

"No, I kid you not. Not that I'm — as you can see, as I always say, there's nobody less nuanced, less complicated than me, I'm black *and* white, so I don't mean this to come out wrong, but . . . well, momma's from a long line of Baton Rouge Catholics, a chain of them, a chain mom had not exactly broken but kept dusted up more like a museum piece. We didn't go to church more than a smattering. A pathetic helping that wouldn't feed an ascetic. But she had a kind of a TV-tray altar draped with a coarse red cloth, and if I got too close — a ball came flying into the room or hide and seek messing with a friend she would swat at you, believe it! When she'd shower in the evening I'd go in there, sometimes, to stare at the pictures of our passed family members arranged between real flowers, some so dead and dried they flaked off like dust to the touch. Some of the folks I didn't recognize. Two uncles lost to crossfire.

"My — " His fork grated against the dish and drew a shriek. "Anyway. Looming above all these crappy family photos — except a handful of professional ones, but those from a funeral photographer set on preserving black Chicago heritage, above them all mama raised up — I kid you not — Cabrini. Can see her clear to this day, laid out for her funeral, but the way momma had the picture set it was like the lady was propped up, tilted, supposed to be horizontal but was shifted, vertical . . . a strange angle. You want to know what's *crazy?* They — don't ask me *who they,* damn if I know, who would be asked or tasked with such a, I mean, such a, seriously? — anyway they dug up her body in the nineteen-thirties and found it, supposedly, what do they call it, not 'not rotted,' but — "

"Incorruptible."

"Right, how did you — ? "

Stella had been gnawing on her lower lip, dizzy and giddy but also sickened by the consonances that were hard to write off as anything other than infernal omens or evidences — no way in hell 'happenstances' — of what Nonna called providence.

"What I meant — did I — say before? My mom's maiden name. My Nonna — a crazy lady, we call her God's firecracker. Cabrini."

"You're kidding me."

"Well, that's, I guess, a big part of why I came down to work at the school, St. Cabrini's."

"Naw," he said, flexing his jaw. "I mean, that whole . . . connection . . . is why I volunteered at the grade school. Usually I do Chicago Public School system. But, so you a Christian. Catholic."

"By blood. Used to be, or, more accurately, used to *say so*."

"You lied? What would that win you?"

"Not a conscious lie, but more like I *thought* I was a believer but wasn't. When something really hard happened it turned out I had no faith. Truth: if I had no belief in the middle of a downturn, it hadn't been there in the first place, so I stopped practicing because to practice was to pretend. So I stopped."

"Just like that?"

"Why fake it?"

"Decisive."

"For once. And you?"

"I'm not a religious person, really — not at all, truly. But not a naysayer either. No angst at God. No angst at all with any of the people who spend half their lives groping blindly down their long and winding hallways going nowhere in search of, what, a ready soothe for what they've done wrong, a way out of the hard prospect that we're the only ones to account for, for all the shit we do to each other. I mean who wouldn't wish for someone else to make right what you made a mess of?"

"No angst at all." She let out a nervous chuckle, an adolescent crack that broke from strained lightness — and the levity drew from his stern mouth a smile whose sides gleamed dental-bridge gold.

"You hear some?" When he stared at her, his eyes asserted with widening irritation that there was only one answer to the question.

"Okay, I mean. Take momma, and — God love her — the contradiction, the just plain obvious *pain* that should have come with being treated like a dupe by the very force that was supposed to be a kind of celestial caretaker. If you woke up at random at three a.m., and if she didn't hear you tiptoeing down the hallway, there's a fifty-fifty chance you peek into her room you could catch momma talking to Cabrini. Like a — my brother said — mental case. (My brother was really my cousin by the way, adopted: his parents were killed and we took him in). Dude was a special mental case. Meant, I'd say, in the clinical sense. No slur. Seriously. She looked on the death face like it was alive and well and listening to her whisperings. For me Cabrini, pale face, put the fear in me, cloaked in such a heavy black costume that her body got kind of lost, and the two crosses, she was holding two, sometimes my eyes would go double because momma told me to look at the cross and tell Him to take it all, and I'd try to look at both and go double, and then Cabrini would come into focus like some . . . what's the fairytale word . . . stately queen from another world, an arc of flowers around her head, an outline of sheets, sleeping — to me — and standing at the same time. Surrounded by candles and the legions of the no longer living."

Peter's eyes narrowed. He struck a matchbook flint with a cardboard stick that barely caught fire, touched it to the little candle discarded at the edge of their table — a leftover from a birthday party maybe, a leaning tower of skinny wax whose texture of incorruptible skin was a shock to the room's numinous light — and he stared at the aspirational orange, the petty flicker fast petering out, a look of longing that also dared.

"So I guess it's aspirational — that 'no angst.' I — even as a kid I was embarrassed for her. By her. And I guess what I'm saying is that I sympathize with that kid's perspective. To the point that I veritably adopt it word for word to this day."

"How'd she come to that kind of . . . devotion?"

"Listen. One winter in our section of Cabrini the heat had to be turned off for months. I'm talking January and February in Chicago. Now to begin with, listen, there was the unpalatable dust and filth particles in every corner and vent and cranny, always appearing no matter how hard we scrubbed. An undying host of motes you could only *see* in a certain light, but always there, outnumbering father Abraham's grains of sand on the ancient shore. As if literally eternal. Impossible to clean. Took me years to shake the wheeze I picked up living in that place. But this winter was the worst. Big rats had started to show up everywhere, right around then. They looked better fed than most of my friends. The damn things had defecated in the vents and the landlord wasn't in a hurry to clean the air system. People getting sick from doing no more than breathing. For a day we kept the dial up high and opened the windows at the same time, but no way that was happening long term. Would still be paying off that heating bill today! So a few days into the debacle mamma moved my mattress in front of the stove, shoved hers to the edge of mine, but in a way that meant I'd get the main breath of the heat. Turned on the oven real low — not too high so we'd not get sick. But one night the gas from the oven was smelling, reeking, and momma dragged her sleepy body over to the TV tray, prayed and prayed and prayed to Cabrini and then stood up, fed up, and told me to fetch my things. We were going to stay at a hotel for a few days. Who cared about the cost. The question I had was not the cost but whether we even *had* that much money. Momma said 'I don't have hotel money but surely they can work out some kind of old-fashioned agreement, surely the world ain't gone so corrupted that an honest barter is disappeared. Diddlysquat, just you watch. I'll clean or do their dishes for a room to curl up in one night away from this, away.' She needed to sleep so she could work. See, it all shook back to the same need. So I got my backpack and filled it with underwear and she packed some food and we opened the door and — I kid you not, it wasn't there a few hours before — there was a big space heater, fancy, expensive. No explanation. Next day she asked around and even called the landlord. Nothing. No explanation. 'Mother Cabrini,' she said, giving me a look that said 'Don't you dare doubt it or I'll give you such a one.' So I didn't. I didn't doubt it at all. I talked to Cabrini all night long. But I didn't have a *thank you* in my bones because I'd wanted so bad to stay at a hotel, which had never happened before.

"Once, after an especially nasty sequence of killings, she called all the neighbors on our floor to come over for this bottomless crock pot of jambalaya and see if they could put their heads together. But at the end of the meeting (my friend Javier and I were spying from under the couch (it had these crazy elongated legs!) they'd sent us hush-hush off to my room to talk grownup talk, which was always an invitation to overhear whatever we damn well could), heh, so at the end of the meeting, she's going around gathering everybody's paper plates and insisting that Miss Arrow takes the leftovers and says 'Now wait a minute, just wait one second,' and now here she is dragging the TV tray out, real careful because the thing is crazy rickety, and setting it down in the center of the room and kneeling there like some pastor leading everybody in a service. I mean Mrs. Jones looks so straight up nervous, stands up as if to leave but hovers at the doorway like she can't take her eyes away as momma prayed aloud to Cabrini, calls on the saint to save our city and especially the part of it named in her honor.

"For a few weeks after that I waited for Cabrini. Figured she was working up something really elaborate behind the scenes or something. Nothing. Another smattering of killings. To a kid — and I guess I'd say why should it be any different to an adult — it's not like the request momma had was selfish or couldn't be squared with God's infinite circle. So somebody tell me why no reply, other than the usual 'It isn't His will' or 'because it was better for the families whose kids were killed, whose dads were downed by bullets, shit, better that they died, for the sake of humility or a dose of dependence, a reminder of humanity's awful smallness,'" — and here Peter broke off and bit hard at a fleck of flesh at the base of his thumb, which glistened, whetted by his mouth. "I mean, maybe Cabrini was the one who saw fit to demolish the building — maybe that was the answer — because it wasn't worth saving and she didn't like the rest of us have the founder's pride that says at all costs I'll drive this Pequod until I die no matter how much damage and carnage? As a young whip I couldn't help wondering, that the sorts of landlords he trusts with his properties is pretty good evidence that God's got — please don't strike me — bad delegation skills, not so much laid back, maybe, as too likely to trust and test the wrong candidates for leadership, to put it into our wretched argot. To say the least. After I saw the layers of hell housed in that vertical shithole ghetto, saw momma expecting an answer that never came, I started to find that there's a species of faith that is hard to distinguish from self-hatred or a sick kind of submission to an imagined entity that — I can't put it more eloquently — hates the living daylight out of you."

When he unfolded a napkin his finger was bleeding.

"Dry skin," he said, shrouding the red, which bled through the thin white abrasive pulp and looked strangely bright and beautiful under the tumble-down light.

"There's a passage my Uncle Cedric, a pastor — always the same unprepossessing gray suit — would repeat whenever he'd visit us which has horrified me ever since. Something like, 'There is nothing concealed which shall not be revealed. Nothing hidden which shall not be known.' Book of Revelation, if I remember right. My uncle was a big interpreter of that book. He'd draw out schemas on the back sides of the graded assignments my teachers sent home. Map out various routes by which we'd get to the end of the world." Peter's elbows went out and his head leaned down. "A good man. I mean, he was more of a father than my own to me by far. Taught me music. Gave me grief if I talked back to momma or slacked on a chore. A good man. But he had this thunderous voice, all mysterious in the half-light of the living room, spelling out the final judgment and every single soul ever lived would be called to account in front of the whole mass of billions upon billions and what's crazy is to conceive of that host of not atomic particles but particular persons, *unrepeatable persons*, and each error — eccentric or old hat — read aloud in front of the rest, which, I mean, that alone seems like it could eat up eternity. And there was nothing you could do to shirk or interject, qualify or defend. Not to mention you were stark naked while God's angel read off your wrongs."

"But not your rights."

"What you did right?"

"Yeah. Merits."

"If so he left that part out."

"Seems — heavy-handed."

Peter wiped his eyes and put out his palms in a plea. His face went flush with little sweat beads. "Don't! I'm — sorry. Not take down my uncle. Without that man I'd be worse than dead. Look at it, maybe, like this, please (and forgive me for getting kind of

66

uptight): he likely didn't want me to get the notion I could bribe somebody to fix the weights or tip the scale to suit my liking. And I wouldn't blame him if his point all along was to scare me into being good because the whole situation our family was in had tilted me toward messing up."

"So he was using hell to scare you? Seems like, sorry I don't mean to disrespect him, but it seems like" — in her one long-held breath he bent his head and hyperventilated through trembling nostrils that widened with anger — "abuse."

"No no no. Oh but I don't think that was his motive. He was a believer all the way down."

"Oh." When he leaned in she didn't rearrange her legs to sit up or scoot away. She did not turn her shy eyes to the side or take back the forbidden words.

After a few seconds he sat back. "But if he taught me terror he taught me music too. No better way to work out the terror." Peter tapped his foot and hummed, his finger clanging the washed-out aluminum spoon against the chipped handle of a coffee cup, culling even from such unpropitious instruments a rhythm and sound that made her smile:

"Don't take it away, Chicago: my childhood my life my *alma mater* of pointless martyrs . . . Sorry," he said, suddenly circumspect, flexing his callusless fingers, "recovering musician. Haven't played, not seriously, since I started my Masters."

"Don't you? I — don't know I would live if I stopped with the piano. Well I do. Because I have, now, for . . . since I've been here. And it's been awful all the way down. Like if Cabrini had even an out-of-tune instrument I'd be there weekends playing loud when no one can hear."

"Do you know Bill Evans?"

"Oh yes, is there a song . . . ? 'Two Lonely People.' Love it. But I don't play him. Can't really cut a page of jazz without feeling like I'm trying too hard."

"Classical?"

"Chopin. Debussy. Some Satie. But sure, I know classical. You — did you say you played trumpet?"

"My favorite, but saxophone and even drums from time to time. As I mentioned, my uncle was a music man. Played with Miles Davis for a time. Became a regular player at The Blue Nile in New Orleans back in the seventies when he was only twenty."

Peter stood as the waitress walked by and tipped his empty cup up under the spout of her chrome carafe. His phone buzzed and he pleaded "*Excuse me, I'm so sorry. I have to take this.*" He kept repeating "*Who are you?*" throughout and she'd wanted to tell him so much more but by now she sensed that she needed to do something drastic to win herself into his attention — though once she arrived there she was certain he would keep her, know her, take her under his bedcovers.

When they walked out into the undead night, the sleepless circuitry reeling all around in whirring cars and parked cars blasting music to rival the sound of Cabrini-Green's demolition.

. . .

Yes again and again and again and again, night after night after night after night, they walked out into the undead light, the sleepless circuitry remaking their minds, as if the switchboard machine of the city slipped wires into the nerves of their flesh. She pressed her hip against him hard, staring at the red dots that blinked S. O. S. from the tips of two tall towers that how in hell could they not fall?

"Look. I can call in sick tomorrow — at Cabrini's. Nobody's coming for counseling anyhow except for you and, as we can both see, it's *you*, you who done analyzed me. I want you to — not feel obliged. To have every possible out."

"I want to see inside your house. What where you live is like. Inside." The audacious words came out only half-convincing, rashly wishful from her bashful face whose blush flushed, red as a fire-extinguisher clamped against a tenement wall. How she flinched from the telltale blood. She could not clear the hurdle of hesitation without her heels catching. She almost tripped on a construction cone and gripped — then ripped off — a bannered swathe of POLICE LINE DO NOT CROSS.

"Can I call you?" he asked, "Not that, I mean, I would invite you out or in or whatever but tonight so much came out it's like I'm *intoxicated* by so much telling, by the way you hear me, and I want to, better be, sober and ready if you ever are ready for . . . I mean, I don't like to . . . I mean it's your . . ."

"I don't have a phone." He had not yet asked because up to now they had played the accident, the "Fancy meeting you here" after school.

"Oh man that's a new one, a first, I mean, as a way of foreclosing."

"Okay. A track phone I've got, but it's so cheap I can only make outgoing calls."

"You *are* slumming it. Or lying. Scared of me, like anyone in her right mind should be."

"I know my kids, my students — they all got me beat with whatever tech they carry around, taking covert hits underneath the desks from their, like, electric cocaine. Technically banned at Cabrini's, you know, but it's an inside joke with all of us because the principal hasn't figured out how to redress hundreds of infractions without seventy-five percent of the students in detention instead of their classes where at least — we can hope — they're less likely to look at, I mean, you know, what."

"Right. Another way I break from the highest standards of my profession. I can't abide this out of tune jive about masturbation bringing relaxation because, 'studies say,' in an age of distraction it's good to focus on only one thing and it's, 'studies say,' psyche-soothing. I can't compassionate — all that airbrushed fake sex. Grotesque. But no more pamphleteering, no more half-cast opinions cast out like they was Brahmin — you know, that was my biological name, Brahmin, legally was my name until eighteen, I tell you this so that you realize who you're in the presence of." He threw his head back in mute laughter. "I should let you leave, leave you alone. It's late. Or early, depending on how you look at it."

Wearing the POLICE LINE like an ostentatious scarf, she flew ahead, looking over her shoulder, testing, to see whether her direction was sound.

"Not too late to ask me on another date. Or to ask me, properly, for the first time outright. Instead of just letting it kind of just happen."

When his eyes went shy she walked before him and turned to be sure, teasing all the way to his room to be sure they were still on the right track. If Blake could see her. What he had left. She felt him watching her fertile hips and felt where she wanted his hands to be, swaying and swaying and playing all the way.

They passed a Planned Parenthood clinic and she crossed to the other side of the street. He caught up quickly and said "Wrong side" but she said "I'm not that kind of girl." He gave a scared smile and laughed hard and dry. "You laughing because I'm not a girl at all. Old maid. Don't be mean."

"I'm — not."

"I'm kidding," she said, sure she'd tested too far, skipping, almost, spritely, ahead.

As she stayed in the lead Peter shouted out directions — "Left!" or "Right!" — whenever she stopped, cupping her ear to hear his secret map. He bridged the distance, was fast beside her, when a cluster of teenagers blocked their path. "Get lost, fast." She heard the elevated, earnest inflection that commanded his negotiations with the group. Tensed tendons and muscles eased. Tiptoed kids fell back on their heels as he flashed gritted teeth that said *don't mess.* She could not believe she had lost her wariness. Normally her right fingers, when she walked these streets alone, gripped the little key-chain pepper spray, while her left hand on the phone poised over CALL because 911 was already typed into the screen. The electric fence of inhuman vigilance had been shut off, bereft of watts, the entire time she had been with him.

She looked back once more from a cocoon of darkness that appeared between twin bungalows whose roofs nearly touched, even though at the base they stood a good six feet apart. Tall in stature they leaned, tired, like sleeping watchmen in the American night. She ducked between and felt the thick cloak of darkness. She stuck her head out, scared for Peter. If she tipped on her toes she could peer over car tops to be sure he was still standing. Out of habit she entered the numbers and suspended her thumb over CALL. As if his sending her here in this unlit pocket was a protection against plausible harm. Her head swiveled and she sucked in breath, eyes adjusting and her nostrils also to a sick admixture of ammonia and glue, burnt metal and fast-food wrappers. Beside an overfull industrial trash bin a plastic bubble waited to pop. Glints of light that leaked down from an exhaust grate like the red eyes of a hibernating predator pierced the plastic coating with scarlet beams. Or the beams were white but the bag bloodied. She shined her phone — a faint blue orb — into the bag and vomited at once.

What at first seemed surely butcher refuse — she remembered the dumpster behind dad's deli, one time a parboiled pig carcass that turned out rancid — this time proved an eyeless baby in fetal position bent dead before her blinking eyes. Her lids lifted and fell like wipers clearing the window in a downpour. The skin was jaundiced with a neon glow that conjured pictures of Chernobyl. Whatever the sockets had once possessed had disappeared; all that remained were flattened jelly sacks, slick and sickly, like a spoiled condiment, that sucked Stella's stare into the hollows of the head. His head or her head? The lips had retreated back past the gums but could not remove the curves of a smile. No extant nose: sinus vacuoles in still-solid bones. A pretty forehead incongruous with the forceps marks and the discolored skin like plastic melted in a microwave or a doll dropped at a bomb site that had not, any more than her former owner, survived the dose of radiation.

"Hey! Back off my baby," said someone, "my baby, my baby," from an open window, elbows out, looking down on her — a spidery woman in a sleeveless T-shirt whose face was all shadow through the aura behind her.

"I'm calling the police!" Stella screamed.

By her sound Peter located her, but not before she was speaking, breathless, with an operator though he said "Call it off! Police'll only make it all worse," but she pointed to the indentation, the concave insect nest of the city, the center of a spider web she had stumbled into in search of safety.

"Yes, I'm sure, it's a baby," she said, muffling her voice as if to protect it from voyeurs and listeners who everywhere lurked. She screamed again, reading off the street signs, trying to determine the closest intersection. "A baby, a baby! A human baby!"

A gunshot ricochet from the open window, the spidery widow.

Peter pulled at her elbow and dragged her, stiff legs scissoring in zigzag patterns, dodging and trying to confuse the aim of their enemy. She moved but her mind died for a time, and then she was moved and not the author of her movement, the density and weight of her body increasing without a will to direct the limbs. The eerie siren-signals of her thoughts grew faint and then faded and when they returned, rebounded off the blocky buildings, they sounded not like amateur radios but more like the moans of a dying animal — and she remembered that Christmas day long ago when her dog had died on her lap, in her arms, stretched across her brother's lap too (how they always fought to be sure they both had exactly a half of him), and how when the movie reeled along long enough all fighting ceased, all the world at peace, and the black and white movies they watched around Christmas and all the fainting ladies they contained and how every time another woman lost confidence her whole family would laugh together...

She woke in the half-life of a limbo world — what remained of her consciousness almost absolute confusion — amazed, in a maze. Shapes and sounds amounted, when she tried to make sense of them, to nothing. They ran in what seemed like predestined circles but everything was — seemed, came off as — completed, determined: like the onset of morphine haze that makes deliberations and decisions impossible, a liberation and a horror at once.

"Here," Peter said, pulling her carefully. She thought he meant a dilapidated house, big front porch, blue-shingled, windows open, wind-swept, empty and clean but inhabited by a mournful absence. A single bulb, just inside the door, surpassed the noontime sun in its brightness. She started to pull then, against his strength, to depart from the track, to ascend the stairs, but he said, "No, there." But as she looked back over her shoulder at the single bulb that summoned her up, the light — if pleasing and alluring from a distance — let loose on her eyes, burned her consciousness awake and she knew, all at once, her every mistake and wrong and she ran back into his arms, huddled, hid, her nose now running with snot, nuzzled without shame into his shoulder, his breaths, the rapid rhythm of his chest doing the work of a defibrillator and as they stood in front of his complex — a thin, five-storied, washed-out brick block and the hallway light was a stingy gold, shaped like the single bulb but half screwed in, and the city of Chicago, because that's where they were, would lose all power if the bulb were fully screwed — not because of what this no-place would take from buildings of officious consequence, but because what the light brought from pain-killing shadows would, when seen, arrest the arrhythmias of all remaining human beings who had not succumbed to the somnambulist dream shot across the millions of screens.

By the time they reached the complex stairs she caught sight, in the corner, of a pair of limp legs and he said "Watch that needle" and pointed at his shoes — "Why I wear boots." A man said "Sweet Jesus" and no matter how hard she stretched the aperture of her aching eyes she could not make out the face of the man but his pants were pulled up past his knees and they reeked of urine soaking his socks and the sores were like craters on an alien planet and Peter said "Ration your sympathies, please" as he creaked the hinges of the heavy door and it scraped like a solitary confinement cell. As her feet followed his — her hand in his hand — they stepped over strewn-out, strung-out bodies whose faces all had the same mouth-slack satisfied expression etched into their fixed flesh like the perished population of a bombed town.

"I could condemn, but . . . I can't not see how you could get to that point, all right? Could have been — maybe could be — me."

The bodies — and there seemed to be some twenty — at first looked wind-thrown, scattered randomly, but as they turned down a widened walkway the chain of unconsciousness could be traced back to one half-open door. A woman's wail sounded strangled within — like whistling through a twisted straw, but then the same voice let out a sigh and said "Thank you," accompanied by a heavy thump.

"None of it's real," she said aloud, and he let out a disgusted laugh fast retuned into a caught cry that sounded like "Why?" His eyes looked violated, struck back. Were they going up or going down? She clutched her heart. Help. Wrong way on an escalator? For some time now in the back of her brain, where the synapses struggled to stay awake, she was certain — for sure — that the baby in the bag was nothing but an elaborate hallucination: the gross product of all her fears. But when she saw what her denials did to him she broke down, hands over eyes, crying, her fingers clawing over the veiled flesh that hid, burning, in her sockets.

In his apartment — 421 — only a nightlight shaped like a flame, gleaming blue from the wall outlet, lit their way to the studio mattress, coloring the white striped bedsheets with the blue hue of a back burner, keeping their faces shadowy, hidden.

He pulled two chairs — scratchy orange plastic — and placed them firmly two feet apart. Seeing her hide the strained stretch of her back, he handed her a pillow from the bed. The scarlet pillowcase was meticulously framed by knotted yellow yarn that dangled downward like a hundred thin abacus lines fixed in fated tallies.

Knees pressed tightly together, hands splayed, white-knuckled, on her hips, she tried to say what she had seen, tripping in surreptitious defeat against all attempted explanations. All fell into elongated ellipses, as if the dead baby were prophylactically protected by the puffed-out plastic, industrial strength bag which was made — it seemed — to keep toxic waste in and to deflect all interpretations as if they were dangerous — acid rain. Impoverished mongering of buried meaning from a dead alphabet — exotic sarcophagus engravings whose letters — etched once with vigor and conviction — failed, now, to signify.

They did not speak, let themselves stare sleepy at their hands and steal little looks and try to give smiles against the facts that they had seen.

"I have to make it right," she said. "It's mine to make right. Who else? Can't offload it elsewhere, can we?"

"Why? Or, I mean: isn't that assigning some supreme meaning to no more than — the random, to *chance*? I mean you know there's countless discarded babies, abandoned. But *one* out of the countless comes your way and — doesn't it require a . . . pretense? To surmise that one little increment can matter against the *avalanche* of indifference, or — no, the right word — planetary *mass grave abyss* — where cruelty keeps piling up?"

"And that's why when you saw those kids, cross-armed and pissed, armed and restless, you crossed like the chicken to the other side?"

He nodded, exhaled, rubbed his chin against his sternum and then leaned back until the chair legs lifted off the floor and she reached out certain that he was about to collapse.

"Why I like you. One of the reasons. Push against my prejudices — like — was it Jameson who said it — *history is what hurts.* Like whatever little good we scrounge could be worth nothing if it's not world-historical . . . though for me, increasingly, the bigger problem is: the poverty of what counts as unequivocally 'good,' anymore . . . all that's survived as always defensible: preventing people from violent deaths, especially children or so-called 'delinquent youth,' like the kids who gave me this scar, here," and as he pointed beneath his ear the parted scrap of flesh appeared as if his pointing there brought it into being.

"What happened? Why didn't you tell me?"

"We had other matters that needed tending."

"What happened?"

"I can't: if I say it aloud that'll only make it worse. Way the world is, the way it is."

A metallic beetle, nose down, passed, golden searchlight weaving between the buildings — a helicopter that came close to hitting a mirrored wall of offices, but halted before it rose in a rush and rooted elsewhere, a disconnected dot in the night, at once meaningless and another clip of low-level terror that acquired — precisely because it meant *something*, but something unknown to her — an ambient anxiety, always there like electronic tonalities that tolled without rest in any city. The search surely had an object known by someone. It was simply the case that she did not know it, and what if she were to know the objects of the thousands of vehicles

75

and the millions of persons? That level of omniscience would translate into instant madness, as whatever was in us — what she once called, what she once again wanted now to call soul — was not a high-powered computer switchboard.

He held her hand through a quarter hour of silence, until she started to hold him back. He stood and rummaged through brown cupboards for crackers, a can of broth, and set them before her with a tray of teas.

She accepted a cup — "ginger, please" — and after the steam whistle warmed his face and they watched the scalding water turn the yellow-gold of congregated sun drops she felt, as she sipped it, the same symptoms her friends with morning sickness told her could be eased and soothed by the bitter heat.

They waited long and said nothing, necks bending like drooping sunflowers, drifting into a haze of half-sleep, and when she woke up, desperate to forget, she sat on his lap and said, "Yes."

He teased by pulling her POLICE LINE scarf, still intact, and holding up DO NOT CROSS. Soon her fingers were gripping and then unclasping the buckle of his belt (it felt so loose when she freed the notch she wondered how his pants had stayed up) and he was unsnapping her jeans' silver button, and she remembered falling into bed with Blake and how he always kept her clothed when they kissed and here she was almost forty-one replaying in her mind Nonna's little lectures against her anarchic, ephemeral, "meaningless teenage hormones, is all" — as if all that sex could be were configurations of immoral chemicals — which, were it the case, then marriage too was just a convenient contractual way to keep the hormones regulated.

She cooled. She asked if she could use his shower. The narrow downpour numbed her mind — the cold water that only grew colder when she turned the knob toward the etched H.

Stepping out, she found a robe, coarse white with scarlet stripes, and buried her shivering body in it, outsized by some seven times. She laughed when he asked if she was ready — "A little late" — but breathed out a reverberating yes that rattled and rose from under her ribs as they found the mattress, and surely she woke the neighbors, with her *Yes*, a shattering of boundaries which became — bizarrely — part of the thrill, but her head was a game of glassy marbles, the shooter sending scattered losses and sudden wins as she raised her elbows and framed her face between two equal triangles as if to lean on Euclid's sureties as she entered this nervous amorphous shape of two bodies merging into one, and as his lips found her ears she could not stop her squinted eyes from searching for signs of other women — detritus, discarded clothing of other girls who he maybe took here too, and as he reached into a bedside drawer and rummaged blind, his prickly mouth — he seemed so clean-shaved — brushing hers, to find the little plastic packet that held the latex sheath he stretched, she said "If you want me you have to risk me."

His eyes, first scared, fell to a steady stare — at the wall, at a future he had long written off and found now not wanting but somehow worth daring. He managed a silent *I do*, but he cooled and his body turned toward the wall, arms awkward and legs tilted fetal like a praying mantis.

Remaining still, stiff, on his side, he reached out with stealth but she saw him tap and sneak a glance at his phone. Disgust and devastation picketed her sacrifice of dignity, held up their handmade cardboard signs, but she shoved them aside to solicit his desire, to make him want without betraying her wants. She kissed his neck, ran her finger down his spine, and felt at its tips the thrilling tingle she meant to coax from him.

"You on something?" he said and she watched as her hand flicked the back of his head, only after perceiving his meaning. He cut short, dropped his hands, cooled.

She could not say "No," could not coax him with a lie, so she kissed the knuckle that hurt from where she hit him.

But as he wrapped his cold body in a thick cotton robe and fell back, fetal-curled, onto the mattress, before she threw herself on his chest, felt him cover her in his wrappings, she could see — as her hips found his — their baby, a little jaundiced, premature, but a flailing free fall of raw life, due to be swaddled in his daddy's blue cotton. A host of needs only she could salve. Peter startled by his helplessness as he could not calm the air-sucking infant. She would hold that baby with fierce affection, not oblivious to her pain after eighteen hours of interrupted labor. And then life would not be, anymore, *about* her. To have succor as her purpose and to succeed completely at something for surely the first time.

He tapped the screen and tried, but failed, to shield the ubiquitous blue-white burst of light.

"I'm sorry, I was just trying to silence it," he said, as she rolled off of him and saw the shape, in the peeled paint of his far wall: a heart-shaped daffodil bulb, buried, waiting out winter to begin the bloom.

"Seriously. Please let it slip. I'm here. Yours. All the way."

As much as any man's heart can be, she silently recited, *inevitably — fated, he'll see — divided.*

"This could be *our* bed, not *mine*," he said. "You get me, seriously, like nobody, maybe. I want to know you, totally, too.

"This could be *our* bed, not *mine*," he said again, turning to silence his vibrating phone.

The florist shop, she saw now — that bulb — had been for her a safe place, a cope, to solve the sense of mute failure that followed her Kairos experiment after college.

"I was once in a commune, for a while. A little while. Full of ideals. After college," she said, surprised at herself for saying so. Here. Now. But her ears tingled pleasingly when she heard said out loud the source of her trouble. "Don't, I'm not talking about being *triggered*, not talking, please hear me, about *trauma* — though you'll be the first to tell me that in fact the commune was the source of my whole life's woes. It's just . . . To this day words like 'living simply' and 'community' and even 'ours' feel, to me, like, like . . . cancer cells on the tongue. I'm sorry," she kissed him and let him feel hers, for reassurance, as if to press against the sick image. She remembered the sure abandon of sharing all, taken literally by two dozen people, executed with exactitude. "In the commune — Kairos, it was called, a backwoods place in western Wisconsin — they disparaged all hierarchies. Not just meals were common but everything." How she'd grown sickly still or started laughing when the leader Jane Galley stood at the table and said, eyes closed, eyelids blue as if painted with makeup but not: "Put the self to sleep and wake up." Though Stella was sure that her fellow members would rouse an equal and opposite reaction, when she looked around everyone only nodded. *Put the self to sleep* was a favorite, repeated as though it were a scripture proverb. "They had us switch bedrooms every seven days to learn detachment, to 'put the self to sleep,' as Jane put it. 'Put the self to sleep and wake up.'"

"But let me guess," Peter rubbed his right lid. A fleck disappeared as his eyes went wide: "All her talk had, in short order, found a *de facto* governance through Jane's careful 'curations.'"

"Did you live there, too?" She laughed, quickly giddy as if his bed were an elevator, dropping, dropping to the ground floor.

"All the same everywhere, I tell you. So predictable it isn't funny."

"And opposition to those careful 'curations' earned you public reproof, let me tell *you*."

"You got reproved? How did it end?"

"Ended with me sleeping in a bathtub rather than share the bed of Jane who had shown up nonchalant in the night and said, tired-like, she'd been disturbed to see how fiercely I was withholding, keeping back my self, she said, and sometimes the best way to overcome what was in most instances an indoctrinated instinct, a combination of shyness and selfishness, was to share a bed with someone you still felt was a stranger."

Footsteps followed Stella's half-naked slip out, ceased at the hall's end when she locked herself in the bathroom and her body, after an hour, across the ceramic casket of a tub, nodded off, "nodded off until the first sign of sun and a headache, neck-ache, woke me up," the ceramic, the bone white ceramic pressed against her skull, "and because I couldn't tell if she was there, still, outside the door, if the footsteps stopped because she left or because she was standing there waiting all night, I crawled out the window and fled through the forest, showed up at a gas station Greyhound stop a day later covered in burrs. Took a bus with the money I'd hidden under my foot since I first showed up when they asked us to hand over all our possessions, 'to put the self to sleep.'"

"Man," he said, propping himself up, badly balanced on an elbow, "I'm sorry. I didn't mean to move so fast. Ours. I mean. Or maybe it's not even, for you, a matter of speed. But of *ever*. Of staying away forever from *ours*."

"No *this*, if anything," she gestured to the space between them, the fissure of sheets she watched her fingers flatten, "we have to own: if we're doing this this is *ours* to own. Not *mine*. Not *yours*. Ours."

The walls of Peter's bedroom looked like butcher paper from her father's deli. Again Peter let his full weight fall back on the bed, let every controlled muscle collapse. He leaned back like a blood-drained thing and turned, like one wounded, and said:

"You're withholding."

"Not as much as you."

"I'm naturally shy."

"Could have fooled me."

"I like to hear you. Don't let it go to your head."

Patches on his faintly red ceiling peeled away to reveal white speckles, asymmetrical whirling stars.

"Before we go any further, Stell, I'm not stalling but I got to stay honest, I have to tell you something, here. About *that* day. That man. And me."

"Which man?"

"You'll see. Give me a minute.

"Used to play wrestle with me when he showed up earlier in the evening. Even then he'd cut things short and say look at this boy he don't know when to stop. And he'd flop down on the fat couch and point me to my room. Momma nodded. Strange even now how no matter what I had no anger at her.

"Enough. See. Something there is about you. Brings things into the light . . . not the naked broiling sun but a lamp, like, with a soft shade."

"I'm glad."

Stella leaned into his shoulder, felt her blood rush there as to a wound. Her legs felt sick still from walking, slack as the spat gum that someone had stretched from a light post — like a tightrope — to a fire escape. She rubbed her thigh and stretched her knee and let her leg rest slightly over his, resting or consoling it was his to interpret, so it was his to take or leave or break whatever little she could give.

"I should tell you now, in case you need to scream and run and," he swung around widely, the pivoting axis of his leg at an angle that matched the earth's. "I should say, fess up, forewarn, that I . . . killed a man, once, or may as well have, and they locked me up. Juvie, the whole works. That was what started my wanderings out West. I knew, then, why so many outlaws kept crawling toward the Pacific, away from whatever wrongs they done, like if you go far enough West you'll — you follow? — no longer be . . . what . . ."

"East of Eden."

"Yes! But the knife thrust — a piece of metal mined a million miles away from who knows how deep in earth's bowels, melted and molded into a perfect point with a sharpness that could cut right through all the fat life throws at you. That blade! Was my best of some dozen I kept under my bed or in my pockets (mom was always pointing out another knife I left on the floor or bathroom counter or kitchen sink, blade out and almost cutting her wrist as she threw blue Comet across the entire surface of the room and scrubbed until her muscles tapped out).

"What I did — was it putting something into the world or taking something out, I don't know, thrusting the blade between the ribcage bars and trying to kill the prisoner that hunched in the corner throbbing and beating and hiding from my murderous rage — it was, I swear it, in self-defense for the sake of my moms, though he did not strike her at least so far as I had seen and he didn't threaten but I knew it was coming, percolating like his perpetual cup of decaf on the stove, back burner mama kept on as if he'd be coming home to stay showing up at any hour and she'd be there, ever-ready, convincing the wanderer to rest in her arms, sleep in her bed on a permanent basis, burning that stove gas like a charm, adding here and there a cup of water, a spoon of grounds when the coffee got watery, all vigilance always, all days, in case he'd show up unannounced, for which mom always kept a jar with purest clumps of whitest sugar 'cause he complained if anything bitter passed between his frustrated lips. You should have seen them curl and strain when the blade cut through his starched shirt and dug into his drum-taut skin.

"And so what if I didn't off him. I was so disappointed that I didn't. So what. What, tell me, is the real difference? I saw her wanting him stable, staying, sticking it out, stuck with us, her desperate wish all my damn childhood without knowing who the man was — she never told me even to this day he was my dad, my uncle had to say it.

"Far from her husband, he was somebody else's, though this she didn't find out for a decade, he's a traveling man she met late one night when he walked, on accident, into a room she was cleaning for cash on the side, a tender dude given to tears and holding his head in his hands before her, begging her to make him feel better and praising her and paving out promises, another working Odysseus who got lonely on the road and maybe missed home but didn't stop him from borrowing a body. He'd show up on cocaine, it seemed, or could have been some cheaper amphetamine in the middle of the night — his eyes like planets beaming this big intolerable brightness, mama'd not hear him so I got the door and he'd walk in and make a wild gesture as if he was letting *me* in the door and so it went for years like a dream that kept recurring: me letting him in and watching him disappear down mom's crowded, darkened hallway where he'd expect to be put up and her, no doubt — I'm the product! — put out. I don't — she to this day won't tell me what it was possessed her to have me on standby on an absolute order to unlock the deadbolt, let loose the chain and slide the crowbar and toss away the other twenty means installed to keep us all alive. (And I'd have to put them all back in place after he disappeared down the hall! I'd have to . . . lock him *in!*) At my worst I worried, worry that she owed him something, but what I've no clue, because she didn't have nothing to show for it and if I ever mentioned the man she shut her lips like with sutures or stitches, closed no matter if she wanted to speak.

"One night I sleepwalked into the kitchen and peed on the floor where they were standing there talking and when he slapped my face — 'a joke!' — she grabbed his collar and he shoved her hard, then followed up with an elbow to her rib, pressing mama against the oven and he held her head over the burner and turned the dial, with his other hand, high and looked in my eyes, his own total bankruptcy bugging out of them irises black and brown and stirred with rancor like some horror show ventriloquist doll straight up escaped from the factory of hell I do not here exaggerate I swear I was seeing a son of Satan all other explanations fall short even to this day, his shock his mop of crazed black hair shiny and pointed in six directions, combed back with his now freed fingers but spraying like springs against his propriety against the gel that was supposed to hold he pivoted and pointed at me and said, real calm, 'Be a good boy,' and said as if I was culprit 'Be a good boy' and I grabbed the knife gramma used to use to gut the pig she got each Easter and I lunged for him like I'd played at doing with my friends in the alleys like this one time man behind Jones Uriah's Corner Variety where we'd dumpster-dive for shiny metal, whatever and we were playing with blades, flipping them out and pretending to spar in that ghetto twilight — golden blue with an aura of pollution — and out of that light and right towards us comes this big kid — skinny but sure of himself like a force — a pistol out, shouting for 'Ugo, you all is hiding Ugo,' and Ugo was behind the dumpster crying and with his pistol pointed at my skull I charged, knife out, right at his heart and he ran away and I never saw the kid again and now I lunged just like that at Mister 'Be a good boy' who had the sickest leer in his eyes, I swear the purest evil I've ever seen, a mixture in the iris like muddied water stirred and stirred and stirred forever, a slow-cooking wrath, a recipe not of his invention, an infinite anger that got in my eyes like splashes of muddied blue when I lunged and he fell back when I fell ahead and if he hadn't he'd not be alive but at the time I was sure he was dying and he said — with an honesty I still find refreshing, his limbs trembling and starting to stiffen like rigor mortis was sped up somehow: 'I couldn't possibly hate anyone more than I do you now. I never meant to bring you here, into the world, but I did, and here's what I get.'"

83

"Crazy thing was what was playing on the record, the table in the living room, on low and so faint you could hardly hear it was some kind of spinoff or should I say rip-off awful riff on Coltrane's *A Love Supreme*, which to this day I can't but feel as some kind of desecration, albeit of a lesser kind.

"So there. I'll spare you the rest. I didn't kill him. He bled but lived. I didn't kill him but may as well have. Dreamed that night that he was drunken and shrunken and caged in a cockfight in a mildew basement, one bulb dangling from a string suspended above the contenders, small as a chicken but as stout as ever he hypnotized his rival chicken and the thing clucked in the corner and cowered and didn't twitch.

"After an ambulance and police fiasco I woke in the police station sad as hell that he had lived to spin the story. I knew — I tell you — the sadness of hell. He had so much baggage with my mom that he abstained entirely like some magnanimous saint from pressing even a single charge but I was punished anyhow — Juvie — and, so as not to bore you, as you can see I'm a gentleman now but buried like that last decaying moth eating decay into my insides like crazy inside a painted sarcophagus is that kid I once was. This is the part where you run away in terror, back there to that officer. Happens every time," he said. "Not that I ever dared to tell the whole thing until now. Something there is about you, Stella, I almost *can't not confess*."

Agitated, like a cat that's been declawed without warning, he slit the blinds of the slender window at the sign meant to flash *Manhattan* but was mangled in a spot someone had apparently dangled from, and instead said only *Manhat*. "All that's missing is the *e*," he said, cool and smiling, and she saw his eyes swivel as he followed a follicle that stuck out, static, from her hair.

"Don't. I am. Not impressed in the way you want. Nothing you could or did do is anything I haven't wanted to or couldn't, though it'd take maybe more than even my Nonna's best pitch to convince you to get right with God. C'mon." She tried to go on, but her will numbed and dragged against her acceptance of the man, of the would-be man-slaughterer beside her who suddenly

84

stood, stuck out his chest, a flex, a strain of confidence against a slumping body that had aged in the telling of too many hidden things. Under the breaking azure rays that blinked from the sun's risen circle his smile, the one that seemed always on, percolating on the slow blue flame of the back burner behind his face, it fizzled out into a cold convulsion. His lips clamped and twitched when he tried to part them.

"Look, I don't feel guilt. Naw. You wouldn't either because there's none to be had. Tell me it's impossible for a patricide to say it straight-faced. To kill your father —

"But you didn't, *you didn't*," and she feared he had but had tried to cover it and now was working up to full confession.

"To kill — Scripture's where it says hate for your brother might as well be murder. If I were going to play the moral game I'd demand to be measured against the most refined morality ever made by gods or men. But my point is I could take that scripture and rip it right out from the Bible and chew it and swallow and watch it turn to shit and still feel no remorse. To kill your father and know no onus. It's one of the taboos for man from the beginning, even when you got Saturn devouring his sons (you ever seen that Francisco Goya, painting so powerful could wake the dead! Whole horror of what happens when you go against the enshrined bond, more metaphysical than biological. Deep, man, deep — I mean I really *believe* it's more than a means of keeping oppressed children trembling. Because I felt the fullness of the horror when I watched him wish he could devour me there, when I knew he would have, too, if he wasn't weakened, would have given anything to eat and unmake the kid he'd had on accident who paid him back by showing up, three-dimensional, an animate curse, a personal message from his bad conscience. A wish he took with him into his grave."

At this she felt again the hitch of fear, tried to mouth "superstitious" but couldn't, was about to tell him "You didn't mean that" when he said "I'm sorry, I didn't mean that," and she fell into a cadaverous quiet as if her strength had petered out. A spinning siren swiveled her head; a store of adrenaline kept in some back cellar flowed and found the ends of her limbs and tingled through her brain matter. He looked almost scared of the mask that had formed on her sad past-worn face. When she reached for his fingers with both of her hands he made as if to retract but then let her warmth hold him still, let her take his pulse and kiss the lips that could not form a word, which showed them both how badly he was shivering. So they laughed a little and parted slowly and his lips slipped lightly away like the last mourning dove departing from the char-stained fire escape that reached up stories lost in the mist Lake Michigan gave like a cloak of morning.

Breathing his hesitation in heavily, she felt her resolve kink like a hose, feared the death of their desire. He went tense, not lax, except between the legs. What if she couldn't rouse his body again? What if, when she could, she couldn't match his form — if her movements came out amateur?

But as her hand fell between his legs and she held him shyly, turning away, she could not believe how easy it was to wake his wants and give them shape. The ease scared her but she still held tight.

The lodged marbles of her thought she couldn't move said *this is how it is, this is how it has to be, inevitably,* like the atoms of her every synapse were planets running their course (of course!) and her thoughts were these same atoms acting out unswerving, unbidden, and absolutely inevitable laws. Her half-admitted, hidden plan to save this man whose pose of shamelessness was sadder for all the cool surety he thought he affected — she found this failure endearing, finally. She covered her breasts with a tense-muscled X and he turned, muttering "No I do. I do. I do," and only now did she know for sure this was the first time she had ever seen him scared.

Part of her wanted a full transcription of the secret conferences he kept with himself as, shivering and pulling a blanket around him, he turned and rose and, cloaking them both with the useless camouflage of the green goose down blanket, he put his palms on the balls of her shoulders: the pressure pleased her, she let him stretch, did not protest the heave of his weight, repeated *here's how it has to be, what it would come to inevitably,* and when his hip bones scraped

86

against hers she did not say *stop it hurts* but counted a crazed pulse of cardiac arrest she hadn't felt since a high-school Cadillac-backseat fuss that lasted fifteen clumsy minutes and left her with none of the pleasure he gave, now, with such gentle recklessness, his tensed jaw opening as she told herself she could shrug him off she could throw him out of his very bed, and the thrill of not knowing when he would come and the thrill of thinking she could still turn back, cut short, call off, continued to trill until his closed eyes slit and she felt flush with his final tremor. When he finished a flick of disgust lifted his lip as he rose to clean and she knew at once the weight of her illusion — her scheme of saving him a bad joke — though if he had taken more than he'd given, more of *what* she could not say because the lively mess he had left inside her — she could see the flagellum kicking like kids, swimming like in the lessons she had taken as a child, sinking more the harder she pumped her legs — the mess could make nothing more than nightmares of the future, could do no more than rip the sepia-spinster photos she'd preserved in amber as if her childless state were a fate or a fact, a surety that her fertile years had ticked to an end.

Stella could not fathom, fully, satisfyingly, where the *wanting* of children came from, really. Was it truly the case that she wanted to give or was a baby something like a *proof* of her existence? After Blake the ache was awful, unsayable, but since Chicago she had figured out how to press on with duties in spite of the desire, the persistent presence that would not die, accompanied almost always by the nagging fear that she could not make a baby anymore, that her baby days were over, missed, the thousands of possible souls she could bring irretrievable, purely theoretical. The fear followed her, still, everywhere, and the child would appear, unbidden, at the end of a workday while she set the children's desks: the shadow of a baby learning to walk but scared into a stupefied stance because every time she takes a step the shadow takes one too — terrifying — until only the shadow seemed real and the baby a fading hallucination.

The sink water sloshed down the drain. The sucking sound had all the bad manners of a late-night diner. He spat and cleared his throat and stumbled, first, then slunk and crawled back in the blanket without a shadow because the windowless room housed darkness well. Was this a basement unit or were there really no windows or were his curtains black enough to block out all messengers of light? Head rested on the pillow, she peered over to where he was crawling, saw now clearly the thin nightlight was not at all like a blue stove fire, not at all, she nearly shook her head *no*, not a gas flame but a tear, a single ossified drop of salt water, blue water illumined by starlight.

. . .

The next morning Principal Halves was waiting at the entrance with a tissue box that was, it turned out, filled to overflowing with a fabric of gauzy baby blue, and the secretary who was Nadine's mother — Stella's best student, who always called her Miss Stellar — was coaching and ushering the swarming arrivals into some semblance of a straight line. All who entered were "asked" — meaning required, meaning forced — to wear matching surgical masks and so the kids were making fun of death and turning the threat into a game — biting holes into the middle of the mouth cloth, trying to blind their passing crushes by covering their eyes with the blue folds, breaking the elastic because it would not fit: "But if you didn't have such a big head," they teased each other, "maybe if you wasn't so *arrogant*, you could stand to put this on for a second and see how you're really not that *important* — "

Stella needed to get her breath. She left the room and passed Peter in the long hallway that led to the ladies' room. Both, mouths masked like visiting surgeons, eyes starved for a clue or a code, made polite bows and passed on by, pretending never to have met.

. . .

Eggs at Genesis Grocery on Pullman were priced at half a dozen for a dollar. They sat at a rickety, propped-up table in the back window corner of Ishmael Jones's, sobered, half-satisfied, leaning, just slightly, into a shared plate of scrambled surrounded by soft-boiled, runny, hot sauce-steeped eggs.

"The way mama made it. My favorite. Nobody but Charon's can match this shack's flavor. Hot sauce, a dash, and fresh-ground pepper."

Her side ached. She put his hand there, felt a warm tingle, but his fingers could not stop the pulsations, the pain that shot through a galaxy of nerves.

Stella nodded to the sign across the street and said, "I'll learn how to make them. Sales. We'll have to learn how to save." His ears perked up as if she meant something bigger, like the SALVATION writ on the storefront sign above the half dozen for a dollar. "If the baby comes we'll be buying there, not here, no easy restaurant mornings, evenings," she breathed out satisfied, troubled by the heady edge of his tone when he turned and said: "I feel like a new beginning is coming. Like, like I can't even stop it."

"Moira."

"What?"

"Fate. Marjorie. She's back. You're with her."

"Not at all. Not at all." The way he bit his lip, the seethe at the sides of his eyes, reassured her.

"Not Marjorie but fate, yes. Circling back to young aspirations now, regaining them, refined. Like they needed to happen but not back then. Whereas they *have to happen now*. Or not at all. So much of my life's like that. Things that have been handed to me you'd have to be a fool to turn away from, let 'em fall to the floor. I know it seems crazy after all I've said but I'm going to run for alderman. It's not about winning the ticket — I don't stand a chance, probably — but the run would give me the chops and notice I need to take on a bigger thing. Something I can't even speak of yet. My boss —"

"Marjorie?"

"Curtis, mainly and, fair, Marjorie too. Both agree. Stella. Trust me. I wish it wasn't the case, really, but no one else is quite the fit. For what needs to be done in Washington."

"You're running for president or what?"

He did not laugh but he licked his lower lip and looked back at the flashing sapphire sign that said, above LOTTERY, GENESIS CERIES. The first letters were burnt out.

89

"I'm sorry," she said. "I'm jealous. Simple as that. Let's not go there now. The more we would talk about it the worse it'd get. No offense to your counseling skills."

"Which I've been calling into question."

"That's not saying anything. You call *everything* into question."

They stayed silent for a long thirty seconds that dipped like a divot in center of the room.

"Anyway, I believe I interrupted. What you've been handed. What you haven't sought out or chosen." She slipped her arm around his rib.

"Half-chosen — exactly. Can only choose because it's been given. Almost all I am I owe to my Uncle. I couldn't dare try to be a father if he hadn't been one to me first. You in touch with your Dad?"

"Strained since I went South. We were close, once, but now faraway."

"Isn't that every family — close but faraway at once?"

"Harder to be far when we once were close."

"What did it mean to have him around?"

"I guess I . . . took him for granted."

"What we do, isn't it? What we do with what's good."

"I'm sorry you had to go through what you did —"

"— not just *go through*, do, too? I didn't just undergo, I made another almost go under."

"Let's keep that scroll sealed."

"Uncle Cedric'd have something to say. 'There is nothing concealed that shall not be revealed.' A father, more fully than most biologicals. He's given me so much I . . . can't rightly add it up. And either he was entirely deluded to see in me the makings of a star (albeit for him not in politics at all), or whether he spotted a latent talent that is waiting and would be a shame to shuck — man, Stell, I *got* to find out. Whatever I do I do for him no matter how much he looks on me as one sustained disappointment.

"When my Uncle was passing through Cabrini once, on his way, this time, not to a show, but to lead one of them big prayer meetings they'd hold in somebody's basement, packed and sweaty and laying on hands, he left his trumpet on accident. Had to come back through just to get it (I wished he'd made the same mistake a million days, every time). But before he could you better believe I took that instrument and blew until my face turned blue, 'til, I'm not kidding you, I lost consciousness. Passed right out without making a sound. Momma found me when she came home from second shift — she was working in refund processing at this temp agency at the time. But that obstacle was the best thing that could happen to a kid like me. It was nothing to do but beg my uncle not to take it away. Standing there pockets full of toilet paper from crying all day like a champion failure. Momma told him how she found me passed out and he laughed harder than I'd ever seen him, stitch in his side, had to sit down. Head in his hands, he said, 'P. C., look, it's not about how hard you blow. And it's not about you. Most people don't know. Think you just blow into these brass instruments and the melodies arrive unbidden. Like angels waiting there all they needed was your breath. Sit here now. Sit back into the cushion.' He put his hand across my belly. 'Now breathe in like God did before he exhaled his Spirit into Adam. Slow, like you're confident in your purpose. Not reckless. Now press your lips together like this, Pfvvvvvuh,' and I did, spitting back his image so that both of us started smiling now, spittle not quite spraying momma, who stepped into the kitchen and filled two tall glasses though the water always came out warm. She set them down on the TV tray before us and uncle drained the whole glass in one uninterrupted swig. Talk about superhuman to a kid, I mean, I was six years old. Stella I — can't believe I'm just rambling so — I'm —"

"No," she said. "Please please go on."

"So," he continued, fast falling into step. "I can still see him holding forth, stopping to spell out the recipe of firmness and delicacy, tight corners and a loose center. 'Now look. The vibration's got to be there by the time you put the brass against your lips.'"

She kissed him hard and he countered her with that pleasing force, that lover's pressure.

"Man, talking about music makes me miss it. Feel old. Used to sing it all out. Uncle'd be proud. Skat that got straight-up soteriological. My worst enemy D. D. shot in '92 while walking his daily

91

elementary way, the kid I hit in the gut with a baseball on purpose as pitcher 'cause he stuck out his punk tongue cotton candy pink in my face, and I said careful boy I'll strike you out and I wanted the speed of the Guinness book of records, quite a hundred whatever miles per hour, wanted to know that power, you know, when he turned on me like what boy doesn't, jealous 'cause I cracked to the fence and over the chain-link left field boys, and war is peace because after D. D.'s death the gangs got over it, leaders saw the collapse of the child as his ma walked him schoolward, crossfire, ma'am, no pleasure in what we done to your son whose bullet was not meant for anyone else except a rival aimed after and missed, rest in peace. But for me, hearing about it at recess, my brain was flashing with a hot flood and I walked to the edge of the playground and sat and pulled up my hood so no one could see me and said to the streets you did it, what I wished to do man, you hit my enemy in the spleen, I mean, man I mean man you did what I dreamed of doing, damn, damned, quite enough already. So the gangs stopped shooting, a true truce that lasted for three years. Did more, that martyr D. D., for me than the mayor, our neighbor for three long weeks. But all this time later my brother I can't shake it he was right, the Mayor wasn't what they shouted on the sidelines, *Jane Byrne is Ku Klux Klan!* and she wasn't some god like Nero neither though on Easter Sunday gave us bread and circus, yes Ferris wheel the merry-go-round spinning me heavenward on mom's horsey knee and I cried she said when the rides all ended said even then I expected more than any one woman could give. *But what do you think?*" he at last asked Stella and when she tried to bow out with an easy "About what, exactly. It doesn't matter, does it, what I think. I'm just a bunch of privileged cells unfit to comment on your —"

"Living hell!" he shouted.

Then he laughed and his jowls plumped like figs, shined with a rounding edge of purple, surging flesh brightened from years blowing hard blowing late blowing long by ear on the unknown notes of the trombone.

"Tell me something other than hell," she said.

"Other than my own wretched story? Easy. And I won't even say I'm sorry. 'Cause at this point I confess I'm coming to need your ears for healing, the way you take it in."

"And she pondered all these things in her heart."

"Huh?"

"In time I trust you'll know. Now — another story: go!"

He told her the story of Uncle Cedric (his nickname, as a child, was C Minor), "the story of my own maker's start," as they passed birch trees caged in wrought iron and slump-shouldered houses with sagging roofs whose dark-eyed windows winked once in a while. "Forgive me if I leave anything out or add an off-key note that grates. I'll necessarily have to riff from time to time when my mind goes dark and I can't recall the word for word.

"He came back from newspaper delivery at thirteen, in New Orleans. Young as dawn had stood, too, in the doorway, after dragging home late — a little before sunrise, to see, he said, a sagging sunflower — so sad, too hard, he said, to see so much bright going bad — so man he rushed over to try and straighten its chin up, to face it forward (the nuns taught him something about posture), but it slunk its bold gold and brown countenance back into a splay both shamed and blamed on the lack of bright in the sooty twilight. He went back in and got a kitchen knife and cut the stem and laid on the ground and pretended the flower was a straight-up trumpet, moving his hands like the man on the corner they passed each Sunday after church service (Baptist then though schooled by the Catholics). Laying there humming at six a.m. That was when beauty broke in and asked not only for a single song but that his whole life be made into music.

"So he borrowed the trumpet from the street-busking man in exchange for all the coins he'd buried like bullet holes beneath his mattress and went way down an alley to play, afraid to wake the white light from a pissed-off somebody's bedroom. Walked all the way to an edge, a ledgelike place, like the end of the world, where the city ceased and the farmland threshold weighed him in its threshing floor. Fallen to the ground like a spent seed, rising and ripening beside water-sucking weeds, he fingered the valves and bled his brain and never was C Minor the same. And each time he blew he carried the sunflower's kiss on the lips from the flower he held with all that he had. Dude headed right down the street and found the man on the corner fast asleep. Looking both ways he blew it all out, bebopped the Name, beat out the blame, please stop the pain, see my maim, again and again until the sun did its game — again and again the mercy of morning — and the cats crept out the alleyway, bronze beauty singing while he swayed, only to get (at best) a bucket of bath water dropped on his head from on high from above, that pissed-off someone sloshing two feet from his statue-still stance, a dull serious deepness saying, 'Raise your own dead elsewhere!' and something about a statute he didn't understand.

"C Minor fled to the edge of the world and, returning, he handed the trumpet right back in the street man's blistered hands, but that old standby was having none of it, he said, seeing the kid's covetous eyes, 'Git! Git! I got another one hidden, now get you gone by the dawn's early light.'

"None of what C was asked to be was planned. 'Pure predestination,' he said. (Don't argue the point with him, don't even dare. I tried. Don't.) Stayed a man of sorrows all his life but the music made melancholy into joy's little sister.

"C could foresee and would not forestall a freedom to play at any hour, a freedom so full that it had to cost — no stability in the fiscal sense — but he could wake up and shake the dust of a city from his feet and find a spot in a field far enough that ain't nobody listening at midnight to his melancholic joy's little sister. And that's where he learned, lost in the sunflowers, like a plant, no teacher except osmosis."

"Sing in me C of a predestined Pastor who sang the sorrows of his people."

"Sing the shedding seedling falling, hops from the hearse heading towards hell. Deliver a hope in a higher ground where the steeple is so high above sea level people stop squinting 'cause their eyes start to hurt. Spell out the backbreaking burdens in bronze — no churchbells ringing, but Uncle C singing: oh it's hard, my people who the good Lord's heard, o Lord let my people go."

94

Peter elbowed, accidentally, a construction worker bent over a pneumatic drill. "Forgive me," he said, stepping back, placing his hand on the sturdy shoulder of a man whose helmet visor hid his face and whose lips did not utter absolution.

"Unlike some of the folks he prayed with, Uncle saw no inconsistency in playing both the churches and the clubs. But he insisted that we keep the sacred 'elevated' (his word, he never said *separated* or *segregated*) from the profane. He told me most of this outside of our house, away from Mama, just me and him, and just to feel his hand upon my shoulder was to sense what it's like to be *created, breathed into being, not an accident.* Sometimes he'd take me walking later than usual in the neighborhood — a 'dispensation' uncle called it — because what we were talking 'bout was too important, and some things that needed saying were so man-to-man that we couldn't, God bless her, let momma overhear. Typically he wanted me in before dusk, and dusk was busking its last light before Cabrini night came and did its damage.

"And then too, Uncle C was the one who got our neighbor Leo King to meet momma at the bus stop each evening; Leo was a retired vet on a fixed income but couldn't hold down a job for max more than a shift. And so old C Minor slipped Leo some change to meet momma there Monday through Friday at ten p.m. in any weather and chaperone her up to our apartment door. Whatever his weaknesses with other work, Leo never let us down in this way.

"Anyway, uncle ran his hands along this chain-link fence, extra high but flimsy, where an unchained Doberman lived with some dude named Golds who nobody ever saw emerge or enter. My friends and I dubbed him 'Gold's Ghoul,' and it was something of a hazing rite of passage to break his bronze tinted window — like the glass of a drunk beer bottle — with a stone you had to hike and scrounge all the way from Lake Michigan shore.

"He said the world was expecting a lot of me. Namely to live like I was double. 'Come again?' I asked in his register (how many of my borrowed phrases were his: *Come again* was signature Cedric). My head hurt as I tried to follow him. Confused as a crack addict in first remission. 'See, already it takes some repeating, the point is so important: *the world demands of you double vision.* One man who could spend his days with double vision and not get a headache.' The doubleness was to be a Bible reader and believer in the pews or in your own private chapel for the King of the Jews, and a son of a bitch somebody else at work and whenever you took that walking corpse without a soul to air it out in public.

"Now let me do a disappearing act and assume my Uncle. Doomed to fail, but the love's so strong — let me see how much of him I can summon.

"'You see,' he said — I can hear him shoot it out like a trumpet creaking through a silver straight mute — 'Jesus would clog the cogs of the machines if he was let loose from the little penitentiaries where the parts of his body's been divvied and tamed, like museum pieces from another era. So it's of utmost import if you wish to succeed that you keep the Lord buried alive under your bedroom floor. Oh sure, you can whisper nice things to the thousands of double-vision damned. Political prisoners, some, who've chosen their bars and free meals bought with eternal blood; others, I don't doubt, damned from forever.' He didn't elaborate and I bit my tongue.

"'You can bring him a birthday candle under a bushel (there's a draft where he's staying, in the ventilation system, and we wouldn't want the twig of light to blow out entirely, am I right?). But don't let the prisoner inspire false patience. Listen to me, P. C., this is key. There's a kind of waiting in supposed humility I like to call a liar's patience, that's compatible with so-called toleration: the assumption that the prisoner's own perspective is just as sound as any other.

"So long as you feel the distance between heaven and hell when you enter his cell, well, you can — and you damn well best — keep up correspondence with the lost souls living in illusions around you.

"'Z' a time to shut up and a time to talk. A time to stop and a time to go. But when you're out on the crossroads earning the bottom line, making your Mammon money just fine, tolerating another day's compromise and He shows you a path that's harder but higher, boy you better take the narrow way, whatever it costs

96

you in time or money ('cause *time ain't money, I can promise you, prove it, time's a portion we owe to the Maker*), but if in whispers or shouts the Maker speaks, best without thinking twice put on the brake. Don't look back, don't balk, don't break! Stop for a holy Sabbath break, or go slower to see about that car wreck that's craning the necks of everybody passing without a one of them — not a one of them — stopping, well, boy, *that's* an affront to the common decency we cleverly call efficiency. See?' He stopped and bowed his head and muttered something I couldn't make out. In my mind it's there, that unknown word he said that could have been the secret code, could have rescued me from unbelief. Minor C was *on* in a major way and when he went on I was ready to step out onto Lake Michigan and keep walking 'til we reached Milwaukee.

"'Forgive me,' said C. 'Please. They used to call me the Spirit's secretary. I used to be able to explain things easy, take something supposedly unknowable, something invisible and inedible, and feed it to folks with all the tang and grease of a buttery, paprika-spiced slice of corncake on Sale a Sunday. But God, the Word, saw fit to weaken my words so as to keep me from riffing over His script, because if fluent versatility with the tongue can free it from stuck scrapes at meaning, the same gift can send by the millions a host of followers into Gehenna's landfill. Same gift that can send souls to the flames can set somebody on fire with the Spirit, it can take a woman to the foot of the cross, standing there staring up and not counting the cost, can set her to seeing things through 'til He's down from the instrument bent from the Empire's perfected, selected, specialized torture, pierced heart suffering it all according to Thy Word. Can set some kids who ain't yet known hormones, sitting there content on a lazy Sunday, skipped church and slovenly, licking the leftover Sunday feast batter for lunch like that's the tip of the taste buds of life's traded pleasures, I swear — I seen it — a good preacher's word can rouse such a lazy one to be a good boy and help his daddy, who God done given authority, delegated to name things and to have dominion under the sun.

"'Now I know it's hot, o'er a hundred with humidity, but obey, P. C., your shadow of a daddy, your tired uncle who needs your

97

muscles to take the millions like God done told me to tell you. Pied-piper them to the foot of the cross, fall down with them there before the tree they stole them apples from — every one — and stare there at Him hanging, a contradicted sign, against the rest of His kind's theft of fire.

"'Ahem, now, enough from me. Ahem. But for the preacher He brought in as one born untimely, can I get an *Amen*:

""'Even so the tongue is a little member, and boasteth great things. Behold, how great a matter a little fire kindleth! And the tongue is a fire, a world of iniquity: so is the tongue among our members, that it defileth the whole body, and setteth on fire the course of nature; and it is set on fire of hell. For every kind of beasts, and of birds, and of serpents, and of things in the sea, is tamed, and hath been tamed of mankind: but the tongue can no man tame; it is an unruly evil, full of deadly poison. Therewith bless we God, even the Father; and therewith curse we men, which are made after the similitude of God. Out of the same mouth proceedeth blessing and cursing."

"'The same fence keeps someone rightfully protected and keeps, unrightfully, someone else out. Seems to me, with the sacred and profane, we need a chain-link fence you could see through, porous so that the Spirit can pulse through every earthly thing that you do. Now look at that dog's drool on the chains, see the bubble, the way it blows in the wind. Like that wind, the Spirit blows wherever it will, but the world wants to get into every place too, and so what we need is a holy membrane that could let the Spirit blow through one way and keep the noise of the world at bay. You follow me, what I'm trying to say is: we must let the sacred *elevate* the profane but not the profane to desecrate and dominate and dictate over the sacred. They say slavery isn't writ into the Constitution, and they may say that separation of Church and State wasn't meant, by the Founders, to keep Christ a private prisoner, but whatever the intentions at the origins of this country we've, like Pilate, put Him in jail and let Barabbas run loose and make sure Judas gets his cut of the cash before his conscience kicks in and he kills himself.

"'Boundaries is hard to draw. Where any of us really begins and the ones we're indebted to ends, how much of our ancestor's weights and levities we still carry, or should, or shouldn't, and how much to let the past lie. I've been hesitating to say this to you because the last thing I want is to impose my ministry on someone I've loved like the son of my own manhood — of loins, don't flinch, I learned long ago was, hard truth, impotent. Because I seen fathers who can't see past their noses and get furious when they look up at forty and find their kids aren't spitting images. The pagans gave us a demons' church of child sacrifice, but they also gave us Narcissus who, you know, fell in love with his own fool self as a sign of contradiction against all fool souls who do the same. And so I wouldn't call it prophecy, though in my heart I know it is, that you, Peter, will be a pastor, who'll be a star to offset the great night that the fourth angel has brought upon us:

""""And the fourth angel sounded, and the third part of the sun was smitten, and the third part of the moon, and the third part of the stars; so as the third part of them was darkened, and the day shone not for a third part of it, and the night likewise."

"'Now the third part of the stars's smote by the light pollution of the city of man. And the same man-made lights have confused the difference between the night and the day so that Mammon can have his millions of minions making him an emperor's cloak whose technicolors looks more splendorous than Solomon's, though if you pulled the plug he'd be barely covered by rags that reek of the pus of soul sickness. But God sees to it, in this coming night, to name a new elect into the Light, and you, Peter, I see in you the rise of a sign that could pull the millions with you, and even your fall could wake a nation of somnambulists hocked up on one third opiates and two thirds amphetamines all to keep the machine paradise humming its filth and covering the skies with the illusion that I am the center of the universe and the other worlds out there, which send shafts of their pain or pure joy in lit-up sound waves from heaven or hell — we ain't got time for them.'"

"But you didn't do it?" Stella covered her breasts with the sheet. She shook her head *no*, draped herself as a ghost, stood up as if ready to go.

"Huh?"

"You didn't get guilted into the suggestion?"

"Guilted?"

"You didn't feel bad?" she settled back down, looked around as if for a witness. She walked across Ishmael Jones's chipped floor and set off at a clip out the door. He threw down some bills and threw down another and left a few quarters just in case. He caught up with her halfway down the block — last year's dead leaves scattering and swirling under his feet with an eerie swish, and when he pulled at her elbow he saw, startled, like contacts left in far too long, a skin of prickling, painful shock in her sad reddened eyes. She stopped, illumined by a passing streetlight.

"I believe that he believed that he was hearing God's own voice."

"But you felt bad, bucking his big idea."

"It's a small price to pay for Fat City," he said, turning in a muscular pirouette as he extended his arm and flicked a wave at Chicago. A man, passing the opposite way with a stack of Ziplock bags stuffed with mossy green clumps, dodged Peter's grand gesture and flipped him the finger.

"Now you're seeing where things went south," said Peter, shaking it off and not turning around but fixing his attention all on Stella's spellbound eyes.

"Is your uncle, is Cedric, still alive?"

"We're . . . I love him . . . estranged, but yes, so far as I know, he's not gone to meet his Maker."

"Hard," she said. "How easy that can happen. Nonna said something I'll never forget: 'Spiritual maladies, like those of the body, are wont to come on horseback and express, while they depart slowly and on foot.' She borrowed it from someone — I forget. But I guess I mean that friendships we can work on forever can —"

"Sever in a single snap of bad weather. So right. Too, too true. And it was three times hard because I owed my uncle my life." He hesitated and looked both ways but they were not at a crossing she could see. "Before he came along I wanted to be white, I mean like easy white. Like just plain white. Try to just fathom, I mean *can you imagine* how awful, for a black boy, it'd be, to be white without being white?

"Let me answer that, no you can't," he said, at the same time that she answered "I can try."

"No," she said, and he grimaced, unsure what she was saying no to.

"You're right, right to correct yourself, to take back your lavish white liberal attempts. Don't need that kind of sympathy or *generosity*. It's all a ruse and even this, what we're doing tonight. As if we can remedy loneliness."

"But you can't condemn me for wanting to try. You can't stop me either, you can only leave me. Like everyone else did, do, and will."

He stopped walking.

"Yes," he said, and kissed her eyes, which closed under the warmth of his lips. "And look, I ain't crazy, I ain't raging against whiteness — I been down that rabbit hole more than damned Brer Rabbit, acted it out, used all my wits and millions of dollars in grants to define and debunk whiteness, but always some unwanted, inconvenient contact with *people* revealed the fragility of my systemic racializing. But I'm saying that there's something soul-sickening twisted about a black kid setting his sights on being white — 'white,' whatever the hell *that* means — as if it were some supposed summit of all human perfection. Not able to see what he is, who he is, as *good*. In itself. For itself. And coupled with this binocular living is a near-sighted blindness to any goods that reside in the folks closest and most intimate. Including, well, P. C., *me*."

"What happened between you two? You didn't do his prophecy. You didn't get — can't find another word but *guilted* but trying, I don't know, *guided* by him?"

"I — well *one big thing* I cannot mention in polite society. But, besides that, I resisted my uncle when he seemed to prey on my vulnerability. Wouldn't have put it like that, then. Didn't know his whole story then. Saw him flashing fine instruments as time flew by and I thought he had means. To me, it seemed he had such money, but if so then how come he never got us out of Cabrini? Well, 'cause he didn't have all he seemed to have. For a kid, that hurt. And then, well, don't we all know the old story? The one you idolize starts out a window and ends an impediment, points to a door too narrow for the both of you to pass through at once.

"I worked at Collard Greens as a dishwasher 'til I was nearly eighteen. Before that, after I —" He looked up at the polluted sky. "Excuse me, ma'am, maybe another time. It's enough for now to know there was about six years where I should have died. Stealing cars daily and getting slaps on the wrist — except the time I drove down Navy Pier and sunk a sleek Chevrolet in Lake Michigan — and lived — like a *chevalier* — to tell the tale (and isn't there a whale story to tell of the automobile and the want of oil)! Running away with such speed and frequency I turned momma into a lifelong insomniac. Police always returning me home, saying just wait a few more years or months, you'll be eighteen and then you're your own man, not beholden to — what? That's the thing: it's not like, from what I could tell, I had any grievances against momma — except maybe her silence about my absent father — so solemn and complete I sometimes wondered whether I even had a sire — her change-the-subject or leave-the-room tactics.

"Mom's wits were torn out. Like the hair clumps I'd find around the house. And we'd had no pet. With the help of a social worker and Uncle Cedric, she made sure I was moved to a ranch in Wyoming. Security, barbed wires, a beautiful juvenile Eden in the mountains for hard-case delinquents no parent could tame. But of course all that beauty — I couldn't stand it. I hated it. Escaped. The mountains were too much for me. Gave me palpitations. Too great, I suppose, made me too small. Police picked me up on the highway, hitchhiking. Dumb — I was out of my mind with thirst in Nevada, seeing shit that wasn't there. Seeing the skyline of Chicago all wavy, and I was a hundred miles from Las Vegas. Escape. Police pick-up. Return. Repeat.

"Until one time my uncle drove out to fetch me back. But *that* sends me further away before I can get us back home!"

"Home." This piqued Stella's interest; she edged in, tried to keep from awkwardly swaying her hips into Peter's but needing, suddenly, to feel him against her. "Home," she repeated, puzzling her chin with the pinch of her fingers. "Home." At first unsure of her irruption, she was encouraged by his look's reciprocated interest. "It's just," she explained, "I've wondered a lot about that. Nostos. Homecoming. A lot lately. I spent so long back in Milwaukee that I'm scared should I ever go back it would be nothing more than a masked regress. Besides I . . . don't really know my mother at all although we've spent a lifetime together and my Dad is still mad about, well, me being here. Love's anger, he would call it.

"Anyway, forget about me. You're sure, it seems, that it's *not*. Possible, I mean. To go home. For anyone? That seems, I mean, a stretch, seeing what happened to you, to think that no one else could crack the code, that no one else could. Come home."

"Wait — but you ain't planning on leaving me before we even —"

She peered around a rusted Yield sign, seeing the shape of the chase better now, and smiled. "Tell me more." So he did:

"Fed up at last with 'farming out the prodigal,' he found me — fucked up with thirst, hallucinating my way to death — on the shoulder of Route 66. Tell me how he found me and then tell me, seriously, there ain't no God. Why people like you and I are useless idiots, cosmic aberrations.

"He got us a hotel on the Mississippi and we took a three-day vacation there. 'Vacation,' I say? It was detox. I don't know why but the whole time I was scared. Like I was stuck in a room with a stranger I'd never seen. But I was paralyzed. I mean I couldn't even get up out of the cot where I collapsed the first night. (He said, his cheek out like when he blew the trombone, 'Young man, I'm willing to endure a lot, but I call the bed, you get the cot.') Uncle C prayed over me at the banks of the Mississippi. Pulled the car over under the Interstate 74 bridge, the old one now defunct, called out, incidentally, for being one of the worst in the country for want of safety, I mean thousands and thousands crossing every day had left it shaky, almost looked like a death trap tilted. Anyhow, he pulled the car off the highway and let it roll, really slow, just tucked under the Illinois side. Always I'd ignored or cared less about such crossings — passing from one state to another over lines that seem so authoritative and real on a map but they're as unseen as any angel of God when you pass from one political rule to another. This time, though, with the slow roll that felt also like a trespass, the car idling — sneaking like — down toward the river, uncle swiveling his head paranoid that some bright lights would cut short his plans — this time was like *coming home*. More than ever before or maybe ever after, I had the illusion that it was possible: to find a home, and to return to it.

"But okay. Here is where the story gets garbled. Hard as hell to remember right. Exorcism? Baptism? Initially I believed the Mississippi healed me, whatever God did to me there through the hands of his minister C Minor. But why then as time tolled on did it hurt to recall that little drowning, little death? Bringer of pain or bringer of peace? And as years go on, whenever I try to tell it I can see even as I say a sentence that I'm embellishing without even wanting to, without even trying, which means where's the thread, the frayed heirloom fabric of truth?

"He asked me, 'Peter, you ever been baptized?'

"'Don't know,' I told him. 'Maybe by momma.'

"'Aw, my sister. She got a good side, but she runs too many risks of the spirit.'

"And when he said, 'Do you repent of sin and give Satan the middle finger?' I nodded without meaning to, but when I felt that up and down motion I wanted to believe what it meant. Then he handed me a blue bathrobe, thick and tough but warm as a womb, and told me to change in the back car seat. When I came out, without a word, he put his arm around my waist and walked with little pelican steps of trepidation down toward the waters and bid me close my eyes as he muttered prayers in tongues I never heard before. Before I knew it — I was so tired, and feeling his arm around my body all the rage that had run me ragged bled into the clay where we stood — or sometimes I wonder if his hands were a conduit that sucked up the sewage I was sick with 'til then — before I knew it he had sunk me under with a gentle but sure hand, submerged me, and when I tried to come up for air I couldn't because he held me there underwater where I could see nothing no matter how I tried until I stopped trying and went slack and heard him praying words whose meaning I couldn't make out. And a hatred flared in my heart, there and then, a murderous hatred, and I wanted to kill him . . . but next thing I knew my lungs were fine and I was laid out on some sand and clay and covered with a Hebrew blanket my uncle's friend brought back for him from Jerusalem when his friend got to go where Jesus walked.

"I tried to hate him, wanted to hate him, wanted to want to throttle him for what seemed like the unforgivable sin. All he did was smile and say 'And, ye fathers, provoke not your children to wrath: but bring them up in the nurture and admonition of the Lord,' and when I asked what in the world happened he said it wasn't of the world and fell into a scratchy silence like when a record player's needle is at the end of the swirling circle. Picking a stick out of the water he said:

""'My son, despise not thou the chastening of the Lord, nor faint when thou art rebuked of him: For whom the Lord loveth he chasteneth, and scourgeth every son whom he receiveth. If ye endure chastening, God dealeth with you as with sons; for what son is he whom the father chasteneth not? But if ye be without chastisement, whereof all are partakers, then are ye bastards, and not sons. Furthermore we have had fathers of our flesh which corrected us, and we gave them reverence: shall we not much rather be in subjection unto the Father of spirits, and live?'"

"Next I knew we was at a hot dog stand and walking aboard a river boat, the only blacks on the whole vessel. Uncle'd just been paid back dues for all his recordings for which he never before received a penny, not to add nearly no acknowledgment on the liner notes at all. Told me, as we took a boat down the river, the story. I know its sound still, so well it scares me, the affinity between the younger P. C. and his uncle is enough to make me sing — make music — again:

"'Let me sing you a song of rage. Let me tell you what I seen in this life. Feel free then to see and say it all different. *Them record company company men!* What I woke up saying the night I died and came back to life. They wrung my body of all material gain: *I'm a spiritual man, God, but ain't no harm in having a body to house the spirit in!* And them men they taken this body for a ride, dragged

105

along in back of a car playing on repeat from fancy speakers the breaths I blew into and drew from the soul of that thrift-store saxophone. *I ain't trying to put thieving claws on the musical master's monies, my Lord. But is it stealing if you take back what was stolen from you in the name of a contract you never saw and never signed but scholars of the law show you to prove you signed your soul away?*'

"In his fingers Uncle crunched a crisp leaf taken from a passing dead branch. A foliage of grief grew across his face. And from that burning bush of pain he pushed out a chewed toothpick that sprouted like a stuck-out tongue. He spat it into the blue and brown water.

"And all at once, as if a muse unbuckled a muzzle, he sighed and said in a rasp, a muscled whisper mustered from nothing, leaning against the railing which supported the heave and heaviness of a body that wanted to at last collapse:

"'Let me tell you what I seen in this life. Ours was an ordinary existence. We stood at the edge of the earth, which is flat and finite not round and eternal. Sort of sagging, always lagging behind. We was never going places, alright? Untied, shoes slipping off, a common cough whooping and spreading, brought to you *gratis* by the local smokestacks of a now dead factory that made plastic angels and other misnomers called 'religious goods.' A charitable chain, to be sure, legally registered as a not-for-profit, but so help me God if they weren't a bunch of chumps, boy. Listen, let's call it as it is. No dazzle to the truth besides itself. We named them pirates when we was young and that was an exaggeration to be sure — no swords out, no slit throats — but cut-throat was their golden rule, took their booty easily, stole not the souls but the fouled flesh of so many — uncounted, lost now — in our town, coming out, of course, with a shipload of profits and good salaries for families we never seen someplace else — a law of the land. God knows who made a law that if you broke you'd go broke. Sure they put 'back into the community,' but at the cost of how many lives a year lost to wheezy emphysema lungs?

"'We was, we were, steeped in midnight. Thelonious Monk maybe said it right: "It's always night, or we wouldn't need light."

But which light — the natural, the God-sent, or the factory-made yellow that filled our bellies and made our lungs hitch and sputter? Through the stained glass windows of industry the light blazed for all to see, stuck at the edge of the edge of the city, on a knoll, not a hill, see?

"'Sneaking out past bedtime we could not help but stare, a gaggle of kids up to nothing. Stunned, we saw only the white bright as it basked our blackness in lackluster. Don't know what that means? Look at me boy, I'll buy you a dictionary to carry round opposite the Bible your right hand'll hold forever, so long as you're living so help me God. Those factory beams seemed situated with intent, with selection, as we baked beneath the teeming white heat, rays that lavished awe upon us from small slits carved out of the factory façade. All the while a crammed cloud reaching like a pillar to what heaven? We hardly noticed the smoke for the windows, the golden yellow, the gilded air.

"'Leaving, our steps always dejected, dragged until a kid called for a game of tag. Then we threw ourselves up in trees and down into dried-up window wells, spent supposedly-sleeping hours inhaling musty basement dust, bare feet against the old coal-room floor, pink foot bottoms painted black. And that coal powder overpowering our senses till our friend Virgil — an asthmatic mess whose nose was always running snot — let loose a series of sneezes, a line of short ones like a firing line of shots, and we fell over laughing, but we felt so bad so we patted him lightly like long-time friends, since we were, but half because we were scared. Then Virgil's brother — who was halfway his dad for all practical purposes — would find us awake and flip the switch, get the switch, give our backsides stitches but he couldn't hit 'cause he fell into laughing. All words lost to a big belly laugh.

"'Ahh, P. C., you can't come with me back then: the way down is easy, but up was a hell. I know damn well that laugh wasn't how, most days, we was, back then. Most days we wasn't just *being* who we was but wanting to be somebody else. Old as Abel's brother Cain. Why my sacrifice ain't good as his? But the bigger question is this: why when I look back to being a child I recall what's good, what's good, more fully, as if what's good can counter so much suffering?

"'Spurned when we went out of our hood we stayed home, laid low, playing chess games without complete sets, but with more laughter than we knew what to do with. Oh the forces and pieces of the game were against us, but that only made us play harder, invent from an absence not a new set of rules but pretend pieces that we could all almost see, geez, uhuh, how fateful it felt, destiny it seemed — to play without all the pieces, you follow, you see, P. C., what I'm sayin? — until eventually when we put to the side childish things, when *seemed* metamorphosed into *was*, and we would lose another friend in a sick black soot-breath, expulsion from a godforsaken choked throat. Yes sir, choked to death by a couple big kids who brought their game pieces into our neighborhood down from uptown.'"

Peter kicked a half-full beer, picked the malt liquor can like a pawn, poured the fluid out until it emptied, and set the thing next to a big fire hydrant: "Check," he said, "But not quite mate."

"So you see, C lived a sad life. And so it was that from all those losses, from the thrift-store saxophone he bargained down to half price, Uncle learned to wring a sound that any who heard would pay a pretty penny to get a hold of. But as he rose in estimation, he was fed up, still scraping for change, in a state fit to kill himself or somebody else. Touched, touched they said — he had always been touched — they told him when he turned young man that he was touched, like an extra tooth that gnawed into the side of the brain, said the men who played beside him in nightclubs and jazz bars from New York to Lost Angels (Uncle's name for the famous city) — they said then that he had an 'anger problem.' That he needed to get help. Seek what they called therapy. He said he didn't need none of their wares and then refused to play until they paid enough for him to do one better than therapy: 'Increase my gig wage so I can study theology.'

"And he skipped shrink sessions and went straight to heaven!

"Can I swear I never seen that gnaw, that extra tooth of anger in him? You asking me, his *son*, to tell all? Oh hell I confess. Confess

I even caught that gene. Learned from him how to raise my fists.

"But," he hedged, cagey, huffing, as if she were pressing him to trot the skeletons in a line in the abandoned storefront, family secrets instead of mannequins —

"I'll digress if I go there, 'kay? Don't, can't lose the thread. C was a calm man after he played, quiet when he came home from all those shows. Sure, sometimes, of course he got loud with me but can I say I didn't earn it?

"Overwhelmed with shows, practically begged to join the famous but never enough of a marquee to make it, he even stooped to play in casinos when he had played out all the clubs, seeing none of the record royalties — and which well-known jazz master's record isn't heard here or there playing on? — the 'royal bleed,' as he liked to call it, went straight to the record company.

"Until, after a long recording, enough takes to break his brain, he follows this fellow out of the studio. (Tells me this after walking the slippery night all along, through the streets like a detective unpaid but hired by God.) Boots he wears too big for him but he found them comfortable to play in, though look now they hurt as he follows the producer in boots that once belonged to daddy, big and black and waterproof, trudge, walking in circles, like he knew he's being followed, not following to demand his fee, but never turning around or giving in, just making circles in the New Orleans night. His father always said his sore feet felt like they was forged in a furnace, twisted at the ankles, red rings around them from where the boots dug in, the bloody skin, bright red against umber, after a factory day's Sisyphus trek.

"Losing the track of his producer, who slipped up into a brown-stone, maybe — or was it a dog in the corner of his eye? — he goes back out to the fields where he first found that sunflower and played it like a horn. His friends would go out there to have their women, but he slept with nobody but beside the stable of — no joke — some overfed hogs 'cause, he said, it was the only place he could get a clear notion of what it was like to be a man, what was a man was not a hog was not he a man, bedside, brilliant, beside a pen of well-fed hogs, good God, he was a man as demanded by the

109

hog whiney, the whine he heard, the line that he knew he never could cross, the line so other than that which demarcated him from his record company man, the recording big wig to whom he threw pearls, the kindly swine who treated him nice and always handed him checks on time though that was the trouble the combination of timeliness and so much niceness with short shrift, bad butcher's cuts, like he was the beef and all they fed him was fat, so fat the fellow he followed home, found him the next night after an especially soulful and final platinum album session, forcing himself through the fellow's door to find instead a hysterical wife — white turban of a towel on her head, like a vanilla ice cream cone melting fast, Cedric not threatening to take his life though thinking it when they said, 'Don't shoot!' both of them at the same damned time, but he did not even say, 'I have no gun,' he just felt his gums gone as bad from clenching and grinding teeth as from jabbering prayers in his sleep all night, and 'Why do I frighten you? I want nothing but my monies, my royalties,' he spat, standing straight up with dignity, a posture the nuns drilled in since kindergarten and called it *dignified*.

"He smelled fried chicken leftovers from the stove and the wife turns as if to offer and he says 'Mind if I sit down? This is business, yes, but we bifurcate our lives to no avail, a lie, who you are when you're there you are when you're here now I've come to collect my dignity. Give me my outstanding royalties. You have withheld them for far too long and I can't keep hustling along to clubs across the country to keep a roof for my nephew's mama, my sister and her son abandoned, this is my life, my life you undo,' and he scanned the whole span of the pretty crafty house, arts and crafts and imported giraffes cut as if by primitive peoples as if of other planets. 'I need a check; I checked into the crazyhouse of credit already, the steady installments stealing my soul, how you say, money kept cannot steal your soul, see how I stretch myself seven days a week pounding on a piano, trumpeting low blows to my brother's timpani, smiling when I steal time to visit my nephew to hold his head up higher than mine. Don't say *help honey he gone kill*— I ain't touched — I ain't even touched his tepid head, your naughty boy who needs a fat slap, needs a pappy's rod, my God . . . but my God it ain't mind to hand, *leave room for the wrath* — even in this here room! — although you control my daily bread you can't touch the sinews of my soul. But I need the dough I need the dough, pre-kneaded dough placed on the stove, bought like that for a couple extra bucks. Whit, you and I's pals, see, see how nicely you invite me in, *sit down have a seat, a glass, something to eat,* it's never too early for a good class wine. Do you like the blanc? I prefer the blood red.'

"Then the producer, this nicest Whit of all, feels — man, he *feels* the fear. Both across the table know its tremble, this is *terrible* impossible happening hits home. Minor C just folds his hands and says a blessing over the food Whit's wife sets down with servility. No C doesn't hit a one though he wanted — he told me — to slit the man at once, to borrow the chicken knife and stick it right through. Whit, catching a whiff of that wrath C's trying to keep breathing away, reaches for the phone.

"C stands without a second thought. 'I made myself a mari- onette, let the hate become my puppeteer.' Before he sees what exactly he's doing his well-worked thumb and pointer fingers have clasped his boss' pulsing throat and the man — why wouldn't he? — looks like he's thinking *now least he cannot pull the trigger,* Minor C getting bigger and bigger and — *honey, careful now, call the cops!*

"Cedric stopped. Left a good meal like it was nothing but slops. 'And man if I wasn't starving just then,' he said, licking his lips in the telling. But he jutted out the door to save a man's life — his, Whit's, maybe both — though when he got to the entrance, exit, could not take another step. Hands behind his head already, readied for the jailhouse cot, beheading all his thoughts, distraught. As if all he brought to jazz would be erased, the circular record like an empty table with a spilled bottle of blood red making what he played unplayable, denying him the keys forever, his cuts on them ebony keys, his kiss on the trumpet he squeezed.

"But the cops never came even when Whit looked out the win- dow and saw him waiting there surrendered and they stare into one another's eyes like two moons orbiting a planet in rival routes that could never crisscross. Cedric couldn't even take a step. Strength sapped. He fell asleep there, on the steps like an offering unable to depart, deferring just in case justice should show up, his hands cupped open for a beggar's royalties.

"Freezing under the sudden drop of a bad gutter's leaf-clogged refuse, he woke in the morning saddling one thought only and rode it all the way to Chicago on what he was sure would be his last ticket before they named him criminal and all his Christian reputation was paraded like a fresh-bought slave from the block back to the plantation.

"What's he do then, when the train pulls into Chicago station and he walks the long blocks to Cabrini-Green and finds mama pregnant by a man whose name she will not muster? Me growing not exactly against but without my own will in her broken womb. He turns back from whence he came and rides a long train alone on cash he'd meant to keep for food and knocks again on Whit's front door and the man serves him a manila folder filled with nothing but legal fodder and tells him to go, kindly, to hell. 'Which would mean to keep hating you, which I do but I won't,' C shot back. 'But I'm not giving up.'"

"He refused lawyers with greater fervor than earlier he'd rejected therapists. Spent another seventeen some years translating the glyphs in that folder without relying on representation — without making it even to the courtroom, such was his hatred of the system.

"'Code crack came like lots from the sky as if to prove predestination!' Cracked the glyphs through a fellow jazz player who was a moonlighter and revealed, sheepish, when Cedric told him his 'Sob Story, Inc.', that he was a lawyer for an insurance company, this after uncle mocked the profession. 'My jibes, my jokes, wasn't even funny. Old hat. What hate'll do: sieve the humor straight out you. How many lawyers to screw in a light bulb? Three? See: one to climb the ladder, one to shake it, one to sue the company that made it.'

"He'd spent decades, he said, lost as hell in a cotton field labyrinth of clauses and all was sorted — in a week! — in his favor and he knew at once what a fool he was for letting his wage-slave master off the hook (for Whit had died already) instead of swallowing his trumpet-head pride.

"Gathering the monies with haste — like he's passing, like if he don't get there it'll all disappear or he'll be six feet under tomorrow — he took that same track from New Orleans straight back to sweet home Chicago and all the way on the train he's singing a riff on Coltrane's A Love Supreme, and he fell asleep and dreamed of me pulling hard on his sleeve, 'Daddy, daddy,' a love supreme, when he finds five seconds through the door that I've gone missing he falls flat on the floor falls cruciform an' his body starts turning like a weathervane and he says, staring West, 'I got to borrow a car for a week if I'm to find and bring him back,' and she knows a woman who owes her a favor so in an hour he's on the road in a baby blue Buick Regal whose bowels are rusted red orange, following the compass of his soul, pushing on the pedal like a spur to a horse, saying 'God it is you who divorced me from my dues, my just dues, you let me lose but now, why this win, to whom should I go if I lose it again, am I to be consumed like a hog, doomed to sing, in doubt, the blues?'"

Peter paused. "You follow me?"

She nodded and leaned against a brick wall, cream dyed black from exhaust refuse. "But let me catch my breath," she said.

"I'm sorry," he said, chin down, cupping her belly with his firm right hand. "Baby?"

"Maybe. I'm not, you know, an expert at this."

"Let's sit — that bench in the park?"

"How romantic. Looking down. On a pool without any water."

"I'll get us something to eat real quick."

"No," she said. "I'm full."

"You thirsty?"

"No. Now go. Go," and as they dropped and leaned back into the lover's bench she scrawled, with a chafed edge of Lincoln's coin, P. C. + Stella into the wood. He kissed her earlobe, her neck. "Now go."

"So," he said, not catching his own, talking as if he was still walking fast, "so, as I said, he found me out wandering and that's how I started to find a home — as if I needed to go faraway first to know, fully, how at home with him I was. Hitching on the side of Route 66, waterless and hungry as hell, hallucinating like a ghost in the desert wandering toward my wishing well: 'God found you, not me, P. C. Car should've broke down so many times I was scared shitless to be caught out here, without gas in the middle of nowhere.'

"After the 'vacation' C finally broke down, on the way home from Mississippi. Let out a big cry that could have looked like a laugh to cars flashing by. Windows down all the way but still sweating, drinking a big jug of water but rasping. 'Strange to tell you, new creation, I know we should be all celebration, but I see you in me and me in you. And that's a double-headed coin to toss — both what's good and . . . what's dross.'

"He pulled from his pocket a sheet of music, a blank score without a single note, and said 'Don't be fooled when you see this here into thinking you're seeing a blank slate. There's only so many scales that can fit and fill and there's only two directions the notes can lead — sort of like steps — up, up, on Jacob's Ladder or down into the Devil's Cellar. And what's your life on these scales, Peter, a same old sentimental favorite, all melodramatic, all *moods*, played out on repetition, slavish imitations of forms that could take you into a man-made heaven or the true blue note which your mother would call an *orison* from the valley of tears, a song that honors the steps taken by everyone else who brought you here, which means that every pleasure and every measure is marked by the frequencies of faraway pain — *My tears have been my meat night and day,*' and while he cried he rode eyes closed, nimble fingers touching unseen keys, pounding pedals kept in reserve for funerals or wedding feasts, then a blur, his fingers at once unfree: liberated from the longing to be without limit, and he started to sob, his head like a whole note bobbing, pulling the car to rest on the shoulder of an unknown bridge that hovered over an unnamed water:

"'*It's alright it's alright it's alright,*' igniting and fighting the little flighty droplets that fell from his eyes like missing measures. He swung the door and stood and hobbled, like a drunk man, to the bridge edge railing. 'Like a raindrop needs rain so my tears seek the Source, wherever they flow may they all find You!' He nodded, snuffled, shot snot out, laughed. 'It's alright it's alright, it's alright. We'll always be more wrong than right.'

"I stared into the river below — but it wasn't a river, because the water was still, so still it sort of scared me. I'd never seen nothing like it before.

"'Don't write my life in black and white or yours neither, figlioccio.' And the next moaned not sung from his lungs played in a score that stretched to the stars, and he sang in a tenor so tender: 'A love to lean on, a love to lean on, a love to lean on, a love to lean on, a love to lean on, a love to lean on, a love to lean on,' and on and on, until I tuned out, lost consciousness and leaned over the railing hard and Cedric saw me start to fall over into the stilled waters and he shook me awake and said, 'Not another, one submersion in the Spirit's enough. You leaning into your death too hard, and there ain't no need to pine after dying 'cause you already dead, my son, in Christ.'

"Things started looking up. Cedric rented a room for us in the Tribune building and enrolled me in Atlas Academy, an elite school for the upper echelon. The token person of color, the exception, the one on every glossy brochure sent out to showcase the school.

"We dragged our shit to Streeterville and watched a groundskeeper throw more than half of it into one of those big green trash bins which Uncle had delivered just for us. Just like we then had a whole second unit to ourselves in — no joke — the Tribune Tower. Oh, you don't know? Man, you really *are* a foreigner here. Time for a tour, I'd say. C'mon now. Neo-Gothic (and yes, I had to be taught, when we moved in, what in the world that meant. Thought before that it was something about ghosts). If you looked from a distance you'd think the thing was some kinda cathedral, which, I mean it *was* home to the sacred offices of one oracle — The Chicago Tribune.

"One of the glories of the city of Cain, and I mean they really *crowned* this civilized center with that building, buttresses, I — the janitor'd take me up onto the crown terrace but I couldn't bring myself to open my eyes. Ever since I almost fell from the boat into the river anything having to do with heights did — and still does — do me in. Sometimes I think it could have been more than a phobia. Something down deep rejected that stance of looking down — not just literally — see, on the city. Always I was more at ease staring up at those buttresses like a peasant awed by some church that's a million times more beautiful than whatever straw shithole he's learned to call home. But it was always *strange* to me to see the belly of the place lit up blinkering with offices, I mean *that you could look inside at all,* even if most of the windows they covered with drapes and blinds, you could still see silhouettes, and it always seemed odd, peculiar, that this place was little more than a workplace hive for people (my Uncle had a connection who got us the unofficial suite, and other than us no one *lived there,* 'less you count the workaholics who came so early and departed so late it seemed they were always there).

"Strange. I don't know why. But the flying buttresses blew my mind, leap from the street to the summit, don't really stop there but keep shooting higher, pointing past the earth entirely and here I'd never, barely, at least in Chicago, bothered to look skyward at all, rather kept my eyes close to the ground . . . or over my shoulder, to be safe. Wyoming, Nevada — those lost days — all was different like another planet, like what happened there and what happened here and the way the world took shape in either had nothing to do and less to say to one another — perfect strangers. Out there all was horizons, enough infinity to make you feel your smallness with every single breath inhaled, feel how puny and passing you were to the point that for me it was almost as if I was, out there, already dead. Under that otherworldly horizon I found something fitting about looking skyward. Guess it woulda been hard *not* to, hard to pretend the world starts and stops wherever our city maps do.

"Let me take you to the Tribune Tower tomorrow. Saturday? Saturday. There's these two gargoyles, my favorite as a kid. One whispering man (rumor) and shouting man (news) that manifests — gets exactly right — the daily war on what we call truth that drives mass societies crazy and makes us happier to stay head down, satisfied with little pleasures because what the hell is happening is too hard to figure out.

"My brother and me each had our own rooms, I mean, and this was *before* they opened the place up to the public, really opened, later, in some kind of need, I guess to pay the billions of bills I bet that place has. 'Lunch tickets' to Howells and Hood restaurant (a very different hood now, wink wink, get it? I'm sorry, I'm sorry — nah, no excuses), a ritzy outfit on the ground floor, where we ate two square meals a day, and then the tutors — it was like homeschooling, I guess, as big as the Ritz. We freaking learned French! And I learned to love it, though it made me wretched then, in my late teens far more taken by the latest video game rage.

"But it sure came into use later when I wanted to read *Wretched of the Earth* in the original — and Tocqueville, too, for good measure: two very different prophets. The latter on the official syllabus the former I chanced on in a French exercise — one of the examples from Fanon's work used to demonstrate the future tense. Dr. Palver taught us history and literature and Miss Acres math and science. Mama didn't mind. She'd come in sheepish and stand behind, tickle the backs of our ears and blink and say 'I know you boys know what you've got' before walking backwards out the door. I'd look down to find a butterscotch candy falling from my shoulder onto my lap. Mama wasn't, let's not sentimentalize. She sure didn't. Let me tell you. Mama, my mama, wasn't book smart. A laundry cleaner. No diploma. But aw how much that misses — in so many directions it's not worth covering. Yet if she struggled to really read a book — still she could read *you*: she was an autodidact of the heart. Cedric was — surely still is — whip of a mind, but she could take *him* apart. Put him back together. Even when he paid to have her put under (to scrape out the cervical cancer) she shot back something about his being so happy to give because he was afraid to receive, something she must have perceived over years and determined, in case she never came back, in the few pre-op minutes left, that was the time to tell him what's what."

They watched the half-dressed branches of trees, moist leaves like laundry drying in the breeze, an empty ball court wrapped in chains, the waterless pool half scraped of its paint — bone white where the blue should be.

"Well, but whatever happened on the Mississippi was a dividing line splitting my life. There really was a before and after. I don't claim to know but I have to guess it had something to do with a father figure looking me straight in the eyes and saying, repeating — at a time when I'd become mainly a nightmare to myself — still he saw, he said, and I can still hear his watery voice, the flush of little waves springing toward a full-out torrent: 'inflections of the Light,' he swore he saw, 'in the corner of your eyes, a reflection, I'm certain, a refraction, sure, I'll grant you even it's warped nearly beyond all recognition, but I swear, still, on my soul, I swear: you're called by the Father to elevate many and even when you fall you'll wake up a nation.'"

"Besides, what kind of twisted pretzel of a psyche would I have to possess — okay don't answer that — to do the work I do and still hold it against uncle for living his fantasy of mission territory through me and momma because we were both: family and broke? I mean even saying that aloud — my position for many years until recently — sounds flat-out crazy. A *Tribune Breaking Headline: Praying Man Turns Out to Be Preying Man!*

"'Cos if you wanted to subject my motives to a purity test, I could be easily accused of the very thing I fought him for: when without the needy my own work wouldn't exist. When my paychecks wouldn't arrive unless needy people needed me, because the luckier and the more self-reliant ones, the saner ones, the folks who can fake it to the point of function, they don't need someone to sort out their marbles because *they* don't need me to play the shooter. Sure as this is water, here, and it's not spilling because the translucent walls of the glass keep it from falling down, they don't have the kind of psychic separations on which I rely for my paycheck. Let me say it simply: widespread sanity would put me out of business.

"And don't mistake my tone here. I been at the brink of what is called crazy most of my waking life. All that's been keeping me from the other side of the rubber room's door is . . . well, now, that's a good question. I always say music saved my life . . . or somebody else's. So angry, at anyone who looked at me askance.

Kept me in my room from three 'til nine, momma's shift most of my life. The folks lived up above stamped their feet but they had nothing on me. It was, as Momma said, a harem and a heroin house in one. Better to mourn in the house of mirth. The screams I'd heard did not seem scary. Seemed more like they was singing my insides. When the strung-out, slow motion laughter seeped through the ceiling cracks, that was when she'd admit her terror I would turn into an addict, inevitably turn, I guess because I'd been exposed, inured, to so much drug dependence. I said once, picking at the carpet like I was scalping somebody's head, that if she knew my heart she'd find far worse things that could come to pass in my future. Then she sucked in a desperate lungful of air and asked, begged me to tell her what was the trouble. I — I tried to spell it out but it didn't deflate that searching rage looking for the enemy it couldn't rightly name.

"Wasn't until you that I could cross over, like, to the right side of that Mississippi moment. Wasn't until you I could start to be truthful about how crossed-out my heart had become. But you, baby, you resuscitate."

Over the next week's-worth of nights, between arguments about his alderman bid — she wanted to want it but *the baby*, baby — he unfolded the story, of which Stella could not hear enough. Yet she was scared of opening her own life, which in comparison she now found paltry — made up almost entirely of the daily — so when he pressed her with questions and even stayed silent in protest of her mum position she would let her sad eyes wane into crescents and press from them wind-made tears and say — in some variation — that the least she could do was listen, if it could lighten the burden of a man she'd so admired from a distance and who now disclosed his deeper identity as — the secret she would perfectly keep — himself a Man of Sorrows.

· · ·

The red cross of the pregnancy test lit her face in the dark bathroom mirror. Stella had let her apartment dilapidate, but needed to come back to take the test. She could not find out in Peter's bathroom. She needed to get to the store for a lightbulb, but the sudden closures and lockdowns kept her nerves lit like a bundle of brittle kindling, waiting, settling for shade after sunset — she stopped and sighed until her stomach curved out, faked it into a full natal swell, stood there stuck in strange relief. Maternity leave. The baby almost an afterthought to bedbound days enshrined by just-read mundane clauses in the far back of the faculty handbook of a school that worked you always overtime and perpetually appealed to a sacrificial service that was hard to naysay without sounding sacrilegious. Cut from a single mold, formed from severe, dignified iron, the same Jesus expired in every hall, set under the tall, peaked arches from nails that looked too thin to hold him, hung asphyxiated from the asbestos walls of every old room in the building. She never passed him without a blown kiss, her habit since she was seven, yes, but now, to be truthful, her desire for comfort eclipsed her wish to comfort Christ — and even the notion seemed so simpleminded she laughed it off: console Consolation itself? To be young enough to believe "without guile" — what Nonna yet did in her old age — how much of that recipe of faith consisted in a blessed, amnesiac simulacrum of senility, she could not stop herself from asking.

Her first week at St. Cabrini's Elementary, after grading until her wrist went blue with ink, colored with a blush of purpose she had not known since Blake's disappearance, she had heard a slosh and slap around the corner. Ten tiptoes later, she watched the janitor stretch a red rag into a perfect square, then jostle and slap it on a telescopic pole, then raise the cloth to the dusty figure who hung by his arms above the washed chalkboard where a scrawled proof stayed half-erased. The raw rag dripped and the dead figure glistened. She'd sprinted into the girls' bathroom to wash the crop of sweat from her face, felt the cold flow from the faucet until her cheeks turned pale again. Look at you.

"And look at you now." Stella could hear Nonna's nagging critique, delivered with a sweetened espresso and a handful of homemade, heirloom biscotti — she often rose at five to make a batch before she hobbled over to Mass — and look at you now. Done the near impossible, what everyone back home had doubted hard in secret while they applauded, proud: tossed herself into South Chicago, lost herself in tireless teaching for the first time at thirty-nine — nearly forty — years old. By now that infamous Milwaukee magnet had lost its pull — as if flipped, so that she barely spoke to her parents anymore and found the distance decidedly blessed, the foreign quiet of her former life happily impossible to invent again. School — her students, their trials — became all. As she had been beholden to no one else, why not work her wrists blue, why not push when strength went south and she could see the horizon of oblivion?

But baby meant she needed to live at least long enough to give him away, give her, no, she was sure of his cells humming like his father, like the music of the spheres transposed into a jazz-scaled hymn that scattered in seven directions at once and managed, still, to summon all comers into a piqued, an agitated reverence, a mellow, low-frequency song that thirsted for justice like a newborn for milk, that croon for more — listen — that croon. Baby meant she'd be swept away from the curve-ball boys who brought bullets through detectors, buried like relish between the bread slices of metal lunchboxes marked by no other enmity than the friendly competition of Cubs-White Sox emblems. Morning sickness? Yes, please, God, yes, please God! And she saw her dress bulge out like with wind blown from a bugling band in heaven, which could not deny her this rite of life although she trespassed the marriage bed — had done the forbidden but was given, for her sins, plenty of scraps, enough to make a "bastard child" from scratch.

She called in sick — it was eleven p.m., which meant the safety of voicemail instead of the seemingly innocent and indirect but in fact fishing questions of Halves — and collapsed into the cheap, concave mattress whose dip mimicked the room's sunken floor: beautiful cherry stained wood like a cabin but done in by more dying than living. A sudden vertigo she'd never known sent the water marks on the ceiling spiraling like a typhoon sea. Spilled bleach from her earlier scouring of the kitchen tiles — what she did while the test was ticking, threw herself into to avoid checking — spread

still and waited to be scrubbed. She thought of Peter's mother —
her scrubbings — and shook her head, for whatever its ruins her
apartment needed no real cleaning. She was bleaching stains that
did not exist to pass the nervous twitch of knowing — for she
knew before the test's plus sign that she had beat her fears — had
sped ahead of fate's hard hand — had been chosen by life at last.
Though the moods she was sure were menopause — too early, too
soon for the great change of life, too soon — what, then, could
make sense of them?

The radio pitched out shoddy waves, shameless over its hocked
wares. The internet here was dial-up, slow but free: it was first hard
to get used to, but mainly she felt she'd slipped out of the cell of
Wi-Fi's former tyranny of constant surveillance, constant checking,
rechecking, rechecking, in unceasing nervousness for another hit,
a message, a chance to be chosen at random from the billions. She
needed to get to the store — tomorrow. Or she could sit at the dial-
up for half an hour and order food to arrive at her door. But the
vision of a screen appeared, always, like a hieroglyph from Uncle
Cedric's Apocalypse or a psychological warfare firework, shiny and
alluring and absolutely deadening. When she shut her eyes the
darkness was edged by a sharp penumbra, an outline that showed
where the darkness ended but also elevated it. The outermost edges
bled with the scarlet of the pregnancy plus sign — the red cross.

Out her window, the back of an ambulance sped where — to
the delivery room? — the vehicle's sirens were unseeing eyes that
allowed its medic to run red lights and forced even the reckless
drivers to bear down hard on their half-busted brakes.

Labor, Nonna had said, was like that: putting on the brakes,
bearing down, clenching to press the baby out. She could feel
herself bearing down, alone, on the angled bed, arms stuck with
IVs, bent and blue-faced prepared to die to see the baby she'd
readied inside.

She held the pillow over her throbbing head, pleased by the
mild fever that had driven her to order the tests from an untried
same-day delivery service that dropped off groceries at your door
for no fee. Strange to stand at the threshold window and wave to

the masked driver in mute thanks: half for the weird mercy of drop-off delivery, the other half because he kept his distance and didn't blink. She'd waited until his car peeled away before she dragged the brown bag inside with winter-gloved fingers, carried it like a sack of dog crap up the stairwell with the wobbly wood steps and, in disbelief that she had forgotten to order two-thirds of the needed groceries, dumped the contents onto the table and took the brown bag over to the window and watched it dive toward the dumpsters below.

The radio, a low and crackling fuzz to keep out the street's night noises, said with polite disinterest mingled with a concerned sympathy: *Two years for tearing down an abolitionist statue in the wake of the strangled* . . . before another station intervened to opine *By every measure a sign of decline, but that's why I tell my clients it's important to laugh, see: at a time like this, what other remedy remains?* And then the first station's stretched-out voice resumed: *clearly the cause of death.* She kept the radio on AM because the frequencies typically kept out these crossed wires and the whoosh sound — if at times overwhelming, like her apartment was a machine womb — kept out the chaos of neighbors and passers-by, all of whose noises lasted all night.

Unable to reach the off button, she seized the cord and yanked it out, three golden prongs cut short of current but flashing blue before they went cold. Three lemons to slice the nausea and an off-brand bottle of acetaminophen to quell the fever that led her to suspect something more than a migraine was the matter. The pregnancy test a last-minute item — just in case, just in case — though the science would only confirm what she knew. She sipped through a straw left over from the restaurant Peter had taken her to on their first date. The cloudy, spry water cooled the low fever that felt almost pleasant because it forced her to be still. She called him but the ring went right to voicemail and she called him again and again — no answer — and she did this, kept on doing it, like a dead lottery game that keeps playing though there is no kitty, no prize to give away. Finally, stilled by the cold sips, she decided to put all off until morning and feared his face would falsify his mouth's forgeries of acceptance.

Stella pulled at the lead weight that dangled from the window sash, shoved open the fogged glass, and breathed well-chilled, gas-tainted air before sighing from beneath her ribs — the exhale longer than the breath taken in. How hard to be still and yet hide from yourself. Covering her ears could not block out the litany of should-haves that came out like the actors of a play joining arms on the stage edge as if poised above an abyss, as if teetering toward the pit, for one last bow — expecting nothing but a rousing bravo, again, play it again and again, why she should have stayed where she'd been.

She turned her feelings off like a faucet, shoved the handle so hard it stayed there stuck.

. . .

Stella rarely saw Peter during the majority of her pregnancy — from May of twenty twenty until late February — as he canvassed and delivered new speeches nearly daily, trying to win another majority, cutting back his counseling hours to the minimum needed to keep his license.

With baby building pressure, fluttering and stretching, pushing wings against the walls of her womb, she curled up to Peter's absence, spent more and more time at his apartment, not just nightly (he would mosey in weary, drunken with exhaustion, falling fast asleep), but passing daylight hours. She could hardly sit alone in her room but found, like a cat, a sunken soft space at the edge of his couch to burrow into. Most mornings the sickness was not hard to bear, but by afternoon she was sipping ginger. Twice she spit it back out, like bile, pining for the flushing gag of vomit that could pluck the taut stress of her vagal nerve, loosen the terror that visited like Furies whose wings fluttered *shush* in her ears, muffling, violently, her baby's faint frequencies.

She let her lease run out without moving all of the belongings she had left behind. The prior landlord sent notice of a five-hundred-dollar cleanout fine to Cabrini's, and she did the math of her account that evening and Peter delivered his speech to the wall, stopped to insist he could cover the consequence, which was mainly his fault for "winning you over." When she went to pick up the check from the school office, there was Jackie Vettrano with the strangest smile, not without sternness but warmer than anything, a benediction over the baby.

The day after he paid that price tag, the baby came. The Caesarean section meant most of the reading and breathing practice she had done were moot. The drugs left her with the feeling of an overdose, an accident in her veins, metallic soporifics that helped her forget the whole lonely longed-for ordeal. He was kneeling beside her, saying "You can do it," gripping the bed railing and her shoulder until he was not there and no one was.

He left her in the hospital alone. When she woke both baby and daddy were gone. The television played Wheel of Fortune. Stella picked up the phone countless times to call her parents but always the dial tone rang in her ears like an EKG gone flat. She pressed the button and asked the nurse if the child's daddy had picked up the baby and the red-faced woman with steel colored hair pulled back her mask and whispered — as if someone else who should not be hearing was listening illicitly — "Baby's in the incubator, be ready for you, God willing, tomorrow."

"God?" she shot back. "Or the doctor?"

The nurse limped quietly toward the door and shut it so as to keep Stella's madness contained in the room which made her rise and start walking toward the hall until the tubes in her arms went taut and she could not take another step without ripping the plastic from her unshaven arm without yanking until the needles pulled out.

"Who took my baby," she asked, dizzied, then settled back into the bent-up bed, curling under the bleached white sheet that was cook against her angered cheek. The nurse was still dampening her forehead with a cloth when she slipped into a tense sleep — her limbs rigid and her jaw clacking when she woke in flashes of fever all alone.

During her recovery, he took a week off and woke to feed Jason his bottles. Mornings, propped on a stool in the kitchen, feet on the table, baby splayed in his lap, he started in with the complaints.

An about-face, as if birthed by her pregnancy. The patience she'd felt in his arms played dead. His evenings were spoken for by what he wouldn't say, but he arranged to have take-out delivered every time he wasn't there to make a meal. When after months she braved the questions — "You think I'm ugly, don't you? You're sleeping around. I bet you're being careful now. Sex with her to keep you from being stressed. With her and her and her and her. Making sure to be real careful. Seeing up close how much it costs."

For the first time since Jason, Peter gave her the eyes he'd worn when he said, on that first date, "Who *are* you?" He cracked his spine and reached for her wrist. "I won't even answer that question. Though I don't blame you for asking it. I don't, at all. Too much. It's all been . . . too much."

"The baby? Me?"

"So much more. The baby and you — that would be *easy*."

"Nobody wants to do the dishes. Everybody wants a revolution."

"Look, Stella," his finger found her cheekbone, the blush there that he'd said he loved, and though she first retracted he found her again and she let him instead of retreating to the bathroom. Her lower lip trembled and her tongue tingled.

"I wasn't wrong to leave politics, but."

"Oh no. Don't do it?"

"What?"

"Doubt your every decision. Again. Please, Peter. Please. The alderman thing, you said, was worth doing but —"

"I'm not doubting the stepping away *then*. But the months spent running for alderman —"

"I wouldn't know what you're speaking of, honestly. That time hardly exists between us. I saw you, what, a handful of times."

"But all of it worth it. Like I promised."

"For who? You!"

"For many, many people."

"Not me. Not your baby. When I woke up after, in the hospital room, there was nobody there."

He knelt on the floor and crushed the halo of his afro into her thigh and sighed, said, "Guilty.

126

"But, hear me, the things that it generated, the possibilities — the ripeness! Stell, hear me. Sounds like a savior complex, but if I didn't, don't, get involved fast in a bad knot over in Washington — somebody's going to be dead."

"You?"

"You think I care about that?"

"You should. Now at least. Not for yourself. I've given up on convincing you *there*. But for your baby. C'mon. Basics."

He rose to the window and shoved it open. A warm wind as if from a field laced with cattails instead of factory air gusted through and knocked over a glass. It tipped but did not shatter.

"What all we think matters ain't nothing, you hear me?" He spoke to her but shouted outside, as if an audience, more sympathetic, waited there. "How can we know? From our little windows. Vantage points small as beehive cells. Shit — forget it: once you've gone up, on the Ferris wheel, and taken in the whole, don't matter if your vision ain't an eagle's eyes. You can realize fast how much our little private lives matter. Or don't. I wish I could leave it behind — but who could, knowing what I know —"

"Which is?"

"Conspiracies. Inside conspiracies. Inside conspiracies. No melodrama when I say, I swear, human lives are at stake here."

"Your son's?"

She kissed sleeping Jason's forehead and after three hesitant steps, hurried across the room to hug Peter from behind.

He did not turn to kiss Stella. He looked down on the littered streets, the cracks in the sidewalk. She followed his gaze.

Months mustered on like one long night.

Mornings he started with exacting critiques, shot out in some short cranky sentence that only half made sense, laying into some inconsequential opinion she had offered, sometimes something she had mentioned in passing months ago, or when they first met — little risked thoughts forgotten until he flayed them. She had been right to try and stay silent.

She had not known a life like his. Who that did would have no wrath? "Rage, Achilles," she would whisper from the bathroom

127

where she learned to stay when he failed to rub the fire from his eye, the one that always looked loose and wild, when all her *whys* were met with silence, his spatula raised not over the eggs but over his head — or hers — like a weapon.

. . .

Stella stopped at the security turnstile and planted her feet there with a stance of some permanence. Sleeplessness had given her a squint. Through thick mascara that colored her eyes the officer behind the bullet-proof sheath looked faintly penciled, his peeved face pale, and the awful sense that he could be erased made her reach out without reflecting. He reeled back, the narrow outline of a half-open mouth muttering through the rounded microphone, "Your time has not come," in a pleasant tone that mismatched his blank face. The man's bold spectacles — dark and circular, the most defined part of his person — looked leftover from another era, and he stretched out the gaze of his outsized eyes until they alighted on the leaning lady whose elbows offset the weight of the counter. She pulled out cotton balls, puffs of tissue, a crossword puzzle "got me stumped, I got me DOWN, I got FALLING, I got WALLS, I got BLUE, but it don't add up. Why I kept my husband around. He always had a way with words."

The bold spectacles magnified the eyes of the waiting officer, protected by glass, whose uncrossed arms spelled professional patience. Lowering himself off the high stool, he spun, playfully, the empty gray seat, waiting, studying the faceless cushion like a croupier at a roulette wheel. The woman searched the wreckage of her purse, turned it over, said "damned this hearse. Where all I own goes to die. Husband was here he'd find my license. Find my credit card afore anything. When he said afore he died 'You're killing me' I didn't think to take it literally. Let that be a lesson on you!" The penciled man took out a pen and wrote something permanent on paper scrap.

This was the station they sent you to when you failed to pass through the one for everyone. The woman pulled at a run in her stockings, a blackened division that ran through the back of

128

minuscule fishnets that caught everything, her pounds of flesh looked painful, barely fit her. The chromatic counter where the woman leaned glared fiercer than the one in Nonna's kitchen on Sunday morning when the sun sent shafts that blinded your eyes as you spread marmalade across the day-old Italian bread toasted past brown to the perfect burn. But, if brighter, the dented counter where the lady dug her elbows was far filthier with the crusted detritus of countless travelers who leaned hard to relieve, right there, their traveling weariness. In Nonna's kitchen counter you could see the oval of your face but never the features of youth or age. Here, Stella saw, even from a distance, the glare threw back a spitting image of every flaw written in your face. Try resting in the reflection of that visage.

When the woman finally pried, with a fingerprinted tweezers, a twenty-dollar bill that had dried and hardened around the long rooted-after ID, she shook her black jacket with a laugh and shouted — to the turn of ten heads — "Lottery!" to the patient officer who looked as impressed as Charon tallying the fresh-arrived dead. Her left hand kept up a loose sequined skirt. Sequins stared like countless little eyes, like the gaze of millions going nowhere. "I'm single, available, a lucky old lady, now show a poor woman whose lot has been suffering some chivalry if you want to stay living." She winked as she shoved her stubborn walker past, her right pointer aimed at the man half-erased who said — with all the polite condescension of a freshly-promoted middle manager — "Welcome to heaven, Mrs. Jones."

Peter, wearied by the ordeal in front of him, stepped aside and patted his pockets. The officer looked out from the plastic like a laid-off prophet who had found conventional, gainful employment, and as he waved the woman through the turnstile he waited for Peter who, oblivious, was rubbing red blotches out of his cheeks with cold, chapped, gray fingers that felt, when he touched you, like life or fate (she always hesitated to think it and could never explain to even closest friends), the chameleon skin that some called albino and others translucent and artificial alien in the tabloid magazines (though they had to try hard to make him unhandsome) and still others as black as can be — a take alternately celebrated or used to make his cut-out image a favorite target at the pay-per-hour shooting range on Grange Avenue.

Behind the desk a wide tunnel ascended slowly, then dipped suddenly in the distance. Framed by dull aluminum moldings that flickered as if electrocuted, the tunnel's walls were still duller: several scarcely distinguishable shades of matte silver faded to gray. Far away, at the end of the tunnel, a faint red cloud the color of whetted dust hovered above the sharp decline. Fuel exhaust? Construction? Her squinted eyes could not descry. Someone in a yellow hazmat suit sucked the cloud into a vacuum and then disappeared down the stairs.

She could see him cramp his hand, which he did whenever the slightest inconvenience even threatened, saw him press the heel of his palm against the pants she had ironed against the tag's warning: Dry Clean Only. His cheeks were wide where the bones bulged but the skin itself was thin and taut. Often he poked fun at the flesh of his face "stretched beyond its god-fearing limits" by too many childhood hours spent blowing through his uncle's instruments — especially the busted, beloved trombone. But to her his visage seemed anything but soft — a fine cliff ridge that could withstand the waves of an ocean with nowhere else to go. If you looked long enough you could see a tremble, subterranean, just beneath the skin, but Peter's secret, sensitive center was overpowered by a tired smile that said to the world "I've heard your jokes and found them, frankly, wanting, my friends," whispering meanwhile through the side of his mouth to the ones he loved — the many he knew through passing handshakes and stares at rallies — "I'd rather die than see you cleave to such inhuman waiting without a whit of real promise, nursing instead the dope of eternity inscribed in the country's DNA — test rats racing the endless experiment in equality undertaken with infinite impatience, telling you all the while to be patient." She could hear the crowds call back "Amen."

"I can't," he said in a whipped-up whisper whose staccato and pitch tightened her stomach. "I can't go. Can't do this. Crazy. Can't." Stella shooed on the next in line, gave the officer a laconic wink by forcing her tired eyelids wide open for a second before she let them fall and let the womb-like darkness return, her head burned, she got lost in a sightlessness that soothed with the promise of her next sleep. "You can't stay," she shot back, and he turned to the right as if struck with authority.

The officer shouted, sharply, "If you step aside from your place in line you have to start over, have to start from the end."

Peter pressed his two fingers together in a crushed peace sign that trembled with rage and he found a place opposite a pillar where the "functionary can't find me."

She waved a sheepish apology to the officer who — busied with the next reject — did not see her desperate amends as she followed Peter to his hiding place and then touched the base of his back with two fingers, the spine bend there where a pinched nerve stressed, pressed hard to relieve the pain, there, where the pinstripe wool had sopped so much sweat, the run-off of his final decision, what insomniac sheet tosses hadn't wiped clean. She would go back to the apartment. The reek of the laundry, if I leave it, will seep under the door and the landlord will break in, afraid some murdered tenant fermented in a backroom bed, or a tenant timely with his rent but overdosed in an heirloom armchair. Flies in the eyes. Hers widened and she pressed his nerve with the last of the strength in her strong thumb. She then took her fingers from him forever and bit her knuckle until it hurt. She had told Peter, who never checked the weather, that the forecast for D. C. was colder than Chicago.

She kissed the base of his neck — just a peck, though when her lips felt his warmth they wanted, demanded the more she refused to give — pressed instead again, unprincipled, her pained knuckle into Peter's bent nerve path until it became a full-blooded highway and he said "You fix me," and she clicked her tongue, "And that's the trouble, I can't do that forever, won't be the one you save all your mess for" — variations on a familiar quarrel. Peter slinking home after undisclosed ventures into the underworld of Chicago politics — Charon's Kitchen was just one of many haunts — tense with the thrill of some new strategy (he said he was now averse to violence but the lids he kept sealed over his doings made her sure that the plans involved explosives). He would not tap her but would sit at the bed edge and rock himself calm with a rude motion designed, she was sure, to disrupt her sleep and then a handful of times he would hand her a condom, letting her choose if to soothe him that way (every time she threw it away) but most of the time what he sought was comfort which was hard to give when he spoke in riddles of classified conspiracies that he boiled down to power plays and almost always begged her, back to her, see, as he stared out the gauzy drapes of their window at the sleepless city's computerized lights, that he was walking a thinning tightrope that transcended "the right side of history," because "the way to do right, in our times, seems to me, is to blow up the notions of sides of history as if any one partisan possesses it all, and the only thing that can make that apparent to a sleepwalking population is a loud enough dynamite to wake the dead. Let's say, for the record, I'm speaking metaphorically." These vague and veiled allusions to catastrophe morphed into talk of his overworked nerves and he wondered aloud how long he could carry in his one person so much weight of history: "Don't you see, when you comfort me you are keeping alive the dreams of millions?" He had turned away from the sleepless city, and though she could tell that he could not see her as his eyes adjusted to the bedroom dark, the pupils seemed like portals into futures only he could see and make happen.

Stella had once relished the role he gave her to play, though she now chose to throw it away, right here, today. She stepped back and followed his stare — halted and blue-faced from the ubiquitous glare — wondering why a strange half-smile formed and flowered from his faltering mouth.

"Cowards." She was not sure who he was condemning. "The unpredictable at the heart of the violent. Only the event can truly liberate. No one knows which way the wind blows except," he paused, "history."

A tall screen half the size of the wall had flashed from forecast winter storm warnings to a live protest at an unknown location (a list of the latest stock market figures blocked the place name, held knowledge hostage). Nighttime trash fires lit up faces whose linked arms made a walking fence, a shifting border blocking out what, protecting what she could not see, a half circle of human chain chanting words she could not make out, shouts shot through baby blue masks and bold red bandanas that looked like dried blood, eyes peering out like well-washed obsidian perfected for centuries to reflect — not absorb. Wind whipped the flames which became — another flash — curvaceous question marks put to whom, asked by whom.

She blinked and the orange looked ostentatious, make-believe, so impossibly heatless and unreal that the burning rage was all in vain. But buildings fell apart before her eyes and poles collapsed and people like dummies or dolls were tested and left there, left there, under the weight, but then a makeshift club of rotted wood wielded by a gaunt older man, maskless but bearded, went wild — wide smile propped up by columns of impeccable white teeth. He battered the gut of a kid, a boy not older than ten and with all the force of a magnet's laws a dozen people came to the youth's rescue, circled the doubled-over child, boy, kid, not older than ten, who rubbed madly at the puffed-out patches that kept his eyes completely closed, frantic to win back his sight, the blow and the tear gas leaving him bent, skinned knees naked on the pavement, palms spread across the pitch black surface until a uniformed stranger with an automatic rifle dispersed the crowd and ripped off the mask and revealed the boy to be even younger, not possibly older than seven, and the stranger, clothed in a decorated uniform, struck the fear stamped on the boy's face, forced from his mouth a silent scream that stretched and stretched until it could not stretch any longer, stayed wide — a broken, oblong oval like an overcooked Easter egg. A baton shattered the camera lens and the world, for a second, disappeared, before a fuzz of technicolor static returned, reassured, a neon resurrection. And in this new life the boy walked away, alone, a spring in his steps toward the orange orbs of fire.

The line to the turnstile, when she looked, had halved, and Peter, fussing with a luggage zipper, made with his mouth an oblong oval, a wince of pain he did not mean to show, a side, he'd said, he only shared with her. That compliment contained precisely the problem. How he became a boy beside her. Something she hated and also loved.

A officer with a friendly pug dog face whose eyes betrayed a well-nursed sorrow ordered Peter to empty his wallet. Peter pulled out pictures of his baby, several of Stella turned aside from the camera — never both mother and child together in the same captured portrait, and never he and she snuggled into a shared frame. As if his ophthalmic gland withheld in protest or an irritant fleck was blocking his iris, the friendly pug blinked and studied the certificates that verified P. C.'s existence. His eyes wandered over Peter's shoulder to where Stella and the baby stood. "One of these things is not like the other," he said and tried to take the plastic tickets but Peter said "Wait you can't do that, legally," which perhaps he could, but Peter pressed for the point where all authority betrays its circumference and steps into mystifying arbitrary territory over which it assumes with a forceful assertion and a shrill style untamable by drops of mellowing mood stabilizers that mine is the kingdom and the power and the glory. The pseudo-policeman stepped back like a child.

Still the man said, with a shout that startled Stella's shoulders — sunk them and strained her elongated neck: "You'll have to wait here." Disappearing momentarily without explanation and returning with grim disappointment, hand-drilled into jaws exercised by failing restraint, he said, "I can't believe this shit. The security room is in use by a woman who's dilated to nine centimeters and any minute will deliver a baby. You ever been in a room when a kid popped out like that, unexpected?" and Peter almost opened his mouth but she saw him annex the answer to that question. The man rubbed his palms together and drew a primitive prison around Peter, circling the suspect with yellow tape that as it twisted for a second seemed to read PLEASE LIE DO NOT CROSS. As if to reinforce the flimsy bars the same man dragged a portable railing and rearranged it with great patience until he was satisfied that Peter's corral said everything that needed to be said, only then realizing that he had cordoned off a drinking fountain that flowed without ceasing, a sign above reading OUT OF ORDER.

Peter below it stole fresh sips from the cataract arc, akin to a desert dweller who mistakes a geyser for a mirage.

The man, nodding with satisfaction, stepped away and said "I'll be right with you," as if they were waiting for a fast-food order.

"Come," Peter asked her from across the rope fence that wound in crisscrossed convolutions around and around with dizzying complexity, as if in the botched job lay hid a secret code geometry, but all that bound him was a transparent labyrinth that lacked, her eyes scanned, a start or a finish.

"Come with," his elliptical eyes waning, closed with wanting — always he wanted — opened into a beggar's question, but the plea assumed a tone of command. Again she covered the baby with her hair — a reddish brown translucent in the light — like a curtain hiding from him the delight and the secrets of home that he swore he found there, somewhere, within her (but where? — because he never could specify or name what she owned, what he swore he would give up all else to possess). She remembered that word, possess, with a pain, and she gave a curt head shake before closing her eyes, peeking through slits to see if he saw her unclasp crossed arms, let drop the weight of the sleeping baby who hung from the sling around her neck, and he saw her arms outstretched, awkward, a bent-elbow tension that would not give, and her palms turned outward, nowhere to go.

She stood before him like a costly statue staring back through its cracks with a sad defiance. That she had something he sought after — at one time she'd clung to it as a compliment — hardened her mouth.

The bright and ubiquitous lights left her blind to all other dwellers. The two of them might have been back in his little living room, and she looked around for the TV-tray table, its crippled leg propped up with dead magazines. She stepped into the scene — the perpetual circle, like a vinyl record that never stopped spinning. Too broken to stay lifeless. Her lips shaped a kiss through the red veil of hair — a by-now familiar routine of cruel teases that she set between them like appetizers on an ornate table whose napkins assume as grand a stature as the food. These little flirtations were reliably followed by self-recriminations that pierced, like the tines of heirloom silver, whatever remained of her confused hatred. Always she did this when the desire for closeness pulled up a familiar chair between them and threatened, like the baby, to bond them together — Jason the famous sleeper who, palpitating sweat, she'd taken to the doctor (she wiped the neck sweat off on the crumply paper that ran in excess of the examination bed) as the elderly man way past retirement flashed an expert smile lit with ivory dentures and acted as if he was treating her, not her child, but to humor her ran a battery of tests and found nothing to fear, here, he said, pointing to her head, pointing to the baby's, here is the trouble (as his mouth said here, here his smile said there, there), here some babies are champions of the unconscious, would rather dwell there than this waking world and you know what, I don't blame them, the doctor had said, and I don't think you can either, my friend, you look worried and alone.

Reading with his left hand a new emailed message — she heard, as he mouthed it in mumbles aloud, something about Affordable Housing and the steelworkers' wages — Peter reached to touch her right hand, as if to relieve the unfulfilled pose. The big and blue-tinged television bared derailed trains and blared the tree snap crackle of wildfires feeding insatiably on a faraway forest. Smog of flames faded into war. The rifling clacks of sniper fire kept another disconsolate silence from threatening to summon explosive regrets into — again — the space between them which was, of late, like the stuffy room that was his affordable housing apartment, windows painted permanently shut, so that every breath was like something stolen. A soldier camouflaged in vomit-sick green raised a rifle like a giant insect and pumped it above his helmeted head, pointing its legs against a skyscraper backdrop before the well-washed glass of the revolving door caught in reflection what he did next to the baby whose mother stood elbows out, asserting her bones against the gun's nozzle which fired and then filled the little one's brain.

O in light of the brevity of breath, how stupid this neverended argument. This fight that could outpace our lifespans, elderly in a nursing home still disagreeing over bingo cards and spilling our troubles to the others around us so that when death comes who would mourn us and who — God — who could blame them? How hard can this really be. Why not just leave without word? She hung her head, chin tucked above their boy Jason whose streaks of hair were set, just now, in the sweetest black ringlets colored slightly blue by the screens that stared, in a series, down upon them. All the way here in the cab, she had twirled the stray muss of graying hair to soothe him, as he cried and spit out his hard biscuit teether on the floor: should she scrape it up or count the cleaning cost covered by the exorbitant fare? She steadied his head between her knees and treated his hair like a masterpiece she would bring to perfection against the swerves and jolts of the traffic, against the strain that scratched at her mind like a brittle comb against her very brain. Softly, as she ran her fingernails along the nerves he'd inherited from his dad, his mouth went lax, his neck went fluid, and she shaped his hair with terrible focus. On the airport escalator his fit pitched higher, and snot and spit rivaled the sweat that she had smoothed into flawless curls to soothe herself as much as to quiet his wheezing, caught-phlegm baby screams. Only when his red hands mussed up what she made did she see, completely, what she had done: her breaths and shush had shaped the hair into the awesome waves of Japanese woodblocks eternally arrested before the sea cliffs could kill them.

The line had withered to two.

"Come on. If I come we'll end up in a game of hate alternating with make-up love, made-up lovemaking, make believe, baby. If I stay, we can long for what never came. Put to pleasant dreams, on an afternoon, what never ever could have happened. Old story. Desire what could never have happened." She stopped shoving his hand away, gripped three of his fingers and held them to her mouth.

"Something I couldn't say 'til now. What kills me. You think I'm taking Marjorie's advice. Which, let's be real, you wouldn't have been worried by if you hadn't read my emails."

"You make it sound like a daily practice. Like I surveilled your psyche nonstop."

He looked from corner to corner of the place, locating in the shade of each a camera eye like an interstice in between the joints of the world.

"Paranoid. Sure. But even with ten or a hundred angles those f-ing filmings" — he hedged his language as someone else's toddler passed under his elbow, a child whose shoes blinked red like airline beacons, far too young to know the taboos of words — "I mean even if they had a million angles they'd fall far short of omniscience, right? But it takes someone on the inside to spy, the ones who don't mean to, the ones you trusted but who can betray it — it takes that kind to really put on pressure. And I don't mean to, look at me —"

"Look? What you don't want, don't locate the — Peter, don't you dare locate the finally perfected stage of the surveillance state in me, as if that feeling we all have of being watched is my fault alone. Once. I swear I only read that one, and even then, even then I was trying to look up a recipe to spare you the usual, same old routine. Shit, I bought scallops for whatever absurd price per pound. You couldn't help but like the meal. I saw the satisfaction through your brooding, moody collapse on the couch."

"Why then didn't you come to me there?"

"I thought you wanted some space one night. It's not like either of us moved out. One night on the old couch."

"Don't dodge. I won't follow your digression."

She smiled but could not solicit the same from him. She feared, if she stayed here, they might make headway and all her conclusions would be crumpled and cast out.

Jutting from a nearby row of seats, a man's hand crushed a spent coffee cup and shot it in a skillful arc, just behind a hobbling elderly couple. The cup swished the rim of the nearly full trashcan, to the shared celebration of several onlookers.

"You think I think you're a risk to my career. Forget Marjorie. She's a veteran, all right, who dares doubt it? A veteran with 'decades of experience.' I can hear her repeating the talking point now, a parrot in a coal mine. But sometimes experience is the blinder. What passes for wisdom is a skewed habit. You think.

138

We fear risk. I mean — you asked me to 'risk you.' Now, when you're pressing me like this, what I'm supposed to do? When I swear that I could care less, you think I'm . . . lying to make you feel better. Like I said, it's not like I'm C. I. A., but I can't share with you what I'm doing, baby, for your own safety. The alderman thing got heady enough. That time we was followed back home, remember? Could I live with myself if what I did collapsed and killed my baby, maybe, and maybe you too?"

"Who?" She whispered. "Who would kill? In response to what? Are you doing — going to?" Her mouth refused to form the words.

He spoke on a frequency so low she had to strain, could hardly hear against the announcements about Lost luggage unclaimed: "I swear to you one thing: my whole work — against theirs — is to save lives. To prove that taking lives, in their way, won't carry all the good consequences they've dreamed up. Not some outright ban on violence. If I take the non-violent tack, they'll laugh. So all I can do is work with what I have: that their goals can be got at in another way that won't turn targeted and random folks into corpses."

She let him caress her hardened jaw and looked again at the child they had made.

"You're not telling me everything. You can say 'I'm not lying,' but that isn't comforting. I can't live with a man who half of his life — who am I kidding, it's like eighty percent — is hidden. From me, at least."

Jason's eyes were invisible, buried under the sarcophagus of sleep, his consciousness sunk into depths unexplored, his mind so wonderfully elsewhere and absent that the airport cacophony could not touch it, although his fleshy arms and striated thighs — fat and relaxed into dead weight — hung from a faded blue sling she had spent half an hour arranging just so, readying the papoose for the long travels home — the buses and train and the walk to her parents who she had not seen for, what now, two years — fixing the straps so that even when she changed him she could snap him back in without incident. Limp arms with little hands no longer clung, spastic, to her shoulder. His limbs splayed in a passive X.

Curtis — Peter called him "the unchecked law, the" — large scare quotes — "'living legislation' of the movement. Talks nonstop about the need for 'checks and balances,' but he's the most unbalanced man I ever met — never seen nobody put him in check." Curtis had wired him enough for a second flight when Peter withdrew his promise, refused to arrive at all before he refused to arrive alone. Which was crazy, because in the email Stella read, Marjorie had said that the monthly amount they would deposit in Peter's account would uptick to $20,000 per month as soon as he set foot in D. C. When she tried to conceive this amount collecting over time, the dollars, the digits, bounded beyond her imaginings and she gave up, breathless at an endless stoplight, the way she felt after the brisk walks stolen during lunch breaks at the Milwaukee florist shop. Baby's breath. Jason's warm against her breast. She could get her job back at the florist and drain her paychecks on baby formula. And en route to his hundreds of thousands, Peter had haggled over two airline tickets. To let Curtis know who would be in control, even if Curtis was officially his boss.

We need you at any cost. The digital note explaining the wire, a line that pulsed on the screen he stared at and showed her twice, and then showed her again, scoffing at but clearly cherishing, was as close as Curtis had ever come to pleading. Peter, too, had been all pleads in the time warp of days that was this past week. The shock of her refusal still shook him: what if Stella was just letting him know that she was officially his boss?

As a couple behind them argued in Arabic and a boy sporting bright blue shoes slid past, leaving a jet-trail of marijuana, Peter shook his head and said "I — he's ours. Not yours. I can read like a palm what his life'll be like if you raise him alone. Without, not without me — it's not about me, but without a father. See?"

She did not say So what you're saying is that you'll let me go in peace as long as I find him a flesh-and-blood father? What of my blood, my flesh?

At four in the morning over clearance-shelf coffee — which meant they packed the filter so chock full you could chew the grounds like circus glass, the kind the carnies had when they came

140

every year to West Allis to man the State Fair Ferris wheel and supervise the funhouse mirrors and breathe fire and gnaw glass shards like some unsung sideshow creatures of Apocalypse.

Peter had promised never to take custody to a "talk-show legal level," so now his sudden assertiveness tensed her jaw like when she was a child at the carnival and saw flames spewed from the face of a mohawked fellow mortal who had locked eyes with her and grinned.

"I've. Got your ticket. You don't want me to make this a legal thing," to which she shot back "You f-ing liar," censoring herself because the little boy whose shoes blinked still slid and skidded past as they spoke.

"Why are you — you're packed. Why'd you pack if you're not coming?" He mussed up the designs that remained, made the waves of Jason's matted hair wild.

"No ticket for Jason."

"He's free. Boy don't need no ticket."

She sped her steps toward the dimmed crimson Exit that flickered a little before it went black. Over her shoulder she watched Peter perform an elegant zigzag pretense toward the turnstile, a perfectly premeditated about-face filled to the cheeks with sick confidence (that sneering grin he made whenever he felt his advantage slacken). She peeked through the window of the darkened exit: he wasn't bluffing, he was back at the turnstile, he was straddling the threshold of security.

Stella took her fingers from the door clamp before it clacked into place and retraced to where she was before, searching for the circumference of their lingering endless conversation as if it were some final destination. A gray-haired woman in hair curlers carried three over-stuffed plastic bags that hung from frayed rungs around her wrists. She stopped and blinked and asked Stella, "Have you seen my husband? He was just here. He was."

"No, I'm — so sorry," said Stella, who saw pupils so dilated they scared her and a wet and warm flush surrounding the woman's eyes. Surrender. With a light touch her fingers found the woman's forearm and she said "Can I help —" but before she could finish a sentence the stranger lifted her hands in a spastic motion toward the pockmarked ceiling or what was beyond it — the skies faith said were up there still, or the God who was not literally up there, actually, though because you could scoff at primordial idiocy that did not mean there was no God, but Stella did not have the woman's strength to stretch into the supernatural when this world was already plenty, thank you — and she laughed at her own unwarranted offer of "Can I help you?" (how precisely could she?) and almost shot after the fading woman who walked away with a sententious sway that left Stella talking to her herself, saying, "Can you help me?" under her breath. Alone she tried to act like a natural, a regular airport character. Right hand resting on waist. Elbow out.

Atop an otherwise empty bench, a small boy hid beneath a baseball cap and held a cardboard sign up high. She squinted to read the barely legible blue letters. NO PLACE LIKE HOME. No parent or elder stood beside the boy. She cupped the base of her baby's head and kissed his fresh umber skin. Soft skull. So vulnerable. A limping man leaning against a column kept a red carnation clutched to his chest, and the plastic that wrapped the ripe flower sent out shimmers of scarlet rays like the blood of a martyr in the childhood books her Nonna read them before bedtime. Peter was waving the printed ticket that someone from D. C. sent him last week. From what she could hear, the clerk was complaining that the name on his license did not agree with the name on the ticket. "My biological father was a Brahmin. I mean, that was the name of my father, biological. My mother, who raised me, was a Clavier. For years I've gone by both, one or the other. Whatever." The clerk looked from the license photograph to the twitching face that stared down on him through double-thick bullet proof plastic, the reflection of his own face in the acrylic sheet eclipsing the officer's pencil-thin existence, and again Stella looked around as if all this could be erased in an instant and if it wouldn't be for many years what was the difference? It was still too mutable, the impermanence too terrible to love, and she hated that she loved her child whose forthcoming sufferings — as if announced on marquee — would pain her worse than whatever she had known.

Craning his head back, the clerk, who — she saw now — was only dressed like law enforcement, in a costume that at once seemed more cute than convincing — a royal blue short-sleeve shirt with military shoulder straps, a big belt, and flat black pants — brushed his mustache with a walkie talkie antennae, then called for back-up as he looked into the future and waved Peter off to the side.

"I can't let you pass. My boss has to look into this." And he pointed at the next in line, an elderly lady with a therapy dog who flipped back her blouse sleeves, unburdened her weight with wide elbows on the counter, and smiled.

Walking sideways with his hands in his pockets, Peter pretended not to be troubled. She knew when conflict came he needed more than a minute alone. Head tilted back like a prayer, he scanned and then scrutinized the blinking departures. Screened numbers and names of cities flitted like a casino machine and she saw him watch and wait, hand on chin, as if the dots might determine some new destination. He shook his head as if destiny demurred, refused to appear in black and white.

Whenever he turned and gave glassed eyes at once she entered, dizzied and smiling, the wide airport waiting room of his mind, seats all taken with spilled luggage and a crowd enervated by delays.

Gathered in a huddle behind bulletproof plastic stood the officer and his two superiors, a lean man with hollowed-out eyes who put his hand on his colleague's shoulder and made violent but curt gesticulations at the computer screen only they could see.

Peter veered close to the fence that kept their esoteric pursuits officially hermetic but at least transparent to all watchers wondering what was the matter, wondering what a person could possibly do wrong to summon from the dim back desks of offices these pale and authoritative lords whose weary stances were already yearning to slink back into bent-over postures. And the atmosphere grew dense with suspicion, people gripped their belongings as if they might soon lose them and what if in fact they lost their lives also. When the shorter of the bosses waved him away and he turned back to Stella like one of her students who had hoped to skip school on a fun field trip but instead of a ticket received a demerit, his eyes warped from winsome to sad. She faked the indifference of a mother who cares but can't let her boy grow up soft in this world — her part to play in the predetermined dance. But God how she wanted and wanted intensely to stay in this place where the one who looks through you first turns and cringes but then looks again, away, again and says I don't care if we lose all I'll love you like we could only and inevitably win.

She could look through him too but had to do so askance, as he tried, always, to disappear under not only glares but even a glance. Why she insisted on his moving away: he would get what he wanted and then what? Maybe at last he would miss being seen. Maybe with no one to witness the scenes he made like over hard eggs in the morning, with no one to see his pale fingers pull at the pomaded baby afro with an anger that tried to rip out the roots and an ire in the eyes that could set off the low-battery fire alarm. She could see him, spatula raised on high, elevated rants of an impossible soul over a fan that sucked the smoke from the overdone bacon he'd forgotten to turn.

The officer was absent, but behind the glass five men held congress, four bent elbow to elbow and one looming, arms akimbo, the purple birthmark above his stretched brow the shape of an unmapped continent.

An unasked question pursed Peter's lips but he swallowed it like a saved coin. The line was long again — "'Last shall be first,' my uncle'd be proud, see unc I ain't a raging heathen though you'd keep me from entering your man-made heaven, though you'd consign me like an infidel to the gnashing molars of the mouth of hell!" — and grew fast as more diverted, impatient travelers raced their roller bags by, sleepy slits with red eyes or tanned, returned from some impossible island. Inside of a corralled corner, behind red velvet stanchions that seemed out of place, second-hand maybe from a closed museum, a dozen Muslims in black kaftan robes kneeled and bent low on prayer rugs. Behind them a yellow police line X forbade entrance to a small side room whose doorpost bore a Star of David, a dome tipped with a crescent moon, and a blocky cross — all in a row.

144

The Muslim men were bent to the floor. All she could see was the blue embroidery of their prayer cap tops. The threaded flowers of pure azure possessed a kind of terrible beauty but the white was overbearingly bright. Her temples — she touched them — throbbed with pain and her fingers could not bring herself the relief which she always managed to give to Peter. She could see her Nonna kneeling before a makeshift shrine — a dozen candles whose wax, when hot, made a sound like *hush* or *shush* — in the narrow hallway of the old family home, why she always kept her head bent down instead of staring up at the woman whose hands were outstretched, palms out-turned but somehow not to turn you out but rather, somehow, to draw you in, without sin, the white cloth of Mary's garb worn away by a century of age, the stowaway statue a family legend, like holy loot stolen from Italy and planted at the center of the home. Her chiseled hands chipped of peach paint or weeping eye now blind without pupil did nothing to diminish the primordial outline of a mother, Mary, the mother Stella never knew on earth as her own, if kept together with cosmetics was as far as she could remember like a famished ghost who you paid your respects to but received in turn only anxious confusion squeezed out of a diminished store of love — a wish, a genuine wish for the good of her child, but barely a finger lifted to make it.

Though Peter's stare stayed straight ahead, she felt, still, so terribly seen, and always next to his piercing eyes others' interpretations of her existence fell like so many cut straitjackets. With everyone else she was accustomed to playing, staying as if — *as if!* — aloof, impossible to know — a posture that required ceaseless effort. After each outing for most of her life she would collapse onto couch or floor, forearm across her face as if to try and block even God's omniscience.

Even Blake she had kept at bay — arm's length when they went out to dinner and looked down from the big bay window at the mother duck who squawked at a fox, the nonplussed flash of fiery orange who seemed to mock her solicitude for the brood of ducklings who floated downriver, oblivious, and as she said something about the strange profusion of wild animals inside the city limits

145

Blake knelt down next to the table (he'd arranged with the waiter that the room would be their own, that no one would enter to refill waters) and spoke the words she had always wanted said, but why did she have to cleave to the table to suppress the recoil like a tedious spring broke loose from its purpose of absorbing shock, releasing instead at unwonted times a tension that warps the helix's symmetry and ends in an edge of sharpened metal that could cut you if you weren't careful . . . maybe this was more than part of the reason he ran away although she said "yes" but maybe he heard hesitation in her "yes," but had she not made, in the aftermath, amends, offered countless little reassurances as when he apologized for the rehearsed deadness with which he delivered the marriage proposal, and had they not laughed at his stiffness, at the fact that he nearly failed to get the words out? But even then when he reached for a hug she drew back she did not know why, still though she was devastated when he called off the marriage and she played into her family's sympathies without hinting at her part in the problem. She knew all along that, though Blake was a basket case, what he called his madness was not all that was wrong. She swore from that point to stay permanently single and acclimated to a lonely life that yet lacked the vicissitudes of bliss and despair, the unpredictable *range* of marriage.

But from the first Peter had pierced the part of her heart she'd let play dead.

Look at him. Talking on the phone. Curtis, surely — or Marjorie. "But the whole purpose is to unite, not divide. And if we can't agree on that fundamental, then" — he darted eyes around before he let it fly — "fuck it." An inviolate yearning spilled from his pupils, his choked silence charged with something like innocence in spite of the bad things he said he had done. Repaying his silence in kind seemed to her a kind of cruelty. The thing she cleaved to in him, she hated to find in herself.

With her he could be so self-absorbed — with everyone else he was solicitude and smiles — but when she got lost in his own private labyrinth she found a kind of bliss, and after nursing her hurts after Blake disappeared, caring more for Peter's hardships than her own was good medicine for tedious wounds she'd ceased to pick at promptly after meeting him, because his problems *really were* worse than any she had faced and at first she believed she could even make him happy, though by now she knew that all attempts to lead him out of the maze made the man more intractable, that the only path toward incremental truce or temporary contentment was found in the back alleys of a complex warren that he'd memorized like a Daedalus who'd never tried to take flight.

Better to play the puttering bird who pretends to be only passing by, feigns fascination with some other errand, but arrives precisely when the need appears. But even when chances seemed to show up and she landed, lightly, on his shoulder, he had no patience for a route out that consisted of anything other than soaring — walking, for instance, instead of flying, learning to press on while parched, to stop for necessary rests along the road and "waste time" in order to arrive in one piece. He was all haste and when the frenzy ran out after a particularly draining campaign, after a day of canvassing that seemed mainly wasted, he went into a catatonic stillness so that she wondered, always, if he had a core, anything permanent behind the fevered ambition. Limits lit a rage in his heart.

The electric ether above flickered out, then burned and blared. He pocketed the phone and blinked against the light, peering hard to see her. She felt her cheek and found it raised in an anger she had not noticed. Her blush blended with the suppressed passion.

"You're beautiful," he had shouted during one of their arguments.

"The temper, your temper," she had yelled back, almost breathless after the last word. The temper was new: she'd picked it up from him. The temper. Not hers. "Yours." Never before had she been so angry so often, and never before so totally smitten, so expert with excuses for his flaws. He'd told her she was strangely gorgeous when she got mad and she did not know what to do with that. What if that meant a marriage might work? Or what if he merely had a terrifying capacity to transfigure the pain he had so clearly caused into something so-called beautiful? Shared heating bills, water from the same tap, the late-night taps on her shoulder when he'd come in with skin hot from the shower.

147

Over the loudspeakers a woman explained that unattended private property would be confiscated and that all passengers should keep alert for suspicious activity.

"My fault," he said staring at her fingertips, reaching to touch them before retracting fast. "I can't not. I know, I know we've talked it to death, but I'm still — whatever you say — yours."

"That tickles!" she said and turned away. "Wait, your wallet! Did you print that other part of the tickets? The receipt — fine print? You asked me to take your wallet, the bigger one, the one with all the cards, off the sink but — did I? I didn't." She saw, for a second, his half-shaven face: the mania and panic of the early morning arguments made them late, and he nearly left for the airport without applying the blade to the blotches of scruff on his left side. He had gone in to finish the shave but left his wallet beside the sink. She saw it when she emptied her bladder and first picked it up but then put it back down. Suddenly she trusted that her stumbling guesses and tormented attempts to do right were being corrected by a stranger's hand. That time at the lakefront park when another couple's baby was learning to walk on a green that declined into the water and the parents — "let the child test the limits" — bit their lips and let the lady who reached down hold the wandering toddler's shoulder, turning her away from the fearful water which was yet a good ten feet from baby's toes but she anyway shook a shaming finger at the father as if to say *she could have drowned if not for me I frankly don't care if you thought all was under control.*

Stella stretched her empty pockets, relieved that he couldn't pass through the gates without the fake I. D. she'd seen but left, and *why,* now *why* had she left it — when all she wanted now was for him to be *gone* — in the wallet he always took on trips, and it waited there for them both to return, to reassume their interminable debate next to the bottle of disinfectant they'd paid twice the price for when the pandemic summoned hoarders and gougers from where they were always waiting in the wings of history for just such a chance.

Jazz — baby Jason — put his finger in his mouth and she rushed to yank it out. Forgot to cut his nails. His cry sounded like a warbled saxophone note played by a destitute man who'd sat up sleepless on the courtroom steps in Chicago mid-winter above a sewer grate that gave off rancid heat. The weary whine drew a smile from a woman who had never relaxed into her chair. The whole time they'd been there she'd been sitting on the edge, as if listening to every word exchanged and watching the unsaid bodily argument with a wisdom she was forbidden to share. The woman had tried to dye her hair black but a big patch in the back was stark white. Her lipstick was so liberally applied her mouth looked like a skinned knee.

"Here, dearie," she said to Stella, holding out a handful of diapers. "I volunteer at the women's center. He looks like he needs a change." Stella checked and felt the sag. The diapers — idiot — were buried in her suitcase, though her purse contained a miniature pouch of wipes for door handles and every imaginable germ-site surface. Even after the experts reversed their initial alarming warnings about viral contagion and imminent inevitable death, she couldn't send that first scare packing: it had assumed a sort of squatter's rights in her soul.

Stella laid the baby out on her unwound scarf; Peter stepped nearer to help her as *Homeland Security has lowered the threat to yellow*, a soothing maternal woman said in a voice so synthetic it was impossible to tell whether she was human or artificial in origin.

The decibels of Jason's scream only increased when Stella removed the sagging clump of waste which would join the debris and detritus of untold millions who took for granted the plastic sack that another would tend and another would empty and the earth itself would swallow and hide under a hill beside some subdivision, and the sun shot through as the rag was weighed and tossed in an arc into the trash can. His son now screamed. A man hidden behind a magazine lowered the glossy pages just enough for his discontent to cover his eyes like the heat that rises from the freshly poured asphalt on a Midwestern summer night. Peter stroked the baby's ears, pinched them both and said as he slipped on a dry diaper scented with jasmine: "Naked I came into the world and naked I'll go out of it!" The magazine man lifted his pages but his belly moved with reluctant laughter. He peered over and ogled Stella without trying to hide his leer.

"Watch him." Peter had started to see a potential pervert behind any eyelid that didn't remain shut. He exercised an abstemious watch over the focus of his own attention. She'd always marveled at that wherewithal. But her jutted hip — a coquettish joke — emboldened him and he was so close she could smell the sweetener that made his breath sugar. She could smell too the lavender he had rubbed into her shoulder last night — the oil mingled with coconut that she'd have to now work in by herself unless the prices for a Chinatown massage fell to where they were prior to pandemic economics. His lips laughed but his big eyes brooded. "Stella. This is not me asking you to let me, I mean. Why I have been acting like today is final, like we got to decide right here, forever, what the rest of our lives will look like. A hundred flights in a day, I mean. You could come tomorrow if you change your mine. Mind. We could, when we feel those hundreds of miles, know what we need to do." He straightened up and gathered his luggage — a gaudy blue gym bag over his shoulder hung like their baby over hers. He blew them both kisses and backed away with the resolve she'd been dying for. "I won't ask you to come with me now 'cause I know you'll say no. But please. Please don't — "

"Come," she said. "Go now. You'll miss your flight. The clerk is waving you back. Look. You have to go to the bathroom bad. You have the look. Bye now. Don't, now, just go. Don't make this so . . ."

"Stella," he whispered, and by now both the officer and his clerkish boss were making waves with their matching hands, like zealous grade-school crossing guards. "Love." The word heaved with the whole of his chest. "I can't. Please. Baby."

"You're breaking every rule we decided." She started to walk away, assuming the resolve she had wanted from him.

"Star," he said, looking over her sunken shoulder as if scouring, searching the breaking dawn for the constellations that could be salvaged before the bright day would make them play dead.

"We just need to social distance," she'd laughed out, once, when they were arguing across an L-train aisle, trading barbs through disposable masks that repeatedly muffled their meanings. A habitual tactic, the joke, pulled out like a formula — like the baby's fortified formula, ready at hand when her breasts were too raw — in the last few weeks of this damned deliberation, and yes that would be hell, deliberation without termination. But here, now, though the coil spring was carrying a weight beyond the heft of its helix — and this was the part where laughter was supposed to relax the spring, save the sharp metallic point from gouging ruthlessly into their hearts — she failed to find anything funny.

"You be the star," she said, settling into the poetry uneasily because it always spoke her more than she spoke it, but she understood why all lovers found only the celestial bodies sufficient sketches for their desires.

I'll see your star rise from far. Leave all ill omens uninterpreted. Barely spied. Belied. Just somebody that I used to know. Stare and awe without needing to blink. By far. The best way to keep love and make it last.

She laughed and touched his unshaven cheek.

We would have gone the way of all. Neighbors complaining about our fighting out loud. That night she slept on the fire escape the first of a series, a gallery showing of contemporary love on the rocks. At a bar with her baby on her breast, sipping watered-down vodka through a little red straw the color of blood from a fresh-cut wrist. Separate beds, elaborate routines to make it all seem justified, right, the pharmaceutical for untold ailments. But the hardening days on the horizon would have needed, in time, a still stronger anodyne. Separate apartments and then separate states. Why not cut to the inevitable finale was her way of hashing it out on the rocks, stabbing the bloody little straw point into the melting primordial ice.

At the very point he swore three times over he would not, whatever, resort to the law — "no nauseating cuisine of custody" — their discussion took a hostile tone that had not diminished for weeks. Combative phone calls comprised of more hang-ups and dial-backs than sentences exchanged.

A glare off the glass made them both turn their heads to the thousands ascending in metallic birds — the counted and searched and decriminalized souls, the cleared souls approved for heaven-bound flights, and how many hurried goodbyes while they deferred theirs into oblivion, look at them almost begging Peter to pass through the forbidden stile where a woman clacked past, kisses blown like saxophone notes wrung from the gut of her waving companion, and on the other side of the barrier she stood there stationary in blue boots and stockings and a feather down hood that matched her mascaraed eyes glistened like feathers somehow not ostentatious but a grand and welcome disruption here, like a peafowl tail asserting pattern and order out of what chaos. A stiff old lady nursing a walker reached into her purse as she passed, blew her nose as she gawked like the rest at the blue and purple feast of a person, pulling out tissues like a magic trick, a chain of relief for so many sorrows masked as a sneeze, as just a little cold.

Stella shrouded Jason's face with the thin cerulean of the scarf Peter gave her. Stubborn, rippling his lips with anger, Jason peeled back the veil, tilting his head to watch dad go. The drowsy baby who had let them sleep, who napped through loudest crossfire of noises, who nearly never woke in the night needing to gnaw at mama's nipples — her body and Peter's a steady nocturne, her back's concave filled with his chest, an exhausted tangle of unconscious peace.

Like a weathervane prone to lightning she could draw him back with a single pout and by midnight they could be in the apartment naked and cold under the comforter which would be uncomfortably wet from their desperate reconciliation sex. Instead of a pout she rallied her anger — thought, in sequence, of everyone who had ever hurt her throughout her whole life — and that was the last look she let him have, over their sleeping baby.

"Stand up," she shouted over the makeshift fence: nothing more than golden stanchions, theatrical red velvet, low-slung rope. She could skip over like in Double Dutch. Jump the rope. Grip his head. "Who in history has been given your chances?" A chain — with a medal her Nonna had given her, silver St. Rita whose dented forehead somehow meant she specialized in broken relations and other lost causes. The chain dangled down as she screamed, the muscles of her neck spraining: "History's what hurts. And one of the things about it that hurts? What makes history is more chance than fate. Well if you don't take yours then what of the millions abandoned? Dealt only horrors? History is what hurts? I don't see any chains on you now. Hurry before they catch you. Be like born again with those rallies. You were made to lead. Now leave."

But as Peter turned his back on them and the ruthless sun from so far away caught nonetheless on the clasp that kept his suspenders in an X — his jacket he'd slung around his luggage — and the mirrored light at a harsh angle bore into the baby's eyes, Jason puffed his cheeks and blew like the trumpet player daddy once was. Though he started out shaking and wailing the sound made by his own sorrow startled the son into stupefaction — a smile of unknown satisfaction — as Peter disappeared from sight.

. . .

The squall dropped no sleet on the lake but its downdrafts dipped and displaced the stilled winter air like a sequence of scared and nervy birds, fledglings too fast for their own good. Disturbed, the waters curbed their gusts and curled them into capsized question marks. Choppy, cold, cobalt blue lapped against the gray-brown pier boards, sending up crests of whitened spray, and from the sepulchers of time foam nestlings that flapped in bursts and, spastic, defied all downward pull, their ascents reaching the pitch of defiance before they fell, innumerable, one by one. Again and again, and again, and again, until what started as a disturbance, a scattering of attention, resolved into a rhythm of acceptance, an assent that set her blood flowing. For the first time since leaving the airport, she stopped shivering in spite of the chill.

Stella stood taller, stood tiptoe to spy, but couldn't peer that far into distances. She turned back to the lone rower, his black dog's head peeking over the stern, the man's rapid hands ruffling his scruff until both of them stopped their tipsy shaking, both bucked up by the bracing air. She checked Jason's makeshift sling and tucked him into the folds of her jacket — an ugly silver one Peter had given her, gaudy like an over-the-top ornament that keeps somehow making its way on to the tree each Christmas — then ruffled the white woolen hat to make heat, which warmed her hand too so she saluted the boatman who could well be Charon because it was all over, her world or whatever. Over. Over. At least the overture of the end. Assent: to the cold and the questions and the contingencies. As when your yes does not mean less because you've seen from the first all these hints of the hard parts before they play out, because the real risks never resemble the omens that announce them.

She watched the man in the worn blue dinghy, leaned as he leaned when the waves slapped the bow, bucking him into an arms-out squat that balanced the boat he masterfully straddled. He rowed. He sat. He rose. The horizon line looked like the broken ruler left in the bottom of Natasha's backpack, Natasha the former student who held up her pigtails with pink gum wrapped around and around. Always late, her appearances petered into an official Drop Out in the grade book column. Before she left, the class was already a mess. One of the boys formed a pistol with his fingers and shot her dead and blew the smoke — "Playing with you" — but it wasn't fun and Natasha, fourteen, newly pregnant, had gnashed her teeth at the boy and raised up the ruler like some legendary nun until the boy (it was Coop, Coop, crazy kid, almost banished from remembrance, who'd been kicked out for pointing his play gun at the principal) hid his head, laughing, on the desk. And Natasha rushed to the front of the room and held the jagged wood edges together to take the measure on the washed-out blackboard while Stella thought *what a dumb martyrdom, dying for the sake of elementary math* (she'd read somewhere of ancient Pythagoreans who had been killed for their philosophies), but she steeled her outstretched arm anyway, awaiting a real bullet through the head as she turned and drew the next problem, made the chalk line straighter but still shaky, Natasha whispering *fuck that Coop shit*, and Stella blushed for having left her own ruler at home: it must be gathering dust, finding strange refuge in the clear textbook lines of grade-school geometries, almost the peace she had first found as a student doing Euclid's proofs in that faraway dream of adolescence that was not a ghost or another person but the same one whose peach fingers flaked with chalk white and sweated with fright, scratching at her heart, metal taste in mouth, stepping again out into the hall to cool her forehead against the tiles of the wall, the long halls full of soothing emptiness that peaked at the exit's vanishing point.

Crazy she had wanted to say to Natasha, "Do you want your baby? I'd have her. Him. I'd raise him if you want a second life." Lawsuits and parents' verbal lashes kept her thoughts from escaping her teeth.

Stella had stood there scratching at her heart, metallic taste in her dry mouth, leaden tongue incapable of speech, then stepped out into the hall.

Here the white-striped boat's sturdy hull was outlined in a blue that stood out idyllic from the dull colored water, the water colored, dyed with dullness. An overcast washrag of clouds kept the sun not just mute, not just dead, but forgotten, as if earth's starless future could be seen from this puny pier at the end of Chicago. Thousands of millions of billions of years. She checked the screen of her phone for calls. Zero. She checked her screen again. Zero. The third time her eyes fled there she tore them free and stuck them through the long chrome telescope that tipped back downcast, hung there dormant awaiting eyes, but she couldn't see without putting in a quarter. She felt herself out there, as if the surface and the lake were made for us to float upon, to defy the fact of sinking to the deep by figuring out how to stay afloat. Because he wasn't purposeful in his direction but — it seemed, as she squinted and then stared — circled back to where he started. Unless the wind was doing him in. No other vessels puttered around and she wondered whether what he was doing was legal in November in Chicago. Silly idea. A police helicopter descending on the man, cuffing and pulling him up the ladder. She should call to him, shout for help, ask for a ride. Let him decide her destination.

Fingers worrying the bus ticket home, she still didn't know if she should stay or go. Peter had not brought up the key, illegally copied, she still held to his apartment. He had to know she still had it. She could turn around and head back there, sleep after the insomniac night that kept them both on opposite ends of the mattress, wrestling out hugs or warped embraces before separating to the edges again. She dropped the ticket and watched it scatter like any old windblown piece of litter. Let the wind decide for me. Stupid. So as the rattling white rectangle neared the water she ran, reached down, and picked it up, clasping until the jagged side cut blood from the heel of her palm.

He had not asked for the keys back. That meant their rehearsal of final farewell was — get real — only an act, another *as if*. Since she had treated God as an "as if" for years, since Blake retracted the proposal at least and the solid, providential future she'd conceived crashed like the cheap crystal ball of a psychic — ordered online for seven-ninety-nine, the cheap grace she'd conceived in her childhood — her horizons and prognostications had remained fiercely and entirely earthbound. Disappointments were easier to bear because the highest pinnacles from which her hopes could fall were always, relatively, closer to the ground. Staying low made it easy to get up, sore for a day, and keep walking into the unknown.

The repeated whiplash shock of these years felt like accident but she could not forget the dizzying happiness. Her time with Peter defied all she'd known prior. It all at once had come to seem parochial, if not irreal. They'd shared that youthful passion, that desperate demand for something total, the sense that this life is a problem or puzzle but might be solved through an act of daring, a scaling of the walls, a perspective from the peak — faith or something similar, close. Now the fractured shape of their future lay like a proof chalked on the board of her mind: predictably, pathetically, but still eerily familiar. Hah, not something so trite as him becoming a god to her: his imperfections, not worse than hers, were every day as evident as hers. The difference was that she had given up on rooting out her fissures, had made accommodations instead of trying (as he seemed to do) to scorch the earth of his soul — to remove entirely all evidence of weakness, all violent or selfish or vain tendencies — because at least in front of her, at least aloud *to her* if there was anything in him he deemed damnable, he worked without ceasing to dig up the roots and rip at his heart no matter how hard it hurt.

But she loved him not least *because* of his weaknesses, which at first she watched with startles and fear, scrunched shoulders and turned-away face anticipating a blow that never came — the comet arcs of his flexed fists as he explained the secret causes of social ills and the recipes either untried or old but cut short before they could take effect — the promises, finally, that his people could rest "in the deferred remedy of disillusioned dreams," he'd said that night in the basement of a church on Division Street, Saint Someone's basement, the first time he kissed her publicly before he went to the podium.

The zealous furor that he sublimated into a sparking Catherine wheel spitting fire from the center like a comet before it crashed and fell and he stood there, blinking, a little boy lost, as if someone else had spoken his words, words that proliferated all over the internet in video and audio reels and articles damning and articles praising and articles damning with faint praises everything he'd said, it seemed, like some approximation of omniscience, everywhere he'd been spied, some anonymous Youtube hosts going so far as to clip grade school yearbook pictures and play with them in Photoshop, placing scans of his beat-down face like stained glass saints in the windows of the Tribune buildings.

Once he'd said, sweaty after they slept together three dates in, "One reason I'm done chasing fame is 'cause I couldn't bear what they'd dig up from my past. Corpses I've buried — not literally: crazy I may be but not that kind of crazy — but long-forgotten spines of things I'd die if I had to relive." He touched his chin and looked at the lightbulb that throbbed like a brain at the center of the room. "A spinal tap of history's ghosts. Why I'll never climb the ladder again."

And the harder he blew on that same old horn, the more puffed up his chest became, with a rage no instrument could exorcise because he denied the existence of the grasping man he was at the core, in the central artery of what is called heart. The gasping but undead ghoul of his ambitions breathed on her neck even when he whispered and tried with tender shushes to ease her mind.

At first she was sure she could straight-face accept it, set to softening or dulling or cooling, but — the one thing she could not tell him — his justified rage, strangely endearing before the baby came, scared her after Jason's birth. What if their child would watch and imitate and maybe — please God no — receive that rage? True, she herself had never been at the end of his outburst, the brilliant displays after his pent-up days. But what Peter's anger, badly smothered, could do to the boy: that was a truth she could not speak — for fear of setting back a broken man who'd more than hobbled — had pole vaulted — a hard arc into near stardom, who'd come so far from his "homogenous sob story, you see, I have to remind you of it, because it isn't unique, it's cliché, that's the point. There are millions who could parrot my life without lying because the story is standard fare for so many."

Look at him, selfless, no aggrandizement. She tried to cleanse her nerves of the fear that, frankly, there was no reason he wouldn't, in time, turn on her. Strange how she held a greater sway over him than the street hoods who would jump a man without the slightest sense that the one they'd rob had given his life for them. How even the D. C. offer he'd finally turned down, after for months promising a departure. He said he declined because the "recruited position" (he relished the favor as much as the secrecy) meant constant travel, twice a week back and forth without breaks unless or until they all relocated to a part of the nation that seemed so other-worldly, alien to her Midwestern mind — the excuse she fed him over a dinner of baked beans and boxed noodles amid tall water glasses. She couldn't, she said, at practically forty-one, suddenly start over outside the known world. Yes, she'd thrown herself into their shared life, his work, her tries too to do right in Chicago — a towering, sprawling, pent-up place so different from the blasé peace she'd brokered back in Milwaukee. But that was before the baby, at a time when, to use his phrasing, she frankly did not care if she lived or died, and may even have been flirting with a way to hasten the latter under cover of sacrifice. The thing that really tensed her stomach — her own dad had been there, she had seen him on the screen, standing beside his childhood friend on January 6th — was how suddenly stuck she would be in that city with no means of her own. Yet he would not go without her.

"And most of all," she said aloud, although this was the greatest lie, "I cannot beg you to come down from your heights" — like the Ferris wheel from their first week's dates — "can't derail you, look at me, from a future that is not just yours but is everybody's on whose behalf you had better go there. So you'd better go there. Deal with the skeletons. When they dig them up, look down upon them as if — as if they are the dead things they are." But the underground reason was *I'm afraid you'll stab me just like you did to that skeleton, that father figure, from your past.*

But then she would swoon into admiration, an undiluted giddy feeling like a constant ascent up an elevator, and the drugged effect would last for days when he was out laying down his life. She would listen to recordings of his prolific speeches as if the breaths through the speakers were oxygen, needed until he returned from campaigns, from meetings and canvasing, and the late night shit-shooting in the dive bars where every other week (the location switching like a lottery draw) a homicide sent everyone home and a pair of shoes hung from the telephone poles in a pathetic dangling double-knot remembrance. When she begged him to choose better risks, he said he had to pass through the constant threat in order to remember what this whole thing was for, that he had to know the risk to remember why the risk was worth taking, because to be inside that terrible mode of never knowing if tonight's shot will be yours, if the murder will come as you throw back a shot having good clean fun with a couple of colleagues or as you strike a delicate agreement with an East Coast funder with a thunderous voice — to lose that risk was to walk like one blinded, was to be one of the billions sleepwalking to death.

When, back then, she was still smitten, if she could think of a being without failings she could keep Peter in his proper place, sorted and filed like the prettiest flowers in the florist's greenhouse — prettiest but utterly dependent on the massive metal halide lamp whose flash presided with a blinding reminder that should power disappear so would everything here.

Whenever, in winter, for that decade as a florist, she had to step into the narrow greenhouse, anticipating the memorized order that appeared so *arranged* in her mind, that would give way before a dazzling burst of green and gold bright in the cityscape of blackened snowdrifts, she would fast feel dizzy, have to steady herself before stooping to retrieve a stem. Such growth defied her sense of the possible every time she visited the place, the reign of winter was so all-encompassing, so inescapable even inside, where, despite the floridity, space heaters and worn sweaters told the true tale of the season.

Across the water the Navy Pier Ferris wheel appeared frozen, poised with the promise of an easy ascent. The pandemic had closed the pier just days after they'd ridden the wheel, with Peter's arm wrapped around her waist, his clenched fist resting over her ovary, her gauche attempts to wipe sweat from her palm before she covered his knuckles, cupping their throbs as if they'd explode — as if the whole of his heart were in his fist.

The city's skyline always seemed by daylight a series of outdated android giants gathered from the ends of the earth, posing for a family portrait. But when he took her to the wheel that first warm night, the skyscrapers' random scattering of lights left on against the velvet black buildings seemed like stars shot through her watery eyes — blurry, yes, from the wind but more from his hand pushing back her bangs and coaxing a blush. She was suddenly sixteen and stupid again and not the forty-year-old spinster she'd sworn she would stay. As the wheel took them away, as the clank and the whirl took them way too high, shrinking streetlights into electric whites of the dandelion when it comes back to life, just waiting there for a wish or a prayer and she pleaded to the God she had tried to deny "Dull the pain, take this *terrible* away, this terrible, terrible loneliness away," she turned from Peter and muttered the plea aloud, waiting for the as-if to answer. And as the wheel cranked and bolts creaked she couldn't take her eyes away from the lights that fuzzed and blazed between her legs like a medical lamp in a labor room, bright against the Chicago night and he asked "What'd you say?" and she tried to explain against the wind, *dent de lion, the lion's teeth.*

Nonna Cabrini called them *dent de lion* from the French, "teeth of the lion," which had confused Stella's child's mind. Scattering the seeds with a big-bellied breath, she'd said "they're so soft, Nonna, too fluffy to be scary," and Nonna had winked and said "the good Lord know how to declaw big cats and turn the lion's terrifying mane into a lamb's tender white wool and make the lion's teeth as harmless as a fuzz you can pinch between fingers, look, like this," and Stella ran after the floating seedlings and stole a handful of lion's teeth inside and glued them to construction paper and drew a big cat whose mouth could fit them and she wrote with crayon *Keep the lion's mouth shut. God!* but when her child's fingers got to the mouth and tried to make the beast smile, the curl came out a nasty snarl and she ran outside to find Nonna in the garden picking big red tomatoes that looked like heavy hearts in her wrinkled hands. When she turned around and leapt — impossible, the old lady's sprightly step — over the well-made rabbit fence and grabbed Stella's hand and said "skip to my lou, skip to my lou my darling," so she did, and when later they stood at the kitchen counter and made tomato sauce from scratch, they prayed no lions would come to West Allis as Nonna's white apron was splattered red, little dots the color of the blood on the body that hung from the cross in her hallway, a plastic Jesus whose face had got smooshed in the factory in the Philippines or maybe melted in a big sea vessel under the deck under oceanic pressure, but Nonna told her brother Jacob when he said *ew*, that the real Jesus' face was smooshed something far worse. When Stella, who was spying, listening to them around the corner, heard what Nonna was saying to her brother she appeared as if by accident, blushing, bad liar, and found that Jacob had taken down Jesus and was trying to wash the blood from his body.

Stella held the place beneath her heart where the statue dripped little mottles like the red pulsations of the Willis Tower peaks and she held her heart now as Peter dismissed the tower as a stupid stunt to be the tallest in the world — "it's not even the record holder anymore, that distinction belongs to some Babel in Dubai —" and waved his hands to make disappear the pomp of the Chicago World's Fair, his city's attempt to revive the spirit of Christopher Columbus. He laughed as he sang with a nasal non-regional voice "The City

White hath fled the earth, But where the azure waters lie, A nobler city hath its birth, The City Gray that ne'er shall die," and rattled as he laughed like a marionette and said "the real crime is colonization through language, as the *rueda de Chicago*, the 'Chicago wheel' has now spread like lion's teeth, seedlings of imperial thought, phrase spoken in Latin America in reference to the Ferris wheel as if whatever happens in America assumes a kind of immediate authority to name and therefore rule the world," and of course she nodded and said of the tower that it was stupid, too dumb to even satirize, and pointed with protruded, mock benignity at the people who sleepwalked for fun beneath, just a smattering of the millions who lived here; she laughed as he said "Look on my works, ye mighty, and despair!" but when she laughed so hard she closed her eyes the pulsing lights of the Tower seemed like two separate entities beating in tandem and when she got home she searched neighborhood listings for used tandem bikes to surprise him with and watched as they traded, breathless and resting, resting and breathless, legs pumping, propelling very different Chicago wheels across the cracks of the paved lakefront where for months now she'd pedaled alone after school, pedaled fast like an unauthorized escapee from an experimental mental ward, because the kids mocked whatever discipline tactics she drew in blueprints on the chipped paint ceiling at two a.m., sleepless and waiting for the six o'clock alarm to order her vertical like a rag doll puppet, ragged in half-light of the half-slum bathroom as she showered and stared in disbelief at her nakedness which her own hands covered first with a vest, a bulletproof anti-ballistic outfit the man at the army surplus shop tossed on the counter when she gave him the brand name her co-worker Kathy had passed along in the faculty lounge like a secret code.

She had wanted to stay on that Ferris wheel forever, to get stuck at the top without an exit. She did not know why or where the want came from but it brought a quick little tremble of horror offset by a stomach-dropped awe, the emptiness of impossible relief. Nothing to do but perch over the abyss below, blessedly suspended over nothingness, undead and yet not condemned among the living to work out her salvation in fear and trembling.

Stella's eyes stung and she laughed a spastic, adolescent sound that shocked her red-pocked face, the high-pitched thrill muffled by wool wrapped tight around her mouth, her neck, her baby. She swayed, felt his forehead. Hush. Shh. Womb sound like they say seashells make. The spiraling conch of the nautilus kind with its whisper of old-world order. God. The virgin seashell strange set against the computer-chip skyline of what Peter called Slaughterhouse City (he had taken to the appellation while campaigning for alderman last year, trying to convince the National Guard to take the place of local police). Sweat pooled under her lower lip, cooled and then heated with each breath. The glistening blue, thin gauze scarf was bizarrely long — like the escape ropes of heroines' hair in the children's stories Nonna read her. *Again, mamma, read it again. Mommy, please. No baby. Mommy's too tired. Go get Nonna.* "But Momma, you read it, *you, read you.*" She could hear Jason rasp from the future, his voice too darling to resist, but her strength too sapped — a "single mother" — with all the consequences of her choice. But maybe by sheer will she could still read to him at day's end. And what manners you have. Please and thank you. Well trained too in your dinner etiquette. Bib situated just so. Fork and spoon set in their proper place. The salutary and right rotation of peas and pears and potted meat. Again she laughed at this false self-portrait — like a sentimental oil from Chicago's Art Institute. How many hours wasted there. No, not wasted, but invested in an invisible bank that paid no interest. Colors keep me alive in there. But you can't pick and choose your life: it's given, lent, not rented really because who can switch, midway, into another, swap, really, with someone else. Why people try vicariously through their children. Jason's future forged by Vulcan.

The vanishing point of the pier disappeared behind the fresh snow's falling curtains.

Rocks, baby crags, the rough edge of earth, circled the jut like stone lions' teeth with cavities as big as a man but starving: useless, mouthless teeth, because the ocean kept hid its sumptuous feast for centuries 'til bones turned to stone and the teeth of these lions were crushing to see. Thick white ice, a thin strip of it, wedged

163

and wove between the boulders, would have invited a step all trips prior but now always Jason, always careful, the baby! — the water below which was who knew how deep and — immersion hypothermia. Though they did it every year, dove in come January's ripe conditions to plunge half naked into the lake. Pretending like little boys, sea lions. You can be whatever you want to be. Pretty. Peter made me that with his lips, silk that he bought and bid me wear, quick butterflies on my face now look bland like that blah turkey water through the baster, my skin is refuse, greasy, seriously, so bland o stop it so vain o God.

Through the fogged window of the pier's cabin — off-white steam turning pleasant cream beside the blasé gray walls of a misplanted prison — she heard a man's bass shouts. He strutted out, a big-bellied hearty elder, "salt of the earth," Nonna would call him, half-shaven with tortured hair and a smile that incited her own. He pretended to tip his hat her way, pointed at the torn-down tape, a yellow ribbon flitting in the wind, that was supposed to prohibit her presence here. Shrugging his shoulders, miming mercy, he made a motion and two younger men in blue overalls appeared from behind the impossibly dull slab and followed like attendants to an abdicated king, one stroking his overgrown beard grimly and the other slapping the glum one on the shoulder as their foreman spat out a series of directives which set them lifting little concrete blocks and arranging them into a plus sign shape. Seagulls cawed like choked hilarity, more than condescending — openly cruel. As the men lifted, the foreman laughed and dispensed cement like Mardi Gras candy made in Vulcan's rented smithy, venting about his father-in-law to the captive ears of his nodding underlings, handing out pretzels and cigarettes, setting fire to the former with a spastic laugh that seemed to give the yeomen strength.

Stella could not stand their compressed expressions of bland embarrassment. She turned away and looked into the distance as if finally seeing a long-expected arrival.

Blurred by wet winter eyes she watched, perched on the pier's rusted railing pinnacle, a ring-billed gull as if inanimate clay — misshapen model of a young child's play. Why does all seem so still here today, so frozen, so fixed-like — the boatman, the yeomen, archetypes that could come from any old age, turn history's page — as if the jaw of time's wandering graze had worn down and been replaced by a lion's relentless teeth that had cut the line of time in half so that all that had happened and all still to come could never hold hands across the divorced centuries. And just like that the gull shivered its feathers and flew away, to defy her daydream, her nightmare of having escaped history, the gull fast joined a raucous fleet of other winged beasts undulating and swooping and feathering the weather towards the shore, where a father in blue jeans that matched the water threw breadcrumbs between the fish spines in the sand. Two children snatched a chunk from his hand and he let the rest sink in the bag and then twisted it shut. They did not proceed with piecemeal skill, the detached patience of the long-game man who has lost too many rounds to rashness. Must have a wedding ring on that finger. But she could not see it, so she pretended he didn't, and maybe in fact that's what made him so good with them, the patience of a slow and unknown martyrdom: as they squeal he just smiles like their sounds just tickle — don't rush through the inner auricle chambers like an inebriated, sonic minotaur of sound trapped in the brain's maze.

Girl tears her hat off, he puts it back on. Boy takes the bands from her pigtails and flings them like rubber band missiles of great significance towards the offshore enemy encroaching — a stray log, mold-moss and ominous. "Fire!" The father splays his limbs like a fool, a lackadaisical anti-missile defense system no joke any longer (he had been cracking up for a minute), now spilling dark fluid from the cup he'd been sipping, Styrofoam from a street vendor, and sharing when any of the children started shivering through their yellow and red one-piece snowsuits, secondhand almost surely so maybe he is a single dad after all as a double income would drive you to do things like pay a pretty penny needlessly for a snowsuit that won't be worn for more than a year at best, at most, for they're born to become bigger and bigger and no songs or screams without vocal chords and no walking without feet or growth without girth but maybe he's just thrifty, has what Stella's mom would call a good head on his shoulders, which, to Stella's mom, meant not brain and not brilliance but the soul of an abacus counter clicking the beads from sunrise to sundown.

Son stretches out his hand to the lake where the hairband missiles are concentric ripples, all that remains of the surface splash. (Why would he have hairbands without having, also, a wife?) A man could figure it out if he had to. Look. Lacrimal fluid flowed from his eyes, sterilizing but not soothing his sight. Textbook biology lesson on tears she taught to kids who laughed her down. From the Latin *lacrimosus* (she did not state that to the class, they did not have a classics class, there was no studying Euclid here, or *Antigone* or Seneca's tragedies, as she had studied at the small Catholic school that seemed like everything before Chicago, a ruse, an alternate reality). She'd substituted for her friend who fell ill and never came back to St. Cabrini's. Merciful — the epitome of pity — how she described the antibacterial agent lysozyme, "a priceless chemical." Surely it is, but the squeeze of it through the secretory ducts feels like the hard labor of my pains, my gestated losses now made plain. She smiled at the poem that had chased her through life, that chewed all similarities into dust, crushed all the beaded connections threaded through the cosmos' chaos and masticated them back together like the *dent de lion*, like a profane prayer that made sense of the world but nothing more.

"Alright troops!"

"Dad, get it!" the boy commanded like a captain, and *this* at last proved the father's humanity, as he fell into full play, the serious smirk that had tightened his face falling away. Like a long-starved ogre he collapsed on the bread of birds his children had cast with such blind largesse and he squeezed the mush, returned to dough the heated wheat. In his own private tantrum he pretended to be them when he called time, time to go home. Oblivious still to Stella on the pier who was walking at a clip that if sustained could kick up a killer dose of dopamine — what would it mean to be freed of such categories, to know nothing of the body's chemicals? Even all the little elementary lessons she'd taught at St. Cabrini's had charged her consciousness with too many names for too many, too many, too many things — so she faux-startled at the man like an old friend saying fancy meeting you here, because yes he had the ring on his finger because, yes, the standard gilded band was stuck, kept snug on the left second finger by the fattening that comes after the vows, when the wedding day's vast promises swell to unguessed dimensions.

He tore the big chunks into minuscule crumbs that he scattered with grace like the sowers of Millet, who painted movingly sheepshearers too, she'd seen their figures at the Art Institute, as well as the little framed Flight into Egypt, Millet's darkened sepia sketch of exile lightened only by the Christ child's face, which made the astrologers' stars pale though they still pointed toward the scandal stretched out across the crèche. As he fumbled to palm the cheap cocoa — bought from one of so many kiosks that had sprouted from the cold by the steaming heat grates that buttressed the bank and the Tribune building and anywhere you could hawk a few dollars — she reached out to take it, reached with her left hand and turned it around so he could see clearly it was empty, her finger, she may have a baby but she had no fixed man, and they could take flight too, two with three children, but he did not take notice of her lack of a ring, for as soon as he thanked her for retrieving the cup and held up a finger to signal *one second please*, a bold gull with a bursting gullet descended and bit bread from his hands, carried the big crumb aloft over the lake where it met a circling of crazed birds whose envious beaks revolted, insulted by his surplus: the whole hefty piece fell into the water and, wet, went under before the resentful could swoop with a speed that outpaced their envy, their raw will to do damage to any who had more than necessity dictated. And she stared where the father stared at the sulking pool but while he smiled, she saw no geometries that would justify a God's pattern but the casual flaunt of a purposeless universe that announced the unchecked will of oblivion. He, however, did not seem to mind.

"No Henri! No Henri! No! No! No!" So Henri darted into the waters, which appeared all sparkle and inviting on the surface, and suddenly her arms were restraining the girl, clasping her wrist without scratching her nails in and then Jason startled rude from

167

his sleepy sailing shot out his limbs like one wounded and she wasn't at all alone, that's the trouble, and the father was up to his boots, bless him, in Michigan chill, the spirit of humankind far deeper than these bodies of water regardless of how many times they outsize us. He seized his son and — maybe because she was here — reversed whatever irate tilt had almost made him snap in public. He gave instead to all the gathered the largest grin he could fit on his face, teeth yellowed by a lifetime of coffee but somehow more soothing for the stains.

"Could you take our picture?" the father asked. His eyes passed over her face the way a grocery-store hand turns over a tomato and puts it back in favor of another. "My wife will love it so long as I get home before they frostbite or worse, c'mon Henri, smile for the picture, c'mon Alice, you too now or we won't be able to get more cocoa at home," and as Alice forged a gargoyle face, scrunching her nose and lifting her lip and squinting over her showcase of teeth, Stella took the phone from the man and snapped the picture with Henri dangling from his snowsuit suspenders like a caught fish that could feed a whole family. Restrained then, the man gave her eye contact for not even an instant but instead offered what appeared to be a bow before he took back his phone and bestowed an out-of-place *Godbless*, turning towards the skyline's seers, leaving flushed Stella with Jason's muffled complaints, a hand of five free hours dealt like a win. But how to kill time before the bus came to return her home? How to kill the need for a father a husband or some other surrogate for her beautiful boy who had — look — his daddy's brows and under them those blinking brown eyes that looked at her like no man before Peter had ever looked (if fully clothed when his full eyes flirted, she felt the thrill of being naked) — stuck and staring and wanting something . . . any more than a squeeze from the swollen glands that pour for the cause of the species' survival.

Always when she walked into a room — at a party or in the faculty lounge, long ago at Sunday School or late to high school dances (determined to skip this one and stay home instead, earphones and sob songs numbing her head) — the boys and then the men with their hungry looks would alight on her like pigeons on a gutter, thirsty for a purer source of water, quick to recover that circling gaze ever at the ready for a finer specimen. They'd rarely even bother to drop and search beneath her face because there were no bulging curves to trace, which came as a relief sometimes when she heard her friends carp about filthy men and their everyday unashamed apish gawks. She'd never taken the other girls' routes — the high school royalties, Bea and Leah — of putting on a face that took an hour to plaster into a porcelain perfection that could if scratched by a nervous nail destroy the edifice at once. How in the locker room after gym they bragged of bras that had wiry cups, that boasted the ample, desirable existence of flesh in fact almost entirely absent. She didn't harbor some religious objection — no zealot of purity held court in her conscience — but feared what would come of so much feigning — the fateful bodies falling in backseats or in the basement when the parents were at work and when the boy would kiss her face and remove the blouse he'd have to hide his disappointment over what was missing, even if he kept on kissing her, breathless, she'd know he'd want, as they say, his money back when finished with her. But what was now even more of a letdown was the father's departure without a tremor of attraction to what she was now — a mother with a child, so now how could even that archetype of ages fail to solicit a second glance of interest? And while all these worries wore lines around her lip her own attention was safety-pinned to the silhouette dad disappearing in the distance, arms outstretched over his children's shoulders, and something about the way he was willing to even hunch and uncomfortably hobble alongside them all — to get at their level — made her stupidly start to cry.

She looked at her watch the way she had once watched her students, threatening to hand out detentions for the slightest twitch of disobedience. Hours to kill. She sat on a bench and the baby burped and scrunched his eyes and went back to sleep and pulling a blanket out of her backpack she wrapped it around them and, startled by the warmth, found herself fading in and out of consciousness, the last wash of adrenaline burning what supplies of vigilance she'd stored. The gray day seemed dusk more than twilight, and her sense of time ticked in reverse, twitching back through the past few years now that she was leaving here.

Though typically if she waited a while at the Pier the sun would slice the hangover gray, today the glum blanket stayed, wet and comfortless across the sky. This place, the shut-down Navy Pier, was inevitably a landmark in memory of Peter. Twenty-one dollars, please, that'll be. What will be? Whatever will be, will be. What would things be like from the heights over the sea when the gears catch and you're dangling your legs into the open oxygen tank of the sky and somehow still unable to breathe, Jason sucking madly at the source, blood red though it didn't bleed, the tense hitch in her muscles causing baby's gums to clench. Can't see the Milky Way here like you wanted when at the State Fair as a girl you asked Daddy to give the man a handful of quarters so you could see the galaxy swirl — who cared about the Tilt-a-Whirl, which her big brother Jacob called a baby ride anyway — and Dad didn't say *You can't because you're in it, like so many things you can't see for lack of distance,* but "Of course, Stella, you'll see God way at the top if you keep your eyes wide open," and how she got stuck up there at age six, alone, aloft, in too much fun, so dizzy when they finally fixed it and the wheel of fortune sent her earthbound again she swore she saw the Milky Way swirl, black and blue and the sepia eye that watched the world and waited what for, what's it for, Daddy, and me, too, "What baby?" *What am I for?* But he brought her down to the cotton-candy line and mom said in the middle of the night she should have had more sense than to eat that shite right after she went on the Tilt-a-Whirl when a fountain of blue dye filled the spout of her mouth and she did not try to defend herself and took great care not to pout the next morning but said yesterday was her favorite day.

· · ·

Now the baby was coming back to where she'd been before he was born. She needed to get to Union Station. Her slumped stupor on the lakeside bench had cost her all those leisured hours and now the train would leave without her if she did not make haste.

Leaning on the L-train railing, staring down the empty track as if her impatience would hasten her ride's arrival, Stella stooped to pick up flattened coins that a boy had balanced on the tracks before the last train screeched past. She watched their warped, oval eyes wink, like grandmother's tilted face in the sunlight (she'd take her to "get light" down by the sand on the other shore of Lake Michigan), Nonna pressing spare change in your clammy palm as if she were giving you precious pearls, begging you to run down the road and up the hill to the Sciortino Deli, to pick up canned artichokes and a day-old macaroon . . . she could feel Nonna pinching her cheek, could see her making her nails into tweezers, squeezing with those tools of affection her son's jowls, half in punishment for his mother's sins but more than half because she couldn't not love him. She blinked — twice — at the useless coins. Faceless elongated Abraham Lincolns. Who would take them, accept them, count them? Not even the boy who had bolted down the stairway at the sight of the man in the bulletproof vest. The strange delight of gratuitous disfigurement. The state of police in the soft police state.

So many people in different directions, departures and arrivals everywhere and mingled in them indecisions, and the perfectly cold blue sky presiding, providing contrast with its unmoving clouds and her pulse a mess, but the baby at breast asleep and smiling and heart beat steady on her skin. Again and again. Again and again. If she had stayed home he would not be here. She could not say *should* have but she could have stayed home.

Stella had always prided herself on being immune to sentimental stirrings — another romanticized falsification that had fallen hard — like Cabrini-Green. As if because she put aside her dignity and bore the insults of her own students and stayed single-minded to the point of asocial — as if this would be enough to reverse generations of dispossession. To her fresh-faced self on the first day of classes, some two years and a lifetime ago, she would tell, if she could, what Peter told her outright: "I like you, but we don't need your help." Though he later walked that position back, and she had no idea what he really now believed, because half of what he said in public sounded like a talking point generated by artificial intelligence to please and upset in just the right proportions. Not that it mattered as much anymore: his alderman stunts had gone mostly unnoted by the gazes that gave the watchers their minds. Like faithless lovers the news outlets lavished obsessive attention, until he lost, when they turned to recuperate with another. Maybe, she mused, that was part of the plan. If he seemed a failure, he could disappear and do some sleight of hand in Washington. The hardest problem, rather than his secrecy, was the harsh fact that he never, publicly, punched walls or apologized for his "bone-deep hypocrisy — soul-deep, covered by skin for now but when they find it out — even after I'm dead . . ." When he said this she searched him for sign of seriousness, a hint of a lead that he was a live target — "my sins will be the choicest flaw that finally discredits, in the eyes of the public, the movement." By the end he kept so much hidden. He flinched and walked out whenever she questioned him, crowned her heart with these prickly sentences, wrapped the pain around and around until she wondered what sins he could mean — his "love of her" (which had never been a given) or his "childhood murder" (which was self-defense, didn't kill, either in her eyes or according to the latest medical definition of death). Or did he refer to some other wrongdoing without handing her the skeleton key that could open the casket nailed shut in the cellar, the storehouse of all his subterranean doings? What, please God, could he mean?

A woman cleaved to the train car railing like the strippers she had half-seen, passing by club windows, in Chicago's well-padded underworld. But when Stella looked again the woman's fingers were clasped around a busted black plastic rosary, her mouth murmuring "Dios te salve" as she brushed her hips against Stella and slipped out forever into the world.

Il Signore è con te. After Blake left, Stella cooked with Nonna most lazy Sundays — the slow-motion day that still kept pace with the Sabbath — arriving promptly after Mass was over and feeling Nonna's hot hands slap her own when they reached for the fresh-baked biscotti. "Did you say yet your il Signore è con te, Stell? Man shall not live on bread alone." "But Nonna, I am a woman, not a man." Strange how these bickering jokes were not funny on reflection, but she found them refreshing and even hilarious in the moment, as if moving in with Nonna meant going back in time to a simpler childhood sense of humor lost not all at once but worn slowly out by the long fatigue she let herself feel on Nonna's couch — a weariness that amazed them both for she slept, the first night, for forty-eight hours without waking or eating anything. But when she slept through Mass on Sunday, Nonna chose not to prepare the food she knew was Stella's favorite, instead offering plain and bone-dry toast, and that was Nonna's way of saying No, *dear, I'm not too old to shame you, and no, you're not too old to be shamed*. But Nonna never, like Stella's mother, soured into a brooding mourning. She let her disapproval be known and then brushed the flour from her forearms and brought her granddaughter into the rhythms of recipes she'd received from relatives born over the ocean, and suddenly they were standing in Italy.

Nonna said Stella could move in but that so long as they lodged under her roof all inhabitants had to attend Sunday Mass. And since for Stella coercion was the killer — she had never taken well the slightest correction, part of why she'd settled for low-stakes floristry — she'd set about finding a room of her own in South Chicago. Whatever the neighborhood, so long as it had walls and was within walking distance to St. Cabrini's in Chicago.

She could have — but couldn't, *didn't*, see! — stayed in Milwaukee, safe in the Bay View staple Miss Beat's Florist when the citizens sported the masques of death, the choreographed global *danse macabre*.

There was no return. No repetition. What if no *nostos* waited for her?

As the early L-train rattled and swerved — too stilted to be a snake — above the city's already-clogged arteries, she smelled the car's stale cologne of ashen menthol and expired sweat, plugging her nose and licking her lips at the thought of Dad's famous borscht, a dish she'd not shared for two years now, an about-face she still did not understand but did not put an end to either because whatever hurt was something like an absence, a nothing where there should be a something. When she'd mapped out a return to her parents', Stella could not see Mom's figure at the end: at the door of their home she could envision Dad, arms out awkwardly but still opened. The strange pleasure of being a dependant, of having an elder take care of you again: and she knew, in retirement, that his constant work habits would be looking for a baby to feed, a bottle to warm, laundry to fold. When she tried to see her mother there, in the living room corner, a shade, as she and her father sorted white socks from black, whatever judgements his bit-tongue kept tied bothered her less than her mother's absence. But she'd learned, through a lifetime, how to placate the shadow. More than her over her parents' pains — her father would rather have her home, under his care, than away and unknown in South Chicago — Stella worried over Nonna's dismissive nod, her dignified disbelief that a granddaughter she'd called her favorite and to whom she'd given so many spoils of her sufferings could show up single and armed with a baby like an affront, a war declared against all laws of plausibility. Her parents preserved taboos (to be sure), but most moral matters were for them flexible, subject to their sympathies and the new conveniences commandeered by life's hardships, by the protean prejudices of the passing decades. They were, she once mused to Blake, a domesticated, distant cousin of his famous former Professor Hape. They "made an appearance" at Mass on Christmas but made most of their negotiations with God — a benevolent grandfather who had retired late and, at the end of his exhausted life and from the privileged vantage of his endless vacation wanted better for his grandchildren — in private. They tolerated Stella's flunked-out brother even though he set their teeth on edge — literally had her mother buying mouth guards so she would not grind her molars in the night. Surely they could spare a relaxed moral space for a daughter who never even bit her nails, who was constantly careful (could they possibly know it?) to protect their fragile emotional statures, to the point that her own barely bearable crises (Blake flaking out the most obvious instance) became de facto a desperate management of her mother's self-recriminations and sleepless vigils of self-pity — all dressed up in the hair-shirt nightgown of "I feel so bad for poor Stella!" who was busy keeping her mouth shut about the "nervous breakdown" that followed, like a new clear fallout, Blake's punishing disappearance.

"No!" — yes, she said it aloud, her lips making circles of fog on the window: No, why, everywhere and everyone (herself a close-at-hand case-in-point) was, these days, a yarn ball of grievances.

Jason drooled and his crescent smile waxed. Through her fellow traveler's headphones she heard — the decibels cracked and cackled, libidinal — "Smells Like Teen Spirit":

> Here we are now, entertain us
> I feel stupid and contagious
> Here we are now, entertain us
> A mulatto, an albino
> A mosquito, my libido, yeah
> Hey
> Yeah

Hey. Yeah. She could have — but didn't, couldn't, see! — stayed in Bay View in the apartment attached to the Polish delicatessen forever. After her previous apartment had remained heatless for three months in the winter of two thousand and ten, for nearly two decades she'd stayed in one place. The deli, Zakorzenienie's, was owned and run by Dad's childhood friend Z. Z. who had grown over the years into her father's "competitor" — at once a sore spot and a family joke. Dad had made a few phone calls, joked about the "political alliance" he was forging by "marrying her off" to the competition, and she did not mind because Z. Z. was an epitomal gentleman — with a cane and a fedora and not an untoward desire. Z. Z. even assumed — by accident — her father's tone and gestures when he made small talk so that sometimes she had to look again, as if Dad had somehow wonderfully doubled. No other living arrangement could compete with the heat included in the rent of three hundred and ninety-nine dollars per month. What she owed, finally, was still ridiculously cheaper because her roommate Eleanor, a grade school friend who received monthly disability dollars, was happy to hole up in the walk-in closet and call those six by four feet home.

They had painted the walls a pale baby blue — to offset the dark, narrow-windowed rooms. The paint can, retrieved from a dumpster, read: Little Boy Blue and as they brushed the acrylic across the blank, glossless, badly-chipped white they sang "Come blow your horn!" so loud Z. Z. playfully took a broom and slammed the ceiling before shouting, "I kid!" To have so few cares — she could not conceive. Those days whose ease she knew not at the time. They talked about "going off the grid." Stella said nothing about her time in the commune — as if to keep the fool's prospect alive. The two of them lit candles in lieu of lightbulbs. Sickly Eleanor, sweet but moody, insisted, maybe monthly, that tomorrow and tomorrow she would this time break away from the whole society and start over on her parents' farm, abandoned land in Germantown, which her siblings kept for fear they'd regret selling their inheritance for fluid money that'd be gone as fast as their hands could grab it. But Eleanor never left for the farm.

And the days and nearly a decade passed with only two unusual swings that swerved the tetherball beyond its typical, predictable circumference.

Stella walked from the florist to Zakorzenienie's every lunch break, her modest wage with no prospect of increase affording all she needed to eat a three-dollar lunch and leave, filled, with a bag of kielbasa all for the bill with Lincoln's face, his aged dream of national unity kept current kept evergreen through each passing of currency across the countless counters of the country. Yes she spent too much time reading the comments left under articles on invasive species or illegal immigration, not just reading but trying to enter into conversation, as Minerva's owl could alight on the ether, which led her to delve into these questions more deeply until she racked up late bills at the library that put a strain on her small budget. More often she paid the fees for missing copies, which had plummeted so low that she played into the cycle of forgetting to return and then mailing an embarrassed check to the library, which was two blocks away — this delicate pretense of distance she preferred rather than walking down Kinnickinnic Avenue and dropping the book in a drive-by slot.

Her hair started thinning fast and she sometimes shed it quicker than the cat, Kafka, who had shown up on their doorstep, circling, circling at the end of a particularly long day. Stella sneezed but said "It's alright," the cat's eyes like two fixed divots of deep-dug fret, softened when she stroked the creature's back but flitting still across the room in search of an invisible, irascible fly that needed forever violent swatting. She watched, beside Eleanor, through her own paralysis, unable to be playful anymore. *Little boy blue, come blow your horn.*

The cysts on her cervix cost a pretty penny, pushed her to consider career changes. She never made it much further than laughing at the logic of a "career" in floristry, which by the time she left had been her means of income for a little over a whole decade, but her laughter didn't humor the oncologist Dr. Khan who said, solemn and sovereign, "Hysterectomy," but when she said she was "Holding out for baby-making, crazy as that sounds," and the doctor's brow bent in disgust she called Nonna and asked her intercession, please — to *be* back then, when she still believed — and she could hear, already, while on the phone, her Nonna scratch the votive match and mutter prayers over the muffled receiver, after which she said "Even now, but meantime however long it takes for prayers to reach the pearly gates you better get a second diagnosis, don't cave in to one doctor like it's more than anybody's guess," so as soon as she hung up with Nonna she scheduled a second opinion, a pricey oracle which wasn't dispensable for two whole months. As she scrawled the date on her calendar the medical college called back and said they had a cancellation and would she be free to come right in and she was not free but she called in sick — the first time in five years — and sped across the pothole streets, out of breath through the pneumatic doors and the circular carousel entryway and passed out on the red carpet. When she woke on a stretcher with an IV in her arm, a kid — couldn't have been more than eighteen — found through a frantic regimen of tests that the cysts were to a one totally benign, to her half-conscious "But can you speak with such absolute authority?" and he smiled and said "In this case, yes" to her "You're not God," and his "in this case, yes." Her letter to Khan received a labyrinthine reply that gave her the same headache she'd come home with the day the doctor scoffed off her fertility. She returned to the florist and took double shifts, using every extra hothouse breath to counter the backdraft of medical bills.

All along the winter of two thousand and seventeen, riddled by the harmless cysts on her cervix, Stella walked the neighborhood late, fed up with wrapping flowers and searching for her fate. The Greek got closer to its core. *Moira. Ananke.* Implacable necessity. The overdetermination of events. For a girl who had done so much digging into determinism, she had chosen an underdetermined life. All that young learning she had loved and let go of returned to ghost her ruminations. She sensed that these ten static years were spent in hiding from some harsh coming waiting for her to finally say yes. Her walks elongated the colder the weather, departing from the familiar circles and getting lost in unknown neighborhoods. Her blue scarf faded because she washed it so often.

Cabin fever struck bad by November, started to infect and inflect her mind so that even in the coldest weather it was better to risk frostbite than pretend to relax in the closing walls of the cheap flat.

One night, her route barricaded and blaring the manic blue and red whir of firetruck and ambulance, she took a detour across the bridge. Below, on the interstate, a hundred cars flew and another hundred in contrary directions, every foot and every pedal steeled against an accident. The woman who'd been her best friend from grade school had recently died while walking across a freeway overpass in North Carolina, the bridge buckling under a large train of military tanks and other land vessels and dropping her friend two stories down into the steady traffic that flattened her on a New Year's Eve, bringing the sum of death-by-motor-vehicles up to 32,393 that year, an impressive increase that put to shame eighteen ninety-nine's modest — quaint — twenty-six.

A young man stood above the median, his eyes her cat Kafka's, come evening, following a toy electric ball back and forth from side to side, except his mind is lost in cars, their breakneck white to the red brake stall. Someone had cut a hole in the wire fence and he stood right there, staring, not caring or incognizant of her proximity. When he pressed his bald knuckle to his lips she tied her shoes twice and feigned other errands, as if she'd lost something in the pavement cracks. But when he did not notice her, even then she tiptoed closer to his planted feet. The walkway was narrow and she could not pass without brushing against his back.

His eyes — like shattered stained glass that had been pieced back together over years — looked to her with an involuntary plea before he took off abruptly, at a manic sprint, in the direction she had already been heading. Instead of fleeing or heading home Stella followed him — ran through a stitch — drawn by what she'd seen of a gaze that did not flinch but seemed to gather the totality of the surrounding city and still not flinch and still not waver even though his wet eyes could be weeping, his high cheekbones half-hidden by the flaps of a thrift-store gray-collar long tweed over-coat — a charcoal fabric that glistened like flint, like the stuff of fire waiting to be struck. There was a gentleness about the tilt of his head, a desperation in the quickened steps that almost tripped on themselves though they didn't seem drunk. He sped down a sequence of obstacle courses — orange construction cones and fresh tarred potholes, perpetual craters culled by winter street salt. She leapt over a POLICE LINE DO NOT CROSS and she laughed as she jumped over a divot and dodged a fallen yellow yield sign. With urgent purpose the man ran — like a criminal or a cop on the beat — into the impossible majesty that marked every mar-ble column and corner of the South Side basilica built by Polish immigrants from the discarded pieces of a Chicago post office. She had never before set foot in the place, which was, at least locally, legendary. He tried four doors before finding a slit that seemed propped open by negligence or accident rather than invitation.

She watched him drop his knee to the ground with a reckless genuflect that reminded her of Nonna, who shoved all gentle, solicitous helpers off her in order to kneel even after the hip replacement, the doctor waving his finger and warning "No more

179

kneeling!" in mock parentage to her straight-faced rejoinder: "You should be jailed by God. You're a usurper. Such a one!"

Not knowing she had followed him into the empty church, he fell flat on his belly, his lips pressed hard to the marble floor. He stretched out his arms, cruciform, and stayed there so still that twice she was sure he had come in here to die, the way an animal finds a place hidden in the infrequented acres. Jotting her number on the back of a band-aid — the only spare paper in her purse — she knelt next to him in front of the votives.

She saw a little note left there by a prior visitor. Worried someone else might take and read, she cast its small scrawled sentence onto the votive closest to her but as she did her mind seized the words which said *Por mi hermana Julieta que se suicidó. ¡Evita que entre por las puertas del infierno María!* Violently, quietly, the little note, written on a ripped off corner of legal paper, flashed fast and smoldered, caught a couple stockpiled wicks below. The largest of the flames, like a generous elder, enkindled the yellow legal with a kiss. Stella's hair, held firmly in a bun, shone out as an untamed outburst of glistening red, a quiet accompaniment to the loose bursts of fire. She had not surpassed the gates of hell. The hungry flames, violent and pretty, rose like a staircase to her Nonna's heaven. The flames prodded her closer to prayer than she could possibly be without them. Arising, her twisted hair glimmering red and wild, she became as if a massive votive flicker before the tiny torches which seemed to blink, blighted, intimidated. As was she. Her body became a candle, her organs melting, hot; dying to hold the wick of her head up.

Aflame with the news, the name of the dead, she wondered whether the man prostrate below her who was totally oblivious to the flare of the candles or the unfurled ragged flame of her hair, maybe *he* was the one who left the note there, though she doubted whether Spanish was his native language. She mouthed one of the memorized prayers Nonna was always whispering (the doctors attributed her litanies to dementia): *Stella Maris.*

A rattling snaked through her and something like a weighted blanket, like a great weariness she'd been wearing like a cloak, lifted as if a wild wind carried it. A rash of anger went through her and lifted. Her hands gripped the votive shelf, wax tears falling to the floor, dripping everywhere, melting against her skin. Blowing a thin wind as if a kiss, palm under her chin, she blew them all out. Shit. I killed them. The prayers. The dead.

"Excuse me, sir? I'm — I. Not from here, but I believe I just made a terrible mistake. I — blew out everyone else's prayers. Like I was a kid with a birthday cake. And that, by the way, is about where I'm at: wishing instead of praying, if you know what I mean."

The young man cocked his head and craned his neck around until he could see her. His shattered stained glass eyes narrowed as he looked out — the light was on her and his eyes should have widened — and then he turned without speaking, bent over, bowed down to the blown ashes, brushing away a heap of gray flakes and raising a matchbook that said Puritan's Pub. He set off thirty heads at once and held it out to every wick and when little licks of blue-veined gold flicked and filled his face he smiled and turned to her and she grinned a bit too, though a sheepish twitch forestalled any fullness — arrested anything like what is called happiness. But as flames flooded the iron candle stairwell, flashed in their alternating upward dashes, stayed and did not peter out, she let out a sigh and he smiled more freely and she more fully let her bit lip go. Fire and smoke, beauty and choke both clamored and kissed above the fifty-cent slots, as though some elemental, primordial rivalry were performing before them for petty change. Her hand held the faded band-aid on which she'd written her number and name. She suspended her fist until he got the gist and put his palm beneath.

"Stella," she said.

"Blake," he answered, searching her face with widening eyes, a thin brow that curved round like a quivering, broken question mark.

She walked at a quick clip into the dark.

Later that evening, not quite tipsy, she settled under the blue flannel blanket, lit the sapphire candles like always, watched the flame ricochet like a spray of fiery flowers off the wall, blink into blackness and come back, but this time her heart reached right

out through her eyes, hungry to clasp the flicker, and . . . Eleanor woke her by blowing out the flame to which Stella, waking,
shouted "Don't kill the prayers!" One arm pumping her chair's
wheel, smelling her friend's breath as she shoved, Eleanor helped
drag Stella across the couch because no amount of her effort could
have brought her tired friend to the raised bed where she slept. But
she brought Nonna's featherbed comforter from where it covered
and warmed dead air and draped the blanket across Stella like a
wide white pall that was far too large for her. She overslept her
shift in the morning but arrived, hair crackling with static, only
five minutes late and no one noticed except a customer who told
her "I don't know flowers, but my wife, she likes them, she thinks
they're really pretty, can you help me pick out a good arrangement
that would make her happy — she's easy to please."

Whenever Zakorzenienie was ready to trash perfectly good food
refuse — a motion that never ceased to pain him, an unsavory fact
of restauranteering he couldn't countenance with a stainless-steel
face — he'd ascend the stairs, pan or plastic bag in hand, and say
something like, "Gówno, Stella, gówno, no, you know I can't do it!"
and she couldn't either, which meant, for her and Eleanor, both a
barely extant grocery list and a stomach sometimes upset, sickened
by what surely should have been trashed.

Over time she started heating up ham and rolls, wrapping them
in aluminum foil, and handing them out along the sides of the
freeway where the men her father called freeloaders waited, doing
nothing for their daily bread. First she went to Eight Ball Eddie,
a vet with a violent shock of healthy white hair, edges afire like a
lit willow-wisp, eyes bluer than Nonna's Sinatra, and a permanent
grimace, hard to pry open. Eddie paced his staked-out beat holding
a cardboard sign that said, in an asymmetrical, half-readable scrawl
that her primary-school teacher would have punished: GOD HELPS
THOSE WHO HELPS THEMSELVES. Though the maxim was, when
you looked long, legible, he had crossed it out with a ruby red X
that had bled its best before he possessed it: the red now looked
like spattered blood. His arms were so stiffly crossed, his mind so set
on the work he was doing — as if he were a messenger sent from

on high — that he wouldn't unclamp them to take the food. She learned to nod and set it at his base like some ancient ritual meant to please the local gods, gods wont to appear under godforsaken guises.

Sometimes, when she passed by without food, he would ask her the forecast or how many knots the lake winds were worked up to tonight, or he'd brag about his pool hall skills, but whenever her hands were full he pretended he did not see her there. To the point of faking blindness. So risible, his pride. When she told him this, once, as to his bitter, purse-lipped scowl, he laughed so hard through his smoker's wheezy lungs that she worried she'd have to call 911. At the end of his fit all he said — scratching head — in a rasp that barely found passage through the man's thick, phlegm-clogged, throat (she was pleased to see his free hand scratching, as this little liberty seemed like a victory): "And what, miss goody, is the sin that besets you?"

That word *sin* was one of Nonna's favorites — not just when grandma was at her most grand, sitting on a barstool downtown and diagramming the bad grammar that spelled a death sentence for the new generations, not just when she declared, so upset she did not bother to finish chewing the big green olive stabbed by a toothpick whose red plastic frill stuck out dangerously from her working mouth: "But hey, the real difference between you and me is not that I've lived my life with more *brio*, because for all that I'm guiltier of greater disgrace, but that I say *Christ have mercy on me a sinner* and you, dear, don't know the meaning of sorrow. Which is a sorrow in itself! I swear if my mother could see your generation. What you know is not real repentance but a vague O I feel so bad! (which, I translate, means *Feel bad for me!*). A kind of self-pity that secretly satisfies — look at me when I talk to you, lovely, and don't go moping about 'I'm not pretty,' because any man here would be lucky to have you" — at which point she surveyed the room for any takers — "But I believe it was a poet, not Dante, surprisingly he wasn't even Italian, Auden I believe, but I'll have to ask my sister, said — you can't know reverence without repentance. You want the highs of knowing our Lord" — she used that phrase even with the wait staff or the grocery checker or the agnostic plumber — "without the depths. Yes, heights without depths. So pray to be given even a glimpse, just once, of God's forsaken majesty. If you saw even a little you'd fall on your knees like a, like a . . . oh, *stellina, tesorina mia,* you know what I mean."

As Stella flinched, casting a furtive glance around to see who might be listening, Nonna only raised the volume:

"Stella. Cut it out. Look see. Cease! For crying out loud — and no I won't quiet down, don't be so vain, don't play your shock and shame card. I'll go toe-to-toe with the worst of them for the greatest sinner in this city. For the sake of Caesar Augustus and his puppet pervert Herod, stop sentimentalizing the elderly. Like the worst we could do was steal a few extra jellies when we go out to lunch with the Bridge Club Ladies. Bartender, my niece here will have another whiskey. No screwdriver. No sour. She needs something sobering. I see I've set her teeth on edge."

She turned around to see Blake, whom she asked to meet for lunch, which really meant to meet her Nonna, which was more of a rite of passage than even the famed conversation with the father. Blake did not even bother to hide his laughter and Nonna pinched his "starved cheek. Now let's put some meat on your bones and you might grow into a handsome young man who could be worthy to woo my darling granddaughter, *stellina, tesorina mia!*" So the weeks went: shared Caprese, Old Fashioned for Nonna, Blushing Monks for Stella and Blake, extra bitters all around, every Friday at Balistreri's, a Milwaukee staple whose red tables waxed with permanent grease were covered with butcher-paper tablecloths covered with endless baskets of fresh bread. And Blake, the believer, passed Nonna's test: he crossed himself and worked for a priest, albeit his groundskeeper salary made Nonna worry how they'd pay for the babies she saw forming in their filmy eyes.

· · ·

Three months later, on the heels of a storm that left the streets bereft of cars, Blake asked her to risk him for life.

The weather had kept her on the couch at the Yourrick house and around midnight he woke her up with the kind of wide eyes

she'd witnessed at the florists but had rarely seen him show to her
except for the overseen gaze on the overpass. She knew at once what
he would do but played along with a "Where are you taking me?
Are you crazy?" Swerving between the scattered snowdrifts, they
arrived at a tower perched atop the lakeside bluff where she and
her friends, in high school, had sledded violently down, jumping off
just before careening into the traffic on Lake Drive below. Bizarre,
almost, that he brought her *here*, where her teenaged mouth had
been first "kissed"— if you could call it that: rather pinned, held,
vacuumed, it seemed, by a foreign exchange student named Frantz
who never managed to pronounce her name right (when he said
the word it came out *Stealer*). But he was the thief while the rest
of their friends whipped down the steep hill not quite to their
deaths. Eleanor had watched from the bench, mouth contorted
between indignant disapproval and squeamish desire.

Blake's eyes, like rose windows, looked dull from the outside but
suggested within a nocturnal vigil, a faint but firm fire protected
in glass from the wayward drafts that wander into any well-worn
cathedral. She strained to remember if he had met her father. Strange
that she would not simply know. Whatever his outward show to the
contrary, her father would wear disappointment for weeks. Who
the husband was did not matter. *That* he was would be his ruin.

Apologetically Blake removed her mittens and rubbed blood back
into her fingers while breathing huffs of heat over their strange
yellow white — like the moon — all feeling lost from the cold that
she hated but walked into without complaint. (He could not have
failed to notice her discretion, as it had become a custom for her to
say "I'm freezing cold," to his "Seriously? It's a balmy winter for
Milwaukee.") After the obligatory police car circled the roundabout
and waved as they shivered, talking weather — he hated talking
weather, but seemed, tonight, to relish the atmosphere, the speeding
cloud with a wide whale belly that swallowed the moon and cast
its shadow over empty Lake Michigan, that infinite expanse that
always *seemed* to end with the forever horizon that could not be
bested but would always remain on the rim of the world — the
unbridgeable distance of mortality.

"It's just so good to be beside you," he said. "You could be elsewhere. I could never have known you. Been known"— and she kissed his scarlet nose, because she could not deny that she took pride (of a variety that seemed good and right) in having heard, as far as he was willing, his ordered infinitude of regrets, and, having listened with attention, not having blocked out the hard parts, believing he had escaped the helix that wound ever down and pointed at the damned. That she believed him he still disbelieved, though he often, spontaneously, *worshiped* her for . . . she could not conjure another word without taking refuge in inadequacy.

Rising from the same bench Eleanor had scoffed from all those years earlier, Blake pointed toward the well-lit cream brick lighthouse, unlocked quick, and led them inside. She felt the adolescent rush of breaking and entering, of sheer joy delinquency. Closing the door behind her he buttoned her jacket top, as if inside she would be chillier still. Trapped within the lighthouse tower, his whole body went wiry, giddy, as if he could not take the next step fast enough, his arms gesturing with coaxing intensity at the spiral staircase that he now bounded.

"What are you doing?" she called up. "Isn't this illegal?"

Later she found that a friend who worked for the Historical Society had slipped Blake keys — procured from a janitor, but he chuckled and proclaimed "What therefore God hath joined together, let not man put asunder."

"I used to think this was a church," she said.

"Honest mistake. Victorian gothic. Dressed limestone trim. Arched windows arrowing toward God. Father Marto loves it. More church-like than a thousand churches. My dad — well you know, he's not all there, memory is fading fast especially lately —"

She felt a fearful vertigo — the thrilling rush of their relationship, how right how terrifying how fresh, how many assurances against their unknowing —

"Oh I know, I'm so sorry, I know. Know, as you know, exactly what that's like from Nonna. Or . . . not exactly. Of course it's harder with him because she's pushing ninety-five and, I suppose, *should* be fading. There'd be something superhuman, something

186

almost overwhelming, should she have her full faculties at that age."

"Funny, I mean *not*, he always joked about being born with the soul of a ninety-something-year-old man. And so it's fitting he's rivaling your Nonna for the watermarks of old age. All that mold in the Yourrick basement. Enough to poison the memory, the mind, whatever he's taking to the contrary: chlorella, bentonite clay, and a whole busted cupboard of a pharmacy. But he regularly recalls and retells the time — as if on repeat, actually, he tells it — he and my mom went to Notre Dame in Paris and tried, for days, to climb the turret staircase that would take them to the top of the tower. The spiraling steps did him in. He literally couldn't take another step. Always at the same spot he'd. Just. Stop. And then bound back down to the disapproving looks of a hundred ascending tourists. He said that maybe if he could reach the top like mom he could come back down with a head full of faith but because he couldn't . . . But, here, not Notre Dame, but we can. You and I. We made it."

"It used to be a lighthouse, right?"

"No," he explained, as she ascended the spiral. "Well, it's called that, always. But was, once, a water tower."

She scratched the corduroy of her azure jacket, self-conscious for having lived in the city for so long and all the while mistaking such a landmark.

"It's actually all just a cover-up," he said, his eyes squinting, spry.

She breathed through her nose with great delicacy, desperate to hide the sudden dizziness exacerbated by the spiral staircase she looked down on as, when a child, she would wait at the top of Nonna's stairs until her dad would ascend and lift her onto his shoulders then stumble down the stairs to the damning glare of his mother-in-law.

"A beauty. Or — beauty. Not strictly necessary — but beautiful, eh? Down there's the pipe that drank water from Lake Michigan and circulated some twenty million gallons across the city. Necessity and beauty meet. This place is like no other. Impossible to imagine the same springing up with the same strength and staying power in this hideous century. Look, though, at the way that spiral moves" — and

187

as she gripped, now, the rusted railing and listened to his soothing tone as much as what he said about the golden ratio, and the grip of nausea that had tightened her throat loosened as she breathed her stomach muscles slack, as he picked up a piece of stone and sketched an equation on the water-stained floor, followed by a spiral that swirled within a growing ratio of squares:

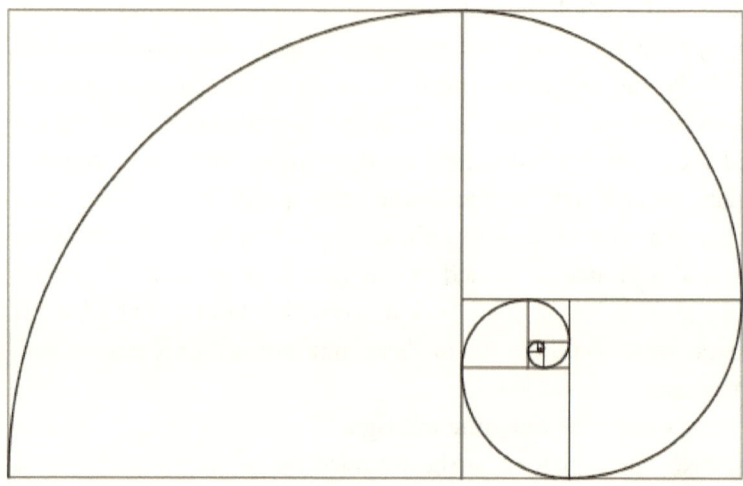

"Something my dad showed me when I was a kid. Hard to forget. Bear with me, I know this seems ridiculous. There's this sequence named after a merchant mathematician named Fibonacci. Oh — here I go, acting like the great discoverer. But — you know it?"

"I — heard of it. In school." Of course she had. But she was slipping into the awkward sleights forgotten since she was a schoolgirl. Not since she had started seeing him had she feared this could be their final parting. She shook it off like a fresh-shorn sheep — her mother's minuscule, marionette tics of perpetual insecurity. "Oh, forget it. You know what I mean."

"I do. Don't be. Sorry. I'm an idiot." With chalk he curved the squared circle swirl. "So it's basically, boiled down, an open-ended series of numbers. Each consecutive set, taken together, equals, produces, whatever, the next: 0,1,1,2,3,5,8,13,21,34,55,89."

The thrill of hearing someone say numbers without the accountant's dull clank.

"And if you transpose the numbers into geometry you get that curve." She almost gave herself away.

"Yes, *exactly*, yes," here he gripped her wrist and lifted it up, and though she checked him up and down for a single vibration of condescension, it was clear — his rare toothy grin — he was totally lost in the elixir of order — the prospect that the world could make sense. "And the thing is, that pattern is *everywhere*. Okay, not everywhere. But . . . maybe." And like a magician who waved his one hand while the other hid a coin, he pointed down and with widened eyes said: "Look at the stairs. Beautiful, although they're washed out and rusted. You could say the rust takes away from perfection or you could see that pattern persists in spite of the rust, *within* this . . . dust. Microscope would only prove what I'm saying. Patterns in drips of water on a pond, consecutively smaller circles of water in the aftermath of every little splash. Don't follow me? Ay. I can see why. I'll show you sometime, the way a droplet rebounds from the surface of water in a perfect circle the size of a marble but then the subsequent splash of the same droplet's remains assumes a smaller but harmonious circle, touching the surface at the same spot. I know, I know, I've got to stop. Whirlpools, plants, galaxies, nautilus shells, the spiraling seeds of a sunflower — my favorite, I think, except the length of finger bones in proportion to the face." Here he lifted her hands and proved how perfectly they fit her face, and she made a mimic of Munch's "Scream" and they laughed when she said "Chaos in the cosmos!" Then he folded, one by one, each of her fingers besides the naked one where a ring would go but he saw that this left a strain in her hand so he let them go and knelt on the stone. His knee shook on the dank cold ground but it did the job of holding him in homage.

"What if we're supposed to mimic that symmetry? The kind that's everywhere, I can't help thinking — no, stronger — *sensing* from the soul. Blah. I don't know how to say it right. How symmetries serve as a way of weaving patterns amidst so many unpredictable variables.

"Stella — will you marry me, please?

"I want to be interwoven with you. I guess what I want to

wonder is whether we might already be a symmetry, have been from the beginning. And if I lost you I'd be partial, imbalanced. Walking like with one leg even though I have two. I owe so much to you and want to be that for you too. Will you be, forever, with me? Will you, with this madman, chase infinity?"

The silver ring — she had mocked gold and diamonds — stayed sober there between his fingers. For a second she thought the ring was dark blue but she blinked and again it went back to dull silver. Her eyes alighted on a shock of sapphire light — bright but not an ache on the eyes.

"You said once you thought it totally silly to waste money on gaudy things, especially — I swear you winked — wedding rings. You're not . . . you look almost sad."

She followed his gaze to the perpetual bulbs paid by taxes — a spray of extravagance from the common purse that kept the water tower always lit. The blue watts pushed penumbral circles through arched windows that conserved their secrets, illuminating the illusory orange walls which were, first-hand, a washed-out gray.

"At last," she said, biting her tongue about the other patterns that would mark their future — the chores and the cycles her parents had perfected to keep the family from falling apart, the rose window of burnt pan marks that scarred the Yourrick table to this day, Catherine dead how many years now? She wiped her lashes of the drops that blurred Blake's craned face and extended her finger until the ring surpassed a wrinkle beyond which it could not slip off.

As he kissed her so lightly — a barely bearable lightness — she saw the story Blake had told her, unwittingly, repeatedly: by now the vision was seared into her lids. As a child, at home, he had watched his mother from the ledge of a staircase that regressed upwards, eternally rising like a cork screw bent on piercing the well-guarded gates of Eden, and he saw, somehow, his mother Catherine, stretched across a number of days, across even years at once, like in camera clips at high speed, blurred into a perpetual present: tending to too many things all day, receipts and doctor's bills 'til she went gray, she could not even scrounge the duration required for her hand to open the drawer and retrieve the ragged hot pads that hardly worked anymore and so she started searing the table with the dinner pans, mostly in the same spaces. But over time she singed the varnished top with a purpose, turning the center a kind of creamy milky white that looked lovely against the deep brown wood. Slowly, with Penelope's shrewdness and patience, she expanded the singes in secret until once, when Dad returned from a very long shift, and she could see through his soured eyes that his mind wore suicide like a familiar beaten Milwaukee baseball cap, she removed the bills that typically covered the table even at dinner. (The table was long and large enough that she could keep these documents on an island atop a plastic wreath that came out at Christmas and never really went away.) Unable to tame the wild smile that stole across her mouth, squatting over the chair because she could not sit upon it, Catherine removed the unpaid bills that had kept her secret unseen, she unveiled the pattern that years of searing had given shape. No one ate for a long time, each of them rapt there over the rose-window S-shapes that kissed to form at once flames and teardrops and drips of blood transfused, translucent, as though flowing out from the cleansing core, symmetrical and the same but as if alive and bent on burning beyond their confines even as they could never escape the petals of the rose that contained them. And for once the perpetual agitated buffeting and shuffling of Mom and Dad ceased as did all even well-intended jabs under the table between siblings. All the world at peace. Sheepish, Catherine said that the searings were "amateur for sure," showed only the blinded outer eye of the brilliant Rose Window at Chartres Cathedral. "Sublimely dulled," she said of the colors that come when you enter the church and kneel there, in Chartres, temples throbbing as you look at your hands covered with the color of blood red pouring, raining down from the dyed shards, lit bright by the dying sun, "lyrical nonsense, sure," she granted, but no criticism could touch her at all, as that is how she saw it still or how it saw her, even from afar, an eye widening and widening in the light, no longer admiring the intricacies of the exterior but captured by the tongues of flames and by the drops of blood and by the massive tears that shoot out from the center of the rose which is the center, "I can't hardly say it — of the cosmos. Don't laugh. Just trust me. I see it. I see it." And Blake's father, lost in her hypnotized eyes, nearly knelt down at Catherine's side as he kissed her very lightly on the mouth.

. . .

On Stella's lips the words kept forming: *at last*. Doing the dishes. In the middle of Saturday dinner with Eleanor. But then Blake disappeared, called off the future he had talked — with abandon — into being. And rather than dare chase after his reasons, none of which he had bothered to give her, she free-fell into frightening self-pity: perched on the high bluff cliffs by the lake, looking down at the midnight waves pulled by the moon to drown the world.

Never had she seemed, as now, superfluous. No one needed her. No, not Nonna. Eleanor, hell no, and not the florist either: a simple want ad, two interviews, a ready replacement, a few weeks of unhappy customers. A few weeks of unhappy customers?

Then Nonna needled her with mention of Cabrini's in Chicago: more than a mention, an oracular assertion. Nonna had straightened her spine and sat at the seat edge with a lost look vacillating between a telescopic gawk and a strained gnat wince, had stared straight in Stella's direction but her gaze went *through* rather than *to* a granddaughter desperate for a clue, their eyes not locked, Nonna's whiskey-jar glasses off so she couldn't anyhow see more than half an inch beyond her outstretched, instructing lips. Sibyl eyes seeing unseeing as Stella took in the giddying prospect.

Emergency teaching certification started soon after, and she became, again, a student before appearing as a teacher in the foggy August of two thousand eighteen, that faraway world before coronavirus cast a cloud of unknowing over whatever was left of the known world.

Stupidest dream, like some bleed of her brain: that she could be more than a seasoned florist who spent countless needless hours on bouquets for lovers she would never know. Why? Because the looks she received when they came to pay, the praises and tips that told their pleasure, gave vicarious thrills without the letdown or the wilt in the vase that would come next week.

. . .

Blood flow of coded zeroes and ones, pliable veins of wide-reaching wires: the automaton kept impeccable time to a T, told it through speakers that seemed shorted out, buzzed, fuzzy, then blared with perfected, irritant pitch, dead tone politeness, computed divinities, sycophants of Chronos all alive and well. *Train arriving in two minutes. Please step away from the doors. Boarding begins in two minutes.* If the L-train failed to drop her at the Amtrak she could wait for the next one in the Central Station hall that lifted, always, her spirits on high like a Chopin concert or an old Polish church. She could get to Milwaukee and buy a ticket back here at once. *There will be no next time,* she could hear the voice warning, malfunctioning, departing from its algorithmic script. *Redeem the time because the days are evil.* She swung back, *you wanted him gone and now that he's gone you're whining about it.* She had treated him badly to scare him away, to save them both the hardest part. No. The hardest part would be the rest of her life, raising this baby without Peter's hands, without the low bellow of his sweet bass voice. Years before she had met Peter he had abandoned music with an about-face restraint, pitched it into the past, no pillar of salt, no resentment over what was lost — *I frankly couldn't have lived that way forever, pay spotty even when we could scrounge a gig, privileged pastime of the decadent* — but Stella heard rancor when he'd laid it all out over grits and bacon and stirred-dust coffee. *So you don't even listen to music anymore?* He'd looked out the window at the police siren's spin, and she heard the scream as if it was happening though the cop had turned on his silencers. *I — if I did it'd all be over. I love it too much. I couldn't keep doing what I'm doing then.* She'd never played the piano for him, kept headphones on and volume low when she sleepwalked into their little living room, sciatica keeping her wearily half awake.

He had a spirit that could take one thing only — counseling or canvassing or campaigning or blown trombone — and she and the baby would be two too many. Renunciation seemed the only right answer. That or a marriage marred by varied motives. And the silliest fiction of them all: he pretended his anger was a thing of the past, something he'd worked through with a trusted mentor, something that had exited his soul in the marches, in the street shouting where his spirit found peace. When he said they could do it, *I'm serious, Stel, I'll drop it all and go back to D. C., Curtis and even Marjorie said I could come back anytime,* she heard the hurt of an arrested man being made ready for a firing squad he'd smile while facing. He never said aloud that his counseling gig could not earn enough to carry a family, but without needing to say so outright she could not fail to see why he had started to talk about the old work of politicking that he had sworn off forever — with a stronger oath than his departure from music. After the pregnancy test showed the cross, he called Curtis and talked for hours, laughing through the shut bathroom door and emerged with a bathrobe over his fresh-pressed dress shirt, wearing also a big smile that made her smile unwittingly back. But later that day and the weeks that followed, when she started seeing him less and less — he was always away, always "busy" with meetings, canvassing and campaigning and shaming the laws so officers who filed false reports would be severely punished for their lies. When they did meet, typically at twilight, he would walk around the room's circumference as if looking for a hidden fire exit before standing with a contracted face, that trombone-blowing fullness of expression, a serious look that said he would never leave. But an hour later he would pound a wall, pace the kitchen and mash potatoes, mash them hard with guttural groans, he would cook and leave them uneaten on the stovetop. Her pregnancy craving for starches being satisfied, she feared to open the fire-escape window, where he sat in conversation with himself, legs dangling with suicidal abandon over the painted black metal ledge.

As the train slowed a husky man busking on the street side played, sorrowfully, "What A Wonderful World."

Dissident. P. C. Damn you. I love you. That morning's farewell had not been their first. She could not count how many false dénouements they had rehearsed before he finally took flight. They flicked through her consciousness like discarded film reels in which she hated the part she had chosen to play.

"Go, lead your leadership workshops. Be a father to the pseudo-orphans who'll gather around you like your own children. Raise your hand over *those* sons. Don't, mind you, spoil the child."

"Come. With me."

"I can't. Baby'd be — in danger. You can't even tell me what you're doing. How can I trust Jason'll be safe?"

He had paced and opened the fire escape window but did not slip through to the outside relief.

"No force. You tried to save me from myself, but look where that got you. I'll not return the favor. If you don't want me I can't — won't — force it." He'd swatted at his chin and kept eyes shut. A V of crows alighted on the darkened escape and when she shooed them away, fearing for Jason's eyes, Peter thought she was sending him. For a moment she feared he'd leap. Then:

"I'll send you a check. Every month. I'll send you a check."

"I know I don't have to worry at all. Not about that. P. C. My God. Go. Go. You've proven yourself. We can't solve *all* our problems. You can talk big about healing your own wounds before trying to soothe others'. But some of us are meant to tend the broken without being able to unburn the marks seared into our souls as children."

"I refuse to believe childhood's so fateful."

"Believe what you want. What you do's what matters. Let's say our goodbyes and keep to it. I'll go back home like so many others. Self-reliance another illusion. It would have come to this at some point. Did you ever really believe we were permanent?"

"I'll send you a check."

Each month, at Curtis's directive, a man named Earl Sorrows would transfer five thousand into his PayPal — or send a check scrubbed for safety. All he had to do for the first few months was send pictures proving he'd been at all of the protests. Slowly he would win trust and direct the passions of a movement whose pains split a million directions.

"Play *their* game and do right by my people. What all I care about, at bottom, is all the stories of young guns gone. On the Southside of Chicago. In Charlottesville, St. Louis, D. C., don't matter. All the same. Shattered pain. They need someone who won't play the peer — who'll harness the agony with authority. I don't think it's lacking in humility — I know I'm not worthy — to say it'll be me."

She said, "Your checks won't buy me, you know." Before she bought her ticket back to Milwaukee, she had visited Cabrini's on a Wednesday morning — without telling Peter — to see about a job. Insane, of course, but so was moving, at forty-one, into her childhood home.

Principal Halves held her hand and praised "such a strong woman, a go-getter mama," and Stella nodded slightly, hesitant, before shaking her head No.

No. God. Go home.

Taking Chicago in swift strides, she felt baby's exposed forehead — hot against the cold, but no fever so far as she could tell. No more kisses from daddy who would turn and kiss, too, Stella's nose, his warm lips soft against his stubble-flecked mouth. Her skin slowly admitted that, yes, full rebellion against her thoughts and the world was too much for her again and so maybe she'd better just turn back around and work the cash register at Peter's uncle's fix-it garage until her fingers turned inevitably greasy and her hearing went bad from the constant clangs and her gray hair hard earned oh God hang it all. Call Peter and beg him back and while downtown why not stop at the courthouse and draw up a draft of their marriage certificate, crazy, her neck snapped and she reared awake fully now and whatever half-conscious half-waking-walking state was replaced by a readiness to earn her keep and get back on her feet so that she could be beyond necessity before she made any big decisions.

Then a faceless man overturned a vendor's grill — Skinny Sam-wise, Dogs for Sale — and ran — and his gray and rained-on hood hid all — but the vendor, heavyset and well-fed on what he sold, did not follow. He crossed his arms and shook his head as the molded meat scattered across the street, jiggling between skidding and swerving traffic. The city's vitals being under construction, all buses and cars were rerouted away from the law office buildings whose countless stories roundly outdistanced the green-rusted steeples that stood shy and apologetic like the pity invite at a big party. A small explosion of scavenging birds erupted from the library gutter. They dove *en masse*, digging their beaks into the more complex fat of pigs — the birds who all at once converged on the same shard of tossed-away meat, look at them alight and tear, violent beaks like swords defending each his own snatched sinewy scrap, relishing that others relish it and unable — her father would say — to harmonize interests the way humans can.

A man shouted to the arms-akimbo vendor, "I can help you sue him. Look at that camera there and there. And there and there. He's practically already caught, alright. But I could help get you what you deserve for being harassed, your business diminished. The long-term deterrent effects this will have on the number of people who'll feel comfortable here, patronizing your fine establishment."

She knew he was a lawyer by the strange affinity his mouth had to her uncle Howard's. A line that could not be called a smile but a stretched rope let temporarily loose. She had to hurry across the street to make the Amtrak. If the Amtrak left she could take it as fate. She could stay in Peter's abandoned apartment until, one night, he would come to collect the rest of his leftover belongings for a permanent relocation to D. C. and instead there she and baby would be. When her eyes locked with the husky lawyer he begged to be trusted but looked, rather, pained when he tried to lift his fixed, fat lips. The stoplight prevented her from avoiding him. To jaywalk would court certain death. Squeezed between the conservative crowd — too cowardly to run against red with the rustling rush of cross walkers — she looked down at his alligator shoes, the way the emptying haze did not penetrate the leather but deflected the water in lovely little gems, amber drops that the lawyer looked down over his nose and nodded in solemn appreciation of his lovely impenetrability. As he blunted her with looks, she tested her intuition to see if after everything it was still intact, if for all her sins her prescience was still a grace she somehow possessed: "You do legal work?"

He pinched the pin on his jacket breast, held it out, delicate and defined. It read: *Mint & Sons.*

"Yes. Civil cases only. Would you like a mint?" he asked, "you look parched," and popped open a golden box engraved with the family legal crest.

"A family business?" she stammered, and the sun skimmed off his lapel label and the heirloom mint case, slicing her eyes like a kid's pocket knife, dull but able to do the job. "My brother couldn't, wouldn't carry on. My parents, retired, had one forever. We don't live in that world anymore," she said.

"The family business?" he said. "I know. Although it seems you're trying to carry on anyhow" — he reached toward whimpering Jason as if to pat the baby's head but she bared her teeth with a primal flare of blood to the gums and he backed off at once. "A simpler world. Imagine never having to go through the anguish of choosing a career, of wondering what you're going to be when you grow up, because it's all been decided for you."

Checking the tower as if he were clocking in, he nodded to an unseen overseer and looked straight at her, perfectly sad.

"No, I meant —"

"I know. I wanted it to work out that way but none of my boys wanted to study law." When he pressed the mint into her palm she let it fall into the slush and then shook her hand the way Nonna did when the feeling had gone out of it for want of use. His eyes darted down but immediately regained a defensive stance that made it hard for her to leave. "One of my life's great disappointments? Yes. But it's kept me honest. Now," he pivoted as the walk sign flashed white its modestly skirted pedestrian.

"No, but what I meant was we don't live in the kind of world where you could accept candy from strangers."

He bit his lip and blinked, pleased. "You thinking about divorce?"

Peter would propose again although she'd said No the first time without waiting or flinching. Admittedly when she envisioned a city-hall wedding she felt cheapened and weightless, like a form of paper tucked away into a filing cabinet.

She saw a frothy shame in the lawyer's made-up face, as if he were embarrassed of something and was sure she knew what — though she hadn't even an inkling.

"I pride myself on knowing people's needs. As a PhD I call myself," sweetening his lips, with loosened tongue climbing the clever ladder, "'Doctor of souls,' ho ho ho," actually chuckling like the Hyde Park Santa she'd heard in passing the first time she walked out of Peter's apartment in the middle of another of their arguments. The melted eyes of the children who looked into not a mask but a magic mirror, not noticing the cellophane tape that she could see glisten from across the lawn, or maybe that glisten only made him more real — the bearer of a translucent light, as if his beard were composed of a dripping stalagmite stolen from the forbidden cave at the peak of the antipode, the end of the world.

"I'm even married," she let loose at last. "I mean, I'm *not* even married. Jeez."

"Well sure, but you will be, someday. Call me." Mr. Mint looked even happier as he turned away, handing her a card, then halting as he reached inside his two-sizes-too large suit and handing her an envelope — sealed, she found, when she flicked it with her finger. He flapped a loosened mask back over his face. "We live in hope."

Mumbling after him an inaudible slur that even she couldn't decipher, she stooped and snatched up the card lest it wind up in someone else's hands. As if a little piece of paper could catch the eye in a world saturated with incessant appeals. She'd missed Chicago Union Station by a block, but before she made an about-face she saw him accosting another woman who looked down on him from her high heels and tugged down at her snug red skirt, smug even through her mask, ready to spit at any solicitous man. Stella did no more than shake her head.

. . .

She barely made the Amtrak before the pneumatic doors sealed the passengers into an intense, endangered silence. A sprinkler-pipe break the week prior meant half of the space was sectioned off by police tape, as if the city were investigating the guilt of the wind which had whipped through the poorly insulated doors and frozen the pipe until it popped. The week she'd ended up needing to leave — she'd forgotten this until just now — was Thanksgiving, a time when travelways across this fair country were customarily congested and clogged like a backed-up toilet or a cholesterol-coated artery. On Thursday, even at eleven p.m., Chicago was a clement thirty degrees. Videos of bombed-out hospitals and stills of face-covered pregnant women (dead, discretion, religion?) being carried on stretchers tilted down from massive screens, sleek and functional on every wall though the drinking fountain was OUT OF ORDER. Stella blushed, a rush of blood known to no one else. She had no idea what country this was happening in, a level of ignorance she had railed against for years: Americans inhabiting their simulacrum, the last place to pretend history's end. But wars wherever did not leave untouched a people unable to fathom total violence. It seeped into the atmosphere, a kind of radiation, images seen without smelling or tasting the aftermath of wall plaster picked up and spat out elsewhere by the damned daily breeze, bitter on the spitting tongues of backpacked refugees trekking hurriedly toward nothing, a musk-like odor mingled with nauseating, gaseous spray.

Gas prices had been gouged or at least tripled in a matter of days, and Amtrak had summoned passengers from the void by offering discounts on all train tickets, half-off for night travelers, and Stella — determined to not need Peter — needed the discounts of night, as did hundreds of others, apparently, as an army of urgent Americans appeared, armed with two and three suitcases, sacks, children — a country reconsidering its *raisons d'être*, millions of amateur cartographers remapping and unmapping their fearful futures now that Covid refused to retreat — they pushed against the habitual paralysis of catatonic stares into computers logging with photographic evidence a slew of new and rising death counts — watch them rush to rash homecomings or risqué retreats onto rural homesteads, computer programmers taking up residence in compounds first designed for family farmers; minimum-wage workers wasting away taking up trucking or assuming the deliveries of a shut-in population that had grown, by now, afraid of the air. But here, after so much separation, the sparse-street malaise of pandemic days was a quick and carnivalesque collision of frantic, manic, private searches, and a body hidden behind Italian suit wear perched beside a blood-eyed, cardboard-carrying bum, piss-stained rags brushing against the stainless, cologne-scented cleanliness.

No one dared to dart into the restroom because already the line at Customer Control was long and winding with ubiquitous defeated men and women milling like revenants in the wrong world without even the gambler's hope, missing luggage and bitter with complaints either waiting to be filed or pitched even now, relentlessly, through the vent carved into bullet-proof glass, to the young man in dapper gray with dreadlocks and a gridlocked grin, who must have been hired because during the interview he demonstrated his uncanny ability to sit looking charming and kindly even, even when the volume rattled the glass that protected him from the pounding hands, hands of one unhappy customer who winced back from the marble countertop he had hit, for emphasis, far too hard.

Stella tried to catch the young man's eyes, prepared to mouth *I don't know how you do it*, to which he, seeing the baby tied to her body in the elaborate blue crisscross wrapping, would say, *I don't know how you do it*. He grinned up into the furies without ceasing, combing his goatee with untrimmed fingernails, dreadlocks tidied in a massive hairnet that arose from his skull like an Egyptian headdress, impossibly smiling above the swirling cesspool of angst that sucked around the barrier beyond him.

Chicago's Union Station was a mixed-up game of human marbles, bodies so urgent in the pandemic mood that the usual effort to keep cautious distance disintegrated into bold, full-body run-ins. A bearded man who reeked of mouthwash limped toward her, nursing right toes wrapped in bandages, lifting the left foot in a spastic stretch which showed and nearly shoved in her face a fungal-infected, neglected toe poorly mummified with medical gauze, nearly knocking Jason from her hands, then shouting at her for *Trespassing, lady, keep to yourself hoity toity*, at which point a bystander who must have been familiar with the antics of the gangrene man — who teased her by sticking out the blackened turds of exposed toes that smelled like plugged sewage — tried to shield her with his twig-thin arm, not the kind of muscle that might frighten away, although his presence as a human shield seemed bizarrely appropriate just now in that the sculpted white hair covered his skull with contours that might have been head armor: "Sergeant! Stop! Sergeant! Stop!" But Sergeant, not stopping, shoved the bystanding acquaintance with a calculated hit designed not to do damage, as if he were skilled like an actual officer, before he grasped at Stella's face, eyebrows raised above black sunglasses, his mouth hidden like the millions by the mask, this one with a hole bitten through. The ovals of his big lenses became her funhouse mirror refracting back, his strange, surgical pincer fingers pinching her clip-on azure-blue earring and then backtracking into a huddle of other men who whistled and clapped as she quickened her pace around a corner and, sure that they were not following, she leaned for a breath against the travertine marble of a Corinthian column built somehow, placed so perfectly just for her, the marble beautiful, expensive but chilly in the windy city night. Better to keep the baby's head visible so maybe these men would leave her alone? Or better to keep the baby hidden in case a kleptomaniac hand decided to add Jason to his collection? — a thought she had previously forced herself away from thinking but one that now seemed as necessary as breathing.

Breathing between statues of Night and Day, the latter, golden, gripping an owl whose gaze contained the sum of attention, she herself looking down, heavy-lidded, a weary watchman over the madding crowd, the former clutching a well-fed rooster as she shielded her eyes against the dawn, neither allegory's pupils visible — a feature (by what design?) that made Stella's lower back sweat with the passage of all these spare seconds and hours that slipped under the unseeing watch of these elevated women meant to celebrate the constant activity of the human race, the race the marathon but what if you ran and no one ever passed you a torch and all your efforts and breathlessness in vain — and rest was anyhow what she needed now, a kind of rest she'd never felt starved for — as if only a year of straight sleep would repair what this last year had taken from her. Another man jutted out from the huddle which was moving, inching, slowly toward her, and he held out his hands like a smooth-talking uncle, hustling each melodious syllable: *See I, I could take care of you, each and every day, baby,* just as an Amtrak attendant appeared, looking officious with a Maglite holster and sending the cock-eyed, red-nosed man back to the huddle which swelled to absorb him.

And then the whistle awoke the travelers, summoning somnambulist bodies to the train, and with one foot on the platform and the other on the vehicle she saw a familiar if fast-aged face. As always when a known profile appears amidst the anonymous mass of practical proton and electron people, an inordinate level of surreal happiness tickled the lobes of Stella's ears. Mary Feckleaf. The one friend mom had maintained since childhood, the one who came over to play cards and who had spilled, to Stella, unapproved secrets about the parish priest, her old cheeks heavy and purplish and wrinkled and hair follicles sparse if long, eyes big as shooter marbles, obsidian pupils searching Stella like her grandmother would when she came home late, her eyes praising what she found even as she tilted her narrow nose in a kind of tacit expectation that Stella not waste what she'd been given, starting at the toes and resolving at the head, elbow bent until her fingers formed a visor over her eyes in perfect imitation of the Day statue supervising Union Station, then shaking her head *no,* incredulous, pupils jittery and lightly atremble as she tried to accept what was happening, and *Seven minutes* said a mechanized voice, *Please gather your belongings from the center of the aisles and make a way for your fellow mortals, and remember amidst your habitual impatience that it's easier to love a perfect stranger.*

"Stell?"

"Mary!"

The woman dropped her suitcase and let her purse dangle from her elbow as she wrapped Stella in a choking hug that made the well-hidden baby suck and then scream the low-volume scream of the very young whose little lungs cannot match their discontent, and silly alibis vied for first place, the automatic crop of shame, the need to keep Mary from telling her mother as if she wasn't on her way home herself and would surely be there before her old friend could reach her in the earliest decent Thanksgiving hours. With a warmth Stella's mom could not approximate, Mary massaged her friends' daughter's arms, pressing cold palms until they flushed with sweat, fixing the cuffs of the worn brown cardigan and saying, as if to save Stella any need to explain, "My sister, Vicki, maybe you met her, oh of course you know her from the family picnics, she has maybe a week of life left and I'm —"

"No! What can I —" but she cut herself short, recalling that she could no longer offer help, not right now, and this thought settled into her shoulders, sinking them.

"Well, at least Bianca's back home for now, with Isaiah, and so I, thank God, didn't have to bring him with, I mean, you know I love Zay but the kid'll need his mom or someone other than me in a minute because I'm *just too old* for that, see, and my hands are always aching from turning over patients for forty-some years," the same hands that Stella saw rubbing her own with a vigor that quieted her whole nervous system — like a maestro who can instantly silence a symphony whose hurry to play left them all out of tune.

No alibi seemed quite right and it was hard to gather which of the alibis would require the least pity from Mary. I apologize. Alibis. The stupidest story she devised involved a good friend, Erica, who had unfortunately come down with a bad addiction to cocaine, which, you know, is very bad for the baby's brain, *this baby's*, and so Stella, trying to be a good friend in return, had adopted the baby and was very blessed to have the kind of job which had a nursery on site, and *this trip home is a surprise for Mom so please don't call her because I really need to tell her myself*, but only that last part worked its way loose from her mouth and Mary, again asking no questions but squeezing her palm in silence, kissed her right eye and then her left, lips flaked by the bleeding mascara when she pulled away and folded her hands to signal *prayer*, and Mary gave her friend's daughter a final understanding stare that almost said "My fault, I'm sorry," and the Union Station speakers switched tracks from an almost unbearable punitive smooth jazz to, the DJ said, all suave, Bill Evans' *You Must Believe in Spring*, a B-minor waltz that felt like the year's melted end, the final tentative footsteps on a pond not freezing fast enough, and would you make it to the other side before the sheets of ice collapsed, perhaps, but you did not dare hasten your pace because that could signal a lack of faith and so you tiptoed totally-concentrated quick steps to the other side of the windy lake, ice-age mistake, looking for lights left on at home.

· · ·

Only after the pneumatic doors sighed shut and Stella could see her own eyes in the window glass, eyes much sadder than she meant them to be, did she realize where she'd seen Mary's look before: in the photographs of soldiers returned from the First World War's trenches, and though the comparison seemed hyperbolic to the point of inconsideration or cruelty — as if whatever Mary was carrying could approximate the terrors of trench warfare — she could not cease from making it again, as if Mary's face were lifted from a textbook high school unit on World War I, and as the train, a sarcophagus capsule of souls buried before their time, speeding to bring them where they belonged, to make time, to set things right, screeched softly at a Racine stop she startled from a bright nightmare where Mary was wearing a blue Red Cross, a uniform unstained, bleach-cleaned, and machine-gun fire was filling the theater with a thousand metallic clacks of applause and Mary was saying "Let me carry you," but Stella stood up on a badly twisted heel and said she was fine, could take care of herself, though when she tried to walk the pain was so complete that she collapsed and, laughing lowly, played dead.

She woke to the envelope Mr. Mint passed her poking her rib. The train lurched. She gripped a pole and let the pull of wheels on metal twirl her around as she switched seats, falling on vacant seats with better lighting — golden triangles above the head like the hooded dryers at the hairdressers she never tried. She looked up: RESERVED FOR THE DISABLED. The car was empty. She stayed put. Nice to have someone else driving.

Ripping the edge off she blearily read — perking up at the appearance of the Latin she had learned so fast in college and forgotten as quickly outside Arcadia:

205

PRENUPTIAL AGREEMENT
PREPARED FOR THE STATE

I. THE PARTIES. Herewith parties prepared after due deliberation on this cold in fact heartless November day in 2021 Anno Domini, therewith this Prenuptial Agreement ("Agreement") forthwith establishes a pre-marital arrangement between the parties following:

> Husband: __Peter Clavier__ , ("Husband")
> and
> Wife: __Stella Tęsknota__ , ("Wife").

The terms "Husband" and "Wife" do not in fact definitively signify or determine each person's gender and are employed solely for the passing legal practical purpose of identifying the individual entities engaged in this binding but incomplete Agreement. When mentioned in a singular version, "Husband" and "Wife," shall be combined for convenience into the single signifier "Spouse," and when indicated together, for similar convenience and to avoid the very tediousness that inspires us to split from one another in the first place — for this humanitarian purpose the Husband and Wife shall be known as the "Couple."

II. RATIONALE FOR DIVORCE. This Agreement shall sustain its significance only in the case that the subsequent rationale for Divorce are met in part or in full: (check all that apply)

☐ Mismatched Essences. The irrecoverable dissolution of the initial attraction and eternal incongruousness of expectations and discordant difference in temperament resultant in the wrist-slitting breakdown of the marriage with no prospect of band-aids big enough. Cut in half. WARNING *Doubt reigned in the celestial councils; the gods were divided between the desire of quelling the pride of man and the fear of losing the sacrifices. At last Zeus hit upon an expedient. Let us cut them in two, he said; then they will only have half their strength, and we shall have twice as many sacrifices. He spake, and split them as you might split an egg with an hair; and when this was done, he told Apollo to give their faces a twist and re-arrange*

206

their persons, taking out the wrinkles and tying the skin in a knot about the navel. The two halves went about looking for one another, and were ready to die of hunger in one another's arms. Then Zeus invented an adjustment of the sexes, which enabled them to marry and go their way to the business of life. Now the characters of men differ accordingly as they are derived from the original man or the original woman, or the original man-woman. Those who come from the man-woman are lascivious and adulterous; those who come from the woman form female attachments; those who are a section of the male follow the male and embrace him, and in him all their desires centre. The pair are inseparable and live together in pure and manly affection; yet they cannot tell what they want of one another. But if Hephaestus were to come to them with his instruments and propose that they should be melted into one and remain one here and hereafter, they would acknowledge that this was the very expression of their want. For love is the desire of the whole, and the pursuit of the whole is called love. There was a time when the two sexes were only one, but now God has halved them — much as the Lacedaemonians have cut up the Arcadians — and if they do not behave themselves he will divide them again, and they will hop about with half a nose and face in basso relievo. Wherefore let us exhort all men to piety, that we may obtain the goods of which love is the author, and be reconciled to God, and find our own true loves, which rarely happens in this world. And now I must beg you not to suppose that I am alluding to Pausanias and Agathon, for my words refer to all mankind everywhere.

☐ Non-Consensual Adultery by: (check one)
   ☐ Husband
   ☐ Wife
   ☐ Both Spouses

☐ Prison sentence denied bail or retrial whose longue durée shall defy chronology or otherwise try the mind's capacity to fathom separation so long. NOTE this "qualifying reason" shall be cancelled in the case that the state apparatus, in order to avoid making virtual widows of the innocent, shall provide spousal co-habitation in solitary windowless marriage suite cells.

☐ The death of either of the parties hereto;

☐ Alcoholism/Drug Addiction of any legal or illegal substance, including but not limited to monosodium glutamate (the City of Chicago excludes yeast-sourced glutamate), the common potato chip (deep fried, not baked), television series, docudramas, or video games (in the State of Illinois "addiction" is prudentially applied using the definition in 21 U. S. Code § 802, according to which "The term 'addict' means any individual who habitually uses any narcotic drug or narcotic adjacent so as to endanger the public morals, health, safety, or welfare, or who is so far addicted to the use of narcotic drugs as to have lost the power of self-control with reference to his addiction"), interior decoration, nicotine chewing gum that costs more than $1.99 per slice (price subject to inflation adjustment SEE CHART S.0.S.0.) and thereby imposes an untoward fiscal burden on the Spouse who — not necessarily through any virtue or merit — does not daily war against the Addictive Personality Disorder (a Disorder that, albeit, is difficult to diagnose, as the Diagnostic and Statistical Manual of Mental Disorders maintains a suspenseful mum concerning the question of its clinical definition, even though clinicians everywhere employ the symptoms in an effort to provide clientele with terminology suited to therapeutic self-knowledge (the sort that leaves someone saying "It's just so helpful to have a *name* for my dis-ease.")).

☐ Pet allergies to the preferred spousal animal.

☐ Other. _____.

III. MINOR CHILDREN. The Couple recognizes that there are: (check one)

☐ No Minor Children of either the Husband or Wife are being brought into the marriage.
☐ _1_ Minor Children being brought into the marriage.

The Minor Children are: (check all that apply)

☐ From the Couple.
☐ From either the Husband or Wife and described in Attachment F.

V. SPOUSAL SUPPORT (ALIMONY). In the event of Divorce, the Couple agrees that:

Co-mingled property shall be divided and distributed to Jane [Stella] and John [Peter] in kind, the appreciation and interest to be divided pro rata in accordance with the parties' contributions.

    c. If it is the nature of the co-mingled property that it lends itself to distribution in kind, but it is not possible to determine Jane's [Stella's] and John's [Peter's] contribution, then, unless Jane and John can agree in writing on some other arrangement, the property shall be divided and distributed equally.

    d. If it is the nature of the co-mingled property that it cannot be distributed in kind and it is possible to determine Jane's [Stella's] and John's [Peter's] contributions to the cost of the property, then, unless Jane [Stella] and John [Peter] can agree in writing on some other arrangement, the property shall be sold and the proceeds of sale shall be divided and distributed pro rata with respect to their respective contributions.

    e. If it is the nature of the co-mingled property that it cannot be distributed in kind and it is not possible to determine Jane's [Stella's] and John's [Peter's] contributions to the original cost of the property, then unless Jane [Stella] and John [Peter] can agree in writing on some other arrangement, the property shall be sold and the proceeds of sale shall be divided and distributed equally. Therefore, when co-mingling assets, Jane [Stella] and John [Peter] should make a special effort to document their respective contributions.

Section 401(a)(11)(B)(iii) of the
Code or Section 205(b)(1)(C) of ERISA
ARTICLE VII: WAIVER OF INTEREST

Stella turned another page, lost interest and stared at the sick neon blues of so many screens still consumed in the twilight.

As the train crossed the Wisconsin border she started awake and flipped the document's final page, pricking her finger on the cheap staples (three stabs of metal whose pincers failed to clasp, leaving little occasions of injury exposed) and thumbing the blood to the base of what she read, leaning back against the head cushion like her father in his armchair after a long deli delivery day, newspaper shielding his family from saying a syllable for the duration of the evening. She read hand-written red letters, scrawled by some underpaid clerk or scrivener but beautifully so, a palimpsest as if prepared for the dead language whose figures carried the curve of the cosmos like the haloed heads of Giotto's saints, like a Medieval painting brushed over a Modern masterpiece:

QUAESTIO 94: *De lege naturali*

ARTICULUS 6: Utrum lex naturae possit a corde hominis aboleri

AD SEXTUM SIC PROCEDITUR. Videtur quod lex naturae possit a corde hominis aboleri. Quia Rom. II, super illud, *cum gentes, quae legem non habent*, etc., dicit Glossa quod *in interiori homine per gratiam innovato, lex iustitiae inscribitur, quam deleverat culpa*. Sed lex iustitiae est lex naturae. Ergo lex naturae potest deleri.

PRAETEREA, lex gratiae est efficacior quam lex naturae. Sed lex gratiae deletur per culpam. Ergo multo magis lex naturae potest deleri.

PRAETEREA, illud quod lege statuitur, inducitur quasi iustum. Sed multa sunt ab hominibus statuta contra legem naturae. Ergo lex naturae potest a cordibus hominum aboleri.

SED CONTRA est quod Augustinus dicit, in II Confess., *lex tua scripta est in cordibus hominum, quam nec ulla quidem delet iniquitas*. Sed lex scripta in cordibus hominum est lex naturalis. Ergo lex naturalis deleri non potest.

"Respondeo dicendum quod," she recited, "sicut supra dictum est, ad legem naturalem pertinent primo quidem quaedam praecepta communissima, quae sunt omnibus nota, quaedam autem secundaria praecepta magis propria . . ."

"I answer that," she tried, not having read Latin with care since college but she thrilled as when Blake had cited the Fibonacci sequence. "As has been said above, to the natural law belong, first, some very common precepts, which are known to all . . ."

The strain of sense-making, at first a stimulant, became, in due time, a soporific, inducing a second sleep so seraphic she did not wake until Milwaukee's Downtown Intermodal Station.

PART II

. . .

In the dime stores and bus stations,
People talk of situations,
Read books, repeat quotations,
Draw conclusions on the wall.
Some speak of the future,
My love she speaks softly,
She knows there's no success like failure
And that failure's no success at all.

— Bob Dylan,
"Love Minus Zero/No Limit"

REGAN TĘSKNOTA INHALED, CANTANKEROUS, the saucepan's surely cancerous breath. Prunes, fiber, he felt his age. His lower back hurt when he lifted the handle and heaved the circle from the back burner. His careless son had burnt the pan some thirty or so years ago, had kept the burner on unattended when they left for church on the other side of town and when they returned rattled from worship—another fight in the filthy backseat—he barred his son from breaking and entering heroic with a baseball bat. He flew—furious, stomach-sprained breathless—through the well painted, unlocked door. That, too! Damn you. As always, the kid—last one out—had left the door unlocked for thieves, spent evenings reading baseball card backs instead of rising crime statistics. Jealous of such idiot ignorance, Regan blessed his nervous wife Mary for being so wonderfully, compulsively scrupulous, for keeping the stove side free of clutter, of heating pads and cardboard scraps—though somehow she'd missed last week's Chinese cookie. The kid had probably taken a bite before they rushed out the door for church. Colored like flesh the remains had melted around the uncurled double-luck fortune that said YOU CANNOT WIN THEM ALL + YOU KNOW YOU ONLY LIVE ONCE. Gathered above the fainter gray mist that rose from the fortune's dampened edge, a circular splotch of char-black smoke offset the burner's pillar of fire like an oracular eye staring him down, summoning him—his oxygen dim, his lips sputtered out the last fresh inhalation—summoning him like a deathbed father who, desperate, stately, and alert, looks for his delinquent son. (He had to breathe the burning in as his consciousness was ebbing out.) As he doused, repeatedly, the undying heat and saved the house from burning down he wondered whether more good could come had he let the whole household catch fire, let all they had taken for granted expire.

All that fury, now, had faded, and the faraway incident, washed by time and hung, a hundred times, on the clothesline, wrung from his red-circled winter dry eyes nostalgia for the years whose currency he had spent in constant and contrarian complaints. Souvenir of that pillar of fire suspended on the stovetop now, the splotch of molten black impossible to scrub or scrape down the drain — but the stainless steel still delivered every morning, and Regan avoided needless consumption with all the stubbornness of a well-heeled dictator — firm but with an about-face benevolence.

The steel-cut oats (soaked since nine p.m. last night) acquired a creamy consistency that required no chewing. His dentist was a damned opportunist for insisting he invest in dentures. He fought his skirmish with Dr. Turncot from the unassuming stance of a baby — a toothless newborn who could only ingest a restricted diet of broths and porridges, of well-smashed peas or overripe yams. The stupid lengths were not lost on him, but they did the trick: the pain in his wisdom teeth had totally subsided, and the molars had lost that metallic pang. When he'd told his wife this she had rolled her eyes and he kissed her, lightly, on a pale, dry cheek.

Peering out the window for the morning paper, he smiled through a swallow of steaming oatmeal. Regan could down a scalding cup of coffee without the least hint of a wince. The steam brought him back to the Capitol, the tear gas whose sting he could taste to this day, and the rubber bullets that branded his neck when he fell on his stomach with a dozen others. Why? Later he heard that Caryle had heaved a ladder through government glass, with one retelling refashioning the feat until the upper rungs lassoed an inside agent officer's neck, but Regan — all alert — had noticed no twitch of belligerence. The mystifying mist of tear-gas rockets whispered fearful things as they passed, and for a passing second he was sure he had been hit and the rubber bullet had projected him straight to heaven, except the place was not as nice, was a plain box, entirely empty, swept and kept neither hot nor cold. He shook to and the *psst* of the rockets shot by like gossipy secrets he could not make out. They hissed their mouthfuls of froth — like the humidifier his wife kept bedside — but instead of Sleepytime

Chamomile the mustard tendrils fingered his lungs like an indigestible invasive ghost. The mohawked man, all in black with a jail-stripe shirt, stood on the ledge blocking the irritant munitions with a plastic shield he had stolen from the police, and as he raised it, boasting his victory, an as-if headless arm reached around the arced window and gripped his mohawk and shook the shield loose, making way for another round of tear gas.

Regan — heels stinging — fell into the steadying muscles of camouflaged men who moved as a unit. As they crawled out of the cracked Capitol windows and lowered into the claustrophobic crowd, easing sideways down the staircase flush with shoulder-to-shoulder bodies ascending, the militia formed a chain and escorted him through crazed congestion. That should have kept him stuck for hours (and if he had been he would have tasted a little hell, hyperventilating as he did lost in numbers). But their leader assumed they were safe and shouted pale breaths of *All clear!* from a tight ski mask that made him look like an ant. Projectiles spat out their white fog and threatened to blind eyes and wound exposed flesh. They had all fallen like toy soldiers, mostly out of shape and sore, poorly oiled G. I. Joe figures rubbing their faces in the winter grass whose yellow could not hide their configuration from the police guns perched on the railing. Regan tried to join their *We the People* chants, but his stomach muscles were stretched so tight — like second-hand rubber bands about to break — he could barely breathe. He had tried to find an accessible bathroom for hours. At least this position allowed him to unzip his pants discreetly and empty his bladder under cover. Relieved, hungry, he chewed the cud, the weed that triumphed through the frozen taxpayer-funded lawn, his first meal at the People's House and not at all bad food (he could not but recall his own father, who during the Great Depression chewed grass when hunger threw open empty cupboards and bellies filled with water still growled, all seven kids in the back yard soothing their stomachs with fresh green blades gnashed between their yellow teeth). When he looked up the dull sky was covered by a film that blurred not only his perception but every conviction he'd come there to claim.

215

The mohawked man who had a stroke and died in jail on January 7 could have been the father of the paperboy who ran the route in Regan's neighborhood — not a paperboy at all but a teen, shaved-headed teen but for two fluorescent pink locks that spiraled neatly over her ears like the peyots of Orthodox Jews. Every morning at five he'd greet her with a smile, his black necktie pulled perfectly tight around a cutaway collar — all of this wrapped in a warm blue bathrobe. Civilization could not be too uptight in these days of the walking dead. Though Mary, who was humorless, had howled when she saw him overlay his tuxedo with a robe. He was no idiot, he'd said, then turned, draping the robe across an empty chair and straightening his tie, twice, in the window. He knew it would be thankless, he'd said. "But you can either cash in your cynicism with interest or do what you can to show a sloppy nation that decency and comfort can coexist."

The most principled needed to remember their rhetoric. He himself had lived in compromising, nihilistic nonchalance for most of his life unknowing, and it had taken just the right means of persuasion to coax him out of his coal-room comfort, chewing the cud with his grade-school friends as if the country hadn't collapsed. Goldilocks and the three bowls of porridge. Only one digestible.

The papergirl covered her mouth when she saw him and he grew mad at Mary, why, at Mary.

"Want a cigar?" He waved a thin one, imported Spanish, his sing-song shout not without melody (beauty even in the little things, something Tailor had told him many times but Eaves and the others could not seem to grasp, with their bowling-league jackets and their half-shaven slovenliness). Either nothing mattered against mass culture or even this early-morning song — imperfect but striving for exactitude — was a worthy counterweight lobbed against the amalgam of missile-screech guitar and militant drum, the screamed-out lyrics that he always strained to make sense of.
"No?"

You had to take the pulse of the people on the street even if he was lying in the public gutters which were fast becoming latrines. When he watched her bang her bald head to the guttural melodies

216

in violent downswings that stopped just before the steering wheel, Regan could see her ten years from now, coming to the massage-therapy clinic where his wife started working in retirement (he had put the idea in her head by crooning and exuding such profuse thanks every time she fixed his bad back): "You got into an accident, dear? The crick in your neck is a new level of awful." "No, but I was a head banger in my youth." Would Mary still be massaging kids raised on false promises and bent out of shape when they banged their heads against harsh reality? God! No, this bald kid would be, rather, likely, a single mother trying to find affordable childcare so she could drive half an hour and back to receive the requisite acupuncture and chiropractic that would ready her for another week of work. And in ten years he and Mary would be mid-seventies. As, practically childless and without grandchildren, with an urgent purpose that seemed, sometimes, pathetically propped up (he shed the bathrobe in sudden disgust, as a pretense that on him could never become serious, though the absence of the robe left him quite overdressed to be waiting for nothing but the weekday paper), it seemed increasingly unlikely that they would even be alive at all and so there was no way poor Mary would still be massaging anymore.

He shivered as he snatched up the discarded robe and walked it back to the outside trash, watching over his shoulder to see if she saw the degree of his humiliation.

She gave him a sweet smile, chin tucked, shy.

The papergirl, like every young woman, reminded Regan of his daughter, Stella, who had, suddenly, in a midlife crisis renamed nobility, risked her life in South Chicago on another bleeding heart, bleeding-out scheme destined from the start to end in disaster and kept — it killed him — bare minimum contact. After a stint without a phone she finally spared him shortcut text messages that could have been computer-generated: Hope UR Exercising or, if pressed, Luv U Too. Never had she ever used such cheapening shorthand. Always — even when he was an unlearned owner of an ordinary Polish delicatessen, before retirement had afforded him the hours to read Spengler's Decline of the West (albeit a faux-leather-bound edition abridged for Modern Readers) — he had corrected his children's excess use of "like" as if it were a four-letter swear word, had scorned such flagrant degradations of what remained of the English language, a language his father had learned late, after a lifetime of half-mute navigation through the corridors of the New World.

Anyone who recalled him to Stella he went soft on, so even the girl's shaven-head Statement (of what? What did it say, that shaven head?) reminded him of her as a baby, suspended over the baptismal font at the unspoken will of his mother-in-law, whose word was — if he wished peace — law. Instead of switching on power to the copper wire that wound angrily around his weakened heart, the shaven-head kid scanning her device, idling there in the dawn's early light, appeared as if a ministering angel who mimicked, poorly, Stella's absent form.

Unfailingly, when her car lunged down the block, brakes squeaking lightly at the next delivery, the neighbor's cat Prince Charming would cut into the street, raising a paw and wanting to play. Sometime he'd click his tongue quickly, thrice, and set out a beautiful estate-sale china saucer filled — recently acquired for a pittance — with a mingling of water and milk. Inflation being runaway and supply chains rattled, he could not justify spending undiluted, unpasteurized Whole, carefully drained from the Holy Hill cows, on a cat. But Prince, a shadowy Russian Blue outlined by silver shimmer, carried himself like an aristocratic ghost, chin up, chest out — as if exiled by Rasputin's magic machinations, doomed like all royalty to anonymity's insignificance, and Regan could only show such a fugitive to his quarters.

Watching the feline's elegant stretch, he did not blame the papergirl, nor did he now think the music was an especially noteworthy sign of decline. The car itself — the very fact of internal combustion, which lobbied public transit into a curtailed backtrack, its enshrinement of needlessly solitary rides, hours spent alone that could be kept in company, to say nothing of the elimination of vigorous blood flow from most living and breathing urbanites — the fact of the car was far more a culprit. She, so far as he knew, had not invented the vehicle.

When Regan needed to travel good distances, more than five miles on a good weather day, he boarded the bus with great resignation, in spite of the barbarically inexact brochure schedules: even in January a driver might arrive at the specified stop — blue-shaded in the schedule — forty-five minutes late. He could see, in the fog of morning breath made hot by a gulp of scalding coffee, one of those big corner stops, wind-shielded but open enough to gusts, full of frost-coated travelers who froze to death before the bus finally came. Lives woefully familiar with waiting and waiting and waiting. And waiting and waiting until anticipation without arrival became the only mode they knew, and the bigger destinations they'd mapped on the horizon were lapped, incrementally, into oblivion the way a tide-rise — albeit temporarily — erases those low, little islands as if they will never appear above water again. A few times he had missed appointments, turning back after doing a foxtrot to help the veins deliver their goods. Mother and father met dancing, would still go out into their seventies. He and Mary could never move that way. The navy blue couch's sunken cushions — nests without an egg to hatch. The last time he had taken one of those anyone-can-be-a-cabby services, the driver did her very best to divert her eyes from the highway's well-made white stripes (civilization's last borders), glancing at swerving cars and the strips of white and exit signs at best a fraction of each minute as they barreled toward what destination, so that he several times cleared his throat to complain and ask her politely to please deposit him, please, on the nearest gravel shoulder, yet whenever he cleared his throat and tapped his steel-toed shoe to the seat, she'd casually stop that tapping on her phone, retracting from the screen her elongated fingernails, false and painted with grade-school glitter. He did so much sighing and clearing that ride that by the time he arrived, breathless, at the doctor, his throat hurt terribly and they tested him for strep although he tried to explain. Negative.

Tonight — this morning — Regan was up even earlier than usual, and after the papergirl was gone from sight, although the shades and drapes were peeled in the kitchen he quickly made himself naked and redressed, with rigorous formation, in his long-sleeve woodland-green marine utilities, a costume he'd come across in an Army Surplus corner, coated with dust that looked like ash imported from one of the World War I photographs, cigarette refuse and shrapnel burn — discarded on discount under a rubbery cover.

For the last five months young men, some thirteen, had been making visits to the neighborhood and the police were unwilling to escort them away. They came feeling for car handles left unlocked, windows left slit, tearing through glove compartments and cup holders to find more than chump tollway change and fast-food wrappers and bad-taste CDs, stealing, it seemed, the ones that disappointed — the theft a revenge against owners who hadn't left out milk and biscuits. Fresh white bread, preferably buttered. His plan was simple. If he happened, while walking with exaggerated steps — warning all advancers, well ahead, of his presence — to chance upon one of these small-time thieves, he would surprise them with a genial grin and hold out a hard candy the color of blood, translucent sugary ossified plasma wrapped in cellophane tinted red, lit by his mag light under night's last cover. He'd snapped the IIIA bullet proof vest the way his wife, on their honeymoon, had clasped the life-preserver on before they capsized the rowboat, laughing, laughing still when they made the shore naked and she quickly clasped her chemise, for him, so he could as quickly unsnap it again. The vest did not fit. He was not getting fatter. For goodness sake, the sternum strap had shrunk. Had Mary tried it on!? — no way in hell. One of the ways he knew he was getting old: the exquisite shape of his wife when young possessed, no longer, excitatory power. Yes, the vest made his tactic less a gamble — was, in fact, what allowed him to pretend the perfect poise of politeness and bravado which, he was sure, would scare the pants off these braggadocio miscreant kids.

The neighbor's broken-legged German Shepherd — an untrimmed and overfed dog, given his own bedroom because the children were all moved out — gave a startled nighttime bark — an alarmed and alarming but lazy yawp, loud even through the thick and tempered glass block winter treated windows. Indigestion. Nightmare. A tumble and thump followed, an echo, a sucked breath, a stealthy shuffle from somewhere around the side of the house. He pulled out his hummingbird pistol, a gun so small it could be a boy's toy, and, back against the brick of his house, scaled down the driveway and spread his legs. The camouflaged garbage can shook just slightly. It was shrouded in a badly trimmed patch of bushes on one of those disputed patches of property: over the decades neither he nor the neighbor or both he and the neighbor claimed the strip as their own, and eventually the hedgerow both so cherished fell into forgotten disrepair. Left alone, once verdant, evergreen bushes that carried the Christmas spirit through the year, bore nothing more than multiplied needle pricks, dry and dead as soon as they bloomed, bursting out in lion mane shapes that did not intimidate. He'd tried to discover the name for the weed. Invasive species, Alice had said when they happened to be waiting in the same grocery line, two tellers and two dozen customers still resistant to self-check-out. Funny how Alice was casually friendly — friendly without cause, without conviction, reapplying her lipstick as she asked after Stella, familiar enough with Tęsknota affairs to know not to name Regan's estranged son Jacob, the "schizophrenic" failure (Regan still disputed the diagnosis, knowing what he knew about the plain old cannabis, the impressive LSD collection laid out like a kid's rare stamps in the attic, the psilocybin poison so different than the mushrooms he grew and roasted in the backyard fire), the scourge of the family — outgoing and familiar at random public crossroads, but when they met back in the neighborhood Alice was mum as the bushes' needles, not a needless word from her mouth.

At the southwest corner of the duplex house (over the decades they had reworked the staircase so that the dualism was whittled down, but the upper quarter still felt like a place fit for boarders rather than family), back straight against the cream city brick, he tripped on the base of a bristle broom. Furious with the enemy pole, he gripped the handle and thwacked it twice — then three times, and a wide-of-mark fourth — against the side of the garbage can, again and again, again and again, like the drums that beat outside the Capitol building, summoning somnambulist America to — what? Throw the voting machines into the ocean? The question thrilled the center of Regan's spine. Not an unreasonable proposition, given how easy they were to manipulate, how impossible it would be to regain trust in a world where every computer could be hacked. So plausible, that these high-profile containers of power would not — by some alchemical coding — spit back results unrecognizable from the numbers they had been fed. But why had he driven across the country, endured the neck crane and tobacco chew that had to be done to keep the friends happy, left his sitcom-and-nightly-news evenings for a place he had never been before, a seat of authority that in his head, until now, had been an unreal fantasy? If he let the answer loose from his chest he would have to admit he did not know himself.

Some "Don't Tread on Me" folks spoke of revolution; others sought to reverse the numbness of dead-end jobs that had poisoned their dreams like a house servant of some other century, the thing that was supposed to win you freedom in fact ending in wage slavery. He used the bristling end of the broom to unclasp the stubborn cover. A fat raccoon with stringy white whiskers — like the thread Mary put Christmas popcorn on — chittered through a maternal leer. Adrenaline obsidian eyes peered out of well-padded squint patterns, and as the intruder perched on the rim and bared her teeth like a middle-school braggart, he pocketed the pistol and held the broom aloft. He had told Stella her heart's compassion would do a disservice to the classroom bullies, but though she blinked and dropped her chin she did not contradict him then, and the messages she sent relaying news of Cabrini's were all coded in neon green, underlined with obligatory optimism. Three streets away a truck idled, pistons spewing a harsh exhale. The mother raccoon almost seemed to sigh as, bored, she let her weight play gravity to the frosted ground, bounding under the brush with a depleted snicker that petered out into purr.

He hated how Alice always asked, "Now where, again, could you remind me, did you and Mary go to college?" His last formal education class had been a culinary certificate finished in two fast semesters at the satellite Milwaukee Technical College situated kitty-corner to the State Fair carnies who camped out long before and after the official events had started and finished. By a hair breadth he might have been of their number, he often mused listening to their ribbing, their jibes and gambols as they tore down rides as he moseyed in the early twilight from day's class to nighttime work, head tired but limbs strong and itching to knife fresh shipped hogs and make the sausage others would eat but not — wincing — make themselves.

When Regan ambled back to the front yard the frost caught the sepia streetlight and for a second it seemed sixty years ago, waking at six years old before dawn and waiting and watching while the world played dead.

From the annals of history his father had revealed — in the voice he used to tell Grimm's tales — the story he used to tell to Stella: how the main stretch of Wallo Street was once home to several butchers who emerged all at once at the end of the day to dump buckets of blood and misshapen meat-scraps into street sewers. Red hands and smeared smocks and caught by no cops, they would form human chains in front of the horses and halt all commerce to help the children fresh out from school, handing out toothpicks poked into venison — "meat pops," the kids would shout and grab, no parents to shake heads and say *mind your manners*. The butchers, too tickled to correct the squealing army of suddenly underfed, starving urchins, the same redhead almost every day choking on the deer because as soon as his friend saw him swallow the treat he'd pretend to do the Heimlich maneuver — entertainment for the ogling others chewing real tasty bites with none of the filler these modern vendors pass as food on these hungry chumps whom the human-chain butchers helped get to the other side.

Things were not that simple anymore, he said, not anymore, so Stella should never cross the street, anymore, without holding his hand, his hand, not some stranger's hand even if the stranger wore the orange fluorescent band across his chest and even when her friends' parents said it was alright, as, through no fault of their own, they did not know how complex the world was, how fast one of their dear ones could wind up in the hands and then the house of a stranger. Later he spilled all, in a rare drunk Pabst spree, as they played Scrabble at the kitchen table and Stella was no more than eleven years old, about sex trafficking and world leaders who gathered on a no-place island to take their pick of the stolen girls. When Mary held up her hand he stopped, did not hand down the too-blunt facts. Still he saw her later through the cracked door and did not bid her cease her spying as he told her mother — and she needed to know this because this brutal world would be her inheritance — all about the stolen children, after he'd pulled the sheets up to her neck, his breath smelling of the sweet lemongrass he spooned into his evening teas, after he'd kissed her quick on the forehead in order to seal her there until sleep but as ever she took this as an invitation to rebel in however a miniature way, so that after he sealed her into bed with the cool of his kiss on her forehead, she stuck her ear to the door to hear all, the horrible things that she half understood.

Always he'd been an early riser. His father, who often pulled second-shift overtime, never rose before quarter to eight, when, all six children already awake for an hour and noisy as hell, he'd shoot up and start the day with complaints, as if they'd not been wrestling at the base of the old green couch where he'd fallen asleep, as now he was flipped into a frantic stance, comb-across against a receding hairline as he palmed a piece of bread, soggy instead of the well-done toast all the watching children knew he liked best, then kiss mom on the lips three times, once on each cheek before he patted the tallest kids on their mops and disappeared out the door.

But that world was gone. Wars and wrecking balls, assassinations, vain devices called innovative inventions. He bent to touch the amber frost and his fat pointer finger melted grass blades green. All flesh is grass. The rest of the lawn was like glass dyed sepia.

He stepped inside, let the new pneumatic screen-door closer prove it had been worth the investment. Its hiss never rose above a hush. He smiled and sat down at the dining-room table, which was covered with crumbs from the prior night's dinner: an apple crisp always had that aftermath, and Mary was getting tired earlier. He was glad, in fact, that she was even alive. Brown sugar clung and coated where the melted frost had whetted his finger. He tasted a crystal at a time, savoring as he splayed the newspaper open and slammed, on top of it, the iPad Mary bought him for his birthday. Once she'd found him here at three a.m., and muttered something about *Some retirement, you'll stress yourself to death, Soldier,* her nickname for him since forever. But what she didn't see was that then, as now, when his fingers swiped the screen's bright surface and he studied the scattered investments he had made in alternate coins that, it was said, could outlast Apocalypse, when he tallied the spikes in value which equaled a total that — projected — seemed wishful, impossible — all this was a stay against the terrible stress that was the sense of his own futility, the utter inconsequence of his capital gains and the ad-hoc militia that he'd been hosting in his basement against the world wide web of deception. Work, that is, *was* a kind of rest. He felt for the pistol he'd put into his pocket and returned it to its minuscule holster.

Down the street he saw another glowing rectangle — like a fantastic portal that linked the stranger to himself. He shut off his screen and slipped out the door, slipping the metal stopper against the pneumatic closer to keep even that low hiss from sounding. Here he was, the night's first intruder, an as-if inevitable arrival, and right at the point when he'd taken a breath and a swim through the Altcoin ether. Now Regan's best sprint was slow, even after all his recent practice, and by the time he reached the edge of the evergreen — a tree so giant you could camp underneath it — the kid was already in Andy Devingy's car — the third of the five-child family's cars, and the one always parked last at night in anticipation for the morning school run.

A hood hid the boy's face, but his frame was scrawny, impossibly young. Eleven, maybe, thirteen at the highest. How could his feet even reach the pedals? If he managed the gas, how would he switch to the brake? Or maybe at that age you forgot about stopping, conceived nothing more than the projectile rush — the raw exhilaration of acceleration.

He found, between pocket change, the hard red candy and held it out like trick or treat. As he held it out, a phone turned toward him, followed by a ski-masked countenance. The boaster was filming the episode to share, and now he would make his first social media cameo.

"Well good morning, young man, and you do look hungry. Would you like a piece of candy?" he asked.

A rush of cold metallic air whooshed under his turned nose, as a theft-protection club launched out the window and clanked against the evergreen's trunk. Regan straightened his shoulders then knelt and reached behind for the club, keeping his eyes locked on the kid who was stabbing a screwdriver keyhole and slamming a hand wrapped in blue latex (the kind of glove a surgeon used) against the steering wheel and saying *Shit* like a surreptitious prayer into the night. His mouth was covered by a Covid mask — baby blue, sucked in and puffed out — and three ivory stripes ran down his black sleeves but the middle strip seemed to veer out of its lane.

That wreck he witnessed the other twilight, the sinuous path of a stolen car that ricocheted down the dead street, hitting parked cars on both sides as it fled. The police operator sneered her tone and asked, when pressed, "What would you like me to do?" "I don't know." Regan was not amused. "I guess I had this strange notion that it was the business of police to prevent theft. To make arrests. To help criminals do time."

As Regan raised the club and leaned in like those drive-in restaurant waiters from a dead era, still with his other hand held out into the streetlight, so the sepia lit on the ruby crystal and painted it the color of donated blood — hemoglobin bursting with vitality, lent raw brightness from a good pair of lungs — the kid reached down into his pants and pulled out a gun which he pointed back.

"Kill you," he said, "I don't give a shit." But Regan saw the orange plastic stopper that tipped the gun and betrayed it as a toy. His wide smile was not forced. There was, thank God, no need to act, because he'd always been bad at faking it.

"This van belongs to a big family. Don't you feel bad for taking from them?" He waved away the gun's neon nozzle with lackadaisical swats he reserved for those houseflies that always seemed to spawn and swarm in midwinter when the sign of life was somehow not an irritation.

"Should have insurance if they haint fools, so the both of us can benefit. Been around this long and don't know how the money works? I get the car, they get new money. Shit. I may even be doing them a favor."

Regan bit his lip before beginning a lecture on the future uselessness of the American dollar, and as the car backed in mad zigzags down the driveway he paused, also, before smashing a window. He had decided against screaming on account of the Devingy children, who would flock to the big bay window and watch as who knew what unpredictable violence attended the theft of their family vehicle. Kids were no fools — they'd absorbed their parents' new worries, a force-fed recipe of pandemic and inflation — but maybe precisely because bad days were coming, because his mind's eye surveyed the way things unimaginable would visit this whole block, the way in fifty years the country could be no more than an occupied tributary of China flush with forced labor and microplastic-flooded carcinogenic farms, Regan clung all the more desperately to the possibility of preserving something like innocence.

Regan fumbled for his hummingbird pistol, the one with the imported German silencer, forgetting that he'd placed it back in the holster, and by the time he aimed and fired at the tires the kid had turned up the radio bass and the earth quaked in celebration. He did not, however, on further inspection — a gawk as the wheels wavered and swiveled — seem to know how to drive. The car lurched and braked like the last drunken guest — somebody's cousin? — at his parents' Polish wedding. (He had heard the story a thousand times, the drunk whose disappearance cast a pall across the wedding dance, whom they finally found running along the highway. Teeth grit, mouth full of spit, the man profusely refused a ride and ran back to the rented ranch and, thinking someone else's car was his, drove off into the stolen night.) At the corner the car pedaled away, by the faraway sound hitting sixty at least past the signs that said *Speed Limit 25 MPH* and SLOW DEAF CHILD and SELF-CARE IS NOT SELFISH.

He ran his fingers on the still hot ground, squatting and staring up at the windows. Not a stir in the sleeping house. How the parents had slept straight through the startling altercation he did not know, although at the last Neighborhood Watch meeting a new mom — Sally, or Celia? — had said she could not sleep without the sound machine loud, "Like crazy loud that should be keeping me wired, up, awake, but I need it, now, to shut it all out, all this crazy. I can't take it." Mumbling heads nodded, and after Wanda Räke said she'd taken to turning on ten hours of a digitally recorded diesel idling, that only this sound and no other had worked to cure her tossing and turning — strange, she knew, but it made her feel connected with her husband who drove freight trucks and was away five days out of seven, and it seemed to drive over the worries she brought to bed these days with the city going shot — to pot. To Regan's surprise, a series of others affirmed her strange practice and a rare feeling of heartfelt unison bound them all together. For a second, whatever differences they knew they had, most here too relied on white noise, soporific in the absence of an active police force, whose absence all agreed was silly, crazy. Melinda's nervous laugh launched the slurp of Coke she had just taken, and everyone — without condescension, with, rather, complete understanding — hurried to find a napkin to offer. A woman they'd all seen but whose name no one knew rushed to the sink and filled up a flower vase for lack of any at-hand cups, fed the slumped Melinda sips until she smiled and said "Oh my God, thank you, crazy. But with double-bolt and chain-lock it does — it has to, I guess — the trick."

He should bring a bag of popcorn to the Devingys, later in the day, evening even. And while the kids would fall upon the kernels he would pull Bill outside and detail what had happened in the godforsaken hours, likely best to leave out the raccoon, but the pistol was probably worth mentioning — a kind of goad to get his neighbor to buy one before there were none left, though he'd have to double-check the statistic about gun sales, since the onset of Covid, rising some sixty million purchases. God knew they were all going to need them.

He wished that smoking were still socially acceptable only because it offered little excuses for goodwill: please allow me to light that for you. I insist, take one, I'll put it on your tab. Whether what was gained by the health of the lungs was offset by the loss of these lubrications was a question more people should keep open. Bill would likely appreciate a Parliament; when he went to buy the popcorn he'd pick up a pack. *Did they even make that kind anymore?*

The basement window wells, semicircles of contained abysses, were barred by wrought iron tied with barbed wire. Silvered by the streetlights, their tips seemed like miniature spires of some children's story he'd read to Stella. He could see her scared smile as she reached across his belly for the faraway rib that eased her fear. All that purpose taken for granted then: the days felt like chores, time like something stolen from other doings that he'd then elevated and pinned up with importance, but which now he saw as dead specimens fastened to what had seemed like marble — permanent and stunning — but showed its shabby cardboard wear. God.

He felt his phone and the fantasy fled. The spires were spikes keeping his family safe, though the children, well, they weren't children any longer. Now the house was he and his wife. Mary, yes, but also her mother, who at ninety-two could not defend herself. He'd read somewhere about a rash of break-ins targeting shut-ins, people with no exit or even ambulation. That the crooks were now cowards made them more terrifying. Criminals with codes at least had limits.

Lately Regan had been half-taken by what Geoff Tailor had said. Two parts fascination to four hesitation. The rest of his friends were all in, but he kept one foot outside the door, into a room where the breathing was easier and claims could be tested before they were crystallized. Tailor had said many things, but one in particular won random head nods offered throughout the day, chin-tuck and rise like the rotated censors from which as an acolyte at St. Stanislaus he had dispensed pillars of incense. He had met Geoff in a dark rabbit hole of the internet, a rowdy room that was hard to find — you could only get there by holding your breath as you clicked through reeking, fetid, dirty laundry, female companions from Ukraine and Russia with toll-free numbers and clothes like lingerie. Neither Geoff nor Tailor were given names — not the legal, baptismal or affectionate nickname given by the anonymous but

229

supposedly famous hedge-fund-managing father he scorned. He went by the handle Emperor'sTailor, lived some fifty miles from Regan on his family's defunct corn farm, defunct except for a barn hand-retooled — through countless hours of online do-it-yourself tutorials — into a food dehydration plant, a vacuum packaging plant called Future Foragers, a business that made most of its money not on powdered beef stroganoff but on a water filtration straw designed by a former NASA scientist who'd died before he could take the product public.

After corresponding with Geoff for a decade, Ulrich Kennan had started addressing his hand-written letters as "My Second Son," because his biological one was a "parasite I can't bring myself to recognize as related bearer of the family name." He willed the water purification straw — GUARANTEED REMOVAL OF 99.9% OF BACTERIA AND PARASITES — to Geoff, whose dehydration operation was not just fledgling but flagging to a halt, because "I confess I spent my waking hours tracking every rabbit hole on the world wide web to figure the truth and do some fixing. I know what you're thinking. Lazy waste, da ta ta," he said, touching the tips of his fingers to the thirteen stars circling a frayed American flag that both decorated Regan's basement cement wall and helped keep the cold out. His finger paused at a triangular tear in the center of the circle, and though the touch of flesh on brick shocked him with an October chill he kept his finger there, leaned his whole weight on it as he turned over his shoulder and said: "There is," Tailor told them, "you know, I'm sure, a natural aristocracy. Some who rule us should be digging ditches and some digging ditches should be ruling. The world has never recognized what nature so obviously asserts again and again across the centuries, and so we get . . . medi-ocrity . . . mediocre compromise at best, at worst . . . chaos." He shoved away from the wall and, looking up at the circle of men slumped on barstools; at Eaves (Evan), standing, hands in pock-ets, waiting to pull out his fists if this asshole started assigning an assured place to the idiots who listened to him for free.

"What governs us now," Tailor went on, shifting his ground, "is not a man or even a minority of men in Washington, but a vast network of bureaucratic minions who, through millions of infinitesimal decisions, feed out fate like a cheap printer from a computer that reduces impossible complexities to categories that keep the machinery moving. Impossible to attack or assassinate.

"Any so-called president has to work against this standing army of armchair soldiers, split for sure but inclined to protect the vested interests of the process, survival over higher goals that in the past made the species proud. They say this is the New World we've won: less grandeur but also less violence. Less greatness but more decent livings for the many. But that's a mediocre mask that wouldn't pass muster at a Mardi Gras. Wage slavery is what it is. You're free . . . to kill yourself working to make somebody else a killing until, in your last decade on earth, warped and worn into a stupor, you can spend your free days having a few bottles or sniffs to unwind and another little pill to fall asleep at night . . ."

Dizzy with the exhilaration that follows when unspoken thoughts are named aloud by another, drunk on round after round of Geoff's statistics and solutions, Regan had swallowed his insecurities and risked inviting the former soldier into his basement. "Casual," he'd written. "T-shirts and beer kind of night." But Geoff had arrived in a finely cut brown Spanish-leather blazer. The man wasn't quite large enough for the thing, and when his layered flesh hung heavy on his face he looked almost ghoulish, pale and pathetic, but once he started talking that did not matter, for the virile agitations of his face gave voice to all the violence of their hearts, and to hear what he said felt like the healing they had sought through after-stroke surgeries on shunts and acid reflux pills and fists pounded on ping-pong tables, reeling over so much more than the missed ball that teased with twists and defied hands as it bounced into oblivion.

Before that night the weekly meetings had been bland, whimpering bottle rockets set off for kicks from mason jars preserved from childhood — jars that had held jam preserves made of Door County cherries picked at a gleaner's price. Forget Florida's arcadian retirements. Ping-pong and childhood at arm's length, revisited.

Even before Tailor piqued them Regan had been roused to gather the lost lineage of his life after he drove to D. C. on January 6 and felt a camaraderie he'd never even longed for because he had not known it could exist: shared thermoses of chicken soup (what the men kept calling "Mama's liquid gold") poured into hand-scalding dixie cups, downed like shots during the vigil campout beside the National Mall. The long ellipses from the yellow grass Ellipse to the red carpets of the Capitol Building. The ukulele country songs sung by a family of seven, descendants of coal miners who'd come covered in "the soot of our ancestors" — gray smudges dotted by darker crystals of obsidian that circled their sockets like thick spectacles and made the whites of their eyes luminous, fully awake in the half-light, all of them working checkout at White Castle or stocking shelves at The Dollar Store, except the father who drove circles in the hills to pick up tire and metal scrap and make more at the recycling place than he had been paid as manager of the McDonalds in Appalachia, West Virginia, woes put in words and then wrenched in the neck of the father for whom all else was harmony, echo — half his teeth gone but no whistle or lisp as he choked out the scales of dead yearning he had earned by living, the lyrics Regan first could not make out — all drawl — and he felt a foreigner to the level of loneliness compressed by the throat of Remington Jones, who launched into a tale of lost children and flour infested by moths and rats, a fat man complaining to a sad guitar's plucks that he'd "never eaten nothing but junk, but I ain't no punk; I know they keep us unfit on a diet of shit, keep our minds as slowed as the cows we rope."

He had learned late into the night, roasting an Iowa farmer's corn and offering an ear to an officer on horseback, watching the rear end of that animal in the impossible silver steak of dawn mirrored from the Reflecting Pool that may have been some obscure lake in a fairytale forest of his childhood. All of the gathered men who drove in his car had gone to grade school together — for their generation, a genuine glue — more than enough to cement instant connection and, whatever their differences, deliver loyalty.

Fun as the back-home basement sessions had been for the first year, they had assumed a worryingly repetitive formula of eating lotus and wishing locust plagues upon their leaders. (Had he learned that from Spengler or Tailor or someone else entirely?) And yet when Regan considered canceling, he could not pull the trigger: three nobodies' sense of meaning was at stake. Their meetings cut against their fear of what it meant that they were all getting old, that their main purposes were decades behind them and the main pleasures to be had from life consisted of replaying their late-night street-smart childhoods. Tailor had put him on to *Henry IV*, the pained exchange of Shallow and Silence, words he and his friends had now memorized:

> SHALLOW: The same Sir John, the very same. I see him break Scoggin's head at the court gate, when he was a crack not thus high; and the very same day did I fight with one Sampson Stockfish, a fruiterer, behind Grey's Inn. Jesu, Jesu, the mad days that I have spent! And to see how many of my old acquaintance are dead.
>
> SILENCE: We shall all follow, cousin.
>
> SHALLOW: Certain, 'tis certain, very sure, very sure. Death, as the Psalmist saith, is certain to all. All shall die.

Andy, divorced twice and childless, was dating a widow, but that was once a week lunch at a French café (Sally had always wanted to live in Paris but her first husband joined a cult and her mother needed her bedside attention after bridge games in the nursing home rec room). He had stayed on for years as substitute high school teacher: "Somebody's sick somewhere every day, so I'm basically full time, but stretched across the city, even sometimes in the poorest ones where the schools is basically juvenile prison, man, I'll show you the wound some kid gave me for a bad grade. But was all worth it because a few years of that and I'm set as far as benefits for the rest of my glorious life.") On the side now he managed portfolios when alimony ate up all of his money, part-time told others what to do with the wealth they earned by their moneyed time, even though he himself had never won at the market — he was always investing in high-risk packages that could deliver big if they ever came through — but that, too, was only a few hours a week: his company had paid him to virtually retire. Make way for a generation who had no nostalgia over the gold standard because they had started their lives well after it had been erased from the face of the earth. Eves had a son when he was twenty, but the boy and his mother lived in California and he had never been granted custody rights, so he followed his son from afar in the papers — high-school football clippings — and, later, on the web, but staring down that spitting image he had never been able to speak a word to left his liver overtaxed. He had never dated after that. Eaves could laugh for hours straight and always, even if he wore a frown, the glimmer of hilarity perched at his eye edges and dared the world to turn solemnity into satire. Flesh wrinkled by a lifetime of jokes.

Sterne — his mother-in-law loved the man, had even, planting a kiss on his cheek, come quite close to the man's mouth — Sterne had confessed to Regan several suicide attempts. It ran in Sterne's family, depression. But still Sterne refused medication, having gone through a gauntlet of therapists who had failed him or whom he had failed: "Not a one among them had any sense of humor. Eaves does me more good than ten of 'em put together. I would fill Eaves' bank account in a second before investing another quarter in a quack." Every Tuesday Sterne rang the bell repeatedly and when Mary opened it he'd present her with a stack of the greasiest pizzas in the city, heirloom recipe packed and baked with the ancient immigrant lard of Costello's, an old-fashioned joint where the dough was still kneaded by a Nonna who wore her head in a red plaid wrap and the tables were covered by those checkered cloths of red and black that suggested roulette but were also — or therefore? — romantic. As the owner — a woman Sterne had "seen" for a decade when he was in his twenties and thirties — Martha made her back-slapping rounds between the Roman Catholic saint candles, heavy on Italian martyrs and matrons — "Lost Cause" St. Rita on every other table — and Mary Mother of God looking down opposite a hack's faithless Mona Lisa whose fraudulent smile did Mary's minor perfections good: all this graced the tables and gave just enough light. All of this indistinct to Regan's sore eyes, because until his son turned the paid-off family deli into Professor

Hemp, recently, he had spent his retired afternoons attuned to the ambient, earthenware tea lights used at his son's old coffee shop job at Rochambeau, the two-story old school coffee house that featured a Bullshit Sandwich comprised of deep-fried vegan delights. It was actually quite good with a cup of coffee, "No thank you to the fancy lattes, I'll take mine black as me heart, thank you," but his son, embarrassed, stopped waiting on him when he came to say hello and chew the news, and the other barista did not laugh, even the first time, he made the black-heart joke. She pointed at the protest poster featuring a lynched police officer.

So many evenings since retirement Regan and Sterne had spent stretching mozzarella and swapping advice which fell short as if by design so that they could do this again next week. When whatever consolations were given failed to solace or solve, neither harbored disappointment but one or the other would order a second bottle of Merlot and every time Eaves's joke about "black hearts revived by the red" came with so much lid-closed feeling — lung-rattled voice, loosed tear ducts, head tilted not in mockery but in absolute recognition — that they'd laugh, then make as if to shake hands, but unsure how to do so directly they'd fake a pretend arm-wrestling match before one of them welled over and the other (as happened twice) had to signal the waitress and ask for water, "These packets of red pepper, the man took too many," but when she looked down she saw all of them sealed and her lips remained so also, keen to let them keep their secret. Before retirement, for fifty years, they had only met there maybe once per annum, but as the decades ticked past like garish canceling Xs scribbled fast on flipping calendar pages, the meals seemed like many, like a single supper that had been there forever and might be, too, so long as they lived. It was there — at Costello's — that they cooked up the notion to rally their diaspora buddies from grade school, gather in Regan's old coal room (his basement, if small, was bigger than the others', and much bigger than Andy's who had none).

Every Tuesday, to please Mary, he also came armed with little plastic octagons filled with iceberg lettuce that always looked a little watery and remained untouched for the duration of the evening.

Sterne's attention to Regan's health — which was always uneasy since the mild stroke — spoiled in the corner and became fodder for rodents, though even the mice didn't devour; the next morning only a few edges were gnawed on the waste pile that made the compost fertile.

Most of those who'd turned down Regan's invitations had grandchildren.

Andy, divorced twice, nearly remarried, had wasted his teens in a lazy rebellion that he could not laugh about when jibed. After he and his "hippie wife" returned from three successive stints in the Peace Corps to a corpse of romance and a pregnancy, he threw himself into high school teaching, reading voraciously against the alternate reality that went by the name of American History, hating the Empire with a patriot's pain. He smiled at Tailor's talk of clean water because from his days as an idealist he knew overmuch about water scarcity and had handed out straws to indigenous Ethiopians on his most successful humanitarian mission. Marshaling statistics that, if outdated, still illustrated lingering worldwide crises, Andy, who hid the little limp brought about by his hip replacement, would savor each sip of his Pabst with a sigh.

Andy was a handyman who had fixed up the coal room until it looked not only livable but like a second home for the old friends. He always arrived two hours early and sat, FBI sunglasses on, parked halfway down the block, in his idling white van, idling, idling. Once, given his suspicious profile, a neighbor — Regan suspected the new couple whose house was kitty corner to Howard Glass's — had called non-emergency police who found — Andy, half-crippled, handcuffed against the cold white paint — several explosive materials covered in the trunk by blue painter's tarps but were more interested in the unpaid alimony Sterne and Eaves and Regan had pooled to pay off in a single check.

Tailor had told them that though he was sympathetic to their "complacent inaction," they had fallen for the exact lie "the elites" had manufactured: theirs was "another America, passing if not already past, the family photo album of flyover country — the Midwest's dead consensus, admirers of —" and here he looked at

236

Regan with a delicious smile of impossible pleasure — "President Reagan. Yes," he'd counseled, "you can drift toward the grave for the next decade or two, hating what your country has become, strewing memories like flowers around the headstones of your grave . . . or you can form a brotherhood already felt, give definition to a movement that is already existent but, scattered, is satellites without a center. No big figurehead to figure it all out for us, a.k.a., let us down when he feels the seat of power and forgets all his campaign promises.

"Gramsci got it right," he said, and Eaves in his stare, Eaves who summoned a nod although the name and notion were wholly unfamiliar. "As usual, we abandoned the enemy's tactics before we even dared begin because they seemed — on account of his being the enemy — bad, poisoned. But that means they won! Their long march through the institutions that rule the masses has led to total domination. Mind control, even. Watch some poor schlep at a parent-teacher association meeting, making some mild-mannered criticism of whatever the manufactured Marxists are serving up in the cafeteria this year. Watch him booed out of the room, almost wrung around the throat for daring raise his right — not his left — hand.

"The age of committees and meetings is over. The parliamentary patience has made pansies of us all. Does a single one of your rulers *represent* you? Have you ever received more than a boiler-plate of bullshit from contacting your representative's office, a.k.a. an artificial-intelligence intern, who lifts his automaton chin ponderously from an online game of chess and clicks a form letter that says Vox *populi, vox dei*? Believe me, I know, it's hard to let the illusion go. It's hard to accept that martial law's a strait-jacket around us in the name of security. But the true victor of the election will soon be set in his rightful seat and then the oval office won't be vacant anymore, filled as it is with an empty mind.

"Have you taken a hit?" Tailor asked abruptly, standing up, his leather blazer creaking as he removed it from his sleeves and lifted his shirt to reveal a red gash — in the swerving, curved shape of a salamander — under his left rib. "Rubber bullet on my bare

237

chest. I'd already been stripped at this point, see, and they can't stop coming for me. Like my sunless pale body was supposed to be submissive, white-flag surrender, but no. I —"

"I was — we were, all of us — there on January 6," Regan said calmly, reclining, sipping from a brown bottle of Blatz, standing (he was taller that Tailor) and continuing: "Can taste the mustard gas to this day. Projectile landed right on my foot. Couldn't move 'cause of the crowd." He hunched his shoulders and pulled his hands together. "Loud as hell — twenty times that firecracker, Eaves, we set off at school — remember?"

"But the police were not as scary as the principal!"

Tailor's left eye squinted in the light while his right one widened against the brightness, incredulous. "You, who were there. That *you* could think that day was a joke, young man?" Geoff was at least twenty years younger. "I saw too many people close to die that day, saw the law oppress instead of order, watched sincere folks exploited for decades dare to shout out only to get the shit kicked out of their deplorable hides. Blast dispersion grenade deafened my friend Phil. He can't hear his daughter when she cries, when he tickles her belly no sound of laughter."

Regan waited to be sure their guest was finished.

"Eaves is good. He gets the seriousness. Why else would he be here?" But under Tailor's gaze he doubted his friends, embarrassed for the first time by their barely-hidden amateurs' ignorance, and he was unable to confirm the question by risking eye contact with the class clown. He saw that the nails he had counted and sorted and had meant, earlier, to carefully and systematically distribute throughout the tower of little plastic drawers, were still balled in piles on the sawdust that coated the workbench. That fresh invigorating scent that came when the blade bit into the wood.

Slowly, like a flag unfurling over an aristocratic balcony in the old country, Geoff tossed aside his suit, unbuttoned his high-cut shirt, and let the T-shirt that said Black Flag show.

"At least I'm not flying the white flag of surrender. At least my heart's still ticking," he said. "Man next to me got spooked by an explosion. Same blast that deafened my friend caused a 'cardiac event' in an old man, a veteran from Virginia who'd survived Korea. Call it like it is. 'Cardiac event'? Saps the thing of all feeling. We need to restore dignity to the dead, not let the narrative fixate on a few crazy performers with painted faces and stolen lecterns. They weren't the spirit of the movement. They don't . . . they don't speak for *us*." And for the rest of the evening he swerved like a Blue Angel over a city, shocking and awing them into rapt happiness — they had not laughed together so freely in forever — even though he mainly gave names to their grievances, locking eyes, winning knowing nods, appealing to common-ground ancestry and bemoaning the demoralizing "flyover fallout" and the faraway regimes that rewrote reality out of the country's history. His earlier gibes seemed strategic agitations to rouse Regan and his friends from slumber, to stir their righteous anger even if he became the initial target. By midnight Eaves and Sterne were convinced that a neighborhood militia was in order. Andy kept his opinions mum, but the way he spat his tobacco suggested he was plotting something bigger than anything anyone had blueprinted aloud that night.

After Geoff left late, very late, or early — Mary was opening the upstairs blinds and clucking her tongue in sync with the coffee drip — Regan and his friends tossed their ping-pong balls into the trash, or crushed the hollow air from their centers with carpal tunnel fingers that suddenly had the strength to destroy. Dried mouths muttered "my God" and Eaves said "this just went to the next level." Although he pointed his finger at the future and mapped out a series of future steps by which the informal cadre could emerge into the daylight, Tailor never returned to The Underground (the name he dubbed their meetings, which previously had just been called Tuesday Nights). He left them as a gift a framed cover of *Time* magazine that featured Francisco Franco in green military garb, a smoldering city of darkness to his left and some sort of restored ruins to his right: smiling, kindly though not unwilling to kill, he hugged himself.

Geoff had traveled in his twenties to exotic locales, to places so secret he kept them quiet from his wife and children and some he hid even from himself. He'd done whatever the C. I. A. said to do, mainly removing the most wretched from the earth or training locals to conduct their own coups. Often the regime change he'd helped along resulted in a replacement far worse than the incumbent, and so he'd cultured a peculiar sympathy disclosed, to date, to nearly no one: there was such a thing as a good authoritarian, or at least a bad one worth letting be.

Within a week the basement wall was lined from end to end with shelves made from orange, red, and brown milk crates held together with black clamps and tightly tied fishing wire. The THEFT OF CRATES SUBECT TO PENALTIES engraved on each had been covered with the taupe sackcloth of emptied potato bags, and strips jutted out, indicating an alphabetical order to the what Eaves dubbed, smiling, "The Apocalyptic Kit." Nozzles of pistols stuck out from a canister Sterne had labeled *Bread and Butter*.

Regan watched as a fog blotted the clear lines of lawns and streets. Blended with the frost, lit by the day's first blue which pierced the sky above the rising sun — fierce like a spoonful of cobalt poppy extract cooked on high heat in a silver spoon — the world sighed, too tired to wake up, but wake up it must and would while he slipped stealthily through the ungreased hinges whose measly protest he wore out with patience as he dipped into his gaping house. Then, the front door blown wide open once he was safely in — WAKE UP! — he bounded the steps to check on Mary, who slept like the Civil War dead at Shiloh, pulling the appalling cover — that color, like a watered-down urine, he had always hated — over her chin, for her fingers had curled around it on her chest as if she was trying to lift it but failed, the patchwork quilt of an evening sky that she'd made for their daughter when she graduated college and who forgot to take it with her down to Chicago, not out of meanness but just plain negligence, oblivious to the inheritance her parents were desperate to foist into her suitcase after she discarded the thing from her lap and left it in the drafty living room the day she left for her teaching assignment.

Strange how becoming Mary's wrinkles were; there was a time when he'd dreaded their appearance, when these slashes of age seemed an affront against a bond between them that had begun when both were so young so that Mary was — he had told her once — "the music of my misspent youth" — and she was supposed, he smiled (*stupid!*) to stay young too for good. But when he watched the crisscross at the center of her forehead, the permanent blue that pocketed her eyes, the faded pockmarks from that decade of sickness, he had to bite his lip to not say *Thank you, thank you, thank you for being, for being there love, my love, my love*, this even though when he saw her later arisen, assuming her standard perch in the living room he would hardly give a nod or a notice of her habitual furniture presence as she hunched there in the rocking chair, catching the daylight as she read from her Bible — a new practice since Stella left, or was it since Jacob started Professor Hemp?

A garbage truck hinge creaked below and she snorted slightly before turning her round shoulder over, evening's last cover still shrouding her body even as the sky was warming, yellowing with the mellow, sleepy sun Stella loved at the end of the pier where they went for vacation — a campground with cabins of cedar wood and hardback beds that no one could sleep on, so they stayed up late trading cards on the pier bench, tossing cans of baked beans, potatoes, Carnation milk into the fire's hot ashes, and Jacob would wake to catch throwaway fish, the thrill of the hook winning out against release. Jacob would make a very good trash man, a good paying job compared to centuries past, the rewards for sorting and hiding others' refuse growing in proportion as the rare places to put the world's unwanted waste diminished, required relocation and reburial. Jacob, he knew, was totally lost — not hopelessly, but there would come a great cost to the years he was spinning like a child's top, careless of wear and of where he would land.

He pretended weightlessness as he crept downstairs and leaned against the thawing window, wiping the gray away so he could watch the world. A man who wore a yellow neon cover like the sturdy old chasubles of his childhood priests cleaved to the edge of the compacting abyss, astride a trembling hydraulic lift. He lifted his hands as a signal and a coworker handed him white plastic bag, an overstuffed circle that dripped some substance the sight of which betrayed the smell. Well paid, at least. Worth it. Well paid?

Well, better be. He would check the average salaries with Andy. He turned away and when he returned found that the trash ritual was complete and in its place stood a bundled woman in black and blue who carried a bundle of something or a baby and a navy backpack packed with a fullness — yes, a baby's face peeked from the swathe that looked like a durable colored cobweb. She hesitated at the end of their walkway that intersected with the public sidewalk which stretched out like arms in either direction — but did the arms point or did they gather? A baby. Whose gathered baby. The winter hat she wore was royal blue, and the thick, flipped-up brim looked warm but wet, drenched enough to catch a croup, he'd bet, a baby. The baby. Surely her body warmed the baby's and maybe the baby even heated her back, so long as she consumed enough caloric content — he would take her to the deli and saw off a foot of challah and the spiced lamb meat she had always loved to eat. He did not own a deli anymore. Her brother, respectable drug dealer, had taken over. By what justice, by whose will had *he* been given the delicatessen? Whose baby? Whose body? He had not seen her without makeup for years, many decades, maybe since thirteen. She must, born in eighty-one, be, in front of him, forty-one. He would fortify her baby with milk, if old enough with all the oatmeal he had made. He would open the Apocalypse Kit for a laugh and pour scalding water on the dried lamb dust that promised "Tastes Just Like Gyros." Hero. A baby. But though she looked over her shoulder and Regan followed her faraway searching, no father was forthcoming on the horizon. The hero — who? He held his heart. Simple acid reflux from a suddenly tensed stomach, or the final farewell he had felt, like fate, was waiting with impatience to take him away — to bury him irretrievably like a lost dog bone?

Suffering appeared across her face. Yet a big smile broke through the frostbitten mouth, lifted her cheeks into rounded coals, kept in the fire for these years and stoked as she saw him peering through the fogged-up window, his hot air renewing the dividing gray which he repeatedly wiped away, away — in a circle, almost an aureole.

. . .

Like the Giotto in Chicago, the Wedding Procession of Mary and Joseph, a picture she'd stared at many hours after she finished her time at Cabrini's and waited out the alderman run and pregnancy. Fixed rituals forever lost but fascinating nonetheless. Not a sublime altarpiece or fresco but a picture on blue paper drawn with brown ink, oxidized with white lead, simple halos around the wedding couple's heads like a child's sketch of an ovular orbit — nothing like the stunning rings of Saturn she'd seen through a telescope at twelve years old — Mary's hands around her ovaries, both of them solemn for such a feast, mortals like angels blowing long, thin trumpets toward wherever God was or wasn't.

She had walked four miles with the still-slung baby — the distribution of weight was a miracle, her back was without ache all the while — but her ratty blue backpack had ripped a block back, and when, like a foreign wanderer washed up on a familiar shore, she knocked on the door five minutes before five, Dad had opened his mouth the way he did when the Brewers' pitcher threw intentional balls, walking the batter instead of risking a home run.

"Dad," she said, "you're all dressed up."

"Yes," he went absent, "I was waiting, the best, waiting for — oh my God, Stella."

As he peeled off the suit instead of a waistcoat he wore a camouflage vest underneath. She wanted to ask but the way he discarded it — like a stiff casualty — on the floor, kept her silent.

"Sit, my God, Stella, sit. Sit. Where did you — what can I — what can I do? My God. Welcome. Here. My God."

His stomach stretched a sleeveless white T-shirt, revealing patches of grayed chest hair that when she'd last seen it at the lakefront cottage lacked even a wisp of wear. He gave a glare as if to someone over her shoulder so that she turned around to see who was there and boo it was no one, a blooming maple that was red with the final leaves of fall and a string of short-circuit streetlights that flickered off and on like her own heart as she turned back with a kind of jump, a shocked step up toward her shaky-handed dad who, steadying himself on the staircase railing, could not speak more than the syllable "Home!" but whose arms were open to the baby she'd brought back with her without explanation or warning — the child he received with a heavy exhale like a reversed vacuum that blows out instead of sucking to itself all filth, a quick sniff through his reddened nose, a startle of tears he completed in private as he retired to the living room faltering with dignity until he fell into the rocking chair's arms.

The dull navy chair of genuine leather — Mary's place, not his, by habit creaked like a dying man's final wish quietly, as if pleased to receive him, happy to help. "Happy to help," he said, the right nouns and verbs defiant, in hiding, his blood flow halted, in a riot. Not even a clue in the crossword margin to name whatever was happening here.

Mom. Stella had not seen mom for two years or three, *three years*, but the span felt far longer, as if the hiatus was lengthy enough to require the small talk and little manners by which you could tiptoe toward the same bridge's center, suspended by boards and rope, no more, above the typical torrent below. The mom she had seen was always already worn. When you leaned in for a hug and "Hello" she could emit a quick but nervous hiccup, a chuckle choked back by a reverberating wheeze, but always it seemed the instant departure was part of a larger, louder implication, a guilt by association with her past of countless offenses in a list she kept numbered against the infinity, the impossibility of ever calculating total hurts, wounds and wrongdoings not communicated directly but tallied and tacked to the dark stucco ceiling where she could review them without craning — for convenience — her neck. The face an advertisement in aversion, confrontation being the mouth of Avernus, avoiding locked eyes, accused you always most of all for leaving *per se*, for the loneliness your departure was feeding, but the whole time you lingered in the living room and hallway, waiting for something you said to scale the wall and light the wick that went out — when? Pale ghost eyes painted hazel, unheated like the gray-edged coils of an electric stove left unplugged. Virile vengeance making violent love to quietist inaction — the self-pleasure of suspended forgiveness kept dangling by the pleasure of pain. Delectation of sadness, Blake called it. Off, the *we'll leave the* light *on* welcome which had never been switched on to begin with: missing a bulb and wires and a switch, but the walls were there, well-kept, intact, and the door was thick, of heavy wood striated by iron crossbars and secured by deal bolts and latch locks and padlocks and several chain locks whose sags rested on the stuck-out knob of a single barrel bolt.

But — and she had to repeat this, here, as her mother reached out stiffened arms like dangling cranes over abandoned construction (a sigh Stella had seen several times already on her walk from the Intermodal Station), as she held her biological daughter in a mechanical embrace whose apparent aim was well-meant, convincing simulacrum that refused and deflected the ready risk of the actual flesh-on-bone touch of two souls — mom had not always been so. Not just those flashes of almost frantic delight as she took out the special kettle for popcorn set aside for Saturday nights, humming Handel and Bach and Beethoven louder and louder as the seeds started sizzling, and even louder as hundreds of little white clouds gathered and stormed against the metal cover and shoved it over the top and mom, sidestepping with a smile, snatched the discus like the Athenian athlete in the children's book she'd read a thousand times to her and her brother before bedtime — before Nonna took over that task and switched to second-hand cardboard bibles and saint books (Jacob loved the unforgiving lion's teeth opened around Daniel's grinning mouth, the prophet's incisors far sharper than the dangerous animals who ruled the den) — and as she finished, poised, with a perfect plié, the whole family was head tilted back for the first time since the prior Saturday and the pent-up pressure of so many skirmishes rose like the steam from the special pan and dad hit the switch of the fan that sucked the exhaust above the stove and sent from their lungs the poison byproduct of their family's special meal, the rattling fan so loud it hurt but soon the smoke and the burnt aftertaste was as far away in some enemy country. Back there somewhere was a good decade — or was it only a year? — where mom's mouth was not taut, uptight, and the lines around her brow were not bent like a scale whose both sides weights had broken the pulleys, angled in

245

the opposite direction of happiness. But as this surety was felt more than factual and the duration of that reprieve happened once upon a time, during childhood's strange sense of duration, she called the whole thing into question: maybe the mom she insisted had existed once and therefore — please God — could come back in the future was, on the contrary, a cooked-up character, the mother she had been reaching out for forever only to find this limp embrace that passed for return, for homecoming, for family.

Her mother did not acknowledge with her lips or even with a lift of the eyes the baby Stella had brought back with her.

Mom left the room "to fix you something," and as she passed Stella staggered toward Dad, suddenly tired, and he squeezed her hand, "Home," he said, "You're here," and he rose, "Let me help your mom for a minute."

. . .

Mom reappeared with a water. "Ice?" she asked, and though it was cold, Stella had a sudden penchant for ice, but she shook her head *no* because the order would delay this whole ordeal she should have seen coming but had failed to imagine.

How this woman was the daughter of Nonna was a difficult question. Usually Stella chalked it up to the pendulum swing, the counterpoint of generations, but from a few scraps her mom had tossed down on the table over poker-face games it seemed that Nonna — whom she adored — had said some things that did permanent damage and had never apologized or even seen what harm she had left behind. One of the family's specialties was being able to nurse a wrong done years ago — just enough to keep it on life support but never with sufficient fuel for rage or anything close to outright conflict.

But she hadn't seen the mom who trembled, now tentatively, now terribly — not the onset of Parkinson's, no — the mom who let out a frank and violent gasp through an unconvincing, bad-tempered smile and then jerked back too late to retract this reel that revealed her real feelings. Stella knew this was not how the family reunion was supposed to play out and she did not know then (but she would much later, keeping vigil at mom's obscenely warm deathbed) that her mom too had been doubly stunned by another revelation in twenty-four hours — as if the end time's horses were hurrying history to what felt like its finale — and all she could think when Stella showed up was this was not how this was supposed to play out, the homecoming mom had planned for a summer day with tulips to pick and hand her with a smile, the kind she had always found difficult to forge, but this would be instant, spontaneous, no fraud but a full-mouth O of delighted disbelief. Oh God but the evening before mom's baby sister Janille — fourteen years younger — had called from Southern California and the baby they had adopted late in life after countless fertility interventions had been dropped or shaken or something (she wouldn't say) by her second husband Ron, a big-rig driver who delivered air filters for the massive lungs of hospital buildings. But she would say that now, near-brain dead, baby was suckled by a ventilator on a high floor at arm's length from its parents now under investigation — part of the reason Janille and Ron had won the child in the eyes of the court was that neither had any record of abuse or even a speeding ticket to their names — though now it turned out that Ron had a felony from twenty years prior. That was all Janille would say, except "Don't come see me, I need to talk to my lawyer and if it works out I'll fly to Milwaukee tomorrow, I do just have this horrible need to *be there* with you, to be by mom but not tell her about this because it would if not kill her then it'd show up psychosomatic in a swell of arthritis that would cripple her permanently."

But homecoming was supposed to be sparrows swirling symmetrical in a DNA helix and fresh lettuce from the frost-bitten garden. But instead mom leaned against her own misplaced reeling and cried into Stella's shoulder as if to mark the occasion of her return but instead with visions of the comatose baby whose pictures her sister had been sending her all day, all black and blue, too photorealistic to deny, her stupid and brilliant and sympathetic sister who had a way of picking the bad ones and so, it seemed, did her own daughter, which meant what about her, which meant failures unnoted coming back home to, to — roost. She mumbled

247

with a warmth at once humiliated and desperate to *be there*, "Good to have you home, honey," nodding at the baby, "And who do we have here? And whose little one are you caring for, Stel?" as she backtracked and gestured her daughter to follow and lifted the recycling in a thin white bag — "Just a moment, this needs taking out, the truck will be here any minute and we might as well get this in can before they come."

The white plastic bag, thinner than a prophylactic, broke in the hallway and soon all three were picking up empty cans of cheap beer that had been smashed with precision by her father's steel-toed work boots in the basement. Mom followed Dad to the door and watched him as he hurled what remained of the stacked cans wrapped in broken white and then ran the container on wheels to the curb to the sound — his wife was eerily right — of the recycling truck two blocks down.

The Russian Blue made little figure eights between Stella's and the chair's legs, the gray hide glistening purple where it caught the cast rays of the chandelier.

"Prince, his name is. He likes you," her Mom said. Stella wanted her to press on, here: *Someone else apparently liked you too, got you pregnant. How could you...?*

Before she had left for Chicago she and her mother had little to discuss, but she distinctly recalled a walk they had taken around the manmade lake in Menomonee, a quarry now emptied but once filled with limestone that gave first shape to the founding city hall and schools, Main Street apartments that seemed Parisian, that widened the eyes when you walked beneath them. Against the efficiencies that had replaced them they always inevitably seemed condescending in a neighborhood made of postage-stamp houses that did little more than keep the cold out — *and that was enough* was the general consensus. The limestone apartments that had emptied the quarry with their European feel seemed out of place in the country of bowling leagues and Bavarian pretzels dipped into big mugs of decent beer. The surface of the manmade lake was silver, and it glimmered like the scales of the perch that populated it. Sprawled across a thick red blanket whose expert weave was

248

textured and pleasing to the passing caught eye — her mother's elbow knocking at her rib recollected her to a level of propriety she had forever failed to fulfill — a Hmong family perched at a cliff and her mother mumbled "That baby's going to fall," but the mother who suspended the infant in a wrap, utterly oblivious to danger, dangled her feet down from the ledge and even leaned in the direction of the poles that her husband and son stretched over the lake, the boy giving his a jut as if a few inches further — whatever the risk — would finally find, as it did before their eyes, a big enough fish for Sunday dinner. Stella joined in their clapping as her mother's quickened step and hung head put a familiar distance between them.

But then later, over leftover popcorn, she and her father, like a long game of checkers, each opponent moving a piece per fifteen-minute increment, mom and dad discussed children living at home, and her mother, mentioning other families whose children seem to never leave, effused sweat on her feverish forehead as she said, with difficulty and needlessly loudly — how proud she was of Stella for "hacking it in a hard world out on your own."

Her mother said she would be right back — she had forgotten the orange juice, and Seven Swans was open now and she would be back to "hear all about it."

Like a skilled pianist her mother played a variation on this theme for an hour, each iteration announced as something original, and Stella almost admired, at times, what she could not help calling genius.

Her father rocked the baby in silence after Stella refused to repeat the same story to her mother again later. Ten times he seized Jason and lifted the slumped child up by the armpits, whispering the word tike with wondrous relish as he shook his balding acorn head.

Later, at Stella's request, the three of them congregated in a kitchen cooled by an awful draft of officiousness. Regan made jocose remarks, none of them memorable, none of them funny, to try and breathe some warmth into the room.

"Mom. Dad. It's Thanksgiving day. Why aren't we eating a meal together?"

"Honey, we stopped having Thanksgiving once you and Jacob stopped coming." Her mother looked hurt but a drop of bitterness did not taint her words.

Mary heated a full bronze kettle of tap water run through the filter. Cryptosporidium had almost killed her. She fetched and set out Nonna's saucers and cups, alabaster with blue flowers that stretched from the shoots to the roots from the rim to the circles, that caught the splashed teardrops of water so delicately poured but sloshed in spite of it over the silver lined rim. She spooned in Carnation tea until Stella's water turned a bloody scarlet, then served Regan, and last herself. Thirsty, she waited for Stella to sip, and winced when her daughter burned her tongue which she played off fast by sticking it out, winning a grin from baby Jason. Mary only sipped when Stella sipped — though Regan, indifferent to these niceties, was on his third cup by the time they finished one, though when he noticed he made a face, a jocose mockery of his own gluttony, and taking the baby he said "Please now tell us. I'm dying to know news of your life." When Mary nudged him he added "Your lives."

Stella parsed and selected the hours, censoring so as not to upset her mother, salting with humor to keep her father happy, and when she finished three hours later mom said "I'm proud of you," and when Stella did say "For what? For screwing myself into such a fix?" her mother continued "But Nonna, upstairs — she sleeps, on pain meds, half the days now — when she finds out, if she remembers you, will guilt you straight into heaven." And she tip-toed over, relishing her tolerance, kissing Jason's thick black brow.

"What's his last name?" Regan asked and she said, "Well, legally, he's a Stęskni. On his birth certificate. On the health insurance card."

"Jason Stęskni," he said, musingly. Realizing the new life shared the initials of his own son's name, he said, "Welcome to the family," and walked across the creaky kitchen floor to bed.

· · ·

Full bladder, too much tea, Mary waited to see if the feeling would fade but the pain grew so she stumbled slow down the hallway to the bathroom and sat on the toilet for a good hour, playing reels of Stella's coldness, even as an infant even when nursing she never nuzzled, just took what she needed, her eventual birthday cards the epitome of duty, quick exercises in minimal respect which she never lost — that respectful demeanor — even when we turned all attention to Jacob and forgot about Stella for a few years there, did not forget but tried to rile her to reach her, to help her stand when instead she was walking just fine on her own and all our efforts in vain if not useless then trapped in, stuck in the game of polite tug of war forever even now I do not know you but I ask you from out of gross ignorance forgive me.

. . .

Where is she now? Regan rolled over where the impress of Mary's body stayed warm but even there his limbs were cold so he fumbled, first from the bed edge, kneeling, next when he could not pull it down, stood and seized Mary's hanging bathrobe, upset bullshit as he walked down the hallway and heard the water trickle, saw the light, continued past to the laptop sleeping, balanced as if waiting for him on the banister.

Election *interference + voting machines* he typed and scrolled to the last article he had left unfinished, shaking his head at the hard facts — they would call them conspiracies, but the machines were victims of not-unverified manipulation — circumstantial evidence unverified evidence his nerve ends numbed he clicked and followed the trail of documented stolen ballots the photographs of votes dumped eleventh hour in burlap sacks she flushed he rushed back down the hallway and pulled the quilt — abrasive like a burlap bag — over his head and played dead in bed a fraud a little fucking fraud Dominion machines the genuine article fraudulence he heard her steps her flatulence as she entered the room he pinched his nose the fraudulence they'll tell us all the shit they did is innocent like sweet incense.

. . .

— a room, her own, calm and stable not immortal but as-if immobile, as if it had kept out the world ever since the beginning of

251

a time not her own, the room where God rested on the seventh day, after he slipped out the rib like loneliness, forever bringing presence out of absence for all, not for some, for some, not for all, not at all for the fallen born who flail, born bipeds crawling across earth's face to finally be known, and she saw herself wretched but not forever, the wretched of the earth faraway, another world, away, away, and here she slept for a full day — her mother feeding formula to Jason who spit out the better part of the bottle, her father rocking the hard-breathing baby whose hyperventilation led him at last to ascend the stairs and wake his daughter, *sorry so sorry so sorry, Stella we tried to let you catch all needed sleep,* and waking felt less real than dreaming —

. . .

She woke in the wild, relentless moonlight, wrapped in a red sleeping bag wet with sweat. Thirsty, she tiptoed down the stairwell that ran from the upper unit attic all the way to the basement. Halfway down she heard her parents' hushed shouts. Listening up the stairs for Jason in her own decades-old crib and hearing nothing, she slipped into the shadows, alert to a confidence she should not have heard, seeing now a scene that made her head hurt and she held the spot where the migraine came, where the ache never seemed to dissipate fully.

Dad's eyes sparkled in the dark. Mom moved and the night light colored the room yellow. She lifted, with difficulty, her shaking arm to touch Dad's sore shoulder, a movement which separated the seam of her nightgown. Looking down at the freckled flesh of the breasts that had fed Stella not just for nourishment but countless times for comfort, too, she said:

"What did we do wrong?"

"Did we? Do wrong? Does it have to come down to that, does everything?"

"Otherwise it's nobody's fault."

"His fault. Or hers. If not ours."

"Nobody's fault. No-fault divorce! What makes these mistakes possible in the first place!"

"Okay. Okay."

"Okay. Yes. Okay. Nice. Regan. So neither you nor I are to blame. Sounds nice. And flat silly."

"Mary. You think I made mistakes in the way I raised her. Say it. Spell out, specifically, what you hated that I did, did not do, whichever or both."

"God."

"No show here. No bravado. It's been a week since you could look me in the eye. Since she came back, I'd say. Around then you stopped."

"I don't —"

"Please. Seriously — just say it."

"Regan, we always were close when the kids were young and I then thought that good, so so good, but how did we do that? We paired up against our own children — their faults never provoked by us, never reflections of our own failings. Don't you remember the exonerations, how many evenings forgiving ourselves our sins, sitting in this room and numbering theirs. Always ungrateful, spoiled children given everything anyone could want or need set against the implied perfect of parents who gave and gave and asked only to be graded on effort, as if —"

"As if exertion alone was everything, all."

"Yes, yes! You see it! Regan. You see it! Don't lose me."

"But so say it then now. What you hate now what you hid from me then?"

"Anyone could have an outsider come into the home like a — what is it that when they go into some tribe and study them like animals, rituals and all that — anthropologist! I'm getting old, God, for my crimes, all the messes I never cleaned up —"

"Mary, you've *got to stop* making a martyrdom where there simply need not be one. If we're going to have this conversation I need you to stop exaggerating."

"Alright, meanwhile mister anthropologist. Just because they're foreign, not adapted, they could report on all the flaws."

"And virtues."

"What?"

"And virtues."

"Sure, yeah. I suppose, those too. But flaws could write them up, tally, rank and file in a special report. Do you understand? I'm not saying *approve*, *agree*, or anything, I'm asking if you get what I'm saying. I've not been ready to look. But I'm pretty sure you could see it right and that's what I want. Not for *me* to tell you but the opposite. Sweetie. I can take it. Or at least I can't take waking up half the week's nights and doing my breathing exercises until the sun comes up, this nostril and then that, six seconds exhale, and I'm exhausted but not rested at all because sleep only comes to those who've done right —"

"Except —"

"Alright, yes, or else asked and received forgiveness."

"But I bet there's millions of criminals who sleep like infants. I can practically guarantee it. I'll ask Geoff, he'd know, have evidence. Did a decade in the F. B. I."

"Were you there when our babies were nursing?" She turned and rolled her eyes slowly, smiled, tucked her chin into her neck and said, garbled through a wearied windpipe: "Not a one of them slept to save their lives."

The moonlight illumined her unmade-up face.

"But that's far afield. What, anyway, I was trying to get at is: honestly who can figure out parenting without first botching it? So much reacting. My parents were always bickering in front of us. Never saw them at peace for an evening, even. Everything could have gone great the whole day but there was this broken circuit in both of their heads that said 'Find the one outstanding flaw and gnaw on it all night like pork chop fat,'" *find the one flaw — which was always going to be there — and fixate on that with all your might, even when you try to swallow you almost choke on the remaining fat, all you can do is try not to hurl as meanwhile your children swing from the trees, swing up and into the sunset and back to do it again for an exhilarated hour while you argue, you think, out of our range, unheard, you think, the absurd nagging and nitpicking insanity it is, really, and almost unceasing, see my head start to hang, mom, your sapling tapped of all joy because you can't stop bartering for impeccability with a man after all*

254

who is in fact mortal, "You never saw it because they mellowed out later, by the time we were married they'd been through three surgeries, the obligatory embolism and a near-death accident, though in place of nagging then they played out this crazy conspiracy of silence," *wearing white flags over their faces, not spouses so much as eternal enemies, low-level threats but still enough of a drag that it's easier to give up than to wise up, I guess.* "But — forget it, you see I'm doing it again: look over there at the failings of others and at all costs don't you dare look right *here*"— and at first his fingers pointed to his head, hand uncomfortably in the shape of a gun, but when he lowered them over his heart they seemed to be covering instead of accusing. "But what if what we did was *worse?*"

Her question covered their talk in a blanket of quiet that made them both lean against the wall, no longer looking through the window but rather to where the faint penumbra cast by the yellow nightlight fell across the twisted sheets of the empty king-sized bed.

Regan scrutinized another kind of silence to see if there too he would discover darkness. His father, a navy officer who had never risen past a subaltern rank, had publicly spoken no more than one hundred sentences per week, a selectivity and silence that gave him, for Regan, a noble aura — activated his attention like a radio station whose frequency is just beyond finding, and when you finally hit it the host remains muffled, whispers at best dressing the words in mystery.

Regan had never complained as he'd heard others do, but that did not mean that he was any better — had maybe only hidden the discontent that had found fresh air only since his trip to D. C. But the vocalized complaints, their tasteless immodesty, always soured him in a few seconds: how he'd wanted to fire an employee in the sweaty lunch room, Bob Greal, was it, jostling a paid-for coke from the machine that swallowed their dollars without dispensing his drink and bad mouthing the fellow butcher who had just left the room, as if Regan would nod, as if this cowardice was not a farewell card to get him fired. Even his sister after her divorce, comparing her ex-husband to their father of course, at which point, previously nodding, he'd instead stopped, dead still, and stared straight ahead — this austere diet of words made the ones he did utter worth more, and besides dad's face — for all his faults, well well well he wasn't spotless! — was a living memorial to an unending war between sweetness and sternness, but you could see in the angles of the wrinkles and the muscles that smiled through the burst blood vessels that warmth outran severity . . . yes, that's the way he was, this wasn't merely another mad effort to make your dead into a fragile-object saint to be shipped across the country to siblings and worshipped at the graveside gatherings. Dad really *did* have a translucent thinness that let shafts of autumn light fall through him? Damn this day that tries to drag all heroes down through the gutters — so shoddy, barely working — that only an arrested age could develop into so-called adulthood. Dad didn't need a statue in his honor, would have torn it down himself under cover of darkness though he nearly drowned off the coast of Normandy, weighed down accidentally with too many supplies, but freed from the strap at first clasped too tight, fidgeting open while his body sank, he made the shore and played the medic behind a rock to a dozen injured and closed with shaking, steadied thumbs the eyes of another seven dead. This fact Regan had to fish from Dad's friend, for he never so much as hinted at his service except to say one night — one! in all his life! One night! One night! And it wasn't even him in the spotlight — around a Kettle Morraine campfire, sipping burnt and boiling coffee at ten p.m. — something'd gotten into him — "I couldn't take what they did to the officers and the sergeants and such, like my friend Fisk (short as Napoleon) who messed up an order and was dragged out in front of the mess and his sins all numbered and named like the bloody hairs on his head, kid, and you'll never believe what he said next, a one-way ticket to dishonorable discharge: 'If anyone tells you that a certain person speaks ill of you, do not make excuses about what is said of you but answer, "He was ignorant of my other faults, else he would not have mentioned these alone."' The damn fool was on his way to Yale when they yanked him away and into the war but you know his superior promoted him on the spot when he said that bit about his sea of sins! Went on to lead me all the way through Normandy — strange the way he was a peer and, forgive me, a father at once. I was sure that promotion would do worse for me, bring out the dead men's bones that take up too many closets of my soul."

Regan let his mouth form the question, rested under the pain it threatened like a dishonorably discharged man, no, the resolution came clear, court-martialed — falsely accused but guilty of worse than whatever formal arraignments were made — a man at peace with his execution: "What if we did worse?"

They shared the terrible thought and clasped hands, fingers tickling each other's palms: *at least we didn't do what they did*, but a question disrupted their teasing handshake: "Yet what if our tactic was worse for the children? One drug addict and one single mother? Though," and here he played the old saw, insincerity biting his every syllable: "even the parents with the fewest flaws can't stop their kids from falling into bad company. Look at the O'Briens. Two jailed, one dead. Albeit four are priests, though, please forgive me, Mary, that doesn't impress me, given the corruption."

"I love you," she said. "And my mother loves you too. Loved you, what have you, now that she's lost her mind."

Nonna. No. Stella slunk from the shadowed wall opposite and tiptoed back toward the circular stairs whose ancient creaks came back to memory as if she were creeping upstairs late, coming in after curfew. No. Nonna. She couldn't. She also left because she sensed that what they were about to say would be too hard to bear or else belonged not to her at all but only to the two of them.

Later, having nursed Jason again, still hearing their solemn voices, she descended and knocked and her dad asked "Stella, did we. Stell. We're sorry. Sorry we weren't good parents to you, as good as we could have been. For instance: never fought in front of you, but went on for half our marriage fighting, fighting, fighting a cold war." His passion slurred his pronunciation and she felt embarrassed for her mother. No. Before her mother could make her contribution — as if Stella were going from parent to parent, begging with fish bowl for true confessions — she said to her parents "Please stop!" She said whatever their faults — "and I surely

257

could list them, but show me a kid, even in his fifties, who is not hung up on his childhood traumas, his parents' mistakes and how they . . . fated . . . the duration of his life . . . to be marked . . . by mistakes made, ultimately, by somebody other than him. Ha! Look, if you want to know the truth," and here she saw the next few years and her living here, her mother's porcelain-cracked conscience, and she licked her incisor and felt her bite hold it, then slowly let go and said, without conviction, that whatever their miseries, they were great parents, all told, and they never had done anything so harmful that it hurt her still to this day.

When her father almost asked, accidentally, "But the baby?" she picked up the baggage of that question and set it aside for later, for when she could come back with a baby stroller and sort out what was fit for Goodwill.

When her mother left the room her father palmed one eye and rolled the other, but as she prepared to force her stiff mouth into an upcurl signaling optimistic futures and good health and paid-off investments, she was troubled to find that he did not turn to her for recognition but remained looking up lost at either God or the spider web that filled the ceiling corner with a triangular handker-chief of white silk. The half-diamond of nose-blowing cloth had gathered a snowy dust coating that gave it the texture of a cotton blanket. Instead of an urge to seize a broom and replace the woven thing with clean emptiness, she imagined herself as she felt when-ever she held back the whole of the truth, shrunken to a few spare inches — crawling up there to catch some sleep. Which was, she laughed aloud, drawing a worried look from her mother — who had returned, having checked on the baby — how those arachnids lure their prey. So though her ears tingled with the spirited apology her third-grade teacher Mrs. Faxe had offered, outlining before a jury of eight-year-olds what tremendous benefits spiders bring to the ecosystem, she gripped a stool and stood upon it and swatted away that diamond of symmetry, that cloth for her tears, with her bare hands. Mom sucked in a single breath and said "It's so good to have you home. You know how much I hate those creatures though I try not to," she stopped, and went on chortling with laughter or embarrassment, "deny that the God who made me, us, all of us made them too." And again Stella envied that ready-made belief that her mother had kept on working like a chore that comes so easy you don't notice you're doing it — the way she'd used to do needlepoint for hours to "work out my worries" in the evenings and would fall asleep with the thimble on her thumb.

. . .

Eyes unacquainted with the dark would barely see the baby-blue walls, but Stella had been sitting there for an hour by now, nodding in need of a sleep that defied her, discriminating between the subtle shades of a color that carried the kind of sadness that remains mostly mute. Nodding, "God," she counted the months since she had been here. Four? Five? Three. No. "God." She scraped together from the mess of her mind a poor excuse for what was called prayer. "God." Bolts of ache ricocheted through her nerves, her muscles, the enflamed white matter of her brain. When she closed her eyes and slipped into nightmare an MRI scan glowed, more ghostly and ethereal than material, the small but luminous lesions blaring like uneven headlights. "God." Pain ricocheted to a piercing pitch and then regressed into the minor aches that hitchhiked the margins of her neural pathways. "Multiple Sclerosis," the doctor had said. "My God, how did the prior scan miss this? Though we'd need to do some follow-up tests to be sure." "Surer? Or certain, completely sure?" "Always the former in this field. You need rest. A baby and this? Because these little spots —" "Firecrackers, or trick birthday cake candles in the brain —" "of light didn't crop up overnight. No wonder your labor, you said, was so awful." "Maybe also why the baby is so beautiful." "There is no question we make sense through opposites." "Are you sure that scan is right, doctor? How'd I do what I do if my brain is on fire?" "It's a free country, Stell" (had she used that nickname?), "but my God, I'd advise you, politely beg you" — here a downward tilt of his sharp and well-shaven chin and an elevated brow over just his right eye — "please, no. To undertake nothing monumental, nothing at all massive or heavy right now, with this on your tests and a baby at home." "You're certain

259

then. The scan can't make mistakes?" "Everything in our business is subject to error. We dwell in probability. Only God, or, our *idea* of what we wish God was, is, doesn't make mistakes." He thumbed the paperless clipboard, then tapped the blank spots of a glowing chart with the erasure of his mechanical pencil, a gesture meant to console her somehow but when he looked up she locked him in her eyes and said, "But God makes the ones who make mistakes." Here he licked his lips and laughed and the well-scrubbed sheen of confidence he had until then emitted slobbered in a string of unwonted snot and as the string stretched across the room, as he ran for a tissue and blew his nose, his red face faded to grayish flesh and eyes unplugged from the upbeat klieg that had been making them hum. "Um," he leaned towards but not closer to her, no, she knew well the routines of flirts and had no reason to recede door-ward, even as his unplugged eyes — desperate to be recognized, to be told *you're handsome, snot and all* — so lifeless now and readied for real tears, here, in this sanitized room. "I wish I could. Believe. I mean I'm not one of these zealots who *loves* his doubt. You could . . ." He seemed stable, square, reliable. Unremarkable. Could she kiss those lips that barely moved when they made words? Not now. Ever. "Doctor, doctor," she said, her tone mildly playful but resolving always on a serious note, "I know I'm supposed to be the patient, but let me suggest a modest change in your regimen. Maybe if you don't have a lot of faith in him you shouldn't be swearing by him so profusely." She sounded like her mother and to be sure she wasn't she risked a flirtatious tilt toward him, then, standing to leave, took his little reflex hammer and tapped him lightly on the back of the head, a place where his hair covered the bald spot so convincingly she nearly did not notice, then tapped him three times on the heart, where his name badge hid whatever was beneath. "Testing to be sure the one in whose hands my life wavers is worth wagering on. You did not flinch when I tapped your heart but when I hit your head you did. I'll have to consult the precedents to see if this is evidence of emotionless bias." He did not laugh at her little joke. She liked his eyes when they went confused. Catlike. Left outside and let back in. She handed him his

260

little hammer. She walked over to the mirror above the sink and breathed hard. "No sign of death. Breath on the mirror. Ancient science. I'll consult the sub-subspecialist next and we'll take a look at your atomic particles and go from there." "My, good . . . God how'd you?" he asked, re-reading the notes that told him what he was supposed to say at the end of an appointment. But she, reaching into a drawer just above the red-lined biohazard trash can, left him with a handful of free samples, mood stabilizers and sleeping aids, their indigo glossy packaging interrupted by emergency red side-effect warnings. "I do need a father for my son, but I'll have to run some tests and see if you might be the one he needs!" She was long highways of pain away, long listless windings through plain lands away, orange and asphalt and constant construction competing against the disintegration of those beautiful Midwest winter snows that cleaned the world and wore it eternally away.

Then she was *home*, here, in the attic, madwoman and child in her parents' attic.

And she told Nonna about the man who had always wanted her to marry a doctor but Nonna, nodding, did not know her name and could not answer with more than a rant she had laughed at now for her whole adult life: "Romance is the scourge of the age. An arranged marriage or some variation would suit our species better. Not material, not practical. *Arranged* by someone with sense." "I promise in this case there is no romance. I don't think, Nonna, I'd have any more children. Nothing about him moves my libido (forgive me for what I know you hate, 'confessional immodesty' — right?) . . ."

But Nonna, taking Jason's fingers and playing this little pig went to market, said "It looks like you already put the baby before the marriage. Can't fool me," and Stella leaned against her grandma's breast, pinching Jason's toes playfully to keep him quiet as she cried "I'm dying. They found on my brain sclerosis. If I'm not dying I might as well be," and Nonna, her pupils suddenly dilated, said "Stella!" "Nonna! You know me. Pray for me, Nonna." "MS sufferers don't die. They just decline, dehabilitate." "Pray for me, Nonna!" "Have I ever stopped?"

. . .

She refused to read the headlines in case she came across Peter's name. It was hardest when, sleepless, she wanted to soothe her mind on the infinite internet but eventually she managed to catch little increments even when her wondering went so hot she licked her lips and left her tongue slightly out as if for a kiss.

When she jerked alert between buzzing, braindead, scraping lapses Stella could make out oblong diamonds that looked out sideways like deep blue eyes — not scandalized but certainly condescending — from the century-old wallpaper that the attic walls wore so well. Better to rest in this hazy blue than burn out in a basement bunker.

Half-awake she saw her life screened on the wall, mirror, mirror, please do not tell how far I am from the fairest of all: thirteen, twenty-three — running around Nonna's backyard, sprinkling the garden but mostly her body, glistening in the pulsing sun's golden — and envied *that* girl's fluent movements. When Nonna had started to stop making sense (she almost literally died, Stella learned — having siphoned the truth from her mother's mum denials — from a hip-wound infection after falling on the ice while fetching the afternoon mail), they'd taken scrolls of the heirloom furnishing from the faraway walls of the East Side home, the heirloom of three generations of Cabrinis not all of whom had no mafia ties, that masterwork of childhood nostalgia none of her children could bring themselves to sell: "You know mom, she could snap right out of it and if she finds her house sold she's not beyond murder." Cashing in on a lifelong insurance policy of mumbled, head-hung apologies, while her siblings elbowed their way into the trove, snatching and even — in Mike's case — stealing, mom had requested, *only if no one else needs them, or even wants them,* the rusted rosary with the blood-red beads kept clean in a white leather Red Cross pouch. *And the wallpaper, whatever's left of the blue kind I had in my bedroom as a kid, probably so old it's got no glue, useless,* the childhood bedroom being in fact a closet in her sister Janille's wide-walled room. She walked away from her siblings carrying ample paper of matte sapphire, rolled and rested on her good shoulder like the stations of the cross — wood carved, impressed eternally into her too often finicky memory — at St. Rita's.

Big diamond eyes squinted and waited with a noble patience bordering on boredom for Stella to wake and *now sit up straight, now, look alive, look alive, child, like anything's at stake, anything at all but not so listless as if you've not been handed the spoils of history on a china plate,* which was hard to understand, for Stella, brain matter inflamed, thoughts maimed, because the plates they used were plastic and they lived far away from where history happened, but Nonna's ethereal voice from the wall was both fierce and exacting and hiding a joke, never able to intimidate even as it asked Stella — in a voice that imitated Peter Clavier — to *justify your existence, justify why you ought to be kept here, alive, when so many other more worthy, less wayward, less spoiled, too young, so smart, so ridiculously full of promise have been swept like no more than wretched refuse from the bleeding surface of the earth.* Her blinking baby, too, the baby whose unclothed umber body glistened with the unction of drug-store baby oil, Jason justified her presence, her breaths, as he stretched and flickered with the agile ripples of one hundred minuscule muscles and smiled before resuming the curved posture the womb had molded his flesh to assume. She answered the unnerving ghosts of the night by filling his mouth with milk and singing *Joshua fit the battle of Jericho* as his father had to soothe his son's colicky cries, over the phone he warmed the melody, melted the lyrics' justified violence. The one time she answered his hundreds of calls. He promised no legal custody battle. She hated the power she had over him; she hated her love of the power.

Here was a hideout, no solution. If she did not find work soon she would have to cash one of Peter's checks: he had sent some dozen since he moved to D. C. and all remained abstemiously unsigned.

The radiator dial remained out of tune with reality, delivering a needlessly long exhale of passion that petered out into a dying rattle, a flash of passion, the strange fact that her dad had discovered after hiring Andy to fix the malfunction (she could still see her dad's friend, the way his eyes followed her mouth before they went south and he about-face turned): though the radiator bred superfluous heat that left you wringing out cool washcloths because the manic effusions of infernal temperature made the attic the hottest place in the house, dad was not losing a single cent for all that rare radiation. *The damn thing's so old it'd fail a safety inspection, but if I was you I'd keep it cooking unless you plan to install new windows, which knowing you I know you don't.* So the window was open in spite of chill that colored the late winter trees lye-white and the shade was slung up too to let in the sky. Rows of as-though-ploughed clouds kept any moon or starlight buried like bulbs and seeds not ready to bloom — like the daffodil bulb on Peter's paint-chipped wall.

Still, Stella knew that baby-blue wall, the place where she slept when she stayed at Nonna's, and ran her fingers across the diamonds, closing the eyes as she traced their outlines, hummed Go to sleep, go to sleep, go to sleep, peeling her brown cardigan off in between tracing her baby's eyes. A sudden suck of breath said that he might now be waking (and that he wasn't, at least, for now, dead). The hours like this. Doing nothing. Doing everything. A mother's hours.

She wished she had *wasted her time* learning to knit when she was a child. When she was a child. When she was a child.

Dad had dragged an exercise device up the stairs to the attic. Not a stationary bicycle and not an elliptical but a simple machine that let you swing your legs freely without pounding the ground. She shook off the low-pulse stupor, now, poised the baby in her forearm's cradle, and started swinging, careful not to wake Jason or her parents. (Nonna's medicine kept her nodding, spending most of the day delusional.) Lacking confidence in her balance, the creak she caused came out nothing more than a starved and fearful mouse sound. Suddenly, though, she flung her legs as far as she could forward and behind, a mad rhythm that made her dizzy even as she felt it as fighting against the diagnosed dots on her brain unless she shut her eyes because then she felt as if she were forever falling and after a time she could acclimate to the free fall that did not end in a suicide splat on the sidewalk. So she shut them. Dad had mentioned, in passing, the marathons she'd run all those years ago, how proud he was — he had sponsored a run by providing pierogis at the vendor stands alongside kvass at a criminal price. Dad omitted in his fond reminiscence the time she blacked out mid-race on a deer trail, face first collapsing into a brittle batch of milkweed that must have tickled but did not coax her conscious. (None of the other runners stopped, or maybe she was last place already.) When she woke to find not angels of judgment and wrath and mercy but a pair of paramedics — one with a laconic, even-keel smile, the other flicking her pointer finger repeatedly against an IV tube, paying Stella no attention — she asked whether she'd ever be able to make music again. The indifferent one reached out and clasped her tensed fist, "You good, you good, girl: you'll make music, I promise you that." "Good," Stella said, "'cause I never could make a satisfactory note before, though I mean to make sounds so beautiful they could read your mind," and she laughed into the teetering spin that was her brain whirring back to life. She had forgotten. Even then something with the brain. Her parents shrugged the lapse off as nothing after the coach explained it away with *electrolytes*. Maybe they could not bear the thought of Stella being unable to run. And she did not blame them. Because the runs had, back then, in high school, rid her of whatever hatreds she had, made her wonder how many of her decisions were driven by petty animosities or preferences, all of which seemed filtered out by the runs. The runs had, Dad once said, made her into a *better person*. She had laughed in the last mile of her next race. Without the furies that the runs got rid of, would she have sufficient motive left over to do anything at all? So she did not protest when her father appeared at the top of the stairs assuming the spitting image of Eleanor with a nervous nose lift and a wavering mouth whose contours contained both condemnatory judgment and something else she could only call — though that was not quite right — a jealous fear: "Winter in Milwaukee, you need to find a way to take out the stress, Stell, inside. Got these coupons for two weeks at some club that will cost you a hundred and fifty a month after the first two free weeks. Just when your body is starting to love that pool, the one without the kids' pee and chemical-warfare-grade chlorine. The YMCA by us closed down last year, after somebody was shot by the junk food machine. This place, in some strip mall off Greenfield, is supposed to be both cheaper and better." She did not protest because maybe her judgements of Eleanor were warped by her own failures and all the stories she had told herself were so much fluff against her hard heart. Her brother, too, she had diagnosed and mastered, but maybe the image she made of him was plaster. He was, after all, the family's piñata.

Sighs alive alas a lie. So many sighs in this misaligned life. Stella sighed long into the large attic room that she sublet now without rent from parents who not understanding the situation at all wanted to badly though they asked few questions. Across the wall posters from the eighties and nineties — Courtney Love kissing Cobain permanently her love's living corpse, a black-eyed Rocky Balboa staring down the singer from The Cure, whose sooty eyeliner mimicked the agony, albeit sweat-smeared, worn by the pugilist, a contest of agony and The Cure played it back again — the boxer's split lip in a minor key. She smiled, now, at the varnished agony, furniture for countless kids across the country, wishing Jake were here to share the joke — they could bob their heads in robotic mock-control until they loosed from their adolescent annals the hypnotic chords that set confusion to measures, the suicide jump precipice fall of bass note strums going down down down, sounds she'd found tedious for so long but now could loosen the knot in her neck to, so it wasn't a joke, was unfunny, in fact, and not even nostalgia but a desperate ache — the clawing of a carpal-tunnel hand trying to outdo the body's gravity, all the rubbing alcohol and climbing chalk sweated off, so that only the friction of your fingers keeps you from falling.

> 10:15 on a Saturday night
> And the tap
> Drips under the strip light

266

And I'm sitting in the kitchen sink
And the tap drips
Drip, drip, drip, drip, drip, drip, drip, drip —

Waiting for the telephone to ring
And I'm wondering where she's been
And I'm crying for yesterday
And the tap drips
Drip, drip, drip, drip, drip, drip, drip, drip —

Jake had kept distance from her parents since her homecoming and she worried for whenever — finally, unexpectedly — she would open the front door and there he would stand, light of foot, ready to run, elbow jammed against the doorbell jammed, setting it off like a false alarm, staring at not her shoes but his to see if he could outrun her still, along the old rural road they raced through years like dirty threaded electric needles their line of communication hanging, unrepaired for miles and miles, the country road, the knee-jerk race after school. He drove them there and they ran it out under crossed wires warped with an especial twist no electrician could fix, fraught with the same convoluted circuitry that stretched across the attic ceiling, mocked safety codes at every intersection, where the rubber coating frayed to copper that sparkled, scary, with the sun's same flame, intimations of inch-by-inch sunrise so wait so maybe they could salvage something after all the copper wire the price they'd fetch if they dragged it down and took it to the paying recycler. Put on The Cure and mock their former sways, fashionable but for real despair, whine their way into sincerity, undoing the years' petty resentments added at each crossing, each intersection, each passing antipodal pole.

As if. His diagnosis, schizophrenia: denied by her whole family: what if he should be here at home instead of unofficially abandoned. Her mother at breakfast had betrayed the mythology: "He's forty-three, see — took time but finally — proud, whatever hurts he's caused, that he's found his autonomy."

What if they were all mad and all used one another in collusion of denial?

She stopped swinging her legs and turned into the shaded corridor. The baby — Jason — was black and blue in the discolored shadows that fell on them there, his forehead a bold rectangular announcement like the animate mind of the man who fathered him, the placard-carrying overtaxed alderman (he had lost the election but he swore interference) who wanted — who was he, she still wondered — to "make it work" with a woman he'd known a week before they'd fallen into what felt, the mush of the overused mattress, like a low-key waterbed that whished out soothes. There she had sought unconditional surrender to a handsome and mild-mannered Social Thought graduate (if she named him her tongue would tingle with wanting) who whispered big and beautiful ideas, an easier life for the needlessly suffering, for too many in prisons who should be made free, free, liberated from a system designed to profit on their virtuous patience ("the political theology of humility"), to say nothing of the inherited guilt that grifters made into a race industry, and she admired his courage that burst staid categories, and she clung to his noble, expectant body bereft of the too-thin plastic piece he had wanted to place between them but tossed in a wanton sign of what was called love. When she told him she had been with no one since high school he wore this revelation like a heavy crown forged from a thorn bush but coated in silver.

When he came her disillusionment disappeared, as did her disorientation in a city whose needles poked heaven like a useless vaccine: all sense of fraudulence, of amateur posturing that had pained her standing in front of her classroom, left her as she let him take her, again and again and again, *take me until you give me a baby, please.* He rooted her to his bed, regaled her with assurances that she did not trust but said *yes* to anyhow because even if he went away her baby would have his mind, his music, a heart like the daffodil bulb on his wall — like starlight hidden behind cumulonimbus.

She swelled and wore the baby well and felt enough health to accompany Peter on his sudden campaign for alderman. All she knew was a donor named Dives whispered confidence and confidences into Peter on a Friday evening after another long counseling week of missed appointments and games of Patience.

At the town hall where he launched his bid she had waited in the back with a panic attack but kept it hid, slipped out of the crowd and stood on the corner, leaning, wrapped around, a tilted Stop sign. She watched him as if he were not a man whose mind she knew whose bed she shared, immediately impressed as he exited the building surrounded by a gaggle of rough-looking kids who tried, in his presence, to tuck in their shirts and stand up straight and siphon an ounce of the alderman's unpretentious confidence — "Call me Mr. P. C." he corrected when one of the kids cried out "Sick dude, P. C., c'mon man!"

For what she had come to call dubious reasons — she now admitted, to the discolored shadows, which stretched toward the ceiling like a man with a spatula, a phantom she was once certain she had seen, a Mr. P. C. who had hovered above her — she refused to respond to his slightest check in and continued to studiously avoid all news of his political rebound in Washington, D. C. Persisting, P. C. sent a steady sequence of text chains, variations on a constant theme: ARE U OK, I WOULD BE DOING GREAT AND AM EXCEPT FOR YOU ARE NOT HERE.

Finally after she tapped out BABY cash came in an envelope so terribly thin she was surprised that no one had opened and stolen its faded mint presidents, no down-on-luck desperate had partaken of his ransom — not fair, not fair, he couldn't be bought, you're doing it again, making him a demon to take the pain out of his absence — which could have been borrowed forever without trace. It was not really a *ransom*, she knew, because he was giving it without expectations, or at least without pulling her down with any marionette fishing-line strings of expectations, and he started giving and giving and giving, mailing whether or not he got something back — and there was eventually no *whether*, because the answer, as the weeks passed, was always *never* — but she couldn't stop the frayed wires of her worries — look at that ceiling, a fire hazard, dad — and her furious suspicion that he, found guilty, of rushing into a baby with a stranger, was buying off the moral hangover.

He had to know, master psychologist, just how very down she was ("your eyes, the prettiest sad I've ever seen"). Not that this

269

made him a predator, but you also could not say there had been no preying, however much she played along with it ("I've been looking for someone to *see* the sadness"), however many chances he'd given ("We can go as slow as you need to, you know. We can stop right now, midstream, and you can clear your head and think it through, though damn you're beautiful.") And why had she taken his repetitious cautions as an invitation to abandon all reserve and wake on the stranger's battered mattress to a synthesizer's scattered beat, the hyperactive love-kill alarm of the morning after and all adrenaline and all alone she rose alone except for a day-old bread crust, buttered, still warm, he had placed beside her where his body had achieved a total stillness that seemed so callously peaceful it shook her. She found a separate blanket, blue like her Nonna's Mother Mary shawl.

Draping it around her, crust untouched, not seeing the note he had left her beneath, she exited his apartment and expected the bodies they had passed the night before to be there, but instead except for a bent needle and several unopened bags of white powder she found not a soul. Still it took her a long time — a good twenty minutes — to find the apartment building exit. As she caught a cab to St. Cabrini's — she could make first period if he ran the red lights or at least dared the ends of the yellows — she had tried to remember from her friends and their babies (friends she had failed to call for months) how soon you could take a pregnancy test, eyeing the back and forth of the wiper that cleared, constantly, the dash window of the constant splatter of broken slush she could see, if she tried hard, a little rectangle of drab gray dry-mouth sky and could keep his safe three feet from the tail-lights of the cars that clogged the street she watched all the nights between now and then, how should she spend them — in abandon with him? Or betting that nothing bad would come of this? She could hear, in echoing intimation, the coming ambulance that would take her to delivery like the siren hearses that passed her apartment every night on Kinnickinnic, where the constant alarms were a strange synthesis of waking annoyance and reassuring comfort. It was as if, should anything happen, she could jump out the window to her death and was guaranteed to land in the back of another passing ambulance.

. . .

The arguments about Nonna and nursing homes started when her mother said, "She hasn't been the same. Hasn't been, in fact, since you left for Chicago."

"Don't blame me, Mom."

"I'm not blaming. I'm saying that —"

"— If I hadn't left she'd be healthy in the head —"

"That your bond with her surpasses all of ours. It's a gift," Mom said, and went outside to water the flowers and leave Stella with her guilt.

"Quality of life. Let death run its course." Stella stayed out of the arguments because whether she assented to or dissented from her mother, Mary would walk out of the room sighing. She did not ask about death and his course: but is he running a four-minute mile or a marathon that keeps on going even when the contestant is weary, is beyond bleary-eyed dehydrated, spitting up blood because there's nothing else left because even the bile exited the body a good mile back?

Three months later Nonna had been in the nursing home for the better part of a single week — "my trip to the moon, and I tell you I'll die afore they ship me back there!" — before she broke out through a janitor's exit without setting off a single alarm. It turned out, after the police brought her back, the little perpendicular window was wide enough for her to slip out at night and wander the neighborhood in nothing but a slip until a "handsome officer, looked Italian," picked her up and drove her back home which was not Young at Heart but her parents' house. Conversations with the nursing-home staff turned up troubling patterns that suggested — in no uncertain terms — it would be best for her either to move into advanced senior care (the cost of which was upward of four thousand per month, and even the monies made from the sale of Nonna's house could not, if she lived a few years more, come close).

Stella had kissed Nonna's hair long when she came, and kept her red hair against grandma's greasy forehead until the oil gathered in the wrinkles perfumed her hair with Lily of the Valley. (Nonna splashed her face with this profusely, as if the cologne were city tap water. "I don't give a damn," she'd told her daughter. "If I'm going to have to live here, hell, I'll use my millions to become beautiful." Her fixed income, if you counted an investment that sometimes showed up as a deficit, amounted to $1,030 per month.)

Nonna had hated the mint green "blouses" (standard pajamas, dotted by "self-satisfied teddy bears" who each hugged hearts with a kind of death grip), scoffed off this mandated "uniform." Often — daily — the "blouse" would accidentally fall slack around her shoulders when the male aide came in to administer noon medicine. Once she declared her intention to marry him. When her daughter said, unsmiling, that Nonna was sixty years his senior her mother pivoted and tossed to the floor one of the many dollar bills she apparently kept under her pillow "I don't know why you put me here, tucked away where no one can see me, where no one has to feel my pain, all that I suffered for you kids, stuck with all these old folks here in the only hell I've ever known. If it's money you need here you are. Get me a room at the Hotel Eumenides. My great-aunt stayed there for a dollar a night in the extra rooms of the top floor. So what if it costs double that now. I know you kids sold my house. Come out with it now, don't lie, my love!"

Her mind was a squeezed, sometimes a wrung sponge, dripping out random droplets of facts she had absorbed some seventy years back or more. Mostly she was elsewhere, her eyes hawkish and suspicious, shifting quickly across the empty bed as though she stared at an invisible game of solitaire laid out there — wherever, through the windows or the walls — and as if some enemy would outwit her and win if she let loose her vigilance for even a breath. Then, the game over, ever the loser, she would say, "Jesus Mary and Joseph, don't you give a damn about a woman, daughter of Eve though I am I am? No one loves me, no one visits me. Why did you give me mediocre children who can't even keep the easiest commandment. I'm not asking love, only honor!" Often she said something to this effect with her daughter kneeling there at the bedside, folding Nonna's hands into prayer. Other times, mom said, Nonna would sing and the nurses would gather into her small room to hear that operatic voice — "that gift of music she gave you, Stell, we've got to get you a piano still" — singing Stella Maris or Ninna Nanna:

Ninna nanna, ninna oh
Questo bimbo a chi lo do?
Se lo do alla befana
Se lo tiene una settimana
Se lo do al lupo nero
Se lo tiene un anno intero
Se lo do a lupo bianco
Se lo tiene tanto tanto
Ninna oh ninna oh
A nessuno lo daro'!

Halfway through one of these late-night sessions her swinging maestro's hands hit a button on the bedside, and a jolting mechanical wheeze flipped her up like a lump of dough against the wall. At Nonna's age, a run of bedsores could become those red ellipses inscribed on the flesh that announce that last long pause before death. Her bed was programmed to rotate her body from side to side, slightly, so that the same hip was never in the same spot for too long, but other buttons intensified the motion so that the bed was a borderline catapult.

Every day that her mother had lasted in the nursing home, Mary had come to play crossword or pray the obsidian bead rosary her great grandma had brought over from Italy around her neck, but every day as she exited the room she heard Nonna pick up the telephone, dial someone — anyone? — and say, "I'm so lonesome, nobody visits me, nobody loves me, they've left me to die."

Growing bitter in spite of expert suppression, enough to confide to Stella, "I hate her, sometimes, I mean I love Mom but she seems to hate me no matter what I do and I start to hate her."

"I know what you mean," Stella whispered. "I'm . . . sorry, Mom."

"Hurt the ones we love the most," her mother muttered, her mouth stuck on the last syllable which went from st to tsk, tsk as she folded an afghan of perfect geometry and threw it against the couch so that it fell open like a slumped body.

Mary planned to cut her visits to every other day and then to once a week at most because her devoted attentions seemed, she said, "wasted. Did not affect the slightest improvement. In fact maybe made mom worse."

She was desperate to clutch her mother's good will, which was slippery now, as if in retreat, but she'd watched the aides coax it out daily and if these strangers could do it why not the daughter? Maybe, she concluded, that was the problem: her familiarity invited confidences, and the things Nonna needed to confide right now were to a one harsh complaints that could not but hurt — however much you could chalk up her rude remarks to neurons that misfired ("She doesn't mean what she says"). No. The voice that shouted, gargling ginger ale and choking, these constant castigations came from no one else: her mother, not a stranger, not a new unknown woman distinct from the one who had scolded her at fourteen years old for eating so many French fries the boys, she said, would never marry such a pig.

This was the worry their family had negotiated into remission for years and years: that the "familiarity would breed contempt." Mom's clichés always chafed when Stella heard them but they carried, if worn out, incontrovertible truth. Why couldn't she — maybe when Jason was crying, lightly *as if she could plan those rare occasions* (she would have to pinch him or prick him with a pin!) to bring an armful of sympathy into the room — why could she not tell her mother "I need a mother but you are like one of Virgil's shades I've tried to embrace in the underworld three times and every one found my hands filled with air."

But before Stella could muster the courage, in those rare conversations in the cold living room, before Mom's conscience could split like the eggs, soft-boiled, Peter tried to keep together, ("Her memory is so bad she'll hardly notice anyhow"), Nonna had escaped from Young at Heart and moved back into her little attic room — a purple place perfumed with Lily of the Valley, with rosaries tangled on the small dresser, spilling over a stash of coins and enough prayer cards to serve as kindling for a year if her father's Apocalypse at last arrived.

She heard Nonna whimpering, banging at her door and saying, "Excuse me. I've got the supplies for the foundlings' hospital. The baby blanket should have been here by now."

Before Nonna had rapped and then rasped Stella had been lost in a great silence. When you really settled into mom and dad's house the noise was nonexistent — with the windows shut, stuffed with shirts to keep the cracks covered — but for the highway package haulers that heaved their tons through the country's veins — a constant transfusion of constant purchases of crossing east west north south desires. "Can't you hear it, Nonna? Coming on the freeway, the blanket'll be here, I swear, any day," and by God it arrived that same afternoon. When the brown UPS truck with the rusted muffler chucked the box that did not say FRAGILE so that it barely made the curbside lawn she jutted out like a winter animal and snatched the treat and retreated again. In a box that felt good to open she ripped away and set aside what could be used as a makeshift changing table on her bed edge in the attic. She buried her face like a Christmas child in what Nonna, on a clear day, had called a "prayer blanket" — a colic wrap made by nuns who lived in an ancient liturgy in Kentucky and whispered soft Latin as they knit fine coverings for "unwed mothers" to keep warm for free, "unworthily," Nonna had added with a wink, "like me. The least, the last, if you don't mind my saying, though it sounds sort of silly, the last gasp of God."

Nonna attributed Jason's great slumber to the prayers woven and whispered into the blanket, smiled at his body splayed in an X. Yes now that the blanket appeared "would you look, that kid who I was going to give such a one for never stopping crying half the night, half the day, not that a baby can help it, I know, but look at him now, wrapped in prayer, have you ever heard a snore so sweet?" The sound always soothed Stella's tensed jaw but just when she let her teeth rest Nonna asked, "Now whose baby is it? Cutie. I tell ya. Or do they drop them off here and leave, anonymous?"

Stella's brain felt bruised from the back-and-forth pull like the tug-of-war games her brother would play in the same backyard of this same Southside house where her family had settled since forever now, and would be until that still fuller forever — if what they believed in turned out true.

Sometimes she found it pathetic and paltry, the do-it-yourself hanging that promised the stitcher and all credulous comers Ye Are of More Value than Many Sparrows, an array of birds made of fat yarn flecks pecking through the plastic as if trapped in a net. "It's to give her some meaning," her Mom had said when Stella, in passing, scoffed and called it kitsch. Immediately she wanted, when she saw Mom's mouth open, to cut out her own tongue in front of the family.

"Would you have her with nothing to pass the time? Are you ready to handle all her idle hours?" When her mother left the room Stella felt weirdly proud that Mary at last had taken a stand.

"Mom," she called out. "I'm sorry. I can't imagine what it would be like to lose your mother, in a way, while she was still alive." When her mother rounded the corner to return she found, gathered, in Stella's fierce eyes, the umbrage of an entire lifetime.

"The doctors call it 'dementia,'" her mother pressed past, cleaving assiduously to the set tracks, refusing to acknowledge to whom she was speaking, as if pretending to gripe before God and not the daughter possessed of vicious eyes. "Sticking to the safe way, I have noticed, especially, in front of the patients' families, but we all know these people they conveniently label have plain lost their heads," and though Mary again exited the room as her shadow still showed on the living-room blinds, Stella was suddenly seven listening to her mother read from Alice in Wonderland while she watched the scene play across thick felt drapes that kept the early morning sun — and the entire rest of the world — out:

> The Queen turned crimson with fury, and, after glaring at her for a moment like a wild beast, screamed "Off with her head! Off —"
>
> "Nonsense!" said Alice, very loudly and decidedly, and the Queen was silent.
>
> Nonsense, thought Stella at forty-one, her mother had never turned angry crimson in all her glaring life. Her fury stayed

silent, played etherized patient. All her impatience was sent back inward in a circuit that shorted out next to her heart, which she was always touching and almost as if clutching, quietly, when no one was looking.

Polite manners. Mad Hatter. Dementia. Her mother had cared for the demented so that she could go to a little college where Professor Clotho had them read Seneca's The Madness of Hercules and she learned dementia from Latin dementia "madness, insanity," literally "a being out of one's mind," from dement-, stem of demens, "mad, raving." Raving mad. Euphemisms like dementia eclipsed the terrifying conjurings of madness that appeared everywhere. In the room next to the bathroom where Nonna stayed, not wanting to be bothered, scared when her favorite granddaughter came to visit: "Who are you? A stranger! What woman! Help! God, call the police!"

. . .

The sky was iron rusted at the edges, and when she watched the sun like a thousand autumn leaves raked and shaped into a single circle she wanted to touch whatever it touched — to be able to bestow that warmth. Jason lay grinning and cooing and splashing, as if coolly floating atop the shallow bath water already dirtied to a degree that shamed her. Stella turned the faucet clockwise to mingle clean in the mess he had made (which was, of course, the mess she'd let him make). Shivering, she stood with her back to the mirror whose ruthless wrinkled portrait hurt — the lines in her face like sharp cuts to her spirit. All tiptoes at the bathroom window, over the fogged-out, blurry bottom, she clutched the sun with faraway eyes, jaded and jonesing for that feisty burn that used to turn a whole room's heads when Peter wanted her, the one time he brought her to the rally and kissed her, sat her beside him at the reception dinner, and the way he looked at her made all the others see her that way too.

When she'd watched, disillusioned, Peter's alderman run — the clips on the news and the hour-long crescendos on YouTube videos — she came to see the need for talking points, accepted without mockery or cringe: the need for repetition and economy.

Peter would come home weary, worked up but worn out from a late-night rally, and raise his fist in front of the mirror, mimicking the slogans he'd bandied again and shaking his head over the sink. (He listened to Malcom X's speeches for practice, and watched himself mouthing Malcolm's terms in the mirror where now he mouthed his own maxims.) Seeing her watch him with a hand on her cheek, he would drink a long slurp, slosh it and spit and say "Sorry for being so poisonous, I just need to get out all the yuck, the sewage and shit that get stuck in my head from saying the same damn stuff every day."

The enemy he cultivated with care and finesse was the mayor of Chicago, who had "handcuffed the police, effectively authorizing murderous criminals to have their fun every Friday night. I sympathize, don't, now hear me," she could hear his voice carry over the crowd. "I sympathize with her calling the officers in question to stand back in solidarity with citizens who'd spent their lives fearing blue uniforms — though the statistics, I dare say, are worth citing, some thousands out of many millions of us. But besides this, stay with me, as the number of dead here in our city rivaled Middle East war zone tallies, as what we do to each other surpasses what 'barbarians' do to the infidels —" here his voice lowered and he chuckled, sickened, "'Barbarians.' What we fool ourselves into calling them, I hereby call upon the National Guard to send its soldiers to Chicago's south side, immediately, yes, in full cooperation with the local force on the ground, but with numbers and weaponry never before seen, please come to this war zone if I'm alderman I'll order it, and, dear miss Mayor, if you fear this will spark nothing but dissidence and distrust I dare respectfully ask you what you're doing from your highrise helm while our people go to hell, and if you want to play the card, then I ask, dear miss Mayor, that you do so plainly, that you send only black guardsmen to keep our children living."

His critics promptly inverted and turned and quoted out of context and milked to the hilt P. C.'s "hypocrisy, an elitist black establishment phony," accusing him of "turning brother against brother," an attack that ached because they could dig up a decade-old clip where he had critiqued the imperialist violence instituted by the very existence of a "standing army, the very kind that the founders of this country used terrorism to send back home. A *standing army*, which is the better name for the phenomenon of the police state. Not only our soldiers in uniform and not merely our national guard, hear, but even those police handing out ball cards are complicit in advancing the police state, for a generous salary giving baseball-card bait."

. . .

Dad is in the windowless basement. Yes there is, was, one window, but it's covered with sheet metal, boarded shut. The floor is furnished with old sawdust softened by beer sprayed from his friends' mouths. She watches him through a hole in the floor, a hole in their ceiling, their hideout, splayed flat and straining to see. The men are bent over at the edges of metal chairs, comfortless things that "could topple if you're careless, kids, look at me, Stella" (what Dad used to say when she stooped to unfold them at six a.m. at the main street curbside, setting up for the Fourth of July parade). Four men gathered around a table of yellow yearbooks, well-preserved since the sixties and seventies, newspaper clippings in between pages and in between stories swapped lukewarm lager. But there is nothing lukewarm in their postures — tense arm clenches even as they laugh. Eaves is talking about the time he walked in on two of their teachers kissing long, both of them married and both of them begging him for the respect he'd failed to show in class, and "Oh you bet I nodded and swore up and down that I'd not say a thing so long as those grades started to rise, all to get out of the room and duck into a toilet closet for long enough to make a cartoon of Mrs. Slatt and Mr. Blanton locking lips and then sneak into the mimeograph room and make a million of 'em and glue a streak across the hallways without any regrets whatsoever, to this day"—"Oh come on, Eaves,"—"No *to this day*, 'cause everybody even the principal Howard, Father Howard, how do you do, knew the two of them met for 'conferences' after school every single day. Damned if I cared about grades at the time, half of my brothers dropped out of high school for time better spent pouring asphalt for interstates that Washington D. C. was conjuring from nothing all across this beloved country. Remember, my friends, my brothers paved the way for our famed trip to Washington! And so I'll stand alleged of the lie that I would not rat out my lover teachers but I'll not stand for the salacious allegation that I sat in the pleather chair of a Senator whose name will go unmentioned by God because it's worse than the swear words young Steven Dobson got clacked on the wrist for saying, so help me God. It was Sister Excalibur — no, Sister Eclipse —"

"Are you kidding me, Eaves? You didn't get served?"

"I don't follow you. Look at those bottles. Your fourth Blatz?"

"And if it was Pabst, would you approve, parole officer Sterne?"

"You do not stand accused, do you?"

"Someone said I look just like him. The man who stole the Senator's chair and tossed it out the window, saying, 'See the ship of state capsize! Moby-Dick open your eyes and bite the captain in the leg, make the president a eunuch and I'll buy you a keg!'" He laughed and belched and held his belly and they all recalled the reel from D. C.

"But," said Eaves, "I'll not deny it. As a boy I needed, benefited from the ruler. Sister Euthanasia."

"You're nuts! Her name was Sister Eustace."

"Sister Euchre! Play us a round!"

"Point is, boys, I dare not blame her for using the rod on my boy's behind. God I needed it."

"Need it."

"Guilty."

And and and and Stella did not know when all this began, but Dad had started to host Tuesday nights with grade-school friends he had not seen for decades, mostly wearied men who'd spent their lives spraining muscles and closing bars, breaking backs, heart attacks, blood thinners, AA meetings, second — and third — heart attacks, divorcing and remarrying from "misery to misery" — she had heard, one night, Sterne mourn. It was hard to hear their stories without staying ear-stuck to the kitchen floor, where a hole let down the telephone cord.

Faithless Eaves waxing the church floor for free — revisiting weekly the acolyte days of thick wax candles dripping warm on your fingers, dared to wait there by half your class who if you flinch will call you a wuss and pile on high at the next recess, forming the wax into a manuscript inscribed with all the catechism answers, easing your way through the test you typically failed "It's sad, you have to admit, to fail at God — though it's a tough subject" — and then easing your way through the math test too, with equations etched on the other side — the scant relic of that dimly-lit place where old ladies with pale faces hid beneath those pretty black veils like babushka hoods in the old neighborhood, Edna with saucy masochistic eyes and Iris whose hands never parted at Mass, knuckles never leaving her chin as she stared at the red and golden cross woven into the stiffened chasuble, and when you looked into Iris's eyes she never noticed your stare at all, your worst flirtations like limp spitballs, her confidence in the host so complete, your thirteen-year-old apposite indiscretions not troubling the holy roller at all. "I miss that contact with good old fashioned faith, you know?" said Eaves, cracking the cap of his fifth beer — this time Miller Light. "I've got to lose weight if I'll get another wife."

"Why the hell don't you dial Father, tell him you'd like to serve again. Pull the jersey out of retirement. The way that parish pinches pennies, the alb you wore is likely still in use. Heck, maybe the congregation's so shrunk they ain't got a server to spare."

"Moth-eaten," Stella hears herself say, that jaded reflex that had gone underground for a decade of *pax romana* — a decade, time unlike the rounded rosaries her Nonna prayed three times a day — a ceasefire that disappeared entirely at Cabrini's and took flight once she clasped P. C.'s coattails, please just carry me away from it Christ she took to using the name in vain though Peter, every time she did it, cringed as if in honor of Uncle Cedric more than out of old-fashioned reverence, as if the faith Nonna had known forever was buried under the foundation stone so if she wanted to fully be rid of it the only answer was suicide.

How now the question of faith had lost fuel, the desperate daily need now to be cured of the self-hatred that came like the worst malaise she knew when Covid nearly killed her, such a malaise her self-hatred surpassed when she left Peter to prove self-reliance, to prove to her baby who knew nothing of proving she could be a source of life to him, if not to herself then at least to her baby — stop that — that downward-sucking vortex that yanks all toward a fossil existence, turns joy of spirit into a museum set piece, guarded by a janitor who makes it hard to remove the exhibit, what she once so disparagingly called in her brother "your jaded, faded, self-pleasing jokes": she heard them bubble up with canned laughter in the uncanny back of her brain and she hated — whatever the wrongs of Eaves and her dad and the nostalgic Olympics being held in the basement — she hated how easily she could critique everything, sink it, blink it all into nonexistence.

Moth-eaten. So be it.

She held her eyelids open, pressed her right lens up to the hole, held her head there and studied the specimens, a petri dish of diseased minds. Except that she could not dismiss them so easily. Their sheer solidity possessed a countering force, an equal and opposite reaction to her science in spite of the fact that they could not see her. They were more real than the ready-made caricatures, put-together others shared across the web, just as real as the motley punks she sat across from at that all-night diner, when Peter was training organizers and all who showed up were dressed in goth, discussing the next organized action — a sit-in on Wall Street or an armed liberation of elementary kids in Racine, "victims of compulsory schooling."

What did any of any of this amount to? The endemic inefficacy made it hard to take seriously. Peter's top complaint.

. . .

After she nursed Jason and fed him pellets of homeopathic chamomile borrowed from Nonna's drawer — she would repay her next week — Stella returned to her perch and found in place of the prior clowning, her father in the basement tinkering, squinting under a bulb with a blackened tweezers, fixing the fire-warden flare as Sterne read from the warden records found buried in the

282

wall and Andy played with the gas-mask strap, pulling it back like he was launching a projectile.

If at home, remain in house and extinguish all lights. STAY AWAY FROM WINDOWS. If walking on the street during attack, seek closest bomb or other building shelter. Do not light cigarettes. Do not strike matches. If in large gathering such as theater or auditorium, remain still and seated and ensure the cooperation of all inside. Large movements of people will cause panic.

Eaves picked up the Verey light signal pistol and pointed at Dad's temple. "Blackout!" he said, and Dad fell back, angled his chair to a risky tilt and nearly collapsed if Sterne's fast hands had not shoved him back straight. Eaves averted his eyes, gasped, laughed when Dad did not go down, and joined him for a flickering reel of faint laughter until, recollected, they crowded around Andy who had made a map of the new formations meant to make their patrols of the neighborhood "safer for us and for the aggressors. Remember," Andy said, above it all, "Our mission is not hate but law and order." Eaves tried to tease, to joke, to bring their gravity back to the level, but something about the thing wasn't funny.

. . .

The next week they were back, each one wearing an identical gas mask. Eaves, the eldest (closest to seventy) and most successful (real estate after years craning his neck painting ceilings instead of selling the structures themselves), who had invested in social media stock when it was obscure and sold when it was ubiquitous (refusing to open any accounts of his own), had sprung for the lot of masks. She knew because she heard when Regan said to him "I still can't believe you went all out with these things, seeing as you're such a cheapskate. But then it's all a hoax, talk about conspiracies, you still living in that run-down bungalow when you're sitting on a million. Why you're not in a new development out on a lake — on your own little oval island, for godsake, is beyond me, but, well, it won't matter where we're living or how many rooms are in our mansions or mama's houses when the bombs really start to fall, the screeching that reaches across the sky. I mean, the military have a mind of their own but how far they'll go to oppose the president's wussy pacifism is, frankly, beyond my intelligence. Speaking of, hey, did I tell you I applied for a position doing reconnaissance for the F. B. I.? Seriously, out of boredom, sure, and I'll never get hired — God help them if they'd hire me! — but it helped me get my head together. Anyhow, you must have death on your mind, Eaves, trying to make amends and set things right by giving gifts to the ones you love. We don't, you know, have many years left and maybe fewer days. I almost want to break open a gas line and test the worth of these bug faces."

. . .

She asked her mother about dad's meetings while she did the dishes one morning.

"Stella, he's worked hard all his life. I say let it be, his conspiracies. Harmless fun with old friends is mainly what I see. Do you see?"

What she saw she could not say. She could not show herself what she saw.

. . .

A clack of wood and the smack of her foot flesh against the floor. *Awah! Awah! Huuhnn, huhhnn. Awah! Hunnhana* . . . Outlandish in this too-still house, the house whose creaks could keep you up, whose basement mice could be heard running across all the house's rafters, from the basement to the peak of the attic ceiling. A cry. A baby. Whose baby? Mine oh my God mine oh my God what time it is mine is it time isn't mine out of mind out of mind. Up Stella's arms shot with a quickened stiffness that made her elbows snap and she rotated her body leftward to seize the baby, whose baby, her baby, whose face had gone from burnt umber to the color of an unwatered rose. Clear snot caught the starlight and glistened in the dark. She wiped the stream of snot with her fingers, wiped her fingers on the sheet. Snot green sheets. God. *Can't. You. Do it.* She shoved her hips into the mattress and bounced her left buttocks against the springs until the wheezy screams relented

284

and Jason's eyes reluctantly shut. She kissed the side of his wide open mouth and, all ease, felt the bed and not P. C. embrace her dead weight. The elm tree's highest branches held the street lamp's nuclear-orange orb and desiring an oblivion that would not end she slept she rattled awake and slept wearied beyond beyond worn beyond motion and nearly time. Again a cry. A baby. Mine "God oh my God I can't," she said, then again not aloud but to whoever was listening. "God my God I can, I can,'" — hopefully more than herself alone, a loyal but unreliable companion.

Before she knew what she was doing Jason was strapped in the portable car seat, her knuckles clacking on the dense and heavy plastic that could repel mortar shells in case of emergency, her own heart shooting out ballistic, arcing over the damned distance, down and exploding in Chicago, landing on P. C.'s front porch and melting the jambs off of his doors, summoning him awake at this ungodly hour, settling for good in his apartment, his bed, he had to be there from time to time to continue trainings in South Chicago. She would find the flame and set afire what false future she had failed to find? "Stella, baby" — in both senses, his eyes lowering from her mouth to the miniature imitation of his face who looks askance, obliviously handsome in a woolen winter cap that pops at the top with a white pom-pom, the sort she always thought fit for little babies whose purpose from a distance was little more than to be darling but not, she thought, as she saw him in the rearview, for cheerleaders tossing their toories with league support of the fully-disclosed, ticket-holding oglers whose pleased stares were somehow permitted and even, she ran the useless stop sign at the blind-alley intersection, fostered, a stadium of oglers, a soft, family-friendly gentleman's club of different degree but not different kind than the tucked-away secret one she and P. C. stumbled into, desperate for a bathroom as they ducked down the cellar stairs of the basement of a bar where he had been endorsed by Wright — the "biggest boost my campaign's got yet"— but when the two, feeling for a restroom, pushed through the bolted bronze doors she found not a sewage siphon but mascaraed women who wore infant pom-poms over plasticine nipples and shook them with fury in front of worshiping faces, the men waiting for their mommies to flare their technicolor milk "Give me more, more, give more, momma!" in the delicious midnight, slapping P. C. when she found him looking, not even staring but "Startled, in shock," and that night had not been their first real fight because the slap had solicited faux fisticuffs as he laughed that infectious exhilarating shiver that she could always only mimic with a sliver, an uptight groan like a broken guffaw. Aw, baby Blue, I'm true, and he'd flicked at her earring and tickled her lobe with a little kiss, the azure earring hot from his breath, but she covered her breast with reticent hands that rubbed her own shoulder as he backed away saddened and said I'm gonna pee my pants as they made the top of the stairs in a hustle, his hand lifting her two at a time, her swelled belly nearly ready, and he spoke his mind as he always seemed to do, telling the bartender this was the last time The Underworld would have his patronage on account of the unfortunate discovery he'd made in the presence of the First Lady, and he would make known to his constituents and in fact to the whole country how the gentlemen treated their ladies, and suddenly she saw him running for president as he swore he was meant to do, proud but worried that, pregnant, she would weigh down the star she saw rising. He stared, staid, startled when she told him this. He did not immediately but eventually said "No."

If she reached his apartment she might find another woman. She should stay, skip the Renault, return upstairs and steal some sleep.

But you, Peter, this a piece of you true with beautiful gemstones of the mineral beryl dotting the border of the small snug hat and all the cute things I used to hate are fitting, not enough, insufficient, on him only the richest dyes will do, and the ball on top dangling from his head gave her a woolen, insulating happiness against the bared and gooseflesh facts — televised cheerleaders and underworld strippers and the cold car she was about to assume, a rattling heater that coughed at random huge lungfuls of scalding air. She pressed the snaps of Jason's hat until his fattened chin felt snug.

She swung the car seat in wide arcs like the smoothly cranked horse head of an oil well, dangling the child in constant motion to keep him quiet as her own soles squeaked against the stairs that Mom had mopped again yesterday and would again tomorrow now that she'd left a trail of faint dark mud. She wound her brown cashmere cardigan around her body as she neared the backdoor and the maw of winter let out a warning, whining breath.

Dad, ascending from the basement, saw her struggling to pull the keys off the nail and helped her raise them high enough. She promised she was going to drive around in circles, put the crabby baby to sleep, and he hesitated and says why not the country roads, "I'd come with if it'd help" — she said no. No, no, no, no she needs to figure how to do this alone, the Renault, the Alliance, is already his and he's letting her use the car without charge she needs to figure it out, alone, how to be alone. Alone all alone without the loneliness. "Not that I'll ever be alone again!" she shouted as she stepped outside and the screen door screeched and she saw his face, plump and buoyant like a helium balloon but ready to pop also, his mind. Some fun he was having in the basement like another life like an afterlife like a life after the one he had lived when they were the only family she knew.

Three dead pumps and the Alliance rallied and she gunned the gas and skidded on accident down the driveway with the mohawk grass. After three circles around the block, the baby screaming louder than ever, she rolled down the window and brought the wind to a pitch that pained her own ears but quieted the spitting baby who had ripped his cute hat and tilted his head come on kid it's not a crucifixion. She found an onramp and drove to the rural roads where she and Jake had run, saw a sign that said Chicago and took the next exit without double-checking, wandering down a serpentine side road whose winds and turns were dizzying, dredging from her empty stomach bile she spat out the window what about the baby's belly must be bad if mine's this nauseated. She passed klieg-lit silos and fancy farmhouses and wondered what would happen here if she pulled right into someone's driveway and dragged her feet to the front WELCOME mat, rapping and ringing until they spied her madness through the petite security peep hole. "I'm going crazy, take this baby!"

She reached for her phone, patted her pockets, rifled fingers through the tight slits and found lint and a few pennies. Insane she left the phone at home. "*I'm going crazy, take this baby!*" Lost, she kept driving straight, the word metaphorical for all roads wound, curling at times it seemed in coils an infinite regress she gripped the wheel, the perfect circle, and cranked it round and round to keep pace with the winding lane lit by nothing but her mild headlights. She kicked her shoes off to let her heels breathe and pressed her bare foot against the pedal, flesh on metal; she felt a cut and blood dripped down the back of her heel. Going and going out into the country until she found a lone silo, fattened as if stuffed to bursting, illuminated like the lakefront lighthouse, stretched oblong like one of those medals Nonna made her wear in the water in case she died when she fell from the diving board, the stars she still found beautiful, miraculous the horseshoe stars grotesque the heart of God stabbed she felt again for her phone and found a faded dime that bought no miracles again and then on Jason's booties, dangling from a keychain Nonna won from friends at a game of Patience she saw the medal she must have seen it in the rearview mirror already. She swerved the car into the shoulder, pressed the brake with all her left foot (her right foot bloodied beyond use).

She tried to find a path to the silo, strapped Jason to her breast with the wrap and slipped in a mottled clay and dirt trench, a deep meridian protecting the cornfield whose husks swished whispers in the untold night, baby still screaming as she bared her breast, refusing the chewed and purpled nipples she had offered unscathed to his father under the play tent sheets her legs had held up, their breath the heat that the radiator lacked, the light casting shadows through the cloth of white that fell like a pall over Peter's spent passion.

She prayed that some man with a gun would not come.

Stuck in the mud her heel felt cool, healed more than manacled. The man with the gun did not come. She stood on her tiptoes to see the silo, the pain in her heel residual, faint. Certain that someone was dangling from the ladder framed by the faintly yellowing horizon she gained perspective as the pain subsided and saw instead that the figure was a scarecrow not one lynched under the old Crowe world nor the ancient hanging God whose gambled clothes she would yet refuse even here, chilled by fear more than temperature, doubting anything sufficient remedy for the creeping craze — divine or insane — that drew her to mimic the solitary scarecrow whose shadow spoke of a sacrifice no human harvest, no mortal could muster. Arms out like a crossing guard on an empty road without traffic or pedestrian, play acting for the real thing. Jason's blue-mouthed, emptied-lung fuss blew hot flashes like fire through and beyond her veins and blood and nerves and brain, and the flames of his pain seemed not an arson — at once she saw with certainty — not a random arsonist's terror but instead a homeopathic fever, a controlled burn in an overgrown forest famed of millennia, impossible to forget, the burning started not by her but by who she knew she did not know if once she did she hardly now could, the burning laying waste inside her, her heady breaths filling her belly, expanding what once had been her womb, each of his screams a new contraction in what new labor toward what delivery, something she fed and was fed by also, was burned by but could be healed by too, a fire she had passed to her son without will, without guilt of the kind that implies intention, except insofar as she would have done it, would have thieved the fig, the fire, would have laid waste to the primordial forest anyway, were it hers to burn — even if she in fact had not she would have done whatever it was, whatever this pain was a punishment for. Shivering, she stared at the scarecrow shadow, his form ragged-edged by potato sack clothes that bore an affront against Wisconsin winters. As if watching the shadow of the clothes he wore were the same as wearing them. "I've gone crazy, take this baby!"

No one takes the baby whose bellows are answered by the barn-warmed cows, the querying who of a stern owl alighting like a judge keeping unbinding court from the gutter ridge of the broken down barn whose cracked wood yet kept the cattle indoors, the judge imposing his wearied eyes, casting them down upon the petty trespasser, as if scoffing as he takes regal flight in a heavy flap of well-fed feathers. The man with the gun does not come. She slinks her healed heel into the Alliance and as soon as she leans the seat horizontal she hears the baby's scream weaken she worries he's dying and longs for his wailing. *"I've gone crazy, take this baby!"*

She wakes in a species of endangered silence. Even her parents' place, which seemed like a monk's cell or a pleasant coffin when she first settled in, sounded — compared to this — with constant hum of machines and fans, heaters and coolers, the undying traffic on the free highway. But here the quietude is in full harvest, a level of soundlessness that makes her nervous. She slips her shoe around the wounded foot and stumbles, stupefied, in the middle of the street, Jason still and at last asleep. Staring down the scarecrow's eyes — big coal pieces she could steal for fire — she melds together from the mettle of her mind a prayer. "God." What meanings you could give or get out of one word when you mouthed it more times than you could tally.

She climbs the rungs of the scarecrow's ladder and runs her arms through his sleeves and hears a hound mewling in the distance, nearing slowly, the sound of hunger, nearing, homing after blood, a hunting dog, she could hear, like her uncles and she tries to descend the ladder but is stuck, arms fixed where the straw had stuffed, her arms also like the telephone poles that reach cruciform forever down the highway, she imagines herself holding wires, telephone cables that reach to D. C., because he isn't back hunkering in Chicago with another woman but waiting for me. When she slows her withdrawal her hands come loose and she feels the sting of the prickling straw as she lowers her body into the first light of the morning that would take her home.

. . .

Regan peeled a single blind back and peeked the tip of his pistol out. A car crept by as if waiting to be caught, tinted glass rolled down all the way, a driver flashing an upside-down peace sign with a solemn nod before peeling away. Down the street, in a sleeveless T-shirt, a kid fed something green through the window and received a bag that glistened like sand. The mailbox contained a prize of coupons (and if you could sit there for an hour you'd find five ways to save five dollars, or you could work another half hour and make up the difference, make up your life) and a single triumphant postcard that boasted white sands the color of the dealer's but far more numerous, kilograms of grains that would put him to shame. "WHAT ARE YOU WAITING FOR?" asked Janille, whose idea of recovering from her loss was taking a cruise with her jailed husband's money, signing her name 'neath a Tijuana stamp and sporting a picture of a twenty-tiered cruise ship that could kill a whale without even noticing were the two to meet mid-ocean.

· · ·

Jacob pried open a Family Size bag of knock-off brand beer-battered potato chips, peeled and stretched with inhuman patience, with a poise that would keep the house asleep until at last the gas of the bag hushed out with salt-tanged bad breath, but the chips themselves were satisfying or at least his tongue told him so. His eyes watered and his nose went red as he tried to chew the crisp concoctions without crunching without losing control and announcing his unwanted presence. If Dad could sleep through a revolution, a feral cat's unclipped claws tapping benignly on the outside sidewalk would keep Mom from sleep for at least a week. It had taken him half an hour to find a way in that would not wake them. In spite of Dad's new security additions — and they chided him about addictions — a crew of cameras with sensory lights and night vision infrared remote control toggle; barbed wire wound around the windows so that their every outward gaze was crisscrossed by barbs that would bloody the intruder's palms; their childhood treehouse worth of boards pounded over window bases; a rat trap fit for a Doberman — he still had a house key, a privilege his parents would have made him surrender if they realized that he was doing this regularly: a missing loaf of white bread on Monday, a can of orange Tang powder Tuesday — all items taken without dire need, without a wince of real hunger. Something about being able to come back and eat his fill flushed him with stability, a grounding sense he had not found through any other available means. Not prostitutes or psilocybin, not video games or government dole. Jacob chewed with less pleasure tonight, licked salt specks one at a time from his extended, guilty finger, checking the expiration date with one eye when Stella came around the corner to catch him, back turned, above the sink, under the double crossed red eyes of the 2:00 a.m. announced by the clock.

"What the fuck are you doing here," he said, not faking his way into a question.

"I think we both know why I'm here," she said, nodding through the walls and ceilings, up the stairs where Jason was sleeping.

"You'd like me to answer the same question."

"Jake I haven't seen in you in two years."

"Three."

"I — I didn't, honestly, have the head space to ask Mom, yet, what you've been up to, how you've been doing. And she doesn't —"

"Know. And, no she would not want to either."

"The last time we talked I —"

"You sent me sixteen text messages in ten minutes telling me I was sick in the head and like a little baby with my big, quote, 'teat' being addiction instead of mother's milk. As if you knew anything about that — at the time, now I guess you do!"

"I regret the *tone* with which I said those things."

"But not the things themselves."

"You. From what I can tell what I said worked. You needed to hear them. If not from me. I've thought a lot about that question. Who could tell you who you would hear. I know you hate me. I know my words are dead on arrival in your ears. But next I heard, after you sent a picture of your middle finger, I heard you were getting off of a federal drug charge by taking a plea deal."

"And that's not good enough for you either. I can hear it. You hate that I turned in my friends to get free."

"Jake, I'm not in a position to hold court. Are you doing okay?"

He crumpled the Family Size chip bag, struggled to get the clip on the top — three times he tried but failed — and spun around at her with a murderer's eyes.

"You think *your* messages mattered that much? You think *your* intervention was what worked. Fuck off. You made my mind melt down. You always were so self-important."

"You don't know self-importance."

"Is that a question?"

"No, Jake, I mean you don't know. Not you at all. Another level. I've got my own wrongs. But. The baby's father. His self-absorption is basically an illness, incurable, fatal." How strangely good it felt to say this, a judgment she had not hashed out, fully, could not speak to Mom or Dad in case she needed to make them like Peter. To tell her brother who had known her forever brought her back to his arm around her at fourteen when he found her leaning against the birch tree at the end of their block, unable to make the hundred feet home, wiping her eyes with a soft green leaf after her first real heartbreak. She tried to say it with pity but her leveled sentence was filled with resentment. "If you make yourself the center of your world it's amazing how many planets will show up orbiting you in adulation. For years he talked at me without hearing me. And I. I played the script he wanted. Became the receptacle of his own invention."

"Stell," Jake said, licking salt from his fingers, "with her big words still. I'm sorry. Seriously. For being such a fuck up. But I'm sorrier for whatever the dad did to leave you all alone with a kid. And because I've spent the last decade assuming the worst of you without grounds I'm without grounds going to assume that what you're facing is no fault of your own."

"I'm not ready to figure that out frankly. I know it's not nobody's fault. I know he wanted to have it both ways, to have D. C. and to have me too." She covered her mouth, keenly aware that what she was saying would make little sense if she went along. "But look at me. Jake. I —"

"If he ever tries to mess with you while you're under this roof I'll leave his body in a mess on the floor."

They heard the familiar fretful footsteps. Not Dad's but Mom's. As children they had learned to identify the difference — mom's tread cautious and nervous and intermittent (as if she feared she was trespassing) and dad's sloppy belt-off stomping. Because for years when the both of them shared bunk beds, after the alternating parent came to tuck them in and bid them swear the same useless oath of silence, immediately after the elder exited they would start whacking one another with pillows, huffs of feathers breathing from the bags, barely-contained hysteric happiness and half of the time they'd get lost in the pleasure of hitting someone with total abandon and somehow not harming the other at all, though the pillows had started to puff out and break and scatter whole chunks of feathers and down across the fresh swept floor, at which point as if he could hear them falling — they were totally oblivious to their wide open shrieks, which had gone from hand-over-mouth to high pitch in ten minutes at most, maybe five, it felt like a whole weekend until Dad, dressed only in bleached white underwear that barely hid his pubic hair, shouted down the hall "Are you trying to kill me?" and then he would confiscate the pillows, one under each slung arm, expounding upon the source of their down because each time they flattened the damn things again they killed another duck or a goose "because this thing you take entirely for granted, this softness you sleep on night after night it doesn't get delivered by a stork from out of the opening heavens, okay, and each one you waste means somewhere someone has to slaughter another round of swans and strip the dead bird of his feathers, all so you can sleep better, which is going to be hard for you tonight because I'm taking these pillows and now if I hear a peep if I have to come back you'll be sleeping on the floor in the basement or worse" and they'd hear him curse after he slammed the bedroom door. If mom came in she was blinking and weary but she'd pick up a fist full of feathers from the floor and hand them to Stella and nod at the sewing box. Stella had learned, even in the dark, to avoid the slightest prick of her finger as she sealed the seam and patched the tears where an untrimmed fingernail had clutched a hole into their instruments of torture.

Like a six-year-old he kept his mouth closed, as if their Mom would thereby disappear — the years, the years, the master bedroom lair that belonged absolutely to their parents dare not knock against the cherry wood door whose grains he had memorized when he was eleven standing their listening to his parents' muffled moans.

"Mom. Go back to bed."

"Jacob? What are you doing here? What time is it? Is everything — are you okay?" She looked him over as if for needles dangling opposite his elbows and then, turning, for shards of glass stuck into his bloody nostrils.

"Jake's here to help with Jason. I heard. At least. Word on the street. He knew I needed a night's sleep and you've been going too hard recently. Mom you give me all you can. Go to bed. Too much injustice for a girl to keep up with. He's going to get up early with Jason so I can sleep in. It's the new — and limited-time — thrilling way to spend a Saturday night."

"Car thefts have tripled this year in this city," Jacob said, splitting the blinds, a spitting image of Dad at dawn, with two fingers to check and see if his own vehicle might be gone. He pried them wide until a sash snapped back, whiplash, a cartilage crack that could have come from his fingers or the plastic. His knuckle cracked out a rivulet of blood.

"Water from the rock," Stella said.

"Murders have increased one hundred percent," Mom added, matter-of-fact. "Nonfatal shootings up seventy five. It's not a place to raise a family. Not a nice place. Anymore."

"I'll only be here for a little while," Stella said, catching her brother's eyes instead of her mother's, assuming that old familiar defensiveness.

Jacob said "I wish you success, but I wish more that we were kids and could take it all out with pillow blows." He blew up the chip bag and, catching his breath, pounded a resounding popping sound out of the single ingredient of air.

He disappeared out the door and never returned again that she knew of — unless he outwitted her sleepless walks, her accidental vigilance. Her waiting for Peter to show up unannounced.

. . .

In the beginning, when Stella first started lessons, for years she despised the piano with her whole soul — not really the instrument itself but the structure, like anything imposed on her from without, all of which to her twelve-year-old mind felt like a variation on the theme of eat your spinach or you'll never grow strong, the old song, play your piano or what would happen? Her mother had no ready answers besides the entertainment she could give to others and the relief that could come with release of her anger and the pent-up things that didn't make sense but could be disposed of anyhow, if you pounded it out half an hour per day, so she'd quicken the *Moonlight Sonata* to a crazed tempo, stumbling over the keys for years, furies, as if the faster she played the sooner it'd end — not the song so much as the fact of being forced to do anything beyond the dictates of her well-whittled will.

When she returned to her parents' house, jittery from all that had happened in Chicago, jonesing from not having played while there, she felt the hard absence of a piano pedal — the pleasant compression of the muting brake, the flimsy vibrato that blurred, with just a tap, the scales of the dissonant spinet Blake had brought her as a wedding present that had turned, when he left, into a bitter parting gift. Even now piano music had the echo of abandonment, still she couldn't live without the sounds. When her parents would watch Jason, for a while she could search the city for minor keys, a beggar, slipping into St. Marquis, the student union at midnight to play that once hated sonata so slowly, a wanderer walking around Milwaukee, seeking the city haunts that housed pianos for happy hours and open to anybody as long as the crowd let you. She learned quickly how very good she was, drawing applause in unexpected quarter from even the most sedate spectators; the stoned man whose face remained hidden behind the dark brim of a badly beaten Brewers' cap, even he lifted limp wrists and pressed his palms together without sound as soon as she finished tempering through one of Bach's French Suites, smiling sweetly so that his yellow teeth showed as he bellowed "Bravo!" stretching his baseball bat legs before he found the strength to stand up straight and toss a silver dollar into the tiny fishbowl that Stella placed at the foot of the piano, a repeated feat that made him proud — every Thursday he'd do it again and then the rest of the room would mimic the man until the chink of thirty coins meant she could buy her Nonna that blue winter jacket at the Goodwill on Farewell Avenue, because whenever her own mom tried to get Nonna a new one the latter would return it and slip the money onto the mantle or into the spice cabinet — besides now if Nonna tried to return it she would get lost in the city alone — but that meant gram's coat was near threadbare, and the fixed income, she complained on her clear days, had no room for new clothes, and Nonna went on to threaten Stella that if she bought her anything she would "break out of this maximum security family prison," knew still in her dotage, damn it, how to return a second-hand thing from the other side of her hometown ("You think I wasn't born in Little Italy?") — not to mention, when Stella defied her, her favorite color was navy blue and despite the fact that thrift was her watchword she had been beautiful when she was young, accustomed to the compliments of passersby, to the second glances of so many men, and though all this was history never to be repeated she'd genuinely come to love colorful things that "did a number" on her life's efforts to be dull, rote, a patchwork of ways to delay death: "And so, dear Stella, when you buy me that jacket which you know like a fool I'll wear like a scarecrow, pick me a blue one you yourself would wear — not some throwaway made for the elderly."

The money came and came and came — in clinks of coin and café checks.

And so she played Bach every Tuesday and bought three winter coats in one month — one for Nonna and one for mom and a sheepskin one for herself. But she would have played it anyway, even if the coins did not come, because she slept well on the nights that she did and the music made sense of an aimless season that obtained no meaning in spite of her sleeplessness, or because of it, because all the ceaseless — say it — sacrifice. She said it, "Sacrifice," and sat there, stupefied by all she had given, certain she should be dead by now if not for — what was keeping her alive? These surges of sound slotted into the scribbled-over calendar she kept like the sky keeps the phases of the moon, showed her wells and bell tower heights of being that were there, always, but could go shadowy, unnoticed, or unknown if the keys were not there to cull these wells and belltowers from the broken landscape she walked without maps, in the longest, darkest night of her life.

. . .

When she worked Miss Beats' Florist she had walked to work every morning gingerly balancing a tall ceramic mug that had a picture of Chopin's sad face. Finally — every day, unsolicited, a passing, solicitous stranger would say, "Oh dear, watch you don't drop that!" — the face had fallen and smashed when a stumbling kid who should have been in school jutted out from an alley so narrow only small cars could coax their way through. He elevated his middle finger until the nail nearly scratched her face. That mug had been hers for a decade, and the notes of Chopin's nocturnes, memorized on her walks, all the scales, and the unusual, almost outlandish oblong size had become one of those inconsequential extensions of herself that suddenly seemed laden with significance. None of the mugs on the undusted shelf earned her approval, but just as she squeezed through the narrow doorway, reluctantly raising her collar for the cold, rattling a vitamin D lozenge to combat the pearl gray that if not without beauty made its way fast into the middle of your marrow and did not depart until late March at best, and at the base of the stairs she caught, abandoned but wrapped with twine, a miniature harmonium.

"The bellows is broken and the pedals stuck stiff," Eleanor reported from the top of the stairs. "That's what Christopher said earlier." Stella could hear, in that triumphant tone, that Eleanor was proud to see any gesture had impressed the elusive Stella who never asked for anything, who never needed anything, as if Eleanor had got the gift herself. As she tried to pick up the harmonium and fumbled with the keys, she heaved and failed, kept breathing heavy as she ascended the uneven steps to where her roommate waited, satisfied, chewing her upper lip real quiet, wheeled to the edge of the topmost stair, she figured — the ridiculous contortions of jealousy killed her, made her hate herself for suspecting — Eleanor seemed to relish the disappointment Stella demonstrated when something so stupid as a coffee cup could cause such frenzied, disconsolate, pathetic stress.

Earlier, as Stella moseyed past, having forgotten her lunch at home, Christopher, the limping old man who reigned behind the counter in the curiosity shop's last days — today was the blow-out, closeout sale — who rarely raised his haunches from the stool because his body creaked with each step he spent, had leapt involuntarily toward her. He must have seen how fixedly she looked. She shook her shoulders and cracked her neck when he said again "The pedals is stuck and the bellows busted. The wood is good — beautiful, see, but not a sound is coming out of them reeds without a pretty penny, my friend. That's why the thing's only ten dollars. Thing's heavy as hell, but" — her fingers reached out for the keys and tiptoed slowly and softly a scale — "it'd make a pretty as furniture, no question." She returned to the base of the stairs and heaved and pulled hard until her stomach hurt and felt her suspicions of Eleanor fall with her failure to move the instrument an inch.

The question, now, was how she would get the godforsaken instrument upstairs — three winding, narrow floors of stairs whose wood was just as "pretty as furniture" but half the board could easily break off if not careful for the uninitiated guest. She and Eleanor had mastered the passage, ascending the steps an inspector would condemn without hesitation or peril, and Eleanor insisted that she loved living there in part because the stairs tested limits and forced a level of ingenuity a Handicap Access would have starved. A wheelchair waited at the bottom, and a wheelchair waited ever at the top.

Tommy. Tommy was the delivery driver who dropped off packages for the florist. She knew him in that bent-over posture, back brace worn outside of his shirt, and by the following Tuesday she had engaged him to pick up and carry this "heaviness of hell" to her lair. (Later she felt strange that he knew where she lived; his voice carried a strained kindness but a childhood of grandma's warnings about "rakes" and "men of misadventure.") She was determined to wring from the abandoned instrument sounds that would compete with the angelic choirs Nonna seemed to see from her armchair, when, slightly sedated from her seven medications and halfway through her third daily rosary, she leaned forward in what looked like sleep except that her eyelids remained separated and she hummed with unintelligible sweetness to whatever she saw. As was typical, Stella did not think to call around for a repair estimate before she purchased the harmonium and paid Tommy to heave it upstairs, directing his every step with shouts that combatted the impaired hearing he'd acquired while working in a packing house.

Three months later she located a woman who could mend the bellows for a price she could pay and in the meantime her dad had replaced the pedals as a Christmas present, his two Saturdays of indulgent handiwork costing only that familiar look of "Stella, you're crazy" and his shaking head when he stooped down the stairs, not knowing she was watching him leave.

And so every Saturday at seven p.m. she set the scores of Bach's Partitas atop the keys and pumped until breathless which was right about the time the harmonium would emit a little wheeze like a pleasantry or a mercy or a pity payment for her novice misuse. She sighed with a fullness known at no other point until Blake bought her the real spinet. (She did not know how to really relax, was unlikely to take a full lunch, and typically she swallowed a peanut butter sandwich standing and reading a newspaper or novel, one in particular that took a long time, set in Chicago and her home city.)

. . .

The gaining of leaves was also a loss. Always celebrated as the end of cabin fever, spring put a stop to the art of survival — the little rituals she and Dad developed — and demanded more than distant waves to neighbors jutting from cars to doors. She had entered the winter's subtler meanings as she hadn't been able to since childhood. Sweet-anise tea dried from the shoots he'd grown last year and kept in the basement, steeped three times until the taste was so faint all they sipped was a shared warmth that somehow kept off the claustrophobic closure that came when she did not leave the house for days, rocking like Nonna in the creaking chair, sipping the anise while Jason nursed, the motion a lull that could carry the years so that she could be seventy and still here.

Yet this season meant too the front yard maple would hide those rigid and fragile branches that had defied death for six straight months, would hide such stark beauty in favor of the kind that pleased too easily, too readily for her. She missed the tree's fingers extravagantly pointing in every single opposing direction as if to say *Look everywhere but not at me!* How she could never be. She missed the steam from her mouth as she sang to Jason in the drafty room and she missed her Dad who now spent nights — when the boys weren't there — tinkering outside.

Retreating to the kitchen's bay window — that ever-open unblinking eye bereft of blinds or drapes because the backyard was walled by pines and fences overgrown with tangled braids of weeds and vines (she did not know the difference) — she inhaled hard at the sight of the morels — the "black foot" mushrooms that she'd pinched her nose at as a child before her father bent down and, his patience to her impatience, identified them with wonder and care, praising the fine hairs that finished the cap ridge and (while picking) admiring aloud the underground *sclerotia* that could store needed nutrients even when the climate waned extreme (she'd later come to find them still standing, more than stumps even into November, when everything else was closed-door dormant and blanched and even the cumulonimbus coughs seemed to cover the earth with death's last gasp). "*Scare it?*" he had asked, and she had shot back "*Sclerotic*" — sending his chin up, serenity threadbare at the stubbly fringes — "It's like Nonna who lived through it all. Hardened. Rigid." "Sounds morbid. Where'd you learn that word?" "Mrs. Wick." "Glad to see they're keeping your eyes on the evergreen future at that school!" he grinned, pretending to tackle her down to the ground and then pointing out the crescent of morels that fed on the death of the old apple tree. "You can pick them," he said, and though her fingers first tapped at the tops of the mushroom with hovering, lightly treading repulsion (he'd later warn her of "false morels" which, if you ate them, could conclusively kill you, a fact which made the good ones taste better instead of giving her double vision). She came to love the pluck because the cap from stem broke quietly — as if the snap was as if meant to be, not as if you were severing the heads of a crop that had been bred only to look pretty dying. Dad had helped her with the harvest when a bumper of them came, held out like a trampoline his rust-colored T-shirt and she tossed in a dozen and tossed and tossed and they bounced but settled and soon he was standing, rubbing his hands, bent over the shoddy gas stove that sometimes leaked and reeked up the house but now sizzled the foraged *sclerotia*, coated with half and half and cornmeal and fried until the delicious black caps were browned all-around. As she chewed and swallowed with relish and milk she again explained about sclerotic Nonna as if he'd been interrupted for only a few seconds. "Not that grandma is *mean* at all — no not at all that's not what I mean." He stepped in when with trepidation she mouthed the rest but refused to say it. "Ah, I see, more this: there's a hardening that has happened on account of having to because of all she's been through. But the thing about the mushrooms' *sclerotia* is that they seem done-in but are really only dormant, storing all the needed nutrients until a less bad environment can come — and then, like they'd done no more than damn blink — the things start growing and nourishing again." "But what if the less bad environment don't, won't come? See. All that good nourishment stored up for what?" He picked up a small cap and dipped it in buttermilk and held the dripping treat out to her: "For you!" Stella nodded though she said nothing. She chewed and stood and felt the pan with her finger first. Finding it cooled, she touched her tongue to the bottom, finishing the refuse of the needed nutrients.

The faint taste of those mushrooms in her mouth, she sat at the table and licked a little envelope. Well-fed, she took out the unsheathed check Peter sent. Her hands had to work hard to extract the extravagance — the wealth that arrived so unspeakably thin, shocking when you saw that the figures were not forged.

She ripped it into a hundred some pieces, and started to brush them into the shaded white void. The heads of zeroes fell into their grave and she inked his P. O. Box on to the outside. Her mouth had joined with the number of nothing, O, O, O — No, No, No.

(In college her professor had had the class memorize T. S. Eliot for extra credit. "Extra credit. Though I'm paying you. Like an

I. O. U. promise with dirty money interest." She had never understood what he meant. But she did recall the Four Quartets —)

O dark dark dark. They all go into the dark,
The vacant interstellar spaces, the vacant into the vacant,
The captains, merchant bankers, eminent men of letters,
The generous patrons of art, the statesmen and the rulers,
Distinguished civil servants, chairmen of many committees,
Industrial lords and petty contractors, all go into the dark,
And dark the Sun and Moon, and the Almanach de Gotha
And the Stock Exchange Gazette, the Directory of Directors,
And cold the sense and lost the motive of action.
And we all go with them, into the silent funeral,
Nobody's funeral, for there is no one to bury.
I said to my soul, be still, and let the dark come upon you
Which shall be the darkness of God.

O God, please, another obscenity, another obscene amount he sends me — more than any mom could manage to spend even on high-end diapers and organic peach pablum siphoned into petite recyclable jars, as if begging to be set aside in a trust fund so that Jason in spite of the supposed odds would become the legendary trust-fund baby, would have enough for a house as a freshman in high school, a yacht by the time his friends were salvaging second-hand beaters from Fyodor's Repairs (the Russian mechanic had given her a deal, a steal on the busted Renault axle she rattled to death that scarecrow night). The payments, which arrived through a foreign account, had started to feel like hush money, though his image no longer appeared in the Times or a thousand Twitter feeds in every direction, saying Look at me! wherever you looked, urgent and omnipresent for a few slow-motion minutes and then half-forgotten as the page was flipped or the tab, the epitome of mutability, clicked off into the abyss of ether, the fans that cooled the internet servers sighing an infinitesimal sigh as they've one less task to keep alive. But whatever the national deficit of attention, his face had been flashed with due frequency — "a lie told often enough becomes truth" — was it Mao or Lenin, not Trotsky, who said it? — that she could find, through a Google search, a hundred images

303

of a man she did not recognize (wearing suits that telegraphed a perfect admixture of authority and cool), that he was not the man whose sweat she had tasted, whose sperm had swum a baby into her belly: he was nothing if not what was called a celebrity.

In the letter he sent separately from the foreign check, return address a P. O. box, and his words slanted at the opposite angle she knew came natural, his handwriting worse than ever — hard to decipher even with the magnifying glass dad used to inspect the morels — he'd confided complaints that seemed at first indulgent, until she came to the page where he picked his own qualms apart — *what a privilege it is to have made it so far that I could take issue with the trials of fame — a level I thought I knew before, but now I know I knew nothing. What it's like to have people you don't know follow your every word and hate every syllable they say you said, with ninety-nine percent of the world not bothering to check the difference between paraphrase and calumny, plagiarism and the real-deal me. The old joke of authenticity doesn't sell well as a commodity. The hardship of folks I don't and won't know dropping my name and dissecting my doings, what it's like to have people who weigh your motives be about as qualified as the mind-readers at the circus. To say nothing of those who celebrate the hate the other side has for me — it's a shit-show, see? Until each side starts seeing in the being of his enemy exactly what he wanted to be. But the worst is this: half those words are scripted, fed, and I'm the great masticator who chews them up and spits 'em back out even when I only half agree. At first I found, what can I call it, virtue in the cause, sacrificing self for the cause, at a high cost, because it's always possible to have qualms of conscience when you aren't the captain of your soul, but I can't, now that I've seen some things which I can't spell out, complete the mission. I wish I could explain the new digs, the new operations, the nature of it all. Suffice it to say that my influence increases even as my public profile fades into a forgotten has-been. Bliss, really, to be done with interviews, to reduce lectures to little venues where the stakes of what I say won't keep me up insomniac anymore. All of which is to say, Stell, that it would be weirdly safe, now, to have you and baby here. My son must*

He had sent the letter unfinished, unsigned. She did not cash the check — whose country of origin she could not identify, though it seemed Eastern European, maybe — but tossed it in the first bonfire of spring in the backyard pit where the mushrooms cooked in the cast-iron skillet on the ashes coaxed from coal, from compacted plants that died a million years back and still had the everlasting lust for life.

When Dad took his paycheck to the bank to cash it and the paper was handed back to him, "bouncing," she, six years old, reached to feel if the thin strip was made of rubber, to rub its texture and see if it erased things like pencil edges. Outraged, her father declared, "Crooks," pocketed the paycheck and passed the ford of carpet to ascend upstream where the bank's attendees waited to serve him, "A family can't afford this shit," shaking the check in the air, he followed, "doesn't it mean what it claims to mean?" the bank teller telling him kindly that the company had declared bankruptcy. He said it. Shit. It was the first he said it in public, published what was liberally leaked in little grunts daily, dividing the devout heart of his daughter, who knew two ways of being, right and wrong, from the beginning, and knew then that he trusted her whether or not he loved her.

When they slumped violent against the leathery Ford seats, he reached out and pressed the cigarette lighter, letting its coils color orange and kissing it to the corner of the check. Red rings coiled into a faint blue glow, as though a child had scribbled terrible strokes of crayon into the air — and, as the smoke accumulated, father cracked the window, the window!, only slightly, as though suicide were already written in the will, in the genes which were science's version of what's his name Calvin's predestination. He rubbed his charred hands on his blue jeans and said, "Sorry darling," as she coughed and her eyes cried of their own volition as a manner of protection more than mourning. "What this means for our family I can't say aloud."

Later that evening — it was Nonna's birthday — he told the story to the whole family, and her grandma said, "I'll tell you one thing. That check's as good as the prayers of a man who's begging God from a state of mortal sin."

. . .

305

Blake remembered the salted mushrooms Stella's Dad made in the backyard bonfire. He tasted them this time of the year although he had only been treated to them once before he fled and she fled in his stead. Sweat poured from the pores of his forehead as he turned the corner with a sudden clip, his left arm chafing against the brittle brick which vibrated with a piano's low bellows, extracting pain from the instrument's bowels — what Father Marto called the bowels of the soul. It had taken time for Blake to shake the sense of bowels as mere intestines, as if confession were a colon cleanse. *Factum est cor meum tamquam cera liquéscens in médio ventris mei.* The sound, resounding, reverberated, rising above the human traffic pounding the cracks in the Milwaukee pavement. The piano must be pressed precisely opposite the yellow brick wall that cooled his cheek. The calm brooding climbed not toward triumph but trod something underfoot, if not death then what, he coughed, Chopin's Funeral March in B Minor resonating in perfect pitch in his inner ear, in his soul's bowels, sending a tremble that weakened his knees until he had to lean to the wall, listening there as if for his life — he almost laughed when he caught the gawk of a passing woman whose miniature skirt hugged her hips so very tightly she had trouble walking, like she was worried her bowels might fall if she went too fast. But fast forgetting her mocking mouth and all the people who ambled past, who pressed with pleasure shoulder to shoulder in the thrill of outdoors after the pandemic, forgetting the passing, his eyes closing, his house asleep o happy chance, the march of Chopin over death, which was already certified and counted for the census, but the fingers were marching during the funeral not conceding as final word the failure to propitiate life, but summoning, solemn, the whole population to ascent at last sorrow's incline, to let it swell you into a stupor until you can see what it is to suffer without the armor of analgesic, hear death's demand to be absolute, maybe — and here he felt in the rumbling, in the ruins of Chopin's civilization, a pricking pain in his bad ear. That walk from Hape's had marked him forever with a cold that kept him prone to flushing and dulled the drum of his left ear, but he kept pressing it against the wall for the trills that he found there, the thrills of the death tread, lifting him from the day's abyss, this was not merely melancholy's milk, the pleasure taken from the pain, he heard his mistakes and their reverberating consequence which you could not shirk off without stiffening your heart into a cold and unsound organ. So that every day he prayed for Stella, for Hape, for all the hurting his hands had not the fingers to keep count of, so by the end of his fifth decade he was left bereft of peace because the rounds of the rosary beads became bullets, a pelting buckshot for all the people he had pained. Whatever God's blood did by way of forgiveness, it did not wash the consequences that tightened his bowels like de Sade's lash.

The distance was too much between, too many bricks, to be skillfully laid. Symmetrical mortar scraped off, it seemed, not by a trowel but by a finger intent to make this building humane. Not one of the city's ubiquitous wrecking balls waited, suspended from a commissioned crane to knock down this well-made wall. No matter how hard he leaned, no fall. He walked quickly toward the apparent front door but was blocked by orange-striped barricades and an overflowing dumpster whose golden rust had consumed the surface, so that the original glossy clover green was nothing, now, but disparate memories — like Stella's Nonna in the nursing home (he had visited her only once, discreetly) — like leaves that Adam's children held above their groins so many centuries, to keep impressed a God who would not ask so much these latter days, their leafy olive, verdant green had faded now to autumn brown, the pieces of the brittle leaf blown by the wind, the wearing down, the sickly whispers of time's thief, nothing left but a spread of veins, not nerves enough to make new rites, to fake new leaves of second sight, instead they stood in naked lights as if with innocence intact. Blake retraced, raced around, to catch the sound of the sonata before the lull, the aftermath, the end of time kept *lento presto*, the buoyant resolution reeling up in spite of its minor chord, the song he heard her play a hundred times before he disappeared, the way she lifted up the mood just like she picked up a crying child and soothed the room, getting lost or getting found — its final measures falling down.

He finally found the front door guarded by a man whose mustachio curled in a smile to save the fellow the trouble, hard enough job the lay security, the unassuming laid-back bouncer, a husky man with red suspenders, head hidden under a hat, the brown pancake ovular kind, what were they called — Irish, right? — but the button bulged like a Russian church top, edges sagging and shading his eyes so he could see but you could not — the little tactics he employed to keep the concert free from crime. Flashing his ID, Blake elbowed through the uninterested chatter of people who had come here for something less urgent, and he entered at once into the center of the notes, separate but strung by the cleft lines together like an abacus, redeeming the time, and the room was the molten core within the charred coatings of rotating spheres, and he was here not for distraction but to pay his due reverence, the heavy tromps paying respects to death and all we have done to dull its sting and sing its finitude into oblivion. Vico it was said *Humanitas* comes first and properly from *humando*, burying. As the seats were all taken, he almost tripped over his own feet while walking sideways to a lampless corner, where he went down on one knee.

The woman at the piano had the same red hair — crochet-needled into a bun — as Stella, the fiancé he failed to marry, Stella, who had tried to teach him piano: her hands hovered over his, directing but not touching until his mistakes began to proliferate and what he played departed from the score so helplessly far that he cupped his hands up over her ears to save her from his savage notes, then caught her fingers which tickled his palm as they kissed and leaned against the drapes that hung low over the bland wall of the little living room Stella had assumed as her bedroom since they started dating, Eleanor claiming the actual bedroom in order to save her their star-eyed sessions. On the other side, inside, the bricks behind him still sent sensations — soothing vibrations — of what the woman over there was doing, her whose scrawny shoulders looked like they were shivering through a heavy umber sweater outlined brightly with a thick thread of bright red, all this over a golden-brown dress that showed the crescent between her shoulders, an exposé he found himself wanting less than he loved the cardigan covering that denied his eyes the rise of her neck. Her eyes were not closed in either abandonment or an acted simulation of the mood she was making. The side of her face — caught only at an angle that made her high cheeks hard to see — was if not loved then admired for its uncanny affinity with Stella's, and when, finally, she turned a page, her full upper lip bloomed like an impressionist rose petal in the still water of her solemn, so serious, so somber face.

In Stella's apartment the spinet had barely fit. She had had to dissemble and trade her ovular table for a dense rectangle, a dark wood Wurlitzer offsetting its smallness with a sense of gravity made manifest when her bare feet pressed the pedal. The living room had just enough space but on one side the floor was dented, bowed under, really, and on the other the radiator, unregulated, would go through mood swings that could warp the stretched strings. He found it on Crow's List, the used goods marketplace, for three hundred dollars and heaved it upstairs with help from his father who took two weeks' recovery in bed but smiled when he heard how Stella's face looked when Blake walked her up and showed her what he'd found her for their wedding.

The two of them had spent so little time indoors. Even in winter at the Bay View café Corazón they would occupy the sole table set still, as if forgotten, outside, albeit under the blowing heater that exhaled coffee scents onto the street. Tilted toward it, they would talk for hours like plants under a greenhouse lamp, leaning against wicker chairs worn down by the dirtied snow, the salt that flicked up from the street, softened and made admirably tolerant by so much untoward frigid weather. And then, the untrimmed and sprawling ivy growth of their two tendrils intertwined came in full at the end of May, after a propulsion of cold that seemed, for many weeks, ready to conquer summer's reprieve altogether. But when June came and they leaned, relaxed, against the wicker gray in the well-lit late hours, they found a ruthless humidity rather than a reprieve and the steaming Turkish coffee that had kept them warm in winter was replaced at once with mainly ice in highball glasses filled with a finger of Scotch for each, please, and he'd reached out for her forearm on a Tuesday after a tedious desk-tapping shift at the office seeking to purchase, on behalf of the city, the guts of a water filtration plant that San Francisco was preparing for a landfill, not because the overstrained guts had lost their grand digestive powers but on account of a new cleansing system dreamed up in Silicon Valley and approved, at last, in Washington. His work, part-time, he never took for granted, no matter how tedious the tasks he was given. Father Marto had found — through friends — a position in the Mayor's office for when Blake was not keeping grounds or keeping vigil at the monastery. He smiled when San Francisco sent a blasé form guaranteeing the exchange, recalling the agitator evenings of college when some self-styled radical would stand atop a chair, bald and stiff like a well-oiled idol lifting a fist and delivering invectives against a city that abandoned its poor and bid them drink slop like domesticated pigs, and here he was, suit-and-tie, shuffling the proper papers into a folder and rubbing his rheumy eyes in the hallway, pausing at his supervisor's door to summon whatever perkiness could be coaxed from his getting-old bones before soliciting — attempted eye contact that ended in a kind of glassy aloofness — a signature from the Mayor's right-hand man which, without any fanfare, secured twelve million dollars toward removing invisible particles of pain from the sinks and showers of several million people. When he looked at the bungalows across the street he saw through to their veins, the lead pipes that would be ripped out and replaced next year. His Scotch tasted especially crisp and the burn it left brought complete throat clearance, as if whatever congested hesitations had been caught there for too long had fallen with the phlegm he spat in the street, cleared his throat to tell her, finally, all of the things he would not do now but which he indelibly had done with other women and a single man — a former professor — and when he finished and she said nothing and ten minutes later her mouth was still shaking to fill the bowl of silence between them and he threw out the word "transparency" and hated its sound so hotly he tried to swallow and take back the syllables but, failing that, stomached the regret. She turned away and her hot ears told him that seeing is not always

310

supreme, that to love the truth does not mean to tell it all the time unadulterated — as if every infinitesimal iota need be said aloud, as if we have right here on earth the wherewithal to undergo the judgments read before all souls in afterlife if we arrive, because if Blake would follow through his logic they would, we would be here not all night, but for forever in an eternal return, playing catch-up with the sins of seven generations dead to say nothing of those he wore like a crown atop his head.

"To maybe tell me one thing one night one at a time would be — to say nothing of loving — humane. But you're inhuman Blake, *inhumane*, to spill it all in a single sitting like I'm no woman but a silver spittoon." She guarded her face as she blew her nose and turned back to him, her eye red-blotches of carnations starved of water for a week: "And what am I supposed to do with all that? Now? Forgive you? You didn't do any of it to me, so why? Blake, are you *trying* to make me leave? You want me to go. And lack the courage to say so. So — my God I've been watching it since I've known you and wishing it away. So selfish. What you just did. *Not* courageous," she said, and stood over him, the unwatered plant of his sunflower face snapping under its own weight. "It's a navel-gazing game. God. Insane. God. Go away."

He had not argued then and he did not now, but why did he frown upon finding the player's face like Stella's but significantly aged, cheekbones like cliff sides, her mouth a door kept firmly clamped, her eyes shut too to keep whatever ceremonies went, concealed, within the ogler's gazes. Because — he looked around at the others and found, tired on tilted-elbow, a cozy and confessional couple, a heavyset man in a pinstripe suit pointing thrice at a growth chart draft — no one else was watching her. He felt as if he were on tiptoes, though his feet had fallen asleep under the weight of his pressurized thighs, legs crisscrossed twice in an awkward knot.

He had not spoken freely to a single woman since. All interactions he kept curt, sometimes turned and walked away with an almost flamboyant rudeness. Too many eyes too lovely or too hungry, too hurt or too hidden by the obvious garb of a widow's mourning — dark lashes worn long and blinking, waiting for him to return, painted black and with blue eye shadow. Where the women surely saw a nervous loser, totally cold or aloof or an idiot or what you will, he rushed away with a hurried suspension of his own reckless wish to hear his own voice tally all the pains he inflicted on the human population, as if he could redeem himself by hurting himself for all those he hurt, as if he could share what wasn't his to shoulder.

How now here now he was not so young, though all that happened when he was — if you could call some three and thirty years young. He was not here now a young man, though the Chopin notes had lost none of their persuasions and he smiled at the picture of him and his father heaving and shoving the piano up a staircase that wound like a corkscrew up two floors to the studio she shared with Eleanor. He was not embarrassed by the keys she had given him because they always parted before she lifted her well-tucked tightly-bound sheets and let them keep her fastened to the mattress, her feet stretching and pressing against the headboard (she slept upside down, she told him, as she traced the place his body would lie . . . outlining a shape that would never arrive). He had tried to explain that to his father as they sweated red and dad rolled his eyes at the dubious cover — the kid had her keys — that the two kids were not dampened lovers in the dark, bent backs and banging piano hammers, as they brought Stella the bones of Orpheus, heaving and grunting up the three flights of stairs, those white keys which when she pressed them resurrected something in him. When he went to purchase the spinet piano — an estate sale number the dead's estranged son was eager to be rid of for change, after he saved to rent the pickup and haul the cherry wood instrument from a gone-to-seed farm to Stella's once-hip neighborhood that had of late been a house of crime, and as he and his father tried to shove and force, love and give and will the Wurlitzer up the stairs, the piano's left leg gouged a hole in the wall and they gave up after two bad-air hours (the hallway windows were, like so many in the city, painted shut). When, heads hung, they exited the apartment, hastening to hide the gift before she came home from work with an awkward canvas splotched with paint — no Pollock this, no sense at all — they found a policeman squatting down, drawing an outline by a pool of blood, marking a square around a patch of asphalt. "What happened here, officer?" Garrett asked, needlessly gesturing towards the undried blood. "Drive-by." The stout officer whose belt was unbuckled rubbed his eyes as if removing a speck, "Eleven-year-old. Gone." A dusting of white left on his lashes, he bent on one knee to finish his sketch, shaking his head, shaking his head. "The name of the dead?" "Julieta," he said.

Blake's head jerked around and, meeting his dad's sheepish face, knew their shared disbelief: how had they not heard the commotion, the assembled random crowd (four of the men were dressed in rags, two wore pants whose tags stuck out) that another officer swatted away, not even the gunshot no regret could shove back down the nozzle. In silence Blake saw them back here tomorrow, loading the dead-weight piano into the rented pickup and driving it back to the farm all alone, the rented hearse. It hurt. His heart.

He felt in part he could not make it up the stairs because he hurt her, spilled his sins and sapped his strength. Told her everything — all the wrongs he'd committed to date. Never killed someone but almost himself, several times (strange how ordinary the inclination seemed until Stella showed him shock, her lips spasmodic, her hair literally pulled out in clumps of slightly-grayed red). And then there was the mass confusion he felt in the face of the city's sufferings. Always others' wrongdoings did him in. A kind of moral hypochondria convinced him that he could match any criminal, rival those depravities only special ops knew of — sometimes even that he *had*. At times it was hard to keep straight which wrongs he'd really done and which he'd read about or heard by gossip.

He nodded toward the apartment door — curved at the top with a blue glass dome that jutted out to give passersby cover. He bounded up the stairs and pulled the canvas alibi from the spinet, tossed it down when his dad walked up and said, mock-quiver in his throat, "Be thou a spirit of health or goblin damned?" Dad's muffled laughter lifted his spirits and he climbed the piano to the other side, then pulled with "Juliet" on his lips, giving the heaves for her repose, keeping it silent instead of spilling it, saving the gift from becoming a giveaway. He slept well at the end of that day.

But she may as well have drawn a police chalk outline around the emptiness that he soon became, disappearing when he tried to revisit, to retract his confession. She would not take scandal at his past. So he cited his parents' own failed marriage as cover for his cowardice — "I'm worried to the point of not sleeping that I'll hurt the hell out of you once we, if we were to . . . *finalize*." Often when he watched couples holding hands, picking up one another's checks, sprawled in parks with heads on necks or in whisper-spit spats at the packed bus stop of a Monday or Tuesday in Milwaukee, the graffiti on the glass saying No Justice, No Peace. He said aloud to his audience of one that the only way to rattle the selfish gestalt was to fail better than he had with her the first time, to fail and then remain there in the headlights of the lover, who would dim them as soon as you walked the line, mutter the lines that you'd mocked as cliché but found, now, to be a map of perfection: "Next time." But, never trusting that there would be a next time, or that there would be time enough for the variations of his heart to prove he wasn't just an algorithm on repeat, he had adopted a cat and learned how to feed it even when he came home tired and kept it even when it clawed him at dawn and he'd only just fallen asleep at three.

All of this, his alibi absence, rested measly and uneasy in the stomach of his mind.

The piano player stopped abruptly in the middle of a mad chase-down coda exploding in variation, leaving the familiar measure for measure torn apart with no repetitions. Stella's uncle who had known the novelist Milan Kundera once — "as acquaintance, I would not dare call him *friend*" — told Blake what the writer told him: "in his Opus III with each variation Beethoven moved away, could have eventually moved in tandem, perfectly, with what we might call the 'great infinity,' making the infinite so much less scary, this man who could sing such utter continuity from such a multitude of different scales, reveal analogy at the heart of reality, keeping the sequence of his initial theme, which resembles the final variation no more than a dried slide of a flower under the eye of a fine-tuned microscope resembles the plant still rooted in the field."

Everyone — even those lost in loud conversation, oblivious to the pounded keys that spilled like atoms, that chased the great changes of the world beyond recognition — clipped into silence and stared at her with the suddenly colluded accusation that she had done something wrong, that, though this was no formal concert, though the piano was always present, typically untouched but there, untouched but for the taking, and though the café did not pay her a single cent although she'd set a tip jar there that read only BABY with a tiny picture of the boy — that though she owed the assembled nothing she had, by stopping, done something wrong. She ran her left pointer finger along her right wrist with an abrasive rubbing action and a mouthed ow, and Blake knew her, unscrewed his denial, unscrewed the clamps that had suffocated his consciousness, this was always Stella's cover for something less socially couth and he stood when she stood and gave the room a terse curtsey, and she caught him staring and then looked away casually and then walked right up to him, standing on her tiptoes to match his height, not in the rival's pose of domination but in order to make it impossible for him to look anywhere else except her glasses — new, they must be, for her lifelong short-sightedness — whose diamond glints along a trifocal line eclipsed her eyes.

"I could feel you looking at me," she said and his shoulders lifted while he bit his lip with the bitter taste of bile swirling like a manmade minor typhoon at the base of his bowels. "Don't cringe," she said. "That's the whole thing. It didn't come off as creepy or, like — familiar — the kind of, pathetic ogling, I've told you countless times I hate. Besides, tell me how a boy and a girl are supposed to meet if one doesn't first look at the other? Angelic telepathy? Pure spirits? God knows I'm not one."

"God knows I'm not a boy anymore."

"Thank God," she said. "I've put away childish things. Having a child helps you to do that."

"Didn't for my dad — not for a long time. Wait. You have a child?"

"Does that disqualify me?"

"Does that disqualify *me*?"

"The daddy's long gone. If that, for a start, doesn't scare you away, then . . . But I have to get home and feed baby. And I, look, there's something overwhelming about even exchanges that pretend to be innocent."

"I — are you kidding me? That's *exactly* what I was just telling a friend, yesterday. Why I don't — why I stay alone. I mean I live with my dad who is kind of, deteriorating fast, but it's also an excuse not to have to get serious in the way of — women."

Finding how completely he mimicked her frankness, how fast and rashly he'd done so without thinking, Blake stepped back, tried a playful note that fell flat. "What's your name?"

"Blake."

"I can't sing you a song of innocence," she said, not flaunting but also not inflected with a cynical sneer. Not infected. For he was sure it was like a disease. "But I'll be here next week. I won't, probably, be as witty, and you won't probably, be quite so handsome (with your hair still wet from the rain outside and your cute attempt to keep hidden in the corner), and I might if the baby's kept me up all night play something even more gloriously morose, but if you can bear it all I'd love to see how we stand, then. To see you again, I mean," and she looked at the beads of electric blue lights that traced the door frame and blinked.

"Stella. It *is* you," he said, having almost lunged after her, his foot catching on somebody's backpack. "Stella."

"As in *Kind of Blue*. Stella by Starlight. That's not what my folks were thinking in the least when they named me but it's what I've become since we last knew each other." She had fathomed what she'd say if she saw him again but the script had been shredded by the scissors of regret, the violent and unremorseful ripping into the petty, unreadable pieces of brilliant showing-up. She shook her head *no* and touched the tip of her toes. "I mean it could be very, very vain, but I do, I do, I love, love, love that song. And . . . the more so, strangely, since Chicago. Instead of feeling it as a guilty reminder."

In the days after he found her again he walked daily around the Din Park Lagoon, after work and without having eaten, worrying over her forthrightness, watching the goose feathers trouble the water, so totally light and untroubled themselves — a way he could never be but she, Stella, seemed at times to possess, a sort of spiritual levity if not weightlessness. For whenever the truth appeared that unabashed, and whenever a self-styled truth-teller appeared, two things (at least) followed in train: the expectations were set so tip-toe high, reaching even the topmost cabinet and clearing out what remained hidden there, that whenever an error remained concealed — by shame or strategy — beyond the spry eyes of the roof-top tell-all who had promised, from his perch, to see and say everything, to cry the town's dirty laundry (his included, free of charge), the disappointment was severe. And then, these self-styled truth-tellers (he was once, God, of their number) almost always were more interested in unveiling the sins of others and the deficiencies of systems than they were in unconcealed confession of their own self-serving designs. Stella had not rubbed her wrist the entire time they talked, so the pain that she had dramatized when she abruptly stopped playing had not been feigned or phantom. He was wrong about many things. Unless she'd forgotten while they spoke, as she had given him those moments of levity, Chopin tiding over him like a flooding Lethe — a sound that stilled too soon.

He hated being weary of the world but could not discover a way to erase the wary face, furrowed and warped, from which he tried to exude real warmth to the elderly who circled the lagoon two blocks away from Stella's old place. Watch them with their walkers and wheelchairs, smiles breaking out of the wrinkles that had seemed at first glance far more fixed than rutted, heirloom, old tree bark. As if they needed whatever kindness he could spare or needed him to receive theirs. He was the beggar there, returning on Wednesday and Thursday — even Saturday at six a.m., after walking, briskly, past Stella's Kinnickinnic apartment, passing but never letting himself look up to where her window would be, not even raising his eyes

to the blue stained glass dome that jutted out to grant passersby
cover (out of the corner of his eyes he swore the once blue brick had
been painted the color of mineral-rich and clothes-staining clay). He
could not bear the thought of a light there. In the park the sun was
young, still a hint of smoldering fire some farmer had forgotten to
put out the night prior. There was a silent triumph that tipped its hat
from these octogenarians who had, whatever their doings, whatever
unworthiness propped up on stilts, simply lasted this long, as if mere
life were something worth savoring and his own ambitions only
illusions waiting — wanting? — to be lost. Hölderlin's Successful
Failure. The stretched oval that was shaped like an ovary brought
forth the good ache of gasping for breath — a feeling of life that
he'd known for years since working in the monastery for Father
Marto: repeated desperate sucks of air because you saw how precious
the air was, the goodness of something so plain as breath as clear
as a clanging defuntos's ploro bell, when you sensed what would
happen if it was taken away. He loved the way a bent-over man with
a boulder of knotted flesh for a shoulder would crane his face up
and shout — squeezing his oxygen machine and inhaling through
the tubes that climbed his nostrils toward his brain — "Godspeed."
When he watched the man waddle away he remembered something
his dad had said recently, something he'd written off then as defeat-
ist: that there's too much feel-good gab about leadership, forming
the next generation of presidents, and too little dignity lent to those
whose self-governance will do more for the world but will never
be registered or recorded. But when they met again on the next lap
the man stopped abruptly at a wooden bench whose blue paint had
peeled away except for a few deep-set lines that spread like veins
through the grains. "Some things, you know, that are changing,
now, will take it-t-t-t" — and here his mouth, unloosed from the
stutter, moved without making a sound — "take it away, what you
wanted to keep. Changes. Hear? So massive you won't not know,
won't be able to no matter what. Won't recognize the world. And not
for the better — not all of it, anyway, for the good." Blake nodded
and began to answer before he had thought through whatever half-
choate broken string of beads he so genially offered, but the man

looked from his unkempt hair to his well-laced waterproof boots, then threw his hands in the air and kicked a pebble into the lagoon. The speck did not trouble its surface.

In the charred log propped up from a fire pit he saw the obsidian outline of her whitened hair, perfectly jagged above her plain face, whose features he blinked to recover but failed. After an about-face he plodded quickly away, his soles aching at how hard he worked them, his thumbnail gouging the heart of his palm with the complex regret and relief of fleeing the stranger with Godspeed.

On his way home, at the base of Stella's place, he saw a mail-woman struggling to open the letter lockbox tucked under the ancient façade of the old apartment. She was red and breathy and checking her watch, framed by mistletoe chiseled into limestone, intertwining until it morphed into the small and smug faces of gargoyles.

"I've no idea," she said to him. "These are the keys that I was given. You live here? This isn't my usual route." He looked at the garish scarlet banner that blew, like a screen, above the dome, blocking the modest gargoyle whose eyes were not comic but harsh, its head squared as if pressured by a vice, as if squeezed out from the floors within by all of Stella's poundings on the piano (was it still there? Was *she* back here?). A newly planted, battery-powered sign — maybe for Stella's apartment, maybe for a new condo whose layout plans boasted from a glossy graphic posted on a realtor's easel — listed the starting price at $1,500 for a single.

"Not a chance," he said. "But I do love these gargoyles," he said, pointing at the nooks where the creature hid, calling her attention to the ousted cretin for, it seemed, the first time. "What in hell's damned?" she asked, her teeth big through parted lips that resolved on a tentative smile. "The world would be a better place if every building had them," he proposed, his tone playful. "Why's that?" "Keeps the water from ruining the masonry," he said, signaling the harsh-headed creature, hallway human not a monster, so that the length of his neck seemed strangely extended compared to the smallness of his face, the pouting lips that were the spout when it rained. "Keeps the masons out too." "Excuse me?" the mailwoman asked, patting her bag as if for mace. "Sure," he went on, "they could do the same with plain aluminum gutters. But what would remind us, in all those perfect lines, that the varieties of evil are almost endless? Rarely if ever are our special wrongs alike." She'd cracked the lock with the right key at last and busied herself with letters and a few little packages. "Forgive my peculiar sense of humor," he said, moving his thumb under his fist as he said it, mimicking the gargoyle's exasperation.

"Don't forget to have some fun," she said, rallying confidence as she stuffed the last batch of coupons into the final slot. Strange how both of his mentors — Hape and Father Marto — trained him to spy the ways he might try for these breakthroughs. Something Stella also aspired to. Clues — cues — he could learn from her.

Could never afford the cost of living. How could I dare to pick back up marriage as if I could carry a real salary? The gargoyle spat a trickle of scum and seemed to say, through its smug hole, "The beast with two backs." *Vade retro Satana*, Blake whispered, to the mail lady's "excuse me, or should I say excuse you," "Please do."

. . .

Next Tuesday, when she said she'd be back, when he turned the corner he pressed his ear against the wall of Corazón, awaiting the throb of that subaltern sound that had so perfectly tuned him last week, he found instead a great silence filled by the chatter of other couples whose joy he had to try hard not to hate.

In the monastery basement Blake scoured the internet, found her name, a few smatterings of evidence that in fact she still existed, or at least did once exist — the feature faculty at St. Cabrini's, a birth certificate for Jason Stęskni.

He returned again the subsequent Tuesday, and was ready to do so into infinity.

. . .

" . . . "
"Stell?"
"Here."

320

"You hear me? I — you answered. Baby. I hear him. How's he doing?"

"Looks like his daddy," she said. The words came out noncommittal, the tone tethered and tugged back in reaction because what she offered might please, put ease in place of an evicted disappointment.

"I miss you."

"..."

"You hear that? Somebody or something keeps setting off the fire alarm. First time was at three a.m. I jumped up and ran outside to find a handful of others huddled there. A handful out of what should have been hundreds. Twilight-zone type of shit. Somebody had a blanket and they were all waiting there for sirens. Never came."

"Peter, you're a mess if you don't sleep. For how many nights has this been happening?"

"Who isn't? A week. But this is the first time it's happened during the day."

"But you especially."

"Huh?"

"Sleep. You need it more than anyone I know."

"This is the first time the alarm's going off at a decent hour. I'll take that."

"One of these times it'll be a real fire. Landlord?"

"You can guess the answer to that. My location's not supposed to be known. My name is Peter Brahmin but my high caste don't exactly mean I can complain to the slumlord. I don't know even if whoever owns the place knows I'm here. This is the third apartment I've been in in three weeks. Not that the — other benefits outweigh, maybe, the downsides. Like I can send money. But they tell me, the bank, you ain't cashing a one. Or, better, you cashed maybe one."

"For the baby."

"Baby. You too, baby."

"Are you happier?"

"You know that's a crazy question. How could I be without you here? Him."

"... "

"A good dose of silent treatment today."

"Peter I wish I didn't have to be the one to say it. But I don't think you can see it. The whole while I lived with you, you were permanently disappointed. When I wasn't working I was trying to make you happy. Cooking this. Listening for a long time. I hear that sigh. Please don't misunderstand me. I'm not taking any of that back, but now that I've gotten some distance, perspective, what was nagging all those months came clear. I could not and could never make you happy. And I don't mean that in the superficial sense. And I don't mean that we can't be together because it was hard or it didn't feel good."

She kept from him the other reasons, the hole in the wall the size of his fist. That seemed, from a distance, entirely reasonable given all the projections and pressures pumped straight into that single body.

"Wait. Now why do I have all these visions of you laughing, leaning off the couch and spitting out your coffee? Don't know what made you laugh, but remember cleaning it up. Best chore of my life. Because it meant you were content. What now, that was an exception? A one-time thrill in a 'miserable marriage'? Don't everybody, when a relationship's strained, readily recall all the wrongs, the pain? But that's not all, Stella. Don't lie now. I — could do better to say it. Thank you. I admit it. I . . . love you."

"I've seen it before. Something about men now?" She knew what she would say would be the worst, like a firecracker meant for the sky but burst in the hand before it could even take flight: "With Blake the same discontent. A bucket with a hole in it. Fill it with the choicest, whatever, wine, holy water. In a couple of hours all that's there is thirst."

"... "

"Does anything I'm saying resonate?"

"I see it in me, yeah, honestly. Don't know where it comes from or how in hell to...."

"Heal?"

He made a choked sound.

"Thank you for everything you did for me. The many knock-down-drag-out sessions. The countless meals you made to make my other doings possible."

"What makes this all harder was, is, I was so *happy* to make them. Every time. Every onion chopped, all the time, I'd think of you and believe I got damn good and damn I's doing good through you!"

"You did," he laughed, harder than called for, trying to forge a higher plain, to forage for mushrooms on that meadow that weren't the poison twin morels.

"What *really* mattered was not the dish but what I poured into it, the wishes that I whispered while I made the meal or ran your signatures over to Marjorie or deposited the donations in the bank — all of this, I wanted to please you. And maybe that was the mistake. No altruism in this little heart. Maybe I wasn't trying to make *you* happy but to please myself with your pleasure."

"But I didn't — I couldn't have been happier. When you were there."

"You're deluding. Peter, I'm not wrong on this." She diluted the anger in her voice, counting her own vices like sheep, until what she said wore a sleepy tenor. "I've been mistaken a million times but this I swear is straight truth."

"What do you want me to do different? I'll do it, immediately. Now that it's out."

"No. You, a counselor, know that's not how things go. As if coming into consciousness of our flaws is enough to . . . *oust* them. And besides you don't even believe what I'm saying."

"I believe because I believe in you."

"But why? Because I mothered you around when you'd lost all sense of worth."

"Oh, here we go. Now what'll be next? All the wrongs I've ever done lined up in the corridor of horrors. Ladies and gentlemen, here lies the remains of Peter Clavier, con artist extraordinaire, called by his uncle 'evidence of concupiscence.' Professional sinner, etcetera, etcetera."

" . . . "

"Stella. I'm sorry. Is there no forgiveness?"

"You yourself said forgiveness gets in the way of justice. That patience and forgiveness and humility have been abused to excuse atrocities. Keep the wretched of the earth waiting for some never-coming day when all their woes be taken away. I can hear you say it. 'Fuck forgiveness.'"

"In *that sense*, not in every. Damn, don't treat me like the press. Pluck from a day's worth of words just one that, like a good grenade triggering pin, blowing the rest into amnesiac particles. I said what I said because I —"

"Because you didn't possess it yourself. Forgiveness. I felt it. I lived it. I saw it sicken you night after night. And as we all do, you cooked up a way to make that lack seem not only okay but fully justified."

"Alright. Alright."

" . . . "

"I cop to it. I confess it. What you want? What you want. But I won't take a full tackle. I'm not going to take the hit for all the men who did you in. For Blake especially."

"Blake is back."

" . . . "

"I don't mean dating."

"Your dad'd be glad. All the winner got to do is show up without being black."

"Don't misquote me. Don't do what you hate to see done to you. You think I don't hate it too?

"I said in my letter my dad's friends are out there, racializing everything. Didn't you read it? Dad acts, always, in *tolerance*. He doesn't see what I see: he thinks he can win everyone around, away from their devils. Dad's loyal in a way I could *never* be, and sometimes his demeanor seems like a virtue."

"Nothing like nostalgia to turn loyalty into delusion."

"I don't need you to notice that. I see it and said it in my own words."

"Woah, woah. I'm trying to build you up. Support, confirm you in what you've seen. Damn. Where'd you get this stubbornness, Stell? Your mother or your father? It's coming out stronger 'cause you been around them now. 'Cause once you start on a tear ain't nobody stopping you until the house burns down. And as you can hear that alarm's still ringing. So go ahead. Finish the fire. I can take it. Or if I can't, it'd be a good way to go."

"What forgiveness actually means honestly scandalizes me. The root of the — separation — isn't only you. I can't — again I've been observing my parents — imagine how two people can stay together for any reason other than convenience and compromise. In any long-term way, I mean. Show me someone who's in a life-long commitment who isn't ridden with a trillion resentments that follow precisely from that fidelity."

"Show me a lonely, solitary soul who's not got envy for the dupes who married resentfully ever after."

She heard a high-pitched, hysterical laughter. The sound had its origin in her own chest.

"See," he said. "My only real skill is undermining from the inside."

"How are your efforts unfolding? Have they discovered you're a 'double agent'?"

"Hahaha. I'm *not*, though. You know I can't say all aloud. What I'm doing is redirecting their movement toward its lost targets, restoring the original motives."

"Sounds like every mastermind manipulator who ever spoke on behalf of the people."

"There is no people without an elite. A people without a still point on the horizon has no perspective. A 'people' without an elite is, call it what you will, basically a disconnected . . . babble of atoms that disintegrates into a battle of electrons, each only knowing its own nucleus, as if each unto his own is the single center of the universe. The more a leader clamors on about 'the people' at a loud volume, the more I fear he is leading them by the nose without their knowing it."

"Oh the money I could make on an exposé."

"Not correct, politically, enough for you? Look at these blood-shot whites of my eyes. I'm tired for a reason and I don't mean to be for long. You won't need to make money. Multiple sources've given me enough to retire, I'd guess, next year. Sick. At thirty-three. Stella. Baby. Will you marry me?"

"..."

"That's not a no. So." He stirred the subdued silence and she felt dizzy, like she did as a child swirling a stick around a pool of neighborhood water that radiated a filmy rainbow, oblivious to the fumes of the oil. "Something really big is about to happen here. I'd give anything to see my son one more time."

She waited for a lighter inflection, a levity that did not come.

"I — well, the ticket'd be free."

"I'm telling you. No need to measure things out in that way."

"And the money you're making — you're not taking it from . . . sketchy sources?"

"Show me, in our world as it exists right now, a bank account that isn't compromised. There's enough guilt to go around. I'm doing what I'm paid to do. Amazing how much money there is for this kind of thing, and more amazing how laissez-faire they are about 'outcomes.'"

. . .

After she hung up she cashed a check and traveled to D. C. on an afternoon flight that was not the regular red-eye cheap she had taken her whole life until that day. She went with the baby without annunciation, without telling Peter her plans, ready to surprise him at a rally — to see his face when he saw his son.

She saw his face when he saw his son. His face fell through the stage floor.

The faithful in the front row reached forward to catch him in case he fainted. One man's bulbous eyes measured the distance from the stage edge to the floor. A good ten feet. His Adam's apple rose and fell. Hot as hell, somebody said. "Quick," Stella followed, tenuous. "Must be more than the heat's making him sick. Somebody run down to the bathroom and fetch a glass of water." Where was the bathroom? Was there one? "Quick," Stella said, softly, so as not to alarm the entire crowd, but her round face, flanked by thinning, silver-red hair, was pink with worry. She could feel it like a cross-section of fresh-cut fish at Dad's delicatessen.

Not a window left opened. Klieg lights too bright. Peter preferred candles. The airless room did not breathe and everything, even time, was stuck inside.

For an unprotected, shoulder-slumped instant, Peter looked vanquished. Self-confounded. Lips stretched grim. He had seen her friendly wave from afar, seen her hold up the baby who giggled and wiggled and held his belly like it was bowling-ball ready, without his hands, to fall. She felt when she waved like a skinny ghost waiting her turn. Get in line. What if he did not let her in, if he bided time until none remained, answering questions from his fawning fans, waiting her out with a filibuster?

He chewed his gums until she saw blood and his lips resumed their grim stretch. Until now he had always considered himself a moderate man, the coolest head in the heady room, proudly sympathetic in the face of his and everyone else's "hidden humanity." But now, albino fingers wet with blood from bitten gums, he's convinced by the single fanatic waving her hand in the back of the courtroom, a strange bird who he's known before, brown cardigan and beautiful scarf of azure cashmere she had covered him with, once, when their walk was long and his blood was stiff and the vendors were closed — not a hot chocolate in sight — her baby wrap suspender-slung, conjoined to her body as if inseparable.

"If it please the court, I present to you a case that will prove to be unpopular," she could hear his tremulous, baritone hum louder than the P. C. she had kept at bay, on the phone line at best some short thousand miles away, made in whose image, she wonders, now, while she, in her own story, is the long-lost lover, arrived at last with the famous man's baby, who no one here knows about, thanks to Marjorie who wiped his history clean of her whiteness, who dyed his albino melanin brown.

"It is this raw *anti-*," Peter proclaimed, "which eats away at every good future and puts in its place an abyss, a vacuum. We would need to eliminate the straight-up anti- if we would not fail to save our country. If we wish not to see all we say we fight for eliminated in short order. Hear me, hear me: we cannot be *just* if

327

we're just anti-. You need to be *anti-*, for a little while, you say. Anti-fascist and anti-privilege and anti-West and anti-white. And whatever will be built on whatever remains of the oppressor's ruins when we wipe him away — whatever will be built is not now our business. Yes, by necessity, we must be the *resistance*. But let this be known. A politics of anti- ruled by art and empty of content is nothing but what we profess to oppose: the total art of oppressive power. If we have nothing other than *resistance* to repeal it with, what we hate will be replaced by one big horrifying vacuum filled with the million competing wills of a people who have nothing in common, nothing shared but their fiery anti-hate. Let us not prostitute politics to the principles of negation at work in the enemy."

She waited for what he would put in hate's place but his voice woke baby from habitual slumber and she had to take their boy into the hallway. Separated by thick panes of glass, she took her breast out slow enough for Peter to see, to see the flab he had made her become, the chewed-on roundness no man could now desire. When he caught the flash of her flesh he cupped the curve of his stomach and faltered on stage, halted his words, searching, searching.

Failing to find the right rousing word, he rubbed at his eyelids, stared and nodded when Stella stood tall in the hallway, atop a blue chair left for security, chest out and smiling, unbuckling his baby, holding up for Peter to see the cute T-shirt bearing the statistics: THE 99%. In small all-caps font the size of a footnote was written the clarifying explanation: REMEMBER: CONDOMS ARE ONLY 98.5% EFFECTIVE IN PREVENTING PREGNANCY. The job was done. He could no way read it. God, how had they let her graduate grade school?

His lips started to move again but their deliberate pronunciations seemed uninspired, Peter able only to keep respiring. Jason fed, she returned to the room, to gauge the extent of her victory. Faces once dotted with lazy eyes and poorly disguised desperation looked up at him with moderate confusion, half the heads nodding halfheartedly, as he spelled out steps for a reasonable reform that were as far from radical as D. C. from Milwaukee: body cameras, no faux reports or an officer is immediately suspended for a year. She, he knows, has heard these strategies before but always from his opponent's mouths. Disappointed to be relieved, she listened to him plagiarize his detractors, bereft of all the grievance drudged up from the bowels of the country.

She turned to leave, to wait for him to field the crowd that formed a half-moon around him.

He waved away questions with apologies, almost elbowed a scrawny woman wearing a traditional green Nigerian dress; holding tight to her golden gele, she kept it from coming displaced in the shuffle. The rows of metal chairs were collapsed with terrible speed by ushers whose ears are filled with Bluetooth buds. When a worried hand clasped Peter's elbow, he turned to find a spitting image of himself at twenty. One of the ushers — his badge read J. K. — started to direct traffic away: "I — I'm sorry. I got another event," Peter smiled against the exodus, as if the sudden exit were against his will, while his eyes, frantic, found Stella's slow-pace tease as she shoved the door with her wide hip.

"Mr. Clavier?" The young man's afro was well-kempt and he carried, clamped under his arm, a hefty book. "I have so many questions. What you said. My name is Terrace. Studying at George Washington University. Law. I'm — what you said is exactly what I've arrived at on my own. I — ."

One of the ushers muscled Terrace's grip away from Peter's forearm, not quite in arrest, coaxed the questioner's hands behind his back as if he had placed them there by himself.

"You don't need me is what that means. To direct anything or offer answers. Those days are over. You know where to go."

"But I don't know what to do." The last word came out like a fifth-grade boy's during after-school tutoring in a subject he's failing. The usher by now was leading Terrace backward through the Fire Exit door. Part of the theatrics that made the famous seem important: keep them at a distance, and the followers will feel fortunate to even touch the garment.

Peter soured his mouth and gave a mean stare to the usher, who was maybe a security detail sent by Marjorie. Another decision against his will. Too many matters outside his control. The mistake was hard to hide any more: as if you could maintain what was called freedom once you signed on to a group.

Seeing what had happened to Terrace, the crowd had dispersed quickly, their questions kept to themselves. Congregated in a corded-off rectangle, a thin third of the main hallway, some clapped as Peter passed and several booed (whether he was the object or the security, he did not know). Many round faces smiled through the familiar pain that filled the room like an odorless gas. Seeing an at-ease security officer, sunglasses and bulletproof helmet, Peter sighed and dug his chin down hard, shaking his head as he found the thin arched exit cut like a man-sized keyhole from the great gray stone building. The wind outside rippled and whipped a taut flag cast at half-mast for a loss he did not know. Clasping his own wrist over his backside, Peter peered through the revolving doors, taking in the silhouette of the last crowd he would ever speak to, the thirty who had stayed to have their opinions confirmed — a straggler courting a direct confrontation. Some stood with hands behind their backs and others, hangdog with disappointment, wrangled wearily with the officer, whose gun handle's glare caught Peter's eye. An elderly man in a weathered gray suit, red corsage covering his heart, who wore his white hair in Uncle Cedric's short top with the same curved, close-cut fade, fingered the flower as if in commemoration of a man being led down his death row sentence.

Peter found Stella at the end of the block, where she gripped the blackened iron cage that kept a fruitless tree from being stolen. Her feet, one in front of the other, covered a crack in the sidewalk. He looked over his shoulder with a jerk, half-disappointed that no one had followed him.

"Let's duck in here." He gestured his chin toward a conspicuously empty back alley. There, as they sat on the chilled cement of an abandoned loading dock, he exhaled hard, aloud, three times. He pressed his lips to Jason's hair and inhaled again and again and again.

"That'll be my last rally."

"That's a new one," she said, no rancor but rather pity mingled with the laconic words.

"I got plans. Enough saved to live without needing new work for two years. You or me. Nothing needed. Health care figured into the equation. Maybe three years, even. Enough time to fade, fully, into blessed oblivion. A quiet job I'll find in Milwaukee. I'll come to you. No more you to me."

She stood and slipped into her Dad's navy backpack, said pacing in an awkward slow waltz, "I only wanted you to see him. You scare the shit out of me, Peter. If you don't care to care enough whether you live or die, baby, I can't give you anything. I came in case you don't live long. It's only right you should take him in. Remember his scent when they take you out. I'm frankly not convinced by your *plans*—and if I can't convince you to save yourself, all I can do is give you the fixings for as happy a death as possible. Here," she held out a plastic bag that crinkled loudly in a sudden gust. "Pictures of him. Of us. And a piece. A lock of his hair. A lost practice. My Nonna reminded me to keep a book, a baby book with his first word and such. Remember? Gog. You said it was a thing. Gog and Magog. Catholic, okay, I had no idea. Still a mystery to me, honestly. Grandson of Noah and city of destruction."

"I'll have to call my Uncle soon. One of these days. Get reconciled. I'll ask him to give me a proper Bible study. Or rather he'll give it even if I don't ask. It's the anniversary of mama's dying soon. I'll call him and ask him. Gog. Oh man." He nodded and chuckled and his knuckles showed as he cramped his hands and fell into silence. "I won't say I love you but I want to show you."

"I have to catch a late flight home. Nowhere to sleep and not with you. Not so fast. Nonna played Patience. It's a game you and I could learn from. Start here. Maybe more. No promises. No plans. Test it all against the calendar. To an outsider, me, your mind changes like a weathervane in a summer storm. I need to see it steady for a time. Kiss your boy, see if we can figure it. Somehow kiss him and stay away from me. He has your handsome weighty smile, heavy, heady, star-crossed eyes."

. . .

The tears dripped like a bad cold snot, like when corona had kept him in bed for a week and she ran three humidifiers when he refused to be hospitalized and found, from a friend he knew at Cabrini, a doctor who prescribed him ivermectin. Whether or not the drug saved his lungs, it never stopped his faucet face, which she watched now with nerves drugged by all the accusations she could make but stuffed back down into the bowels of her heart like backed-up shit, sins saved like computer files doubled across several servers. She knew she did not know if they were true — the time he held the spatula high, over her head, was it a lie, swatting a fly, not frightening her eyes? But if they were true, the searing pictures saved on her soul's second server, her very mention of them would ignite that wrath that kept her up at night back in Chicago where it all began.

. . .

He watched her sway as she walked away, heard her say, so he could hear, "Your Daddy." Doubts. She might have said diaper, hungry, baby. Daddy? Maybe. Two cars clacked around the corner, scent of tires starting on fire, freeway speed down the single lane boulevard. The black corvette beat the BMW but both stalled tied at a red light. She swayed, so slight, he would not beg. The red light raised like rouge in the night. Like a dog he would not follow. A cab appeared, she disappeared. The checks would come, and more would follow. The account was full, he was not hollow. He'd call his Uncle Cedric tomorrow.

. . .

Peter entered the unmarked room to find a defunct cubicle, bad light, bad air, and a dozen masked volunteers — some with sunglasses and blue surgical numbers, others with ski masks, and still another several strangers who wore, outside their already-ski-masked mouths, the sky-blue coronavirus cotton.

"It will be the starting point of everything," said a pink-faced man, skinny, spry, blushing, long forehead like a mule's stubborn nose. No-nonsense wizened eyes, adjusting his bun and looking around at all the clacking and packaging happening across the alabaster tables. He coughed into a busted fist, either badly chapped or fresh from a punching bag suspended from the bathroom ceiling. Following Peter's stare he relaxed his fist and mussed up his hair and said, "Revolution. Simple starts. Lenin and his friends. A dozen to begin with. Now look. Jesus." The words lifted his phlegm-stained mask. Spittle stippled his chin. With his other hand he sorted white capsules filled with tiny black particles into small blue cylindrical bottles that read, in bright red: PAIN KILLER. A woman whose hair matched the chrome pipes that wound upward like upside-down tree roots peeled labels and stuck them to the bottles before she tossed them, delicately, to the far end of the table. The concentration in the upper room was as tight as the boiler in its center.

The man with the mule-nose forehead turned, his eyes like snouts, as he snuffled out his maxim, as if to test Peter, to see if this in fact would be the beginning — the beginning of the end of the end of history: "It, what we accomplish together, if we succeed, and we will, my friends, will be the start of everything." His crescent mouth showed coffee-yellowed teeth: a sweet smile like a doting grandfather's, shocked to receive a visit from his grandson.

"Perhaps, but history is typically what hurts, my friend." Peter counted the capsules sadly. "Are you ready to burn? The wretched of the earth tend to fare badly — turned like martyrs over the coals, but without the same destination."

The pink-faced man with hollowed-out eyes — his glasses truly were like the nostrils of a mule — turned a light shade of purple, coughed into his elbow and said, "Better red than dead. What my father always said."

"Have you ever been dead?" Peter could not help asking. "No? Hard to compare then, I'd say."

"Look, I'm here today because my godson cannot be. He was brutally murdered for a routine traffic stop after reaching for his wallet in the glovebox. Don't you fucking fuck with me. He gave his life to try and fight the policies that never passed that left him dead without a chance."

Peter bowed, said, "Shit, what's his name, I'm sorry. It's hard to play about anything anymore." His rash jokes, once a signature, seemed smarmy now, where they once seemed dynamite — doing away with the last pieties. "But I had no idea, of course, if I did — I." The man gripped his hand, "Brother. We got to learn to live together."

"Edward," he said. "His name is Edward. Unarmed, fatally harmed. Officer — I say without relish — stabbed to death in prison the next year."

One by one the man's muscles loosened and as he returned to his task he said, with finality, "We'll never learn."

Peter, sneaking a check of his watch, shuffled into the adjoining office space.

To the adjusting eye, to the newly-arrived, the long room's inhabitants worked without ceasing — the walls were exposed, no drywall even to cover the wires, the pipes, so the place assumed the look of a computer chip's underbelly — all admirably fixated on the tasks assigned by whom Peter needed to find, for always there was a center of power, especially in such a gang as this: all, no doubt, inevitably allergic to structures and systems of any shape — except, of course, for the horizontal leaderless circles of community too typical in the idealist's annals. He felt his jugular vein start to vibrate. But here, as each worked according to his need — a handicapped man counted caps for the bottles with the two fingers he had left — the uncanny devotion moved him. As though, through their common pot of stew, they were feeding the fate of the world. The pink-faced man in particular screwed up his face and shook a pill bottle and sent the cylinder skidding down the table as if fate were hungry as hell and only he could keep it fed. The sun's fire paled through the tinted glass, the last of its light captured then possessed on the cheeks of the veteran revolutionary: he looked as if he had travelled with Trotsky, or at least transcribed his dying thoughts. Had to be at least in his eighties. His high forehead was incongruous with the wide blown-out, weathered cheeks. Peter studied them as the man coughed, his mask ineffectual, slung from an ear, tickling his throat, stimulating a smile.

334

Two coals. How many died to harvest our heat? Quick deaths, young or hacked out over decades, consumptive coughs of fire and blood. Costly in our time. Sisyphus. The room was a furnace. No air conditioning. Dehydration just standing still. Sweat like sparks leapt off volunteers as they poured powder into big canisters. A woman with nails elongated like coffins — painted dark metallic too — clawed at the controls of a cylindrical mixer that clanked and completed what she could not do. She nodded her head to the rhythmic clack, tapping prescription-bottle plastic with her nails.

Peter watched, rapt, impressed, quickly learning the system that followed. The first man filled five packages in five seconds and passed them to the next, who, with one hand holding up a black bandana over his brown face whenever the other came close, then peeling it back to take a breath when his co-worker swayed the other way, kept on filling the packages. The third in the line, seasoned russet face that said he had seen everything, and did in fact say "I've seen it all, success and failure. So what if more missions fumble than hit? Even if one out of a hundred finds its target — well, we good, we good!" — he turned blue, discolored by the plastic cylinders stacked in makeshift pyramids everywhere, bluer still from reflecting the screen of a sleek computer with two wide monitors where a ski-masked woman with thick black glasses lifted them up as she counted the completions.

"Four thousand five hundred and twenty," she said, taking a tack that looked like a hairpin out of a cushion molded in the shape of an overweight Barbie. She stuck the pin into Chicago. Her curled hair bobbed and spilled out, getting in the way of her one good eye. Peter caught himself staring at the scar that seared through her opposite eyehole. A sick green gash, the stitches still in, yellow pustules signifying healing.

"P. C." he whispered into Peter's ear. "I'm sorry I snapped, earlier. I know you meant no meanness. An honor to meet you in person at last." He looked both ways and raised his voice. "This will be the start of everything. The Senator's fundraising dinner is scheduled for seven p.m. at the Lincoln Ball Room." The man in the sleeveless tee wore pinstripe pants and alligator shoes. His eyes stretched in irritation as he put on, poorly, the submissive look of an unthinking underling. Peter restrained himself from slapping the subordination off his face.

"Wait. Haha, very funny. You're shitting me. The event's been long scheduled at the National Press Club." He felt a foreboding in the switch. As if the action he had not taken and had not even fully explained was already anticipated by someone who was watching him.

"Man, if you don't know where it's at we are in triple trouble. The National Press Club kicked them out last night. How Senator Ivors's been talking sufficed. You read the papers?"

"I try not to when I'm working. My team keeps me up-to-date. Otherwise it can feel funny, demoralizing, like everything's already been done."

"Where you are going? What you are doing?" said the pink-faced man to a well-masked boy whose exposed flesh was plastered with pimples. He could not have been older than sixteen — barely-grown facial hair where the mask ran out. His eyes, Peter noticed, held the deception: aged by all they had already seen. "Pull it up. Fix that thing. For your own sake stay well concealed. If I scream atcha it's because I love ya. And when you're finished with that over there, can you carry this box please to 1B?"

"We're fortunate with this crop," he went on when the youth had slunk, stomach held out to manage the package. To Peter it looked like a two-person number. "For as long as I've been doing this we have a handful of folks who are totally in, but most show signs of being doubters — admittedly to varying degrees. But this year — look at what history can deliver. Look, my friend, what history can make happen. With a little help from Curtis and Marjorie. Amazing organizers. Top-shelf shit. Nearly the whole crew is nothing if not zealous." He continued to discourse as Peter pulled a real ibuprofen from his breast pocket and crunched it between his teeth, satisfied by the bitter silt that gave his face a gritty shape.

A fresh arrival in a Hawaiian shirt — badly buttoned, or left wide open — elbowed the man whose eyes glistened like mule nostrils. Peter wanted to ask the man's name. He thought, from what he'd observed, this could be him, a legend — Pierre? But to ask was against the rules here. Every place had its taboo foreigners. Anyone who asked around for names gave himself away as a rat. The policy did not protect famous accidents, but it was instituted for the anonymous volunteers, not for them. The fresh arrival elbowed the mulish man, a second time, when the first failed. He blinked eye drops into his right lens, sighed, soothed, but the burst blood vessel still looked ominous — a tangle of unearthed roots set afire. "Forgive for being late. Someone called in sick at the store. I had to work a double. Won't get a single cent of overtime either." He threw down a newspaper, unfolded it roughly, strew several layers down and let them overlap before he poured out a cloth bag filled with pharmaceutical samples. Fast he tore the two pill packages — "What a waste!" he shouted — and lined them up like rosary beads across the disinfecting news: GOVERNMENT SHUT DOWN, read the biggest type, next to a picture of the president smelling a weed in the rose garden.

"Placebos!" he said. "Plenty to go around. Good to have everyone who carries the explosive prototype keep a cylinder chock full of these pills. It's all spelled out in the kits."

He straightened out his neon blue collar and buttoned the tiger's head — which his shirt's involuntary parting had severed — back together again.

Peter looked up. Thick cables painted white, whose purposes he could not guess, all conjoined at the center of the ceiling. The rafters behind looked like the belly of a capsized, intact ship.

The pink-faced man held his hand over his liver. Little liver spots dotted his chin. The liver sausage Uncle Cedric used as bait when they fished the Chicago River from the Canal Street Railroad Bridge. When Peter asked if it was legal Uncle quoted Paul on the law: "For through the Law I died to the Law that I might live in God." "Huh?" "What shall we say then? Is the law sin? God forbid. Nay, I had not known sin, but by the law: for I had not known lust, except the law had said, Thou shalt not covet."

Embarrassed, Peter fished around his brain, the backwaters and shallow lagoons, but could not recall the stalwart face, unamused, in the legendary pictures of Pierre protesting the gleaner's wages in California, offset by officers at seventy years old.

"I do not much care," said Pierre, pausing as if he was finished speaking. "What we have accomplished elsewhere. All of that was necessary to get *here*. We can say this, and should, about all of our lives. All of it was necessary to get us *here*. Where? A world where it's easier for a kid to be good. Hear me? This," gazing around the bustling makeshift first-aid factory, "This will be the start of everything. Of the second civil war already inevitable. A necessity. Just a matter of who fires the first shot. Do you mean to be dead in a gutter, goggling up saying 'Oh my God, I thought this was America!' Oh it is. It is. Yes. An honor to be involved in the inception of the nation's second life. I do not care how much hours we wasted trying to retrieve professeurs from the pleasant fishbowls. They'll bottom-feed on 'til they literally or metaphorically die. Did they believe radical politics can be worked out on Scantron tests? Shadow puppets on the classroom wall, teaching liberation from the cave? I bet they did! With benefits and retirement to boot! It is still possible — though hardly — to fool one's self. We do not need that type. We need," he reached out his hand and rapped Peter's shoulder once, gripping the bone and then turning away. "You. Now. Tell us what to do!" He pulled out a silver fork from his side pocket, reached around the back of his jacket, and retrieved a can of sardines. "Excuse me. Brought this with me from the camps. Old as hell. Makes me remember. If I ever cease to remember I start to complain.

"Anyhow, 'Future of the Movement,' I realize as we're chewing the bit that I have not eaten since breakfast. And that was a bite of black toast and blacker coffee. These kids all came with their fast-food wrappers. I worry they don't understand the system. It's a great pleasure to play at being revolutionary. But," he cleared his throat and wrapped his nose in a handkerchief, "they are ripe. They are ready, they are . . . in some way they may not even know, in some misguided way, longing for a world beyond this one that we have given them, they are right. This will be the beginning of everything." He stuck the fork tine through the fold of metal and the reek of compressed fish filled the room. "Excuse me. Would you like one?"

He dangled the black-scaled sardine and tossed it back with a strange civility that lodged confusion in Peter's throat.

Berragain, Pierre Berragain, this was the man, one he'd admired from afar for years, conversed with even under a pseudonym during dark web internet meetings, but had not met yet the dying breed until right here in this plain room, the man bereft of any aura except the awful blinding neon, this model of the old school radical who knew that anti- was not enough, knew how to choose actions that could matter for years. The man cocked back his head and poured a stream of silvery water from a tall canteen, gulping loudly, like a child come in from recess. He offered Peter a draught several times until decline gave way to a gulp. "Brother," said Berragain. "We'll do whatever you tell us." In the dusty, metallic air of the dank room the fresh water was so good.

Peter passed another stack of white packages, following Berragain who had turned on his heels marvelously, like a farmer tired from a day's hand weeding suddenly handed a fine steel rake, dragging unkempt nails across a white-board chart that featured four differing strategic positions, alternations for the detonators.

"He just came from solitary, you know," Berragain said, pointing at a skinny man in wide black mask that pushed up his nose, tight black jeans and a black jacket that looked like an elongated cape. In another milieu the man could have been the Lone Ranger, minus Tonto. "But they pampered him there. In jail. He told me. The good thing about solitary, he said, was no fights or rapes from the other criminals. To say nothing of stabbings." Peter ran his pointer finger over his mouth, looked at a warped and grayed shaft of light that reached into the basement room. Something struck Pierre's pink face suddenly. Violently. Berragain balked. "Workaholic. Bad, bad, bad I tell you. You turn into a bat. To get to the point where light is an annoyance. I miss the fields. Living with the gleaners still the highlight of my whole life . . . Nostalgia — always. Something to guard against. As if the past possessed that sheen we paint it with so liberally. Anyhow, that man's one to watch. Stamina of a psychopath. Could be useful but could kill without qualms. Though once, when the supervising officer was getting settled, they didn't change the shit bucket for weeks," he went on, picking up a cylinder of pills, re-reading the fine-print side-effect list:

Swift, smart, spontaneous elimination of white privilege from the face of the earth. Funerary cavalcades that clog the streets. Justice sans mercy sans statute of limitation.

As he held the fine print up to Peter, Berragain smiled in anticipation but Peter's mouth went pursed, miserly. "We've come a long way since the sixties."

With a glazed-over glance at Berragain he made, with difficulty, an approving nod. "Impressive. There's enough pills here to kill the pain of the whole world. It's just a matter of — organization. But whose pain are we killing?" Then his gaze landed on Pierre's crazed smile as they turned around the corner of a thick steel pipe.

"Are we shitting or emptying the shit bucket? Here's the question: how do you win a war of guilt and shame? You and me both know there's no knowing what the outcome of the action will be. The key is. Heh. The key is. Hmmm. Quite, quite. To invert my grandmother's scolds: quite to make a bloody mess. Out of chaos comes what? We can't know until the chaos comes out."

"And what — don't take this for chicken nerves, or doubts that violence is justified in a world where fully legal states are apparatuses of terrorism by another, more benign name — but what violence? Whose? What cost? Whose and what cost makes this kind of risk worth it?"

"Everyone in this room is vetted. All allies triple-checked through and through." Berragain leaned against a wall and flipped a switch that lit on a piece of crinkled loose leaf clipped to a brown hardboard. A hand-written list of names and numbers. "Had to keep this off the computer. Obviously. F. B. I. Here's the part that should do us proud: no one who will carry these things has not made them. Because alienation in the mode of production must be, you see — no, has been overcome. Not everywhere — but here. Yes. But also because conscientious limitation decreases risk. Fewer folks involved, fewer chances of possible defection."

"And they are being paid well."

"And they are being paid well. Especially the 'volunteers.' Unimpeachable wages. More, maybe, than you. And I've heard rumors about what you bring —"

Three masked men hurried past, the head of them clipping like an overburdened donkey Peter had once seen in the mountains of Peru. He made a friendly pose, poised, tickled and terrified by the hate in their eyes. Berragain bent his elbow out, shoved Peter in the side, and said: "Siblings of Contin Weevil, all. Came in yesterday from Georgia after the officer was let off with a sentence unfit for an afterschool detention."

Berragain rattled a cylinder and Peter stepped back.

"Hah. This one was a dud. We tested a dozen this morning. Eight out of twelve without defect. Why we're having it all done over again."

"Must feel like Sisyphus for some."

"You seen a one not smiling — some, admittedly, smiles hard to figure in faces who have known so much affliction? No accident, I say, that tonight's donors are all pharmaceuticals professionals. Tonight's targets."

Peter had waited already too long.

"What if instead we target a statue?"

"What? Cold feet? No need. They're getting torn down without our help, one at a time until not a one's standing."

"Oh some will escape decapitation. Some that should be returned to dust will still stand."

"Why the statues work is the drama. The crowd. The raised fists, the swarm of bodies."

"Dionysius."

"What?"

"Nothing. But this is basically the reason I am here. To talk to — I guess it would be you? — about a change in strategies. Marjorie and Curtis signed off. You can call them if it'll put you at peace, but I hope you know I ain't shitting you about something so serious."

"Did you run this by Ray Kee?"

341

"Ray Kee says he trusts my judgment. Hands off on this one. 'Your mind is my mind,' to cite him verbatim. I have, he said, to be able to make decisions alone if someday I'm going to take his place. Which, we all know, is almost written already. He's old — though younger than you — and the cancer keeps him real weak. 'Your mind is my mind.' Even if I make a mistake. He said that."

Berragain's eyes went white with heated visions. "In my twenties I helped derail a train with nuclear waste. In an unpopulated part of Ohio. Demonstrate how easy it is, how fragile, how falsified the narrative about clean energy. The news went crazy on it, feasted for a week, fattened everybody up on fear, and then went back to sleep. I've lost faith in the tactic of symbols. A shame, but death is the only thing that talks now."

"I disagree. Strongly, actually. Bodies falling left and right. Ideological shootings ubiquitous. Meaningless cycle of terror and head-scratching. Tired dichotomy of gun control or rifles pried from cold dead hands. But what if we tackle an unexpected temple? Residence of man-god. Object of so much respect and reverence."

"The Lincoln Memorial."

"You are sharp."

"You said temple. The building is literally a new Parthenon. Hmm, now tell me, what are you dreaming up?"

"I have a dream. Think of it. Better. See it. King's speech on the memorial steps. I have a dream."

"These ears were there. Heard it first-hand. Agreed with him then, though Malcolm's now more my man. Phrase it wasn't e'n part of the draft. 'I have a dream'! It's all most remember, but what's most remarkable: it wasn't included in the original plan. Let's scratch the Senator's fundraiser and strike at a more complicated, complete, compelling source of power. Something that'll have *staying power* long after it's long gone. Might seem strange at first, but it's exactly the ambivalence that'll give the thing heft."

Through the half-closed door, across the long room behind him, a young woman laughed and clapped. Peter swung around as if overheard, but the scene looked faraway, underwater through the treated glass. Two men leaned back into their laughs, then shot

342

forward and down, about to fall over. The woman motioned for the others to deposit their cylinders into a metal kit, then clacked it closed to a cloud of white powder that rose, rising around the pale gauze table, the crowd of chorus voices humming with satisfaction, then bragging after a victory that had not happened.

"Man has to relieve himself," Berragain said, with a wink, and he took long-legged strides toward the closet labeled Ladies' Room. The laughing woman through the glass had Stella's red hair but grayer. Stella would never say yes. Peter tilted his head like the stuck needle of a broken clock, the second hand — of infinitesimal but infinite consequence and — clack, click — unfixable.

He waited for Berragain with impatience, pacing back and forth between the six-foot threshold, ready to throw his shoulder through the glass of the aquarium. Join the bottom feeders brought to the mountaintop. Would any of them be able to breathe in the future he was helping to author?

"Enough," Berragain said, appearing under a threshold packed with sandbags slung in piles like food-pantry potatoes. He went on lowly if surely. "If you try to celebrate your gains like that you'll go mad. Before you get them. Nothing is certain. I used to do it. I did it too. And then they had to put me on pills much stronger than these. You know that, on some level. We can't afford the noise. You know this. We work diligently and quietly and then later we relax with all our might. But let's not celebrate ahead of time. And even then. It's not for us to measure the weight of what you will have done for our cause."

Pierre stepped over to the table and pulled a plastic glove snug around his wrist, then pressed his decriminalized finger into the light coat of powder. "I do not wish to spoil your fun. I am sorry for — speaking overboard. I mainly want to keep you innocent. Please. Carry on. And thank you for — everything."

But when he returned to the side office Berragain's firmness had not run out. He held his unscrewed gaze on Peter, visibly trying to turn the tool counterclockwise. "No. I lie. Either we do the donor dinner or nothing."

"Do you have the authority?"

343

"C'mon, captain. Authority. What is authority?" His pink face darkened like burnt salmon. Back from the restroom, long hemp shirt and bun untucked, mask pulled above his forehead to keep the strands from his face, he looked like a grade-school lunch lady.

Unexpectedly Peter laughed inwardly, but he kept a nonplussed façade over the absurd pleasure he was suddenly having. Stella would never say yes. Not a single string connected his giddiness to the stern expressions he forged. A total severance. He was good at that, but unskilled in the arts that Berragain had long since perfected. Cutting cords, power lines, wires, what have you.

"Another ubiquitous public murder," Peter muttered. "And if you could measure the weight, if you could establish with certitude some oh so definite purpose or meaning — some historical dialectic that would serve what we're after — how long would you be able to hold on to the surety that you were right?"

"So because we can't have absolute certainty we should favor the ambiguity of Lincoln. I can't — I mean I gather what you're after. I'm no idiot though my father was a fishmonger. Lincoln's delayed action on behalf of slaves. His speaking, apparently, two ways at least for too long. The image — literally made permanent in that other statue — of the Great Emancipator saving the slaves. As if their freedom was impossible without a white man. Father Abraham."

"You see. You just said the statue was permanent. Proves my point. Exactly what I'm getting at. The statue has outlived most human lifetimes. Almost a century he's been presiding from that seat, overseeing his civic temple, his Memorial. Looking with unquenchable longing over that Reflecting Pool as if a simple human mortal who thought he was a nation's savior could do so for so long without becoming Narcissus. And so the consequences will be felt more fully than if we pick off a petty (and I mean that in every sense) race-baiting senator and her donors. I mean — if you're gonna go for a person you ought to really finish off the president or nothing, because, in a state of breathless complexity, of a thousand nodes of power scattered and pulling in a thousand directions, the assassination could only be clarifying if it decapitated the peak of the pyramid, the eye. Which, mind you — you mind my meaning? Only the sophisticated scoff the freemasons into conspiratorial insignificance. First president for sure. And how many that followed."

"Fuck it. You are sharp as a whip and dumb as a June bug throwing its shell into the phantom of a shut-off light. I mean pharmaceuticals is an issue with . . . unities. A common pain that *truly* unites beyond the wild ideas of professors and provocateurs. We've discussed this through protected email with Ray Kee and Dimitri. Funny you and I already had a back and forth there, before we met I had you right. Smart as a whip, but a suicidal June bug. Pharmaceuticals — rallying around it. The senator wants not only a nation of white nationalists without negotiation. She wants to give the corporations free rein to hold our health hostage. And her friends in the Senate are about to applaud her sick scheme into being. The exorbitant profits and the forbidding prices. The crony-capitalist fascism. How much it costs to have a halfway decent lifespan."

"But Lincoln's absence will live even longer, will reveal for all that you can't make a martyr out of a man whose ideals you've delayed or denied or diminished to such childish steps toward full reparation of all that is owed to the nation's backbone, the millions who have hoisted and carried from obscurity all our ideals, forcedly, for free. Lincoln is our national symbol of infinity — of ideals impossible to fully fulfill, and that is precisely why he's *ideal* as a target to galvanize a more perfect" — but he could not say the word "union," could not even summon the first sound from his tightened stomach muscle.

People talked this way, in these places, Peter mused. He had forgotten how good it felt. After all that self-indulgent talk therapy of Psyche unbound. Berragain looked back at him like a candy store clerk awaiting the order of a moneyless child. Standing here.

Someone with a plugged nose announced, "Ready, Ray Kee is, to meet Mister. A Mister P. C. please. Here. Is uh, a P. C. here?" Shivering, a stocky woman with boyish hair appeared and led him, hands behind her back, down a crooked corridor. She wore

345

a brown blazer over a white turtleneck whose collar was curled inside the shirt. The blazer bore stains of white powder.

"You have something here," Peter said, making a brushing movement on his hip, the small of his back. Where Stella touched him before he flew away.

"Excuse me. It's mine to dye the special ingredient. What comes out black begins white. I wish you would wait here."

"Here," P. C. said, peeling a thin stack of thick card stock from the outside pocket of his green combat jacket — fifty cents from Army Surplus, the tag said, laid like a stiff casualty across the back counter like a bed made for his arrival, draped across his person now, frigid lifeless dimensionless uniform now made warm with the still-fresh scent of laminated new I. D. that read P. C. *Brahmin* and boasted the famous photograph of him from the Internet, the one where his backward cap pressed down on his 'fro to forge a Che Guevara spinoff. The insulated jacket, two sizes too large, made him look as though he had not only eaten but had not known when to stop. He was hungry.

Pierre turned and washed his face in a drinking fountain. Washed what was friendly in his countenance clean beyond recognition. In its place his paling features started to sink under a sea of ambiguities.

Peter pulled out a thick scrap and turned toward the wall to scrawl. The bleeding pen blurred his words. "Stella. Are you there? If the next steps we hash out end up passing, I have no idea how long I'll be here. How long I'll live. I'd ask only that you live. Tell my son nothing of my existence. Not a word. In love, P. C."

Berragain slurped loudly at the fountain, sighing long between little sips. Peter folded the tough bit of card stock into an outsized manila envelope he had been carrying around unthinkingly for the past fifteen minutes, and scrawled the memorized address of Stella's parents on the front, in blue ink.

Berragain finished his slurping with an "Ahhh" that lasted.

"Berragain. I'm sorry we — it's not for lack of respect. I could never do what you have done. Be what you've been for all of us. So if the strategy ends up switching, please don't take it personally.

346

As a show of my loyalty, I'll trust you with this," and here he thrust out the envelope, still gripped tight in his dry fist. "I wrote these only in case. It's getting late. Mailman picks up at the box down the block in ten minutes and she isn't here. Can't explain, but this needs to get to her. I'm as capable of illusion as the next. I was sure she would stay, return. It can sicken the — for a lack of a better word — it can kill the soul if not basically suicide it under another guise. Get me? To have things to say, messages to deliver, and leave shut-mouthed, swallowing your heart with your, last breath knowing damn well whatever you would mutter would end up filed in a dead-letter office.

"Don't remember me this way. God. It's good knowing you. Wish there was room for us to be friends."

"There is a room! Where all of us will feast together."

"Wish to God I had your faith. Don't even know if I'm seeing you straight. But I pray I see you — all alive — soon," he said, without conviction, without enunciating a single syllable.

The woman with the stained blazer, boyish hair and broken English, plugged nose and sweet rabbit eyes returned and stood there silent for a second, poised on the drab concrete. She seemed to be counting under her breath. "Come." Swiveling her eyes in every direction she let her arms move swiftly back and forth at her sides — as if time was shortening. Soon they were winding down a narrowing hallway that seemed never ending, the narrowness ever growing larger, replaced by ever smaller panels, and what was left of the sun slit the seams of his eyes as it would a prisoner who until now has been packed like a canned sardine amidst a company of dead fellows.

When he tried to turn away from the sun he found himself squinting into a radiating doorway from within which the rays were still stronger, and in the center of the doorway Ray Kee reached out a friendly hand. Kee, well-tanned and looking rested, felt his mustache between his fingers and pinched the edge of his lips.

"How watertight, or not, are we?"

Peter squinted at his untied shoelace, stepped down to fix it and, as he squatted, said, "I've something I need you to hear. You

347

said my mind is yours. Your mind is mine, whatever. We cannot attend the donor dinner. Our contact with the caterers is unreliable. Because this has been months in the making, many others are impatient, breathing down my neck to press on anyhow."

Key closed the door behind them and the undiluted sunshine was so overbearing that Peter, sneezing, kept his eyes closed the whole time he retold the shift in his thinking to a man who, instead of enumerating disappointments and meting out admonishments, seemed happy — hysterical — to hear it.

"I thought when you alluded it was joshing. But all night I dreamed you were right." But then he added, through tanned jowls that had fed on pristine island fish for the better part of a disappeared week, "But before we finalize. Before I take Pierre in here and get assurances in blood that all you say will come to be . . ."

"Try me."

"You have a child. You wish to retire from the harsh sacrifices of a life poured out for others. You wish your motives were salt of the earth, but if you look long enough you'll find — a dearth. You have come up with an eloquent means of covering up your cold feet." He looked down at Peter's sockless ankles. "We are paying you enough to afford socks, no?" Peter tried to mimic his smile, a little coin of social grace, but he could not muster more than a wavering line, a mussed-up mouth that moved without sound, and eyes that betrayed a sudden hatred.

"You told me I was to decide. That in the state of exception we have entered, all old rules are held suspended. *Successor*, you called me. And now you will not let me act. On my own. Like a big boy. Unimpeded. I'm not a kid who's peed his pants. You said that even if I should make mistakes I needed to be let alone to do so. That a puppet marionette was no way to carry on the . . . organization's aims." He had never told Ray Kee or anyone that this would be his last week with them. After the Memorial was defaced he would quit. He had hardly told himself he was done, because if he leaned too much into that exit he feared he would not pass on his legacy at the very instant he became successor — feared his last intervention would fail.

348

"And all these bottles of painkillers? Those who have put them together for weeks believe that they will be widely distributed, one apiece, to a thousand revolutionaries worthy of the name. They'd no idea they'd be centerpieces at a donor dinner, mind you. Let alone bombs for a stone. Why not honor their labor by spreading the shock around? Please. Proceed with President Lincoln. But coordinate a hundred middle-sized actions across the country simultaneously. Or, on a smaller scale, a thousand."

"We circled around those strategies for weeks. What for, if we're starting over?!"

Key stepped back and cocked his head sideways. "So what you are saying is that you deem yourself unfit for your present position and you wish to thank the organization for the solicitous risks it took to catapult you into an — well, it really is an almost otherworldly level of politics that you would otherwise never have sniffed at the pissed-on bottom ladder of but, thank you very much, you are moving on to another line of work where your talents may be more ably applied. And the organization in turn wishes to thank you for the many important contributions you have made during your time. Please accept this miniature golden pin, shaped like the cap of a pharmaceutical bottle, in commemoration of your year of service." He held up the pretended pin and pressed its needle into Peter's heart.

Peter reached at his side for a knife that had not been there for decades. He swung like he had in the little sandlot when his uncle called incendiary insults to get his gumption chewed up like gum and the ball — a lob pitch — into left field, knees bent and twisted in tandem with shoulders that edged down at a sharp angle and his folded fists struck Kee's face with the smack of flesh like when mama made meat, the tenderizer announcing a dinner that, for once, would not leave him hungry.

In five minutes, when he'd caught his breath, Peter's measured voice exited his mouth in ten directions, a painfully amateur imitation of Kee's, but this did not matter because the app's voice distortion hid the fact that it was impossible for his supervisor, passed out on the floor, to announce in a stern and jolted tone the new direction P. C. had chosen. "And I, for whatever it is worth — and we know that it is not worth as much as we've pretended — with whatever authority may be vested in me, I wholeheartedly sanction this switch as superior in every way to the original plan, which has been fatally compromised anyhow." The microphone plugged into the phone stuck out like a shriveled sponge before him.

. . .

Stella was not waiting in the apartment lobby. She did not enter after him in silence. She did not ask *what's wrong, baby*, when he would not speak. He would not speak. Inside he stared down despair's bloom. The sink stunk, like him, filled with weeks of aging dirt, the fruits of spurts of hope deferred. Fruit flies weaved between uneaten breakfasts. Weeks of her egg recipe — paprika and olive scrambled to a sear, folded on soft rye toasts at sunrise. He could not crucify the faith Cedric gave him, refused to concede his own concessions — directed it all at her arrival. She would come some morning, any morning. She would come again and they'd begin at last. Clean the sink and obliviate the past and cook up a genesis.

. . .

After the boomerang from D. C. back, Stella had taken to doing the laundry. No one had asked or imposed the task. Although on her own she had never adhered to her mother's practice of doing separate loads to bleach the mustard T-shirt armpits, yellowed unspoken underwear stains from pee dribbled throughout the days — she had always shoved all into the same stuffed washer — she immediately conceded to the way things are, filling the scuffed measuring cup with a milliliter of bleach, duly diluting it before dousing the underwear and socks and sleeveless T-shirts with the purifying agent. Most of the underthings she recognized from more than a decade earlier when, in high school, this was her duty three days per week — as announced on the "Chore Wheel." ("Wheel of Torture" her brother had called it. For him getting his body to rise out of bed was hard enough. A scathing vine wound around her spine as she saw her brother set up camp in the kitchen, his

350

unkempt hair obscuring his eyes as he ate a microwaved burrito for two-p.m. breakfast. But he hadn't filled a fling's womb and then fled.) She folded the clothes in her brother's old room, now well-swept and kept for the rare guest or the friend of dad's who'd had too much to drink and couldn't find his keys when he got up to leave because her father had confiscated them earlier, delighting in his suave thief's success. But tonight the bath towels seemed impossibly heavy. The pleasure that their thickness brought when you stepped out of the shower was now only a weighted blanket that her laconic fingers could not fold. She ran them along the frayed borderline, turned then to a cloth napkin, worn so thin it was practically weightless. But this too she could not move. A flash of sweat made her temples hot, then chill from the breeze that stole through the slightly cracked window. She watched as a shadow, apparently there for an unknown quantity, overcame her own, cast against the wall by the hallway light, much brighter than the dusk which was all that lit the room now.

Dad took her fingers and folded them into fists, nodded towards the kitchen with a mischievous smile. "Peach cobbler. I made it. No promises but it's all yours. If I eat more my doctor will kill me . . . before I do the job myself. No joke. But you're as skinny as a skeleton costume. I don't want to scare you, but you look like hell. You can't keep up with baby and then work, er, chores — er, on repeat, without taking some time to sit down and eat."

"But it's Tuesday. Aren't the boys coming around to chew the cud and save the country?"

They had kept politics stored away like a plastic bin duct-taped in the basement, stuffed and overflowing with incendiary files. She tried to wink but her eyebrow refused. Even moving her mouth almost hurt. There was no way she could force down the cobbler. She could put it on a plate and bring it in the backyard, walk along the fence and flip it into the neighbor's yard. Dog — was it Darwin? — wouldn't even like it. Abused and adopted at eleven years old, there was not enough time to teach trust.

Her dad said "I'm starting to doubt some of that. Seems like the same single story plugged into a machine, a set algorithm to prey on disillusioned and demoralized saps like *moi*. But I've reviewed the tapes enough to know something is stupidly wrong with the story we're supposed to believe. Not to mention I was *there*. Eaves — he doesn't like to speak of it, laughs it off like it didn't happen. (His dad was a high-ranking police officer, did half a lifetime of selfless service.) Eaves got hit by a baton until his stomach was blue, almost died then from low oxygen. If he had they would have blamed it on blood pressure, bullshit. You get it? But I'm not an idiot. Remember in the nineties when I was sure the end of the world was nigh? All those bestsellers I read? An animal at the trough, licking lips over chaos as if I was sitting down to a meal. I tell you. But all that straw, that golden straw that tasted so good I stopped then eating anything else, started to make me sick. The constant adjustment of remnants and dates, guarantees about raptures that kept expiring. Something like that is happening here. The dates when the military is supposed to take over and reinstitute the rightful president. They keep on bumping them back and back and . . . shit, Stell, I was hanging on it all so hard it's amazing no heart attack put me under. I want to see. I, it's hard. I want to see my grandbaby get older. But I don't want him to be as far less free as I can see him in my mind, far more deluded than a serf of the thirteenth century, okay? Who had it better in so many ways. No surveillance state."

Why, when he said it bending over the bed, fishing sock mates from the sprawl of hot clothes, picking bits of exploded tissue from the legs of spandex pants — why, here, did his claims not seem so crazy? She leaned, tired against the stained oak frame, the coating they had coaxed her brother into doing after threatening to kick him out.

"And here I am, a true hero. Talking you to sleep when you're just waking up, and after a promise of ten minutes' respite. Get gone. Get yourself some of that cobbler."

Sure enough, even as he talked, Dad had finished the whole batch of clothes. He'd been folding with a crazed quickness, the way he'd once packaged high-end breath mints in the shipping room, a side job to pay his children's tuition when mom's nightshifts were not enough, the swathes of soft cloth he'd clamp around the little candies, spearmint drops lost in their packaging so that (he often suspected) not a few who'd receive this gift would think they were getting fancy wash cloths, oblivious to the dots of refreshment. He'd eaten not a few that had fallen, and they lived up to the packaging's flowery hype, as if lightening not just the tip of his tongue but the ease of breathing through opened passages chronically clogged by allergies no prescription could chasten.

He sneezed. The baby was awake, again, upstairs. She did not need a monitor with that pair of minor-key lungs. Wide open.

"I'd better get going." She rolled her eyes upward, realizing as she did so she was mimicking one of his signatures.

"If you need to nurse, fine, take fifteen minutes, but after that I expect to be given the baby because I can't stand to see my own, my flesh and blood baby, so low. Your eyes" — he couldn't complete the sentence, but did he choke because what he would have said could hurt instead of helping her stand another day and do it again? When she found the mirror in the hall she saw exactly what he'd cut short: *they look like those blown dandelion globes, seeds all sent and the spent stem's head reminding every onlooker without fail of the orb of ethereal white that had once been before the wishes were all blown away,* and she almost shoved the heel of her hand against the heirloom glass that hung there, angered by how readily self-pity came. Unclasping the hook of her nursing bra, she did not stomp up the stairs but tiptoed until she saw Jason's propped-up body, eyes peering through the crib's prison bars, squealing when she squeezed at the leg fat that gathered like sausage links tied up with strings, tilting his guzzling nursing head so he wouldn't gag after taking too much at once, then bringing him back down to her Dad's ready cradle before she forced herself to chew at a peach, wanting to wash the sugar away because otherwise a bite would be a hundred calories, and besides (she couldn't *believe* she was being this picky) this wasn't the way he used to bake them, all through childhood insisting that pies are only worth making if you raise them from scratch, inhale the flour dust and hammer the dough, pluck the strawberries from the backyard fence that doubled as a trellis behind the blood-red rows of rhubarb that lift their shocks of green toward the sky, but these peaches were dumped from a can and the crumbles of crust like something sprung from a frozen canister. A conflagration of nausea, like a counterargument that shut down her position, sharpened her focus to the fierce hunger pang that clanged and bloomed like a painful cavity vacuuming what crumbs remained in her stomach. She needed to eat because Jason because Jason because he does and if you don't he won't, any questions.

"Dad," she said, her mouthful of bitter — a piece of rhubarb without any sweetener — "I miss Blake. I miss Peter. I'll not stay here and have a father for a husband. Please — all the ways you could misunderstand — I was so scared of every future I tried to erase any at all."

. . .

As the cabbie approached the Arlington Memorial Cemetery his speed disappeared completely. Peter, who had purchased a gaudy car seat for Jason — "it's heavy enough to save him but it'll break your back, and who's going to cart it around the city, not me!" — had been eyeing his son with all-alert tension and the sudden grind came as a relief. Two grand cranes, fresh paint yellow as if just shipped from the factory, unmanned and awaiting their next act of construction or destruction, suspended black and empty hooks over the shut down side of the bridge. The muddied blue of the Potomac River looked clean contrasted with a rusted barge across which a solitary construction worker trod, playful tiptoes followed by stomps that seemed to test the structure's strength — that satisfaction of its staying suspended! — smoking and gesticulating and talking into either a phone or walkie-talkie.

Stella sipped pricy coffee, careful not to swallow the cardboard which was so coated with plastic it seemed ceramic. A jagged headache from poor sleep made the water seem to waver and teeter more than it was, and the distorting prism of pain showed her impatient rants of last night in a tasteless slideshow of impossible demands. For several slowed minutes they stalled before the Arts of War statues while an orange-tanned man chewing a triple hamburger held up his other hand in lazy forbiddance. A muscular man, nude but for his beard, sat without saddle astride a wild horse with stately force.

"Maybe on the way out we'll see the Pegasus. Another route. The Arts of Peace. Aspiration and literature. The wings of an open book carried beside the lifted wings of a Pegasus. Beautiful."

"Half my existence I spent in books. God. The better half. The longer I live the more I admire. Soldiers," she said. "But what is he doing to the woman who's lock-step with the horse he's riding? And why isn't she astride the animal with him. The back of the horse's plenty of room for her. Is he leaving the lady behind?" Her intricate braids were echoes by the horsehair, especially the patterns in the downturned tail.

"Look at the other one. There. Right across. She's holding his arm up. He's holding their baby."

He put his hand, palm up, between them. She did not place hers atop.

"Decent of them to cover her nakedness. At least at the waist. Weird the lines we draw."

"In war."

"In peace," she said.

When the car shot forward like a popped champagne cork Peter put his arm around her and pointed. "Look. I've spent a lot of time staring down that one over there. Arts of Music. Can't quite see it. Across from the man with the bow pointed backwards. Ode to paranoia? Heh. Surely a hidden meaning I'm not familiar with. But across from him — the woman with her harp. A happy Pegasus."

"But alone."

"Harp," she whispered, "like a wing. Half attached at the shoulder. Like an archangel's wings."

The cabbie smoothed out the plastic black beaded rosary that dangled, tangled, from the rearview, turned up the Norteño music, and, checking the mirror, clacked his knuckle against the dash and surreptitiously circled a cul-de-sac curve around a dark green patch of broccoli-floret trees, swearing in Spanish as the clog of small trucks and cars prevented him from accessing the inner sanctum street.

"Drop you off here?" he asked Peter as he pulled over to the side of the circle. "What party blocks this. Maybe parade."

355

Peter turned to Stella who said — first with a bitter bite that she over-sweetened like coffee sugared with too much creamer — "If you're ready to carry that car seat let's get out."

Then, as the cab kept curving, she leaned across the seat and whispered in his warm ear, "Honestly I don't know why we came." She heard her mother's perpetual discontent but before she could correct it he laughed and said at the lowest frequency she'd ever heard before, a quiet *pst* that yet quivered with courage: "Look, I'm not trying to make you a believer. Stay skeptic all you like. I don't even know for sure that I'm right. But what's cooking on the stovetop is about to boil and there ain't no way to bring the water back to simmer. It's scalding water on the face of a senator or . . . a simple, harmless — to humanity — defacement. If anything helpful."

She could not laugh and said "I'm sorry. How you put up with me. I didn't sleep. Not last night or the three leading up to it. Nerves about this trip. Nervous. Seems there's no way *not* to fail. I'm afraid, Peter."

"Pull over, please, that'll be fine," Peter said to the cabbie, then pressed with tenderness the triangle tip of flesh between her thumb and pointer finger.

The cabbie's shirt of green-purple plaid had slivers of sweat under the armpits as he stood, arms outstretched, outside the car, stretching and giving a beat grin that revealed a mouth half tooth-less. He'd deposited them at the Watergate steps, plain gray curving planks that ascended from the mute blue Potomac toward an empty stage. A shirtless jogger barely covered by a bra skipped breathily past them, pumping up the steps in red shorts that did not hide thighs as well-proportioned as the statue of war and the woman assuming almost the same posture — one arm outstretched behind her and the other curbed into a concentrated fist. Stella searched Peter's eyes, as if to make sure that they did not wander. He was trying to tie his shoe with one hand, while walking, while balancing Jason's car seat over the outstretched, fretting hand. She thought of her decades of endless walks, alone and then at last with Blake and how P. C. had taken his place. Their wounded innocence hard not to kiss. (Harder still to kill her lie — she knew it was a half-truth at best — that either of them were innocent.) How hard it was to stay in shape since baby came, how fast middle age arrived and had its way with a body she'd taken for granted as spry. She slurped up the last of the chalky coffee and said "I think you could hide that thing beside that bush. Besides, who would take it?"

"You'd be surprised." After he hid the armored car seat and she secured a sleepy baby in the sling — strange, he screamed half the trip on the plane, but what baby is so drowsy all the time? Dad's doctor. Cardiologist. No. Another set of specialists just for children's hearts. What leads to sedation could be anything, other things. Stop.

They walked hand in hand up the steps. "I could have strapped him onto me." She could not confess her worry that he'd take Jason and run. Surely another of the worst-case fantasies that played variations across the murmuring refuse of her brain's arteries. He sneezed as they crossed the fresh-cut lawn and she handed him a baby wipe when the string of snot got stuck across his cheek. All so strange, how easy to acclimate. Picking baby's snotty nose without a blink. He's embarrassed. Marriage. No shame over the thousand blemishes. Brushing teeth in the bathroom while he pees. Furniture or familiarity? Same thing. No. There are several kinds. He sneezed again, stopped and sneezed again and again in quick succession. She handed him the baby's bottle, twisted off the cap and took pleasure in the gasp, the sigh of satisfaction he gave. Several kinds of familiarity. The kind that erases what's at hand into oblivion. The kind so accustomed to the other, so bound with his habits good and bad that what would shock anyone leaves you nonplussed. Knowing and known. Marriage a hair braid of both kinds. The intricate pattern on the Arts of War woman. What was she fighting for, bare breasts pointed? Stella ran with Jason to the street edge. Parkway Drive conjoined with Lincoln Memorial Circle. She paused, looked back. "What's taking you so long? I'm a patient lady. Used to be. But I can't wait an eternity." Looking both ways at the quick snake of traffic, she poised to accentuate her chest curve in imitation of the Arts of War. "Noticed my shield's down," she said. The outside air, if poisoned by exhaust, was still exhilarating after the stuffy cab whose scented pineapple tree ornament had been overpowering.

She stopped at the top of the steps. The sculpted tussle of his messy hair, a violent sea of competing waves. The statue's necessary symmetries tempered his wild, half-ugly visage, the well-drawn melancholy of his wrinkles reduced to several streams across a brow whose arches presided over sunken sad eyes offset by the sanguine illusion that a smile, if not visible, lay in wait — or was at least possible, which wasn't nothing given who he was and what the world he was gazing at looked like. The tranquil, unclasped, open right hand was offset by the tensely shut left, not a fist but at attention to become one.

Peter stood back, lost in asymmetries, his face all wince as if struck by shrapnel, though the afternoon air, with indifferent patience, carried and then cast down bright dandelion wisps, pale stars falling softly, softly falling from the suspended flag.

. . .

PRESIDENT LINCOLN SAVED FROM
SECOND ASSASSINATION ATTEMPT

At three p.m. on June sixteenth, sixteen men — eight white, eight black — were arrested between the shadowed pillars of the Lincoln Memorial building after a single detonation blew off the president's loose left fist. The scattered shards of Georgia marble have all been located and collected, but forensic experts and consulted sculptors doubt they can put the hand back together again. The F. B. I. discovered eight of the sixteen suspects in possession of several dozen pharmaceutical bottles containing a highly volatile black powder. Matinée Ro, a veteran janitor, tackled the perpetrator down the stairs and chased him into the Reflecting Pool. Falling backwards into the unmoved waters, the bomber tossed an explosive after Ro. Ro was running upstairs to apprehend one of the others when his heel kicked the pharmaceutical cylinder, which exploded as it arced over his shoulder, and exploded a slice of his scapular into infinitesimal living pieces scattering, falling down the steps. Ro, who has worked the grounds since before Martin Luther King Jr. delivered his "I Have a Dream" speech on the same steps, said this was "the happiest day of my life." The F. B. I. was aware of the "domestic terrorism, threat" prior to the incident and is unable to reveal classified information concerning their reasons for withholding arrest prior to June sixteenth. All remaining suspects have been arrested without incident. Political activist Peter Clavier is under investigation. His lawyers, denying comment, have indicated that Clavier's case requires no pre-trial detention. Barring Ro, who is in recovery, no one was harmed.

. . .

He took three greyhounds and an Amtrak back under the alias Barrek Cephailias — an I. D. Marjorie had had made months back but one he'd never, until now, needed. At Chicago's crowded Union Station, customer service behind the bullet proof glass had muttered to a colleague out the side of his mouth, "Check this name. Bro's got syphilis. It's certified. Check it out, bro."

"Huh? Sephalius. Kind of a name is that?"

"Real question, if dude's got syphilis, is how'd he get some in the first place, bro? Steal a look. Like —"

"Shit, man. Seriously. God was asleep when he got made. Like —"

"A mistake."

They laughed.

Peter took the ticket back and said a pleasant thank you, pretending the vents hadn't leaked their laughter, pitying them even as he boarded the bus, relieved his desire for Marjorie had died. As he had stayed home the day of the Memorial, and as the forgetting he longed for was finally happening he likely could have travelled as himself, but all his involvements, too many threats to number, would remain embedded in his nerve endings until — after years — all the fears were forgotten.

As if a *tabula rasa* were possible. Even now a new worry was born. Marjorie's bitterness, her last terse text: U O ME. He'd rejected her firmly, said over the phone, through the poor reception, sorry, *I'm sorry, but the sleeping together we both expected, as a given, for years — let's be honest, won't ever, now, will never come to pass.* She hung up and sent the same message twice — by accident or for added accent? U O ME.

359

What if all the protections she had taken to cleanse his involvement of even high level tracking would disappear, what if — worse — she set out to expose all the actions he had authored or ordered? She was not wrong. He owed her, yes, the kind of debt he could not now pay.

Each passing mile west put him at ease, but the original reason for his return to Stella seemed implausible outside of the vertigo, the dizzying pinnacle of Washington's heights. Peter tried three times to practice his speech, "Baby, listen, I couldn't keep away, not another day, couldn't keep away from — " Who? He could not move his cramped mouth. His tongue, still tired from the endless speeches, the late night sessions, the failed persuasions, could not pry through the edge-set teeth which gritted like little ossified stalactites from the center of his sunken face. *Who could he not keep away from? Her? Jason? My son. My son.* He wanted to be able to hate her for refusing to follow him to Washington. Raindrops splashed against the warmed bus window like a million sperm dashed down to their deaths. He needed a drink, felt his Adam's apple burn. The complimentary cup he'd bummed at the station — that read RETURN TO THE EARTH on the side — he'd filled with plain hot water meant for tea, nerves too spent for free caffeine, but the water now tasted of steeped cardboard. He couldn't — a gag — but he did take a sip from the still-scalding cup, steadied, steadied. The bitter water soothed his throat, made him sweat, perked him up.

His arrival at her door would attain no more than a final inevitable, deferred, rejection. He could see, already, her long face warped by a lifted nose, eyelids closed after irritated blinking, his son kept from him, held beneath the bulletproof glass of an ovular window engaged in gratuitous bars of iron. (In her letter she'd told him of her father's paranoia, which invented, nearly weekly, new security measures.)

What if she *wouldn't* show him his son? To send him, furious, forever away? A cruelty? A mercy? To save him from attachment?

What if she called the police when he rang? At least their sirens might set the baby crying — break the staid silence that made him seemed dead.

When he started to imagine how Jason looked now — those eyes, his mother's, that mouth, his own — it was hard to write off, as heartburn from a hotdog, the strange pulsations that passed through his chest: one of these times it would be the real thing. His mother had died, so the autopsy said, not of the early Parkinson's, actually, but from, rather, cardiac arrest. Which was never as clear an answer as it seemed because what had caused the cause of death?

He could not bear to see the baby at all if she would not let him kiss his boy's mouth.

As he switched from a bus to a sleek new train and found in the rearview his sleepless face he could fathom her rolling, blinking eyes — the look she gave that said *get you gone*. Maybe *that* was why he had come, to put an end to the tetherball swings that kept him orbiting the impossible question of whether they would ever make a way. If she sent him off he could wash his hands of all of this. Who cares? As if you could scrub your son from memory.

The Amtrak bathroom reeked of air freshener, a chemical lemon that made him gag. He washed his hands and then spat in the mirror so as to not see the eyes that stared there. He splashed water on his fever dream face, again and again until a hand knocked hard against the door he had forgotten to lock.

As the train cleaved to the rusted tracks that gleamed bronze gold under a sudden sun and the captain called out downtown Milwaukee he was sure, without reason, she would believe him this time. He held out — to what jury? — the simple rightness of boys needing fathers, dropped it on the rusted-out scales against the weight of his tallied wrongdoings, what Uncle C would call the wages of sin. He would prove his mettle even when he wasn't wanted, wash dishes and send her weekly checks, live hidden, who cares, in a hive apartment, a miniature of Cabrini-Green, minimum wage and late nights listening to Coltrane through a turned up headset until, at two, the last cup was cleaned. The risk of being betrayed by Marjorie. But the Lincoln debacle could be forgiven because in that circle the sins of others were celebrated more than scorned, were welcomed, convenient, as counterpoint fixes for nasty cases of bad conscience ("My God, at least I have never done *that!*"), albeit also a blackmail check that would keep him silent about their doings and could be cashed in the case that the police sought a culprit for their scattered, anonymous crimes and the movement demanded a ready sacrifice: the finger would point at Peter Clavier — the patsy to purge their shared guilt in a single concentrated condemnation. One damned so the many could be saved.

Damn. Uncle C had said, when they last spoke, he would rather be a busboy in heaven than the king's jester in Satan's court. If only he could counterfeit the faith C had, but the easy way out — all your sins are forgiven — came off, to him, like an unjust cope.

Peter would keep his head down, not even a busboy occasionally applauded for clearing spent napkins and chawed on crusts: an unseen washer of others' filth, unknown in a dim dispensation that could hide him even from his very self, soap pans greased with burnt pig fat, scrubbing and scrubbing with the heel of his hand until he bled in the backroom, no one to honor or worship or reward him when she turned him away from her father's house and he still sent checks made out of his blood.

As his feet touched the ground and the train brakes hissed he decided to forego the cab he had planned. It wasn't a matter of saving money, though he knew how fast you could spend even thousands. He needed the miles to make out his own mind, to be ready for whatever fate she dished out.

But the dragging suitcase whose one wheel was wobbly, and the labyrinth of crisscrossed streets that assumed strange angles he couldn't find on a map, and the broken traffic lights and busted glass of single shot bottles that dotted the sidewalk demanded, all the way to her house, a fierce and animal alertness, putting his thoughts to sleep for a time.

He approached her door too tired to be tortured if condemnation, with a spray of clove cologne just in case she might see the sorrow that showed on his unhandsome face.

The idea of a God who made mistakes might justify an act of faith.

Three times the bell garbled digital *ding dongs*, each off kilter with
the church tower speakers that rang out static chimes above the
sleepy neighborhood, single-story postage stamp houses, brown
and drab and slumped, most all, punctuated only by the red bell
tower and the sharp ascent of the Tęsknota house, a dull silver
affair whose attic punctured the sky like a slightly bent needle. The
cracking sonic shock of high notes blared like a tornado warning
or fallout shelter test. An elderly man walking his dog, thin and
holding up his pants with one hand, bent and covered his animal's
ears as the mutt emptied his bladder on a tree. A passing kid with
a blaring headset whose band slid down and hid his eyes sneaked
several glances at Peter, who felt the pain of the eczema scars, knife-
dug divots on the kid's sickly face, two large ones at the edges of
his cheeks looking out like unseeing sockets in the absence of actual
eyes. The kid pulled a sweat stained white T-shirt over a belly that
made it hard to hurry, hurry out of sight.

Peter heard the clicks of at least three locks and then her mother
was there, chin down, in a sapphire blouse Stella had worn on
weekends in Chicago, not her now, but her mother, chin down,
fixated on his shoes, which he tied as if in answer to her eyes, raised
enough to nod him through a threshold protected, just a moment
before, by a cast iron gate and thick chain locks that hung down
limp like gibbeted bodies, her fingers gripping the chromatic clasps,
three bulging heads at the end of the chains.

"You must be —" she said, and then stopped, as Stella's feet
bounded down the stairs with all the skipped steps of adolescent
thrill.

Her parents nodded slowly when she said, irritated, "This is
Peter. I didn't know he was coming."

Peter's suitcase collapsed like a child having a rigid meltdown
beside him. He ignored the noise, the fall, the fit, as if the handle
would come around, would right itself as soon as it saw it couldn't
win his stoical attention. To face the three of them — her father
had rounded the kitchen corner and stood there, tie-tight, chest
out, breathing — Peter pivoted his whole body instead of turning

his head, which was stiff, and though he said something it came out stilted but no one requested he repeat it again.

She leaned into him as much to test Mom who would not admit open disapproval as to take the small pleasure of comforting Peter, wrapping her arms around the belt of bone waist that meant he had, like her, skipped meals, the strange affinity drawing her closer, almost whispering "I missed you" in his ear before she caught the thought and took it captive, collapsing the risk into a sigh. He rested his forehead on her neck, heavily, compressing the pulse of her jugular vein, taping on his hip to the beat he heard there until she pulled without warning away and watched her parents as if waiting for their exit.

Her mother pulled the window blinds down but did not swing the door shut.

"Behold, the man," her dad said. "It's better to meet you, man to man, than have you racing around my head like a pixel coughed up by the internet. I — can't agree with most of what you've preached," he went on, standing back, shied, shaking Peter's hand from a distance. "But" — his voice fell into a gutter of barely-mustered, muttered praise, "you're onto something with the steel-worker's wages, and the waste plant, too. Old-school concerns worth keeping live. Stella showed me. The articles. Sharp. Clear. Practical. If only your *movement* —"

"— I don't belong anywhere, believe me, I don't. The *movement* is moving on without me —"

"Could recover your common sense. Ditch the luxury elite ethics. Focus on the hard facts. That either certain people get protections against exploitation or whole neighborhoods'll be treated as disposable."

He spoke to her father in a tone she'd heard him take with waiters and waitresses and grocery checkers. "I don't know what good the pieces did. All those words. What wages to show for them?" Peter looked over everyone's shoulder. "Mainly, my concern is: where's my son?"

Regan nodded, flattened the grimace that was growing across his bit lips.

"The heroic sleeper," said Stella, "sleeps."

"We ate already," her mother said. "And have to get on to — plans. But I know Stella'd be happy to heat up anything you like, though, not knowing you were coming, I'm sorry we have nothing special to offer."

"Thank you. Thank you. But am more than full."

Her mother, with effort, looked him straight in eyes awaiting, until then, even a gloss.

He squinted and touched his lower jaw as if overcome by a returned toothache.

"Well," said Mom, not knowing what to say, "Stella'll show you around, I'm sure." And she shoved her hands in snug jean pockets barely visible over the stiff red flannel Regan had left on the recliner. She had slipped it over her mismatching blouse after Peter had entered the house.

Peter's stomach growled as Stella turned to her parents and said, "I will." She took his hand — almost seized it. Both of their palms pressed awkwardly together like first-date teenagers prior to prom — both cold and faintly sweaty — and they disappeared from the dining room, ascending to the darkened, dank room to look down on Jason's shallow breaths. She watched Peter's eyes adjust to the dark, search his son for some sign of life.

Stella had covered the crib with a sheet to keep the humidified air around him. He peeled back the sheet and pressed his nose against Jason's, stayed there, still, for several minutes. She saw the pain he must be in, stomach concave against the crib railing, but he did not move, Peter did not seem to breathe. She reached out her hand to gently wake Jason but Peter waved her, rashly, away. "Thank you. Thank you. But it's not about me. You don't need to mess up the routine for me. No routine no sanity. I know how hard it's been for you. I want to make it easier." She felt her nose wet with startling tears, but would not be taken in by what she feared he was doing: premeditated moral posturing that would fade in a week, in a day. The cynical thought make her choke on the snot that caught when she blocked the tears from coming.

Peter rose and replaced the gauzy veil that turned Jason into a night-lit silhouette. He shot out a pocket of air from puffed lips.

"Something you should know, if you're going to stay. Because, please do, let's give it a few days. See what happens."

"An experiment," he whispered, thumb propping his chin up, a bitter current released, electric, from the curt words, "that's what we've become?"

"What else is there?" she asked, voice rasping under the enforced hush. Where could they meet here that was not hidden? Wearied by the idea of a walk outside, she tried to recover equilibrium between them, or to put it there where it had not been.

"Dad," she said, "for all his sacrifice, carries Jason with an aura of possessiveness. I tried to tell you how torn it's made me. No such thing as love, I swear, that isn't poisoned by self-interest. Sick, really. That's not metaphorical: I'm eating less — I see you've been too — and need more and more caffeine if you know what I mean. A mess. Not hard to see why we're all on drugs. Why my brother's cannabinoid business is booming. Or so Dad says. He could idealize his children even when he hates what they're doing."

She leaned over the crib to adjust a sheet corner that did not need to be adjusted, disgusted with herself for venting a complaint fully knowing she would never confront Dad to his face.

"Not sure I can be so glib as to claim that I would readily return all those hours Dad's spent rocking and feeding and changing the baby — Mom's mainly checked out, no surprise — I mean. It's my fault. I took the easy way out. I should have moved back in with Eleanor. She offered. I — thought I was doing, without question, what was best for Jason. And I was scared of things I can't, don't want to revisit now. So I took what I thought was the right way out. Moving back home. Which it turns out is a mess. Dad's every sacrifice inseparable from his possessiveness."

"Damn," said Peter, tracing Jason's outline, the little humidifier's single red eye casting shadows from under the sheet, taut in spite of the gathered moisture. "Not surprising doesn't mean it ain't, if I hear you right, sickening. Mind if I step into the bathroom for a minute? I got to call my Uncle Cedric. He hasn't returned my calls in a minute." And as she pointed him to the room that dad and

Eaves and Sterne had fitted with a shower and a toilet, she heard him mumble — for her, against her, "The heart is deceitful above all things, and desperately wicked: who can know it?"

. . .

"Shhhh."

The baby still slept three steep flights above them. "Ducts carry sound too well to worry," Stella had said, "As a kid I heard *everything* my brother did in the attic. Everything my parents said that was supposed to be kept secret." Jason, she explained, was an either / or baby: placid to the point of unbelievable stillness or screaming at outsized decibels of despair. She could bound up and console him in a minute.

They slunk down the steep stairs that sunk to the basement — patches of carpet torn up, cast aside, the concrete freezing cold on their feet — and fell into the old coal room now clean, fresh off-white still tickling the nostrils.

Peter kissed the back of her neck, beneath the held-up tower of hair that glistened grayed-red under the hallway halogen. Stella held out a finger and waved it like a windshield wiper. A deep stomach giggle stopped the façade and she smiled and ran her hand over his lips, the thrill of trespassing resting strange on sore ankles — no tiptoe romance stolen kiss of childhood.

"Shhhh. *Stop.*"

"Seriously?"

"Can you *see?*"

Eaves and Andy were backs to the two of them, hunched over a map of the United States that stretched like a sheet over a circular table once, her father said, used for séances but her mother had had the thing sprinkled with holy water and at least two pastors and three priests had blessed it since Stella was a child. More than a dozen half-smashed Miller cans made a mock circle around the zoned-out men, elbows bent at awkward angles like the bones on those rotisserie chickens mom bought when her weary knees couldn't stand at the stove for a day, chicken bones that threatened to break when you wound the wings outward with hunger.

Andy's thinned-out gray blond hair looked like a faint fire smoldered into ashes, but his red face was the central coal keeping the room warm. A cellophane of sweat coated his face, brought out jagged geometries, and when he saw Stella and Peter stumble in he stood up and with forced composure, clearing his throat, he extended his hand.

"My name is Andrew Pomsta," he said, and he ran a finger over his dimple, as if to be sure he was in fact smiling, "retired sometime high school teacher, jack of too few trades, grandfather of too many to number, so long divorced I may as well have been single except for the children who are walking proof I did at one time have relations with a wife." Although no one had taken his hand, he'd left the gesture there, statuesque. "Stella, I remember you from when you were *this big*. Your father has good things to say about you." He ignored Peter and proceeded. "Now, I have to say you came just in time. I've been struggling to fix something broken, over here, and hoped you might help me make sense of it. I'm as mechanically inclined as your dad, but this problem defies me, I admit it."

He led them across to the workbench. "A visitor sent this as a gift after he left in some heat one session (we meet down here some nights to chew the news, play a round), having denounced jazz music as 'elite chaos,' I believe it was. 'Made by colored, consumed by white. Commodification of the underclass — the *master* trying in a masochistic manner to consume communion with his slave.'"

The man did not once glance at Peter, who did not take the tired bait. "'Impure,' was another word he used. I admit the man was a little . . . indelicate. For being so supposedly cultured. We'd been developing a pretty good rapport with this man, so the argument — which I'm sure you'll see was obviously not about jazz at all but the history and meaning of America itself — left us all pretty down, for a week, until this came with this little note:

> This may not be a white flag but our own decadence is not better but worse. Far worse. A corpse steering a hearse. A curse: Black Flag. Have you ever, like me, in a deep rabbit hole of white-hot resentment, listened to 'Nervous Breakdown'? Epitome, in concentrated form, of the mental derangement dumbing us all

368

down! Sick fountain of the resentment that poisons the rest of us. Can you imagine the priceless thumos spent in basements banging out waste? The respectable would rather point at Punk and pretend they've nothing in common with the delinquents, but Black Flag is a brother of the millions of plebs and lumpen proles and middle-class men who could take back their country but would rather take pleasure in muttered complaints and sweet lotus eater basement nostalgia. An adolescent dress rehearsal of romanticized Achilles rage.

Affectionately Gone Berserkers,

Tailor

He pulled back a dust-caked canvas, crinkled it fishing for a key that was hanging on the wobbly nail where her family kept all their spares over the years. He wound the crank of a miniature ceramic she'd never seen before. "Well would you look at that, here's what I'd meant to ask you about. This pretty machine hadn't worked at all until now, and — amazing, what a treat." Eaves's unfocused eyes stayed put, staring at a map dotted with red pins from sea to shining sea, a circuitry of interconnected events either preserved from the past or forthcoming — riots, protests, Civil War battles she did not know.

The ceiling of the ceramic miniature, which at rest was an unbloomed blossom, unfolded like a phonograph horn, golden and coated with blue flower petals that darkened to a strangled purple as the horn fell all the way open and the central attraction kicked into motion: figurines like those found on wedding cakes jostled their drums, raised their trumpets and stand-up bass, heads nodding and big teeth showing through permanent and garish grins fixed with fuchsia on black faces.

"Minstrels," Peter whispered to Stella, his mouth a gaping hole in the room.

Andy winked at Peter and then closed his eyes like one lost in the music: "Oh when the saints, come marching in, oh when the saints come marching in, oh how I want to be in their number, oh when the saints come marching in." He showed his teeth like the figurines and pulled his lips back in their pained smiles as

369

pleased as if he'd bit into a peach. Peter reached into his side pocket where he'd shoved Jason's little trumpet while cleaning the attic before they descended. He wrung from the toy, a glorified kazoo, that military dirge that found its first home in the Union army and crossed enemy lines to the Confederates, until Taps became the common hymn for all the fallen of the country, spare and haunting in its gaunt notes.

Peter's knuckles darkened atop a muscular fist as he held a beer cap over the bell and siphoned from the silly item a loud and reverent funerary feel that drowned out the ceramic saints marching in place.

Andy shook Eaves's shoulder and, pointing at Peter, bid his friend clap. Feeling the two men's unspoken fight, Stella's mind felt like a badminton birdie as Andy blurred into a proxy for her father, an approximation of dad's worst secrets kept contained in this cleaned-up coal room. She could not fail to see her father's barely strangled embarrassment, had he been present — not, like Andy, to do with his color but, for her dad, because of the baby, whom dad had adopted as his own.

She steadied herself with an arm around Peter's waist when Andy, waiting until Peter pressed his pained eyes as if permanently closed, winked.

The sweat at the base of his back had shed fast. She soaked up the wet with his V-neck T-shirt, forgetting — or deferring — the constant hesitations that had her walking in heart-grasping circles around the block to breathe better ever since he'd been here to visit.

Now, not just averting her eyes but shielding them from Eaves's wink as if he were a blinding glare on an otherwise lovely sunny day, she leaned into Peter fully, surrendered, and as he slipped the toy trumpet into his pocket, flipped Andy the finger, and departed in silence she watched herself chase him up the stairs, felt herself treat Peter like her man.

They bounded the stairs two or three at a time, blood flush with fear's awful thrill, waited on the landing for Andy to follow but heard instead Eaves's heavy laughter. She went to tell her Dad in the living room but he was snoring in the laid-back recliner, the red flannel her mother had been wearing wrapped over him as a blanket that barely covered the bulge of his belly.

When her room in the attic had been Jacob's he had sawed a small square in the door and filled the empty space with two bolt locks. As they rushed, out of breath, into the warm room, Peter flipped both knobs clockwise. He held her for a good half hour and she let him as a way of reversing the things that had happened in the basement. Pretending that words could excuse or placate would insult Peter so she kept silence and swayed slowly with him until he said, "I'll sleep on the floor." She stayed awake long after he did, listening for creeping footsteps on the stairs.

. . .

Mourning doves squeezed their melancholy songs from chests that swelled with the world's sorrow. Pausing, they fought with morning blackbirds over the seeds that fell from the feeder. Mom meticulously kept the feeder filled but either this day's flock was especially populous or she'd been too preoccupied to mind stray birds. When he heard movement on the floor below, heard the pale bacon fat slap the cast iron skillet, crackling in sustained competition with the radio that sounded especially manic at a distance, smelled the burning, seasoned flesh and had to restrain a descent down the stairs, Peter blew reveille through the plastic play toy trumpet and Jason, stationary but rocking on his rear, screamed for the horn and squeezed outsized tears from his squinted, pink-puffed, mystified eyes. He looked almost like a newly-born animal whose habitat was under the earth. His Daddy could not get him to laugh. When he tried to tickle Jason the baby looked pained, passed gas.

What started as a game took on a grim edge. But as Peter went on playing, would not cease, she relished the absence of his cascading eloquence, felt bad, then, at the anger that twitched the blank eyes that stared, scared, or furious at the indifferent child.

A rose, bereft of its mystery, whose petals were wilted and almost dried sclerotic, was yet intact on the brown bedside table, imbalanced but upright next to her bed. Peter had sent the dead thing living. The persistence of the petals long after life gave the rose something even a fresh bloom would lack.

"Too young for Thelonius. Got to titrate. It's hard, too young, to take at once that mathematical madness." As soon as Peter passed the instrument Jason bit the bell's bulge, messed up his face in disgust, and threw the thing against the wall.

She could not look the Daddy in the eye but she saw him wipe a sleeve, there, drying his lashes and trying to laugh it off. He seemed faraway, at the end of a hallway that she could not traverse in a lifetime.

The pan on the hotplate boiled over, slightly. She seized it and poured the steaming liquid over a French press chock full of grounds.

"You may as well be doing cocaine," Peter said. "Not that I'm complaining. I need to wake up." He reached down to retrieve and return to reveille again, his spine cracked and Stella shifted, curved herself around him close, held him and kissed the bone that bulged at the uptight base of his neck. She moistened her hands from a pink bottle and rubbed the lotion into his skin, which felt especially sclerotic this time, as if he'd done nothing to moisten it since she stopped rubbing in coconut oil and lavender. Feeling for Peter's taut muscles, with the hardened heel of her palm, she gave everything she had to heal the pain they had left unspoken.

When all of her familiar efforts failed, she stopped and stood and said "You're hurting," and he said, "I'm high-strung. Every time. I try not to get real angry somebody's got to do something stupid, a caricature of a caricature, but every time you tell your-self so — every time you say so-and-so's a caricature, look deeper, dredge out complexity, you run into these flat-souled folks who seem to be waiting for incarnation."

"But if it's stupid it still hurts. Hurts worse because it's so dumb?"

"That kind of fool could do a lot of damage. Not to me," he said, looking scared, standing and taking both of her hands. "Don't worry, baby."

"He was drunk."

"All the more reason to worry. Lets down his guard when inebriated? Means he'd normally be able to hide hate behind small talk and a feigned face."

"But what do you need his approval for?"

"I don't need him to *recognize* me?"

"You won a public debate with Barack Obama and you need the recognition of Creepy Andy."

"Okay. Thank you for saying that. Not the first part, because how do you calculate who 'won' a debate that ends in a . . ." he paused, closed his eyes as if to see the University of Chicago stage, and, "Well can you even say something ends when the final act is a circling circus of semantics? Yes, yes, the time ran out, but nobody won because we didn't define our terms, couldn't, by the end, agree on words." He laid back against the wall, rolled up his right shirtsleeve. "But that — you said *Andy*. Man, he really is creepy. It's always cathartic to hear a spade called a spade."

"And that's what I'm doing. Calling you. You want him to see you. Give some token of approval. Admiration."

He ran his palm in an oval around his face, then took two fingers of each hand and, emitting a disgusted note from his nose, covered his eyes.

"You don't?" she asked, and when anger flashed before he could blink it away and his brow furrow bent into a tilted cross she said, "Say he welcomed you into his home, which apparently is what the basement's become — I went down, in the night, couldn't sleep, to get a coffee filter — and he was sprawled out snoring across that table. But what? If he welcomed you, would that win you, if in spite of that welcome you knew the hate cramping every inch of his intestines? O, oh, an even grander delusion: you're dreaming of the day *he'll* want *your* recognition."

"Nah. Yes. Tedious, that we keep provoking and hating over such petty caricatures. I mean that's more painful than anything. And even my complaining about the caricatures is a cliché. Predictable. Rote. God. You think I'm insulted over his highfalutin minstrel machine? Man, I need something much more impressive. If he pulled out a switch, shackle and slave block and bid me stand

and sing an old Negro spiritual saying 'See the sweet fruits of the suffering we gave you!' even then the pain of the past would play dead so well I couldn't hurt or hurt back. See. All of this lacks subtlety — the little reciprocities of real history. No. The whole game has grown so.... tedious. Take the bait? Am I fish? It's hard enough to breathe without somebody cutting gills across my ribs. What if I'm genuinely tired of being homeless, in this country, in this world, of every yes being tinged with a no and every nay a halfway maybe? I believe many are similarly exhausted. I've seen it giving talks across the country. Was a time when two people opposed in every way could sit down to play a good game of cards.

"But what if — what if what's wrong is simpler? Been thinking this through — in all kinds of ways — lately: Look, ideology's an idiot's refuge, a prison of oversimplification. But in fleeing it, there's another prison we choose to live inside without even realizing. And that's the perpetual prism of infinite nuance paired with *perfect* tolerance. The avoidance of even an implicit position, a straight answer to a given question whose meaning matters to millions — millions — but which in the name of anti-didactic, amoral *humane* manners, remains at best a pleasing riddle in the endless conversations of those whose drug of choice is chattering . . ."

"Dilettantes. But Peter. What if what's wrong is even simpler? Funny what passes for simple. Old times, good times? Intellectual enemies touring the country giving public debates to prove that there's a better way. You know that kind of 'unity' is not what you're after. You'd spend hours after such shows of politeness throwing darts, spewing critiques — I remember, remember too many to count, nitpicking this or that. Venting in proportion to the repressed pain under the game of unity." She feared her meaning was mangled on arrival. "All that hedging. All that trying to say everything at once. Forgive me if I sound dehumanizing, but you're a hedgehog at heart. Handsome as you are, you are no fox. Another gift given by the Greeks. 'The fox knows many things, but the hedgehog knows one big thing.'"

"That I can't deny, entirely. That is the" — here he held his temples, playing out the drama draining his brain — "tragedy." He

374

held the toy trumpet in his pale palm, the golden paint chipped and chewed off. "There is so little nobility on the face of the earth. No — you hear me right — honor in our wars. No winners, even." He sobbed in one, quick, chest-out exertion, and his shoulders lowered and he watched the second hand of his watch, shook his wrist as if it were stuck although the time kept running out. "What world is this, with visions of winning so woefully — terrifyingly — small? But what, next to a nothing, would it be? A game of cards. Wouldn't be nothing. A game is better than a vacuum. We lost more than we knew when these little rituals ran out. If we'd known I swear we wouldn't have let them go. All games aren't about winning or losing in the main. They're playful spaces that put the mind at ease and open up a wide field to shoot the shit of life."

"Well, join them. They'll be back at it tonight."

"What game were they playing last night? Did not look like a game at all."

"Who knows, some kind of Risk spinoff."

"Didn't look like a *game* to me at all. I didn't want to say so there. Been around enough disgruntled characters I picked up this uncanny intuition. Even as a boy, I called the next murder like predicting a tournament winner. Should have gotten a bet going. Brackets. I see your face. Sick. *Too close.* But that's what folks do in war zones. Make up games to up the ante against the absurdity."

"A prophet. You're a prophet. Would be. Could have been. But reversed. Reading this world instead of the next."

"My uncle said almost the same thing once. You're laughing, the edges of your lips, the way you say it, that's *too close.* I wish I could do more than *believe* in a God. It's hard enough not to, but the next step escapes me. I respect my uncle — but I can't be like him. I'm a hearer (he once told me) not a *doer* of the Word."

He shook his wrist and wound his watch knob, counterclockwise because the seconds seemed to speed so fast he got palpitations. He wound and wound and looked around, as if he could keep time from running out.

"Baby," she said, her mouth line as straight as the level grandpa gave to dad when he died. The gray one with the golden glass — the magical bubble of the level that she thrilled to see centered on a board balanced between a horse in the basement. "I hear you."

"Anyway, here's my guess." He hunched over like the men last night, elbows out, and pinned invisible deaths onto the floor, then took sidewalk chalk from the cloth bag slung over the door handle and traced the outline of a corpse. "I suspect the stakes involve somebody's lives, not a bin of dead plastic pieces. Bombs like the other side tried in D. C."

"You speak of them as if you'd had nothing to do with it. You were the one who plotted the explosion."

"You know why I did it, whatever I said aloud, in public — I'm ashamed you came into that meeting at the very moment I was mapping it all out. But you know — why else would you let me in, why else wouldn't you have called the police and had me arrested the first day I arrived? Not that it would have worked; I mean, like I told you, my lawyer got me good and clean from any pre-trial detention. As it should be. Unless assumed innocence is abolished. Look. The situation was a sphinx. There was no option for 'remain peaceful,' for calling off all violent stunts. Something or somebody was 'bout to get blown up. Why, anyway, are we going back over this? We talked it to death a week ago."

"Do you really need to ask me that? Who could let go of something so massive? Show me. Who. When you left you said you would undo them from the inside. The votes that night were unanimous."

"Oh so because all the votes went my way I'm somehow following the mind of the crowd? The crowd is untruth."

"But what he meant to say is that the crowd helps you hide your conscience behind numbers, distribute responsibility 'til it practically disappears. As if you could divide a moral act by a number."

"Right, why I love you. Keep me honest. You'd never let me ride on your good qualities, or mine, Stella. God. Mercy, Stella. God. You always ask me. Give mercy. Give me some of what you got. All of us got to take a break from the ruthless mirror held up to every fault."

"Stop. I'm not that mean."

"That's not what I mean. No facetiousness. I'm dead serious. Why I love you. Will you marry me?"

376

"I — there's somebody else. Someone's been coming around to see me." Something her grandmother would have said, with her cultured euphemisms which were increasingly euphonious as the common language grew gauche and crass. "I'm seeing about seeing him too."

"Him . . . who?" Peter followed her gaze across the room, but from his angle instead of the window his eyes fell on a propped-up mirror from which hung clumps of the clothing Stella insisted on hang-drying. Back in Chicago, when they'd been living together, when he first furrowed his nose and said he couldn't go to work in a shirt so wrinkled it'd look like a too-clever cubist painting, she first said "Stop being so self-important. As if anybody'd notice. As if the world is awaiting your arrival on Division St., and all the parades will cease if you show up looking less than starched." Then she pulled out an iron and straightened the shirt, the smell of hot cotton and orange essential oil steaming the apartment until the wrinkles disappeared and his scrunched nose rested between her knuckles as he kissed her ring finger and kept his mouth there. Back there in Chicago.

All that softness gone now as Stella shot back "Who? You surprised anybody else would take me? You think you're the only hero I know? That same lost boy who called off our engagement, I, I know I told you about Blake. Weren't you list — don't you remember?" She pulled at her earlobe and shook her head *no* though he said, "of course. First love. I remember."

"First love? We were almost married! He. Came back. I mean almost as if from the dead, okay? I told you — not that you'd remember —"

"Wait, insults in passing. I remember everything you told me."

"Oh, because you —"

"Talked too much about myself, I know, in the beginning. The eternal beginning. Always always you're going back there. Another regret I would have you forget."

"Blake?"

"No, *my* indulgence. My mistake."

"Well Blake is back and don't give me that look that says 'Must feel good to be fought over.' It feels awful and I'm all indecision. I've never been, done, this sort of thing before."

"Didn't dude disappear last time when reality showed up unannounced? But now, oh *now* he's *here* for real."

"Peter either you're nervous or mean. I'm risking everything right now. I could have kept it hidden. I hate it. You think because I rushed with you I haven't learned a damn thing? I'm a mess and anyway all this talk about old mores lost forever, an infinity of nostalgia. My Nonna had a half dozen boyfriends at once. So two is hardly too many." She covered her breast without conviction as he hung his head in silence, stressed breaths staccato and loud.

"How many of her boyfriends got her pregnant?"

Stella shifted, felt her foot asleep, and stood to shake it out. "You want the truth?" she looked down on him, and he stood as if to answer *yes*, bring it out. "I want to love you both but can't. Time. Envy. A bad recipe. Not enough hours. And though Jason might suck both breasts dry there's only one heart hidden in my chest. And yes, hidden, because it's heartless what I'm doing. Telling you the truth."

"And no, thank you. (I know how insecure you are about appearances. Your appearance.)"

"Not insecure. Certain. Certain that I cannot be separated from ugliness. Not appearances. Actuality. Besides what the fuck are we back in high school, suddenly. It's not about looks. He's only. Half as handsome as you."

"Why did you kiss me then, twice since last night."

"I hate your pain."

"Sweet of you. To try and salve what you cause. You can't get the satisfaction of salving it if you don't accept all the consequences. Like," he said, tapping his fingernails against each of the diamond blue eyes that surveilled all he said from the wall. Hundreds of blue condescending eyes. "I want one woman all my life and I'll have that one woman, whoever she is, to want one man — me."

The scales would switch in her favor if she said how scared she was of his wall-hole-making anger.

"You of all people know about broken promises." He held up her hand: "I can still see the place where the ring you wore settled in place. You taught me — too late, it's my fault, what I took from you when I gave you the baby. Gave you before I barely knew you."

"Gave me."

"You think you could cook one up on your own?"

"God, I'm sorry. I — I hate what's happening. Every word that's escaping my mouth. Too much, Peter. It's too much. Please. Let's stop, take a walk. Get out of this house. Separate for an hour and come home. Try again."

"If at first you don't succeed." He patted Jason who had fallen asleep, narcoleptic on the attic floor. Stella had shoved the corner of a rug under his cheek. "He's got a chill," Peter said, and he took off his shirt and covered his child, the diapered rump ruffled in a hump.

"We're not animals, inanimates, what have you. If we get jaded for a time, it's not irreversible — the burnt-out heart, immunity to bonds we don't get to choose. Understand me?"

"I can't hear anything. Nothing's making sense. Please, Peter, bring it to a finish."

He shook his wristwatch as if it were stuck now, although the time kept running out.

"Even were a man to sleep around to the point that his lovers become in his mind interchangeable, reduced to the mechanics of slight variations in the twist of the torso or the sound of the moan. Even such a practical animal could recover his senses, no, not quite — recover, recover. What. The soul? So that slowly he could regain sensitivity to the littlest ways we give away and take — to the smallest kiss on the nape of the neck. Where you marked me with your baby's breath." He moved behind her and she did not protest. Her bare arms showed no gooseflesh. He kissed her where she kissed his neck — on the curve of bone between what she shouldered. "And so though from one angle I've no right to say it, I'll be so bold as to lay myself down. 'If you want me, risk me.' Remember what you said. Here's all. I couldn't risk more if I tried. If you kiss me and leave me I'll be much the worse than if I never met you from the first. I don't deserve to say anything but there's something higher than justice between us."

"Amen. I mean. I can't deny. But, for now. Peter. Are you done?"

When Peter had put his shirt over Jason the baby had stirred and now his rounded face rotated, eyes peeking out of the shroud. Peter lowered, squatted, sighed. "My son," he said. "My son, my son." He ran his palm over Jason's head, curled his fingers into circles and framed them around the baby's waking eyes. "Boo!" he said. "Who's there?" Freeing his right hand, he lifted the trumpet, stuck it to his lips with ceremonious pomp, "Man boy I'd like to play you some Thelonious but maybe let's wait 'til we're older, ready to reach for those dissonant harmonies hanging out at the edge of existence." The blue nightlight, borrowed from Peter's Chicago apartment, blinked when a vacuum sounded downstairs. Beneath the blue light, behind the dead rose, she had framed a picture of Peter from five years ago. (The frame, forged of popsicle sticks, she had taken from a grade-school present she had once presented to her mother: the two of them kissing inside some semblance of a heart coaxed from brittle popsicle sticks.) She had found the frame in an attic corner, covered in what seemed like a handful of dust, and swapped the picture of her and her mother for a handsome one of a younger Peter.

"Some truths are perennial," he said, staring at the blue light, making out the youthful portrait. "'It's always night, or we wouldn't need light.'" When he blew the sound that came out was comic, a cosmic mess of crying and laughing. Clearing phlegm from the depths of his chest, he spat into a tissue and folded over, but not before she saw the blood there. When he started to sing the bellow tone rushed around the room in a resounding circle, and as he followed, faux marching steps, the agitation whirred round and round, Peter's dizzying body a blur, his sung hurt like a circumference of bricks.

> Joshua fit the battle of Jericho
> Jericho, Jericho
> Joshua fit the battle of Jericho
> And the walls came tumblin' down

Nagged, lost — no found, she found in the rare tenor of his notes a sweetness she had first known under his sheets. Stole, there. She shook off the bother. He's here, is the point. The simple stolidity of it. Boys need fathers. My boy. His. She smiled at Jason's guileless gape, his tilted head rocking as he studied daddy. She started to stack the blue blocks into a misshapen but still-standing wall, a solid defiance of fragility, but all the while any moment tipping, the flaunted accommodation with a fragile standing that fretted but did not fully define it, perfectly symmetrical and in a circle, and every time she sat back, satisfied, Jason would swipe with both hands, scattering the blocks in every direction, giving them both a big grin.

Peter, who'd been playful earlier, was — as if in a trance now — lost to them. She had poured a third round of coffee into the little porcelain Italian teacup Nonna had bought at an estate sale, but he'd left untouched what he'd greeted with a "yes please."

"Whew," he said. "Dizzy," he said, turning away with constrained giddiness. She stared at his shut eyes, the jugular vein that rose from his skin like a worm writhing, reaching for life after the rain, his face flooded and flushed with blood, dangling Adam's apple swelled as from a shook tree each time he blew, and again he blew out the highest harmonies, leaving the standard melody behind and reaching beyond what he could comfortably hit, so much struggle kept score in that body, stomach and facial and so many muscles finding the tension that would loosen what was taut. The way he held the trumpet so tender but not as truly as he'd held her that first night, thieving back some of what she'd taken, massaging the hardened tendons in her side until she fell asleep. While she set out to rehabilitate the symmetry, surprised by the satisfaction she found in this block-by-block model of what he was singing, she eyed the baby and outstretched her backhand, keeping his wrecking ball fists at bay. But remembering destruction was part of the flourish, she retrieved her arm and watched as the blue blocks faltered and then fell.

> Joshua fit the battle of Jericho
> Jericho, Jericho
> Joshua fit the battle of Jericho
> And the walls came tumblin' down

Through the door Andy stood there, arms bared at the top of the stairs, akimbo bold and chest out, only his toes on the lapis lazuli floor dad had painted the week before, bright colors for his first grandbaby. Peter balked at the flush bolts. He had turned them clockwise last night. Had they been unlocked then all night?

Andy's heels hovered over the air, his grip on the railing bone-white, the wood glistening with grease and sweat. Tiny pupils, fully dilated, rushed from east to west but found no place to rest, the sound of creaking boards like a forgotten curse. His wandering eyes made her skin itch. Like a rash. Instead of reaching out his three fingers as he had earlier in sheepish hello, he pulled from his pocket a full hand formed into faux pistol.

"I'd say if you touch her you're dead, but it looks like you already did," he said, gesturing to Jason with his fingers shaped into a fake gun. "Don't worry, safety's on. But it's about to come off so for your safety, Stella, I'd ask that you step out of the room. What needs to happen is man to man."

Nobody moved. Just a jerk, she was sure, toward Jason, would set the animal in that direction. The stark geometries of Andy's wrinkles made his blued lips look cerebral. Peter gripped the trumpet like a weapon.

"You know I too have thought long about Lincoln. Seems like we've," his shoulders slunk forward and the words that followed were dragged by the fatigue of last night's drinking, "got more in common than I realized. That's what they say, right? People tend to hate on each other only because they don't know each other. But are we not too different, but too alike? Well — wait! Let's not get carried away. Had we been contemporaries of his we may have both been in cahoots with John Wilkes Booth, just from different starting points. Either way, the man got the job done."

"How long have you been listening. And no. Hear me. No. I stand against any, whatsoever, sanctimonious justification of assassination." He looked at Stella as if to settle forever her qualms over the statue's blown fist.

"A brilliant gentleman of a bygone era — that ours is lacking the likes of him is both a cause and an effect of our petty, resentful age — praised the sixteenth president as, if purportedly a product of parliamentary election, a dictator who 'suspended the Constitution in order to protect it.' You see we both agree that there are two Lincolns and only one of the two is true. We, both of us know that the Great Liberator single-handedly suspended our sacred law of *habeas corpus*. Without that act tens of thousands of American citizens would not have been detained, without trial, during the Civil War. When the judge (forget his name) came after the president, saying the suspension violated the constitution, the great man, that sainted man did not humbly concede. He authorized the immediate arrest of anybody who benefited the Confederacy. The Great Liberator oversaw the most terrible suppression of free speech in American history. The suppression of rights. Rights that can be suspended's no rights at all."

Peter hurried out the sentence like a down-the-mountain train spilling its ore before it reached the valley. "You left out a matter of considerable concern in terms of Lincoln's largesse. I've cited the passage a million times, one that marches goose step through my mind: 'It may seem strange that any men should dare to ask a just God's assistance in wringing their bread from the sweat of other men's faces; but let us judge not that we be not judged.' Second Inaugural Address, no less."

Andy, without taking his finger from the trigger, pointed it toward the basement while he pulled out an old blue Brewers kerchief and wiped the sweat from his upper lip, blinking and shaking his reddening head, resolving on the grandfather smile that says *Clever, I grant you that.*

"Not to mention Peoria!" and here — as if a retired schoolteacher who, at sixty, had a hang-dog look that brought him closer to four score, weren't looking at him with a century's worth of hatred.

Andy stepped back and then lunged forward, his faux pistol fingers cramped into a fist before he did a strange skip and said, "I'm playing." Peter waved Stella away but when she went toward the door Andy's body was there first. She asked, over his shoulder, casual as can be, "Hey Dad, you down there? Something I wanted to show you."

"The old man stepped out," said Andy, his voice smarmy, "and might you, too, for a minute?"

What? Why block the door then?

When Andy stepped aside and she would not leave, Peter pulled her back with his elbow, patted his boy's head, and slipped a black phone out of his pocket. Andy assumed a stance of defense, then held the heel of his palm between them.

"Back off me." Peter shook his head. "Just a phone, man, not a weapon. Man to man, you said, let's go. See if you can go toe to toe with my mind." As Peter scrolled and found what he wanted Andy, strangely, breathed easier and leaned against her brother's high-school Cure poster, knee stretched out and heel to the wall.

"There now," said Peter. "We can work this out. Since we're having such a rich conversation, I wanted to present evidence of our *other*, thus far buried Lincoln." Stella saw that he pressed record, and held the camera toward the hazy man barely visible for the sunshine that the skylight lavishly let in. The atmospheric pressure, as if hissing, became heady as all bodies went lazy.

"Let us listen to the words of the Great Emancipator," Peter said, and he rose like a preacher lit by the Spirit, pacing the room as his wrecked eyes bulged even though he needed to narrow them to read: 'If all earthly power were given me, I should not know what to do, as to the existing institution. My first impulse would be to free all the slaves, and send them to Liberia — to their own native land. But a moment's reflection would convince me, that whatever of high hope (as I think there is) there may be in this, in the long run, its sudden execution is impossible. If they were all landed there in a day, they would all perish in the next ten days . . . What then? Free them all, and keep them among us as underlings? Is it quite certain that this betters their condition? I think I would not hold one in slavery, at any rate; yet the point is not clear enough for me to denounce people upon. What next? Free them, and make them politically and socially, our equals? My own feelings will not admit of this; and if mine would, we well know that those of the great mass of white people will not. Whether this feeling accords with justice and sound judgment, is not the sole question, if indeed, it is any part of it. A universal feeling, whether well or ill-founded, can not be safely disregarded. We can not, then, make them equals.'

"Sure, sure, my brothers and sisters, you can find all kinds of evidence to the contrary. His assertion that the Constitution confirms equality for all, not 'none but rich men or none but white men,' for instance. It's complicated, you say. Yes, but complication is not a synonym for absolution of a sin so serious it made millions of lives walking graves — walking men who *wished* they were graves, for stone cannot feel the lash.

"Yes, sir, I've long thought on it. For years and years stared at Lincoln. For complication let us substitute that enemy of authenticity: *compartmentalization*. His letter to Greeley, who begged emancipation, is a pointed case of the disease we diagnose: 'If I could save the Union without freeing any slave I would do it,' he responded. 'Caught!' you say, 'white handed.' But don't let your spirit separate out the letter: 'and if I could save it by freeing all the slaves I would do it.' You ever tried to walk two directions at once?" Peter asked, then fixing his sad eyes on Stella he continued, "You ever tried to love two people at once? Who here in this room has never done the right thing for the wrong reason? A just act from an unjust heart. Keep that in mind when you listen to Lincoln's letter to Greeley, judge not so you be not judged, because," and here his tenor turned hilarious, as he gasped at the air like one drowning, "this sure looks like the sentence of a sinner heading into the hands of an angry God: 'What I do about slavery, and the colored race, I do because I believe it helps to save the Union; and what I forbear, I forbear because I do not believe it would help to save the Union. I shall do less whenever I shall believe what I am doing hurts the cause, and I shall do more whenever I shall believe doing more will help the cause. I shall try to correct errors when shown to be errors; and I shall adopt new views so fast as they shall appear to be true views.'

"The Union. But what comes next is division, as if by locating two persons in one he could escape the accusation 'Two face!'"

Peter paced in a tiny circle, stayed close to Andy as if to keep him consoled, convinced that he was in control. He held out his phone and scrolled and scrolled. "'I have here stated my purpose according to my view of official duty; and I intend no modification of my oft-expressed personal wish that all men every where could be free.' Love, Abraham Lincolns. Plural. Might as well multiply them all, like Lincoln, in a Ford Motor Co. luxury line. Americans are an inventive people. Multiple personality was discovered in the States. Out of one, many. Am I right?"

"I seen you say those lines before."

"Guilty as charged. Of plagiarizing myself. I'm flattered, though, frankly, that you took the time to listen. As a former high-school teacher you'll agree that the questions I've spoken on are of momentous consequence."

Peter pretended away his fear, buried it in a filibuster.

Andy's eyes, glistening, darkened.

"Ready to condemn him? Guilty though uncharged. The catch is he'd already outlawed slavery in D. C., held in his fingers any man's property found guilty of supporting the rebellion: confederates. Degenerates. And at the scripted dénouement of his cut-short life, assassinated mid-performance, he'd switched so cutthroat concerning slavery that the issue became a single-minded engine that disregarded damage to the Union. You know what happens to a man so driven. They recur in every generation. If victory comes, they cannot celebrate, for pain over what they defeated.

"Who of us has not known some refraction of this feeling? That ambitious aim you lost your friends over so that all alone you poured the champagne, down your throat instead of across ten sparkling shared glasses, drunkenness to dull the day set aside for feasting. If it be so with one man, what of a whole generation? Smug, astride the tensions of the times, mathematically certain that they've taken the right side, as if history was a baseball game fought on a field categorically clear: Cubs," he laughed, "is the chosen, and Sox the depraved. Seeing hypocrisy, we shake our heads. Contradictions make us crazy, but some busted nerve in us keeps hankering after what we know damn well to be impossible. Take just one thing. Absolute equality is an existential impossibility, in history. Ain't never happened and can't. Won't. Am I clear? Can we divide *never* and divvy it up in equal pieces? Some hard-won things do appear, here and there, for a decade or a year, something decent or even good. Seeing or hearing that somewhere sometime some measure of Eden happened, we spend our whole lives bent on that fleeting year which we run after like it'll last forever — as my Uncle said to me once — more than once to his congregations — *no instant of infinity . . . no eternity in time . . . that is the great mistake we make — seeking the fixed in the flow.*

"Not even for that hard-won year, a year that came at the cost of centuries, will we *really* rest content, 'cause we balk, nauseous, over what it costs us and we fear, each passing tick, that what we've found is about to trickle out, get stolen, squandered, all our efforts forgotten. No victory here without heartache. Now don't mishear me. Please, sir," a breathy hurt broke through his words. "Striving for some lost grain of the other shore that got left behind *here*, my friends, whether patiently or madly, is unequivocally worth doing. The alternative is directionless itinerance or total surrender to animal settling. A mule wandering his forty acres in a merry-go-round forever. But no, do not you ever dare believe there'll be a triumph here without a tragic aftertaste — the burnt edge of Prometheus' proclamations of liberation."

Andy, catching the phone's red eye, the little giveaway under Peter's thumb, played his right hand into a pistol. Peter put his hands above his head, elbows out, feigning arrest.

"Don't joke with me. No time for your — preachy minister —"

"No time for my minstrel act?"

"Not that, for me, it's about your being black. I've not a racist inch in my *alabaster* bones."

"When he died, my slave ancestor in Georgia, his skeleton was used by the master to teach anatomy to his children. He did not hesitate to use the skeleton of a colored man. Not a racist bone in his body, eh?"

"What's happening here and now has to do with the state of exception this country's come to, been stuck within for far too long. You get off when you did what you did?"

"And what did I do?" He coughed and muttered into his sleeve something that sounded like "Who? Me?"

"Don't play the albatross. What you didn't do but wished you could have. History's what hurts. *The Wretched of the Earth*. All you've argued amounts to nothing less than outright assassination absolved of any sense of wrongdoing. Assassination as an ethical necessity." His flesh was the color of picked over supermarket peaches grown in soil severely depleted.

"What? What you group me in for?" She watched him rub drips of sweat from his neck, scratch there and then his head, stunned. "What *they* didn't but could have. Lincoln's saved face? You spend too much time in internet holes. Alice-in-Wonderland hallucinations."

"I'm not buying it. You're hiding out here. And no one, apparently, is doing due diligence."

"If I was *hiding out* — from who? — why would I head straight to a known address of my son's mother?"

"Plain sight. Oldest trick." She watched his leer, his eyes alight on her mouth. "You'll get off when they take you to trial. Concerns of justice straightjacketed by race. They'll either acquit you on account of it or condemn you because of it. Two outcomes but from my view the same. And in such a scenario, such a state of exception — when law and order is surpassed by grievances, when grievance and endless guilt replace liberty and justice and all the rest — it's *not* crazy to assume the unpleasant but necessary responsibilities that will make sure justice is served. I don't honestly care anymore how they'll spin me. I've been sitting on my hands for over half of a century watching my country go to shit. I share your target, your Lincoln Memorial, but if my kind were to try it we'd be given a life sentence."

Andy wore an outline of irreality. Looking at him, looking at Jason, sure that if she tried to snatch him he would crack, Andy, and kill them all, Stella shook her head, unable to convince herself that this would all end without death, that the vigilante presence stood tall but lanky with the awkward stance of an adolescent posturing more confidence than he possessed. Looking at him you apprehended next to nothing but nonetheless he was *there*, here. Slowly she stopped the scream that gathered, first guttural, then shrieking in her constricted throat's tower like a fierce burst of birds rising from the bowels of the earth and her throat a belfry beyond which they could not ascend, but before they dipped back down into her belly their beaks pecked into the sides of her throat and departed with pieces of her flesh. Slowly she felt her throat with both hands, fingers formed the sign language for choking. Slowly inched toward her sleeping child, squatted and seized him by the armpits, shielding his body with her shoulders though she trusted Andy would not hurt her, though he seemed ready to lunge or punch, but his eyes when he found her were filled with desire.

Stella tried to make sense of his sentences when he played the preserver of law and order: "Before I die I'd like to write a single sentence of history that might be read a hundred years from now — that could spark others to say *enough*. To take governance into our own damn hands!"

Andy now pulled from his pocket a white-handled pistol that looked like a toy, like the very cap gun her brother would point whenever she invaded his secret base in the basement coal room, cushions stolen from the couch and stacked, a pretended defense, just so. He pointed the nozzle at Peter's head. The tip was not orange, was not plastic or capped. The barrel's mouth was wide open, black inside under silver lining.

"So come with me now, hands behind your back. Citizens' arrest. Hypocrite! You'll cry. The only thing our age has left: all these citations of . . . imperfection a justification for . . . decimation. Suspension of habeas corpus? Though, I'll point out, we have reason to do so."

"Hold on, now," Peter pressed 911, "just one second here, *habeas corpus*, let's see about that," whispered "*Police please*" into the speaker, flipped his thumb madly as if something the phone could conjure would save him from what was happening here, read from his blinking red phone: "'The Privilege of the Writ of Habeas Corpus shall not be suspended, unless when in Cases of Rebellion or Invasion the public Safety may require it.' *Unless when in Cases of*

Rebellion. And here: '(c) The writ of habeas corpus shall not extend to a prisoner unless — (1) He is in custody under or by color of the authority of the United States or is committed for trial before some court thereof.' *Habeas corpus*. Yes, You shall have the body."

Once, at the florist, a man had come in and pointed a handgun at the register, the manifestation of a nocturnal vision Stella had woken to at three a.m., the figure no more than an outline of a human — a chalked sketch, easily erased — and therefore somehow more scary. Her fingers — healed and tough from a thorn prick the week prior — had not even shaken as she opened the drawer and handed him the petty bills pinned there under the metal tongues that depressed them. All had gone as slow then as motion was going now.

An itch to shake Jason for being here at all, a scary itch that shook the room: she nearly dropped the baby, who cried because the blue wall was broken and because daddy was singing with a gathering force that took as if two steps down before leaping up an entire landing, the sound commanding, his eyes demanding she leave him here alone with the gunman.

> Joshua fit the battle of Jericho
> Jericho, Jericho
> Joshua fit the battle of Jericho
> And the walls came tumblin' down

When Peter tilted his head toward the hall she started that way but then threw herself over him, in front of him, and clung. "You shall *not* have the body," she said.

She heard a creak, a step worrying the stairs, coming closer — *Daddy* — she almost called out but again to scream seemed certain to trigger the gun, the collapse, the bath of blood which now would take life from not one but three. *I'm crazy for not stepping out. A world where he dies and I'm still here. Even if Blake* — even still — *never the day would never fade 'til she died.* Nonna's cough from the other room.

Siren lights purpled the walls but there was no sound as they spun. Nonna rested her hands on Andy's shoulders. "Excuse me, dearie," and she entered the room as if to water a plant — her "thirsty clematis" whose leaves were brittle — or adjust the blinds to let in some light (several of the blinds were badly bent and she did not know why Regan did not fix them). The dead rose Peter had sent her living.

The cat, Prince, who cleaved to her heels, would not follow Nonna past the threshold. His yellow eyes seemed to roll.

Dad. Dead. Andy. Shit. You did it. She could not slip past him to see if her father's body lay slumped on the couch, no longer napping but corpse. Andy widened his stance, blocked the door.

Things she thought impossible. Nonna's nightgown was half-undone and sagging breasts gave way to a diaper. Her silver hair, meticulously braided, wound around her blue-veined neck. "Can I hold the baby," she asked, stretching out her arms in a confused appeal.

"My friend," Peter whispered, walking across the room, angling the nozzle into his ear. "Trigger me. Go on. But allow the victim a last word."

Stop, please. Just plead. Silence.

Andy let his arm fall. The nozzle again aimed at the floor. Dad what errand. Bacon burning in the kitchen. Officers where are you. Toast. He liked it black around the edges. Bad jokes all through childhood, "I like my toast like I like my heart — black and cold and hard as hell," and here he'd pat mama's black hair, run his fingers all the way through, slowly with an intimacy that startled her. How barely they kissed.

Stella held out the baby and let Nonna believe she suspended Jason by her own strength. Her phone was nursing against the wall. No more silent siren colors. Another call. Plenty of crime to go around.

When dad bounded up the stairs and into the room she stumbled back getting out of his way and found her feet down five stairs, standing on tiptoes to watch — why? Without really registering what she had done she had pulled Nonna, by her blouse, out, and shoved the woman into the bathroom. She heard the door latch and behind it her humming the hymn Peter had been singing before. Should have joined her in the safe ceramic tub.

The three men grunted in a puzzle of arms locked and —
there — even bone-cracked. She could not see and could not rise
without becoming a fast target — accidental or otherwise. Andy's
gun a toy, a model. If not somebody'd be dead by now.

A ricochet like the slammed busted door of Peter's Chicago
apartment.

He called her name. "Don't tell them," he choked out, "it was
tragic. No it was not 'so, so tragic.'"

Another ricochet, more hollow and harder, like the busted door
of Peter's room, always propped open when they came home and
he'd kick the brick away, breath heavy, and they'd fall, again, and
again, into bed.

He moaned. The baby opened his mouth and winced but no
noise came out.

She ascended and saw first his phone cracked by a heel into a
hundred pieces.

Nothing revealed that would not be concealed.

Dad's grip around both Andy's wrists, a chokehold that did not
blanch his color but concentrated all the red irate in the fists cuffed
by her father's weathered fingers. Andy who was many inches
taller and far stockier seemed to be letting dad shake him, dad
repeating "You drunken bastard," Nonna back from the bathroom,
God, whistling the same song through a mouth without dentures,
Stella hovering over Peter but unable to look down yet because
though she too like her father was reaching out and wringing a
wrist there was no pulse and she screamed aloud, Jason curled
against her breast, "There is no pulse! Help! Call the police! Too
late, too late," and mom was gone, walking her five miles through
sedimentary trails that laid the centuries bare through a gash like a
wound in the earth. And nothing shall be concealed so she looked
and his face was intact why it mattered so much that the bullet
had not found his face the hands who touched dead bodies daily
like a factory at the funeral home would find a way to make him
smile, to give an upward tilt to everything but would the hands
that reached to embrace her would they also hold out accusations
and what if, what if she'd said yes, yes, yes — said goodbye to the

392

fret that Nonna always called scrupulosity which meant you never believed God forgave you and this was true she barely believed if she did at all so what of God's alleged forgiveness so forgive us our debts as we forgive those, as if God held back his mercy until we showed ours, but that was the point, the diminishing point, what — yes — that was the point yes that was the point she believed but doubted that her little flint-scratch of faith was enough to win all that followed she winced and she swallowed between screams and dad was there unclasping his metal kit with the thick red cross bright in the center but the rusted hinges protesting like ghouls as he wrapped the dead in a tourniquet madly he had to know she was saying *he's dead, he's dead, he's dead, dad, he's dead, dad,* she heard his voice but could not make out the meaning of his utterance her head awash, no aflame, with the news, the name of the dead, her mouth pieced together a last ditch trench-warfare-scattershot of puerile prayers; reading off the long list, lingering in the sunny solitude of room filling with all she knew, all she loved. Why was she still here? Here at all? Languid, she lit a candle for each outcry, letting them be, there, like the place she'd found Blake cruciform on the floor, tongues untightened telling out loud what she wept, kept within.

Then the smolder came like second-hand smoke into the lungs of her learning depths, formed her from without, from within.

Nonna was pouring plant water on the floor, washing Peter's blood without knowing it.

The white-bronze edge of Peter's face offset a blue that said death by water or grade school contests to hold your breath. But he wasn't passed out in playful or pleasant or reversible unconsciousness. No return. The fact felt hard. When her pain rubbed up against it, or when the hardness rubbed against her pain, what seemed impervious stone cracked away like a cake of soap and an unbidden desperation for what Nonna had been mumbling about ran like a rivulet over the rock and turned the terrible fact into clay. What even was it she said, leaning back until her neck cracked? Stella grasped after it with both her mind's hands but came up with a lack. Wait. The resurrection of the dead. I believe in. Nonna said.

Gingerly, one at a time, she descended the rusted out L-train steps, both arms extended to the guardrails, baby sleeping, smiling in the sling, brown cheeks round, good eater. He'd nursed all the way from Union Station to here, covered by her grandmother's veil, a blue lace mantilla embroidered with a border of first blossom baby roses that circled a central bloom, a spiraling thing that flickered at the edges with an aura of ivory white explosions like the effusions of a Fourth of July sparkler. When Stella sorted the boxes Nonna gave her — an inheritance before she passed — she'd folded the mantilla and tucked it beneath the lace underwear she'd worn — for Peter? or to cover her worry that he'd see the unlovely tributary wrinkles and varicose veins that ran up her thighs? He'd had a red light that kept the room in a soft mood and dyed her body and his in illusion, but she kept wearing the draperies anyway, assured by the thousands of tiny baby's breaths that hugged her skin, assured by the deliberation required of Peter, who could not fall on her with the first night's spontaneous tearing of clothing but had to remove what kept him out with care. Every time this slowing made her smile, but now she blinked away his outstretched arms, his bowed head, worried that what she'd wanted was worship. Stella had tucked the mantilla beneath the underwear she was certain would stay unused, could not toss out what Peter had touched, taken off; nor could she discard the blue veil that had kept Nonna hidden, "as is proper in the presence of God."

An elderly woman in a ginger sari, heaving two slumped brown bags of groceries up the L train stairs, hairs of fennel and pale heads of bagged chickpea peeking over the top, nodded and made a grandmotherly wink, leaving in her wake a waft of fresh ginger and turmeric, but what remained in the woman's aftermath, as if the mist and raindrops had been distilled with drops of its oil, was a dense diffusion of frankincense and another scent familiar from the church of her childhood. Again she peeled open the printed directions (low ink in her dad's printer, dad had insisted he would drive her here, how she slipped out of the house without him knowing, vigilante, she didn't know, but she feared he would appear in the funeral crowd, worse than sitting beside him: seeing that familiar face, tense with tenderness, waiting for her reply).

She hailed a cab with the digital hand that waved back and whirled across her phone screen. The next leg was too convoluted for a train or, having never found her bearings in this city, she was oblivious to the shortest distance between two points. The cab fare was impossible, exorbitant, but she did not care, she needed to get there, though a violent nauseating cramp came when she recalled whose money was funding the ride, why she could spend without worrying, for now.

From the corner of eyes cast violently upon the cement cracks, she caught a vintage baby-blue car that slowed down beside her, rolled leisurely until she kept on walking. Peter always said *keep on walking. Whatever you do, no eye contact, k?* She watched the tires outlined in white rolling without condescension, flaunting shining silver centers that protruded out like alien eyes, jerked up to see a cab driver peering under his pancake cap and rapping at the glass to get her attention, gesticulating madly and finally slamming on the brakes.

The door creaked with something like class, as a butler might announce a personage of unknown importance, making more noise in proportion to the obscurity. "My window broke, no roll down. You Stella?"

She almost shrieked. She'd only "ordered" a cab a few times, after the first instance when the lady who drove her tapped on her phone the whole time, swerving around an obstacle course of humans who materialized in the mid-city street as if to make her trek a torture. Clutching Jason's head, she stepped back, as if automatically admiring the curves and the chrome of the Corvair, which bore remarkable resemblance to a toy version in dad's basement. She leaned into the elegant vehicle and Jason gave a dry cry as the driver, slinking with dramatic relaxation into his tipped-back seat, called out "Western Avenue North Western 7070?" She tried to double-check the address on the paper but flustered fast and yelled back "Yes!" And then, as the car entered the endless asphalt river, "I thank you very much." "Happy, very happy. Every day a good day." He tried to coax the tone toward a lilt but the words came out reluctant, stiff. She pulled the veil over her eyes and tucked the edge under Jason, unbuttoning her bra and awakening him with her nipple and tensing her teeth until he took the first slightly painful pull, crying still through the milk gulps, after which they could both breathe easier.

After several sharp-turn, weaving blocks, they crossed into a section of the city where the traffic lights were not working. Drivers alternately waved others across awkwardly and asserted the noses of their cars across. A white van without license plates kept the horn down without a break for a good five minutes as the other metallic fish, one by one, parted for the bloated whale who tapped his central knuckle repeatedly and then raised his middle finger from the dead.

"Did you hear what I said?" the driver asked. She hadn't. Her hands peeled layers away from baby's face. "I say make your arm into a seatbelt for baby." The Corvair steering wheel, lined with leather, spun beautifully, hypnotically, as the car swerved and circled the front right tire, swinging the back end around counterclockwise. As a thump sent the car on its side, Stella clamped her forearm around Jason, jutting her elbow out to fend off whatever the terrible force would send her way. The dense scent of oil and exhaust, the flittering light as the capsule flipped over, the choked noise of a scream that came from her but seemed to beckon or warn from elsewhere, as if she hadn't authored the sound but a wheezy, metallic fury from elsewhere had injected its awful arrival.

When she blinked she was belted on the elevated end of the capsized car, with Jason dangling. He was not harmed. Her shoulder was hot, flesh burned by where the tightly wound strap chafed at her skin and rubbed the bone like a manic shoe shiner. Her washed-out navy Milwaukee Hardware bag, a duffel she'd used since childhood lake trips, was a deflated clump discarded like a corpse, the contents scattered in a makeshift triangle. Even as hands above reached to hold her in place, as the driver tried to help her legs down, swung them around and then patted the bald egg tip of his head before he felt the thick hair over his ears and grinned and breathed an *I'm still here*, she watched another hand the color of chalky charcoal, dark but dusted in a trillion specks of white, reach for the Roman Missal that had flapped out its wings, flipped atop the gutter wrappers, what Nonna always called street lint.

"The Lord shall save!" said the man, whom she — suddenly standing upright through the sideways car — saw. He wore a smart, black woolen suit with thin pinstripes of light. The legs and arms were all too long. He held high Nonna's black book, the red-edged miniature Roman Missal. Under high cheekbones in a narrowed face, concave dents looked like eyeless sockets and his regular eyes were shielded by sunglasses. A woman in scrubs with massive eyelashes motioned for Stella to "Give baby here," and she did in order to scramble upward through the sprain, heels shoving off the passenger headrest, up against pains that ran from her toes through her leg and did not stop until it spread, throbbing, like a hot spider web against her abdomen. Ovary. One leg out, she felt weightless as several hands, all of them firm, lifted and then lowered her onto the crosswalk white line.

"Witness this, you who believe! We say on Sundays 'The Lord shall save!' but today we need no hope of *shall*. The Lord *has* saved this true believer from the mortuary on Division. Doesn't matter," he squinted at the print, "that the Word is too small to read unless you got goody-goody lenses. Don't matter if it's Roman or Greek. Without the Good Book they'd all be limp, strapped onto the ambulance stretcher for one more joyless ride down the strip so the doctors can diagnose cause of death: *trauma to the heart, the brain*. Always the same. Nobody adds, even in fine print, *Adam's Fall* as the first reason."

At *ambulance* Stella took back her baby, nodded and shook her head at the nurse, and lunged through the gathered crowd — some two dozen stood shoulder to shoulder, except for the vendor in his wheelchair beside an unharmed barbeque stand. Famished, she tried to do two things at once — grab back her grandma's missal and get a hold of a barbeque sandwich. Quickly she threw down a five like a gambler and retrieved one of the warm aluminum rolls. Broke a bit for Jason who was slumped. She was scared. Felt his neck pulse. Still there. Ambulance. Listen. Police. Questions. Admitted. Tests. Safe side. Hide. Need to get out before all that. She turned without waiting for change and, amazed that her right hand did what she told it, disrupted the man who was making her a witness, patting her shoulder when she took the book, her pursed lips managing a cheap grin. "A testament to invisible angels, bending their backs to save us from these streets!"

"Seems God gave us more reapers than angels." The nasally, phlegmatic voice was a woman's whose short height almost hid her behind the crowd.

"Angels of death aplenty," said the man, nonplussed. "Why his messenger spared you I can't say! You should be dead. But who shouldn't. I say," he said through shining teeth so clean they looked lit from within.

After shaking his head he tossed it back, and let out a laugh. "God assigned his angels a death to folks who need more help than you, sister. You still smoking them menthols like they oxygen tubes. I'll be burying you soon if you don't quit." He straightened his suit and continued. "Should've been a cardiac arrest, oh yes — oh yes, the old cardiac arrest! Put your hands behind your back. You're under arrest! And God's the jailor."

For all his promises and contrary sureties, Peter would have been in jail by now. Had he lived. Better dead? Doubt it. Stella, halfway down the block, pulled down her blouse to be sure she wasn't naked. If you could see my soul my *sins* — why always when she rubbed elbows with others their way of wording was so easily absorbed? — my soul so undercooked you'd vomit that special recipe right in front of the crowd.

The last thing she heard the man yell, a bellow that ricochet from the bricks that laddered her eyes up to the sky: "Some He saves, some He damns, and which among us knows who's who?!"

The time dad ran a Sunday sale and it turned out the kielbasa had salmonella. Nobody came to their store for a month. Nobody died, but nobody came. Damned kielbasa. The more he lowered prices on the sign the fewer people came. Fear that cheap always means crap.

398

Somehow she had also snagged the baby's Cheerios and her purse already had a water so she left the contents of the duffel on the ground. Her dad's address was written on the tag. Send the body bag back empty. Andy's gun. Nothing could touch her. The blessing of being able to die. Running round the corner walking dead out of sight. Jason's sling exactly intact, hadn't sunk a stitch in the accident, steady though she pressed ahead reckless, the ache of his weight offset by his warmth which bled and tingled lightly through her body. Sinking not a stitch though she went about reckless. Sinking down, on her knees, begging death.

Baby Orpheus. Blues for Orpheus. Orpheus, baby.

Two blocks away, nobody behind, she cracked open a gas station door, hand behind her back, and slipped in. Unfolding the faded directions she set them down on the counter, pushed them through the three-inch tray, and bought a scratch-off called Lost Causes. As she scraped the edge of Abraham's face across the cheap silver that colored the penny she chewed the barbeque, desperate for every distraction, and asked the long-necked clerk for directions.

"Duct broke," he said, when she shivered. "Nobody free to fix today. Sorry." He patted the multicolored Mexican sweater he wore. "One of my customers let me borrow. Anyhow, you are close. Two blocks that way and left at the lights. Light isn't working. Watch out."

As soon as she reached the lightless crossroads she again unfolded the enigmatic instructions she had folded and unfolded compulsively since she departed Milwaukee, double-checking that the creases had not erased the necessary next steps and the address. A tilted street sign slung with gym shoes and the wrapped-around red ribbon of a helium balloon told her where to go — down what appeared to be an alley. A jagged line of identical duplexes, weary and wearying, wore brown shingles above their off white sides, eyes half open (blinds or drapes almost all at half-mast), the remains of their glassless windows shattered long ago, harmless under her hurrying feet. On fogged glass, in another era's regal lettering, For Decent Ho — s at Decent Costs. Hopes. No. The wholeness of hope flapped against all decency, took to dizzying flights. Homes. Decent homes. The condemned but still occupied houses (in three of the windows women looked down on her, sipping and smoking and hanging laundry from a makeshift nylon line) exhaled the dankness of utter dereliction (one of the women had little balled-up tissues in her nostrils) and Stella looked over her shoulder at the street where hope comes to die or fly.

Without meaning to she'd been fleeing — bolt fast — and had to backtrack to the building marked 770, a red brick storefront defined by a sign that said *Pale Beer Here* and, ballooning from a cartoon policeman whose buttons burst over his beer belly, raised a chalky bottle on high, exclaimed *First for your Thirst!*, bent back at a steep slant. On the concrete window ledge that crisscrossed two Ionic columns whose tops were curved with what looked like the elegantly wound bodies of serpents, etched below an awning that kept it so hidden a passerby would be hard pressed not to mistake the church for an old tavern, a thoroughly oxidized copper historical plaque proclaimed The Blood of the Lamb, Established Year of Our Lord 1917.

When she pushed with the heel of her wrist the thick bronze door with three rectangles did not give to her push with the heel of her wrist and then the ball of her shoulder. No hinge screech from infrequent use or from the arduous demands of the passage. No movement at all.

Turning, she found another entrance where the window well would be, this one a beaten bronze, thoroughly scuffed, propped open by a brick that had fallen from one of the window ledges above. The parking structure on the Southside of Milwaukee demolished last year because a block of concrete killed a child passing under, pushed in a stroller by the mother who was put on suicide watch for a week after she survived, shoulder-wounded and shocked, unresponsive when family and friends asked after her. Stella looked up. The red brick building, some seven stories high, did not dwarf you like the Sears Tower but rather directed your eyes up beyond it, ledge by ledge up the building that at first she thought a two-story affair, a back-alley storefront shack and nothing more, my eyes so sunk what else am I missing, but above the illicit embrace of incongruous Ionic columns and boarded-up plywood a symmetrical series of storm-cloud gray entablatures kept their old, skyward offices. Windows, busted either by anger or time, bullets and fists or gravity, waited to be filled or fully hollowed out. The black metal fire escape was taped off, charred, defunct. Burn marks left by bursts of blue orange suggested that this too should be leveled, but a single bulb flickered off and on from the topmost floor, and a hand scattered ash down upon the lily plants that bowed in the window well next to the entrance, desperate for the light that barely filtered down between the cluster of buildings that kept the church obscure.

Stella saw above the door a fresh and unrefined stroke of red paint that marked the place like Passover, but the record of past faded scarlet and claret that marked the decades like sedimentary rock, but horizontal instead of vertical. The illustrated Bible of childhood. How she and her brother gravitated to Exodus — the weirdly graphic picture of babies impaled by Pharaoh's police (in the illustration his men all wore officer's blue uniforms), who licked their lips as the spears removed the surreptitious crop of children that threatened to mock the ruler's might. There was something satisfying about the black-and-white contrast, the smiling infants and the murderous goon squad. Even now. Sometimes painting morality's finer shades meant covering over the easy cruelty — obvious to all but the self-styled refined.

She looked at the funeral invitation. There was no time change from Milwaukee to Chicago. Why was no one arriving? Firming her lips and constricting her throat, she threw out a tone that was tender but loud. "Am I here? Is this where I belong? Peter Clavier. His funeral." She half anticipated another widow rocking another baby he left behind, as he'd been blunt about his past looseness and the possibility that another child of his was alive but unknown. She strained in the dream-gray twilight hallway, hearing no steps and seeing no long line of mourners attracted by the perfect spectacle. But after she rounded the first turn in what felt, obliquely, like an underground catacomb, she searched in vain for skeletons lining the sides, for unnamed graves scraped on the wall.

Then a shadow stepped forward, his uniform illumined by a shock of light let in through another direction, as whatever electricity the building contained was not in use here. The guard had cold, coal-piece eyes, but when he saw her they lit fast, went warm, anticipated her questions and lostness.

"You?"

"I'm — this here's his baby —"

"— lady for the day, came in the back way? My condolences. World's chaos. Whatever can go wrong can, for some, it seems. I'm sorry, ma'am."

"Well we didn't do nothing to bring it about." Her voice was a whisper that slipped through her throat. Terrible constriction. Like contractions.

"Not my place to say. Anyway. Folks were out here not five minutes ago, hands over their eyes, preacher spitting in that barrel when I said I hadn't seen a single woman. Showed me your picture from the paper. But I," he grew shy, his tone tenuous and mild, "I already seen your picture in papers and in the station. You're the widow."

It came out not a question. When he watched her crows' feet cleave to her skull. She could feel them there, strangely protective, talons hiding eggs from prey. A mimicry of Mom's signature irritation that she'd felt, recently, form on her face with a frequency that was all humiliation. "It's the safest place in the city today, Ma'am. Why I'm stationed here. We, I'll take the liberty to tell you, received a few threats, likely — almost definitely — false alarms, but . . . you're the widow. Officer Evers is waiting inside for you. He'll escort you to your seat."

"We weren't married," she confessed, as the radio static snapped and he muttered incomprehensible secrets into the ferrying airwaves.

"You loved him."

"Don't go easy. Path down fast. Back up hard as hell. Love. I don't know. I wouldn't dare claim so," but the syllables of her words disappeared as she spoke them and he asked, "I'm sorry, say again?"

The tremble under her eye died replaced by rare despair, wrinkles reflected in the dark sunglasses he wore like a corsage on his chest.

His smile creased fast into a pained grimace. Motioning over his shoulder, he turned, about-face, and let the emerging officer take over, tip his ballistic helmet before leading her to a brown door.

"Funeral's begun," he said, and as she could see the questions he kept quieted — how in the world could she be late? — she mouthed, blushing, "Missed train, accident. I can't —" she released one violent cry, cut it short. "Believe."

He nodded. When she didn't move he said, "We'll wait here until whenever you're ready. Take your time."

All at once the rush of the hours, the single-minded fear she'd not get here that frayed the map of her weary mind — all at once her face went flush and she felt the saltwater cleanse her eyes.

The door's mullioned windows contained colored glass pieced together into a shattering mosaic of red shades that grew brighter and impossibly more intense in proximity to the glossy cross cut and culled from the dull mullion. She was breathing harder and stayed at the threshold to pull slow lungfuls into a chest that creaked and tingled until she exhaled so hard her breath shook the door. As he had come to do since his father died, Jason slept with his mouth hanging open, spittle dripping from his parted lips and discoloring his shirt with a dampening river.

The first thing she saw inside was a woman in a posture painful to look at. Her neck was craned at the casket, open but obscured to Stella. She had made up her mind on the train to avoid any eye contact with his corpse. Corpse the same shape and fashion as a body but not — no more — a man. The only person she would have wanted to meet was Peter's mother, who in spite of her estrangement with her only living son would have surely still come if she were not dead. She would keep what Nonna called quaintly "custody of the eyes" — keeping, thereby, everyone at bay. How many here blamed her for his death. All. None. Take a poll.

She slipped into the pew as if for Sunday service.

No need to reconcile with his passing. No need for a second sighting. She had seen enough to scare her through two lifetimes. The medicine the doctor prescribed made her nerves fuzzy but failed to win against the night's panic attacks. Since the C-section she barely remembered, mind-altering drugs felt familiar, fitting, needed for living. The dose of hydroxyzine the doctor had given she had doubled on the train ride down. Safe for baby, still suckling plenty, though surely her anxiety passed through the milk. She could curl sideways in the pew and fall asleep with her knees to her chest. She had waited, last week, in another pew, an hour before the priest arrived, clicking his hearing aid on as he sat, hearing her number and name her wrongs, a wresting that put her in mind of Jacob who slept afterward on a stone. "Forgive me father it's as if I don't believe. Or maybe, I'm not going to get this right, I can only posit God *as if.*" He did not say *well why are you here if you have no belief, if you've lost your faith?* She was not certain he made out what she said. Again she said again at the end of the confession she was not sure he heard. "Forgive me father," — she shouted, "It's *as if* I *don't believe.* I have no faith that I know of, now, or if I do I do not understand it."

Jason awake was all colic. O to be hardly ever awake. The doctor had said: be at peace; the hydroxyzine will not harm him. The priest had said: "Go in peace; your sins — do you hear me? — are shriven."

Drowsing — the drug was mere material. What she wanted was what Helen gave in Homer's poem to Telemachus. A drink that could numb more than your nerves, more than your neurons — could unwind the strands of sorrow that wrapped their tendrils around your heart.

Suddenly her chin snapped up. I'm here. Where? The wood of the pew looked out-of-place, new. If the flipped car had killed her she would have no spine. The resurrection of the dead. She averted her eyes from Peter's casket, let Nonna's mantilla fall around her eyes.

Through the holes in the incensed veil she saw drops of blood splattered everywhere; she shivered although she was hot when she found with relief that Jason's face was brown and unstained and fast asleep. Just refracted red light from the glass. The doctors said his heart was whole. They would call on Monday with the blood lab findings, but should her baby show any strange symptoms, she should find the nearest urgent care. Like he knew — he did! — his dad was dead.

She pushed back her veil just far enough to peek about and find her bearings. The entire floor was covered in red carpet, but the fabric that ran down the aisle gave off a richer shade than anywhere else, and the slight incline of the basement floor (she could see the pipes covered over by cloth; she'd nearly tripped on the open drain near the front of the room) made the carpet climb, ascend, and spill over the altar, so that what was trampled on by the congregants' feet became, as it rose, a red-wine pour permanently poised. But it split like tributaries through each of the aisles in a subdued but not at all muted shade that offset and accentuated the scintillating center. Precious silk turned to blood.

She stared at the Reverend revering the coffin; he hummed between a sermon he'd given here often: "Truly, truly, I say to you; except a kernel of wheat fall to the earth and die, it abides alone, but dying it bears much fruit."

The choir gowns stopped swaying and their occupants stood with folded hands like acolyte angels at attention.

An unprepossessing plain gray suit that silvered in the light, well pressed so many times that — Peter told her when he went through the legend — whatever irons and chemicals the dry cleaners tried, they no way could nix the mold of the body that had worn it so well, so long, so old, that the suit would fill out without him in it. She resisted as optical illusion the sense that the tail stretched out and lifted him heavenward like Nonna's apotheosis paintings stamped in her brain since she could first see. His body leaned forward, his arms stretched out as if to catch himself in case of a fall, but he sustained this posture for the entirety of his sermon and presumably his life. One of Uncle's eyes was hidden behind his lid, so all that looked out on you was red-veined white until all at once its beam would fall, aimed like a grapeshot of God at someone who would squirm, sit up straight, remove a triangular, laid-back leg from a relaxed knee that now knows not the hour, trembling a little with a readied attention. This even though he couldn't see through it, or maybe because you could see he was half blind, the Adam's apple sagging, extended, well-accented by the scars of a surgery, but the lines ran in symmetry with the tie that he'd tried two times to stuff behind the buttons but protruded again over his slim chest, the pattern a swirl of purple stars and azure suns announcing end's nigh. He pulled the pocket square out of his suit, blue with stippled rows of white from which you could conjure sundry constellations, dabbed thrice at his dried lips, wiping the ashy flecks away, and licked them with a saxophonist's suavity before his mouth opened in a cosmic roundness like the bell of Gabriel's horn.

As he summoned the music his visible tiredness, the bent wobble of waking night exhaustion, gave way to a church organ's verve. He switched off the dampened microphone and waved aside its warped wire neck.

The voice that came out surprised him also — an asphyxiation reversed: breath brought back into a body that had lacked it. It shook his shoulders; it rattled the poorly-set, punched-out windows. He looked up, waiting for the colored glass to fall, waiting without worry for the world to crash, to come at last to its tympanic end. But the cut glass rattled in its panes, the elongated pieces stayed stuck in their frames.

"The words of the Preacher, the son of David, king in Jerusalem: 'Vanity of vanities, saith the Preacher, vanity of vanities; all is vanity. What profit hath a man of all his labour which he taketh under the sun? One generation passeth away, and another generation cometh: but the earth abideth for ever. The sun also ariseth, and the sun goeth down, and hasteth to his place where he arose.'

"Now. Ain't nothing been promised to me or to you. Mind this. Not another millisecond, sister. Today I stand here, erect and loud-mouthed; tomorrow I lie in the next casket rolled out, quiet as a country midnight. Amen?"

"Ayman —"

"Don't sacrilege me with a *Hey Man*. Give it to God!"

"Amen!"

"*That's* right! So let me say straight off something you might, I believe, be surprised to hear. You've heard me so many times, some of you, you won't might for a minute believe it. But given why we're gathered here, the death of my nephew, a genuine genius, I guessed it right to set the record straight so he can stand his own man.

"But before I go do that, I got to tell you who it is you're hearing speak, and I got to tell you who to give the glory if, turns out, what I say's passable. I ain't a genius, ladies and gentlemen. Nothing that follows will be original. If you're looking for genius, someone who can see into the atoms of the Mysteries and name them, well, I'm bound to disappoint you. You would be better off bounding out now. Bow down and pay your respects and head out. I mean it. I'm afraid for whatever reputation I've garnered of being — so some say — a master persuader. Most all that's worthwhile escapes my mouth is just a footnote of a footnote on the infallible and sometimes, life proves, unspeakable, Word. Given us out of God's own mouth. But last time I checked, I ain't infallible. Last time I checked — let me keep you in check, before you get a too big head — you, my friend, wasn't either. No intellectual, not a wordsmith. I can eke out eloquence — at best. At best. Not original. Not a genius. I pray God when I die He might dare call me a Christian.

"But just a word in my defense before I push you to doubt my sanity: sometimes what we need to hear, Amen?"

"Amen, *preach*, let me hear it!"

" — is not the titillating, easy-uplift word, the flashy and newfangled up-to-date verb, but rather, ma'am, the ancient adages, old-fashioned proverbs matched to each particular suffering, a Verse for every replayed curse, our age-old agonies not so different, turns out, than our ancestors' across the centuries.

"Now how many here have had a friend come in your house, scratching his head and slack-jawed like, heavy with burdens heady to bear? It's late, the eleventh hour, and you done taken your melatonin, wishing your melanin made for a darker pigment, darker than pitch, so he might think you a ghost. Cause you may as well be, hear me, a ghost. You long ago stopped looking like the living. But you hold out your hand and pull out what's polite — the handshake, the have-a-seat, the something-to-drink? He stares at a spot on your living room table that he can see but apparently only he, because he's looking long at something really ugly. He says 'I ain't looking for no cup of water, like I don't have a tap in my own damn kitchen. You could serve me up ten tall glasses and I'd be no better off than I am right now — except of course it's a small daily soothe to relieve yourself, I'll grant, I'll grant.'

"He's ornery, now, and you get the water anyway, to dilute the drinking he's been surely doing. When you clack the cup on the edge beside him, he starts searching every crow's foot around your eyes, every lipid in your heavy-hung cheeks for a pinch of skin that can spare some sympathy. But — and you suspected as much lately, the way you drifted and said *uhuh* on a phone call without hearing a word whoever was saying. And here you go point at that cup a water, 'cause it turns out that cup is all you got. Can't serve up as a late-night snack the burnt-out heart you thought was still ticking. Can't hardly see your friend's suffering through eyes that too long squinted at gnats — ruined their eyes — who seemed worth the crazy chase.

"Now Somebody — and I hope you know him — said the eye is the lamp of the body, amen? But your two vacant lanterns that wouldn't sell at an estate auction — no not even, hear me, at the Gun N' Pawn down on Bond St. across from Chicken Shack — I say your lamps ran out of virgin oil long ago, dipping and double-dipping in day old grease fried a hundred times, because you spent your virgin oil on a trillion little trifles, little trials you mocked up for yourself, erecting judge and jury from the dust like you was God making Adams from the clay. But it got away. Oh, Lord did it get away from you now.

"What's real? It's a question we got to ask with care, because we all got a knack for makin' life into a whole puppet show of marionettes. Think we lookin' at a real person and all the time we just makin' up little men, fakin' up little women in our mind. Set 'em up and make 'em dance by the pulleys of our fears. So we follow this or that phantom in a fit a passion. Dress up our crazy chases to the nines, like a series of mistresses we know we can't marry but we figure — am I right? — ways to tarry, ways to make the affairs last years, yes I said *years* of nights."

"Reverend, reverend, take me away."

"We already lost! Hear me! Let's get back hold of the parable, please.

"Then allasudden — Knock knock. Who's there? It's your *real* friend, fool. And you been wasting your time. The thing about pain is, hear me, pain may be *one* in that nobody can evade it, in that whatever form it assumes it hurts us, but pain comes in a million frequencies. A hangover headache is easier to soothe, to see, to save, than a convoluted torment that comes off as no trouble at all but is keeping our friend here wide awake from twilight to sunrise turning and tossing and twisting the sheets into a passionate mess as he makes love to dread, to anxiety, to despair, these expert immaterial whores. Saying he hates it but calling out for more.

"Or your friend knocks at eight p.m. — he had the manners not to see you in pajamas — with a son who got shot too young. What's that? Oh. I see. Hmm.

"All sons shot before their fathers die, they say — 'it's a tragedy' — too young. What if all sons that die 'too young' left this place at the precise right hour, not to say predetermined, but He promises not a sparrow descends to its death — shot by a BB-gun kid for fun — without the Father's permission. I can't comprehend some long division by which a sparrow shot down falls without the deep permission of God, as if only the sparrows are in his will whose organs finally fail in old age. Because that amounts to an absentee Father, farming his children out to a hired slum landlord. It amounts — let's do the math, son — to keeping him on the sidelines a lot, keeping the best Player, the Prime Mover, bound and gagged and blindfolded when the time to kill comes. Because there is, after all, my brothers and sisters, a time to get killed. Quoheleth says there's a time to kill and a time to die. Somebody's time will always come. To *get* hit, to cease, to get cut off. But please let's not say 'cut short.' Hear me. Such is not to be spoken by a true Christian. For Christ himself got both 'cut short' and not. For He gave himself more than he was taken. This ain't some hairsplit of theological niceties, like how many animals Noah brought on the Ark. This cuts at the heart of *ev-er-y-thing*.

"Listen. You hear me?"

"We here! We hear!"

"Let's bring it close to home. When dozens is killed in Chicago every weekend you'll grant, I would guess, we got to *do* something. It sure ain't enough to have tea with your auntie and pray grace before you sip and sit back. It sure is true — and I'll tiptoe through softly so as not to have to hear, come Monday, from half the congregation how I gave this party or that short shrift — that some policy or other cuts back on murder. That law has power to slow the killing. That man has power to make a law. But there's a law that's prior to all. A *primordial* law. And *that's* the law that anticipates and applies perfectly to every scenario, every soul, with — Amen? — transcendent equity. That ever has been, is, and ever will be. Hear me? Hah.

"Still we balk. For one is taken and one is left and we see, as real, only the pain of the leaving. Why'd the time come for this one, not that one? Why am I, with my suitcase full of sins, still walking these city streets when my son, who outdid me in every manifestation of faith, has been favored by a bullet to the spleen? We can't help putting the Maker on trial. Old as Job. Get a job, preacher! 'How, Sir, if all your children *are* your children, can you so slight some and elevate others of your so-called sons, Sir?' I know you hear yourself in this voice. I know I speak for all of us here. Amen?"

"So be it!"

"I confess."

"A sinner I am!"

"'How, God, can you bid us call you just when you distribute your rewards with such reckless unevenness?' Your will is above what can be reasoned. Ah, yes, the easy equation — the infinitely convenient solution. But man. I don't know about you — sister, sit up, don't slouch in God's house — I fear such a God like I'd fear a tyrant who fashioned himself above the law, his *whatever* word a *codified* code of morals and commands that change on a whim. Damn. So here's where we are then. Back at the beginning? Deserving of death, so that a day's life is already all gratuity.

"Grace — amen — is gratuitous. Meaning free. Freely given. And so, in this way, if God makes unequal gifts to children who are all, equally, His, can we really rightly resent it, take for a mistake the roundabout way he evens us out — makes it so not even a one of us begins at a divine disadvantage, starts setback from seeing, with faith, one day, His face? If a gift is a gift it must be given gratuitously. Given any other way, it's a gift no more. Last time I checked ain't nobody here won or earned a paycheck amounts to such and such decimals, tabled accounts of each deed's especial grace. You followin' me or am I losing you now? Likewise, I surmise, not a soul in this place has received a tax sheet from God that shows all his deficits laid straight out, where you should have paid when you withheld. But because we ain't seen them don't mean they ain't real. And He'll show us the math of his mystery only after we pass from the kind we use to get by on this uneasy earth. You follow?"

"Hmnn. Hmm. Hmmn."

"Listen. Sit up straight. Show your respects to the dead we here for. So long as the Lord deprives no one what he's owed, what is due to him in the measure of justice, you cannot tell me God is guilty of injustice. The measure with which He measures ain't meted out before his children gasp their last. Whatever's still loose he'll bound in time. Beyond time. His Eternity, will never run out. But one day, our time will.

"Now here I am, standing scared, at the corner of digression and indiscretion. When we get verbose on the things of God we risk the ditch at every little twitch. Add a word here, your truth turns to babble. Exaggerate this attribute, and you may satisfy your hearers who're convinced the obscure is suddenly clearer, but you've lost the fact that some things, finally, are willed to be hidden, are better for us if they be black ink written on a black earth. A terrible mystery. Transcendent obscurity. You hear me? Deliver me from being inscrutable, God."

"You're not inscrutable, Pastor, not yet."

"Peter would have us be very precise. To follow the nuance without hastening to judgment. So lest we get lost in the usual conclusions — that this appeal to the inscrutable actions of the Creator is either an easy but ultimately unsatisfactory get out of jail free card played when the believer sees that he's got too big for the britches he's been wearing since birth, that what passes for the name of 'inscrutable Deity' is another name for — God help me — 'Non-entity.'"

"God help us all!"

"Or, even if we don't go so far as 'Non-entity,' we can get a hold of, with the other hand, a strange and troubling contradiction: that the God who put in us the want to know Him hides Himself to play hard to get. To be sure, Scripture gives us God as Lover, let Lover be one of his Holy names, but a true lover teases only to unveil, always to take away what hides piece by piece, until we arrive at bliss, at peace, whereas there's a real temptation here to see the Lord as sustaining that cruelty and keeping it coded eternally. Saint Paul had something to say about this. 'Now I know in part; but then shall I know even as also I am known.' Damn. If it wasn't canonized in the Good Book I'd worry such a claim was blasphemy — stoked in the furnace of infernal ambition. But do you realize what this means? It means when we say 'inscrutable' as if the truth were lost once and for all, at that moment we forget, in our pride, that it's rather our corruption that blurs the vision with bad prescriptions and leaves us certain that those who talk of 'God and his ways' try to throw the wool over our eyes. One day — I do hope, not dare, not overbold, not with arrogance, but still I do, daily, with all my heart and mind and soul — I hope — one day He will so purify my heart's eye that I'll know even as I am known.

"Now: 'Preacher,' you say, 'you tossed out the script. This is a funeral, not a Sunday service of three hours and some — still counting.' So let me ransom the time. Let's get back on the train track, shall we? We scaled the tallest hill around here. You can see the whole town from there. But it's easy to forget we're still on comparatively level ground. What Peter's dying means has got to carry more, for you, than it can, for me, today. I can't let us get

412

away with doing our mourning for the one without the many. The despairer who don't know his days are numbered by the sickness unto death. We got to wake up or I've not paid tribute to him, to my," he swallowed hard, "*son* — the only word I could ever use to duly name who he was to me."

He hung his head and inhaled and cried. He waited a long while before wiping his eyes.

The faithful in the front row reached forward to catch him in case he fainted.

"He needs a cup of cool water." A heavyset woman wearing a scarlet choir robe floated across the altar carpet and set a small glass at the edge of the podium. Pastor Cedric nodded, "I thank you," took a sip, spit it out, and said, under his breath, "Lukewarm." He leaned ahead, recovering his form.

"Now what, tell me, is worse than a father or mother holding the dead body of her son who just a week back had smiled in thanks to the midwife — note I don't say the Maker — of life. But I'll tell you, it's easy, what's easily worse. It isn't the father whose son, like Absalom, was in outright rebellion against King David, who could not hear the claims of justice. 'Absalom, my son. My son, Absalom!' What if outright rebellion be not the worst? Because the father has days to reconcile himself to it, to the terrible fact lodged in his artery like a coal-black cluster of emphysematic plaque. He has years to make a cold-war peace with the kid he put through diapers and school, the boy he taught to kneel by the bedside beside him each night with arms lifted up. To not regret all the good he gave simply because there is no gratitude. To not blame himself for the bitter, heavily burdened, intractable boy who brings ruin wherever he works or lives, who wears out lovers like their living souls were pop-up dolls for him to spend his angst against: pleasurably, pleasantly indifferent to their feelings or minds.

"But what about the son who does his duty when he sees you? Who asks 'how is your health Dad' and 'how was your day,' but whose questions are so much mud scraped from some dried-up well within him? Whose bucket dips down and comes up empty, the rope wheel ran out of grease, the bucket dredged up not a drip?

'Cause the fact is and the forecast says there's no inch of water to make his care flow. You see, all the words he says pressed out of a rag that hangs limp o'er the empty pail — oh my, you all look pale! — you all know the kind I'm talking 'bout; some old cloth used for cleaning long ago and, left crumpled, never quite dries out. There's always a fetid bead of water to be found living in the damp musty thing, full of who knows how many deadly amoeba but still passing for a living water. Look next. Soon as the son says his drip-drip-drip duty, as soon as he says them he wipes each one up, gathers each pathetic drip, each recycled life-support droplet, to save 'em for the next duty-bound performance.

"Now. Hear me. Duty, on the level of what's good for a city, a country, is surely superior, surely to be preferred o'er defiance. But who here's been on the receiving end of a duty done with polite nose-plugging? The dude gets the job done but the whole while you can tell he'd rather be tending to hell's rotisserie, turning the damned eternally. The look in his eye as he says, 'Thanks Dad!' means, translated, 'Only a matter of time 'til he's gone. I'd better do my duty while he's here, the old fool.' For the receiver, then, what could be worse than rote manners, passing-time niceties, phantasms in Sunday best, detached from the soul and trotted out like they're the real deal, son. A ruse by any other name, feel me?"

"Warmer, warmer. You're getting warmer."

"Aight son: it's one, two vehicles set you in motion, one of nature and one of grace, and yet now you act like God snapped his fingers and made you appear out of a magic trick. Or better yet, like you are the Mover, the cause, the origin of the breath of life that keeps you breathing, in being at all, even when you done ceased breathing. I brought you into the world and now you spurn the vehicle that set you in motion. Live as if the human father weren't no different than a bull serving his biological purpose and forgotten, nodded to, maybe, lazily, in the field, but only in fulfillment of . . . politeness.

"Here we come upon a complication, and if I didn't fear more that common misconceptions is far more dangerous than speaking imperfectly on something so sublime I'd shut my mouth, close up the casket, and head, good day, God bless, home. Oh but I promise you Peter'd want this said. You all, half of you at least, been here a hundred damn times and you know I'm not inclined to speak for the dead. And Peter's no different for being my beloved. I strictly refrain from making proclamations about the final destinations of the deceased. It does nobody any good and a lot of people a great deal of damage to declare, in arrogance, such special knowledge. Yes, yes, we can say God is inclined to move this or that way, and likely act in such and such a way in such and such a soul's case. He'd do such and such, given your so and so, but that's all guesswork at best, you know? If I make it my office to say 'our brother's in heaven,' I'd better change my business card to Reverend G-o-d, hear me?! At the grocery store: 'Yes, Reverend G-o-d, that'll be $14.40.' At the doctor's office: 'Yes, Mister God, there's no easy way to say this, but given your identity there's nothing I can tell you you don't already know. So: your disease is advanced and you got seven days and six nights to live!'

"Peter, hear me, was a hardheaded kid, hard-knock hard-headed kid from the cradle, the kind that look up at you as babies and wear the face of a total knock-out. And it's a good thing they do, ain't it, 'cause how else you gon bear livin' with 'em? Still, mischief and all, he spent his whole life drawn to the good. Now doesn't that sound like I'm cooking up a saint? Setting aside the infamous allegation against him — unproven, as of yet, and I wish it were famous so that if he's proved innocent it'll reveal through the media to the masses our proclivities to arrive at judgment too, too hastily — there's a million other ways he said no to the good. Ha! Now I have you. I don't mean to say that Peter in some singular way went out of his way to get freed by God from all the deceits and self-deceptions that threaten to offset our proximity to Him. In fact, I'm sorry to disappoint you, dear sirs of the jury, but I'm not saying nothing special at all about Peter, per se. Because everybody is drawn to what's good. Nobody and noplace can take that away. But who, innately drawn to the greatest, executes each day's uncounted choices to climb in a staircase up to Paradise? Now some op-eds is blaming this reason or that for why he's inert and coffin-bound here. But don't let's pay that rabble no mind. Chosen by the father for otherworldly greatness, Peter was a hardheaded Jonah who never was blessed by a whale, I fear, before he heard deep calling unto deep. Only way we could get him to fold his hands is to have him die and turn his body over to the funeral home. Now they arranged a nice pious kid, and at under forty he was to me a boy. But I watched him from the time he first wet a diaper and he had that stubborn streak e'en then, a scream like the cry of Moses before Pharaoh, a scream that said *people, let me go.*

"And here's the crescendo — I'll cut to it now — there could be no circumstance found on any block in any city anywhere, no force, I say, strong enough to cut such a soul away from faith, if he had wanted it. What is this false form of predestination that would say material things could ever have such sway?"

Stella, rocking an irritated Jason — all asleep or all irate! — lurched forward in her seat and bit her lip, so Cedric could surely see.

"That'd be the case if circumstances was the same thing as grace. Life — like all grace — may be a good gift . . . Barring all else, life is an absolute good. But life don't ever exist, on earth, barring all else. Boys and girls is born into circumstance. And in certain circumstances, see, a thing considered absolutely good might become, for you or for me now, bad. See, I been up to the mountain with a saint who set me right.

"Now take the man who did this to my child. Say *that* man's a through-and-through murderer. To take his life is better than to leave it, if inevitably he'll kill tomorrow or tomorrow or tomorrow, a ticking bomb no time could ransom. Woah, am I flying too high? Let's try something all too familiar. Who here brought a purse or a wallet? Hey! Oh my. Look at all that cash. Time to take up a collection, I reckon. Hmmm. But the point is this: if I lit the grill in the backyard later, you wouldn't toss in your money as kindling. No. You cling to it as something good. But if you're getting out of your car after dark, and you had to park far away from your apartment 'cause the evening crowd's gotten rowdy on the corner, and a dude in a mask says give me your money, you give him your money to save your life. Am I right?

"Now God plants each soul in circumstances. And from some stations it's a long road to the White House . . . but let's not lose sight of Heaven. If circumstances may be such as to conspire against some person's being president, ain't *nothing* — no thing — not a thing outside the soul that could prevent him from being in Paradise. Now, some would give us a God whose will is dependent on circumstance and choice. God waits to see what Caius will do with the mixture of vitamins and air quality, number of books in the home, and whether mom is there to help him learn his prayers and wash his ears. Once He sees Caius' free choice — because he didn't know prior how Caius would respond to this circumstance — he *gains* knowledge and gives grace accordingly. Now. Woah. Such a God is dependent on his creature. And so such a God is not the highest can be thought. Such a God is a man-made mockery, and I say to the man who made him up, 'Get behind me!' Amen?"

"Yeah. I hear you."

"Again. Amen."

"Again and again and again Amen. Now. Been mulling on this a long while. Brought it to prayer to be sure the Light scours off as much of my own inventions as can be done in spite of me. I know Peter knew what he was supposed to do. Here. Hear me. If we had police of the soul roaming the streets, patrolling lost souls with a host of dogs trained to sniff out self-deception, here's what would happen, you hear me? Just one sniff at my nephew's heel — dust motes stuck there he shoulda shook off so many years ago. Just one look at my nephew's neck, the way it kinked, enough to convict him. Last time I saw him living I saw by the way he was folding his hands he was hiding he was living he was dying in sin. With a woman. And a son." Cedric took care not to look at Stella. "Didn't say it, but I saw it from the way he put his hands behind his back. Said it to his face, and he threw out a fist, telling *me* I was trying to kill him. With conscience! Well . . . that's some explosive.

"Just one gaze at the ink in his eyes that never dried, a wet well of it, ready to sign off his inheritance left and right, right and left, a single look and the spies of God policing the streets for the sake of sinners, they would have seen, clear as day: the suspicious figure needed arresting. Needed a rescue. To figure out in solitary confinement, cut off from the spotlight for more than a few seconds, bereft of what kisses his woman could give him, emptied of the distractions of changing diapers, taken to some maximum zone of insecurity, like some desert-dwelling monk, well, man, what then? Amen: what sentence would the Word have given him? What sentence? Hear me, for He'd spell it out to you too, or to me. What besides inescapable death? Now what do we do with such a sentence besides say, from the bowels of our souls: my God, save me!"

And Stella, back straight, slapped the scratched wood, shouted *Amen* louder than anyone, waking the woman next to her who was half-asleep on a sequined purse overstuffed with multi-colored cloths. The woman's wrinkles were set, perfectly, with a perpetual smile that gained still greater definition as she saw the baby's repeated spit-ups projecting a pallid, chunky liquid onto the shoulder — her useless, bare black, borrowed dress (the spaghetti straps were so thin it was as if there were not any). The woman, laughing now to herself, pulled tissues from a side clasp pocket. She passed one to Stella who only now noticed the line of saltwater below her eyes.

"Nothing's concealed that shall not be revealed!" Cedric's prophecy came out choked.

She stared ahead at the cross without a corpse while the casket, out of the corner of her eye, carried the corpse that was Peter once away. Her fevered head dizzied in the church which was dank with sweat and creaked as they watched the pastor clasped by a terrifying silence, waiting either for him to fall or for his body to defy the grave and ascend, watching watch out — help him — apoplectic God, stop him, heart-attack, a stroke, what have you — the secret, buried second sight wish — wind of a seraphim's quickening wing, the angel of death not a gremlin reaper but — "Save your servant!" an old man screamed — "Lord let your servant go in peace!" came the response of a half-dozen women, their sung sound something like a supple weave of thread so subtle, so soft, but sturdy as wires, bringing the swinging chariot low where the pastor's head bowed over the lectern like a captain at the stern as if the ship was leaving maps and setting out with argonauts for the unexplored country, bright eyes blinking in the dark.

Someone had shut off the lights. Someone else stood beside Cedric with a Japanese fan, sending wafts of fresh air in tandem with the angel's wings as he started to clap and sing "Swing Low."

When the song died down Cedric rose and limped a little toward the emergency exit then stopped, winded, and turned around, leaning hard on the podium ledge which trembled under his shaking weight so that the Bible nearly slid to the floor but before it did he pinned the book down, then kneeled and looked up with imprecatory eyes — calling down judgment on himself.

The woman beside stood, suddenly, gripped the wood of the pew and made as if to approach the altar, on tiptoe, but, seeing him tremble, she just blew a soft kiss and departed, looking up, shaking her head. Stella followed the woman with her eyes but she could not rise from the hard seat. Several hundred scratched-off sequins decorated the continuous sequence of thin white wisps that kept coming out — like a clown's magic trick from the old State Fair of Stella's childhood, there, where she saw for the first time lost in the crowd Blake — a dream or a destiny it did not matter — buying buttered corn and the red of his mouth against the melting golden yellow caught and fixed her shy stare, and he bit the cob as if he were starving, spirits lifted by the crystals of salt and fully oblivious to the scrappy-shirted girl whose leggings were too wide — they were mom's, because hers were in the wash, her period starting later than her friends', always a surprise and her one good blouse was in the washer, what an embarrassment that she had to wear such mottled, fashionless things to the fair, but she played the outfit off as if punk rock and had caked half a can of spray in her hair, she who would one day — impossible — assume the life of a woman, a lover who in the cliché would become *the one who got away* and as the sunlight kissed the corn and blessed each kernel with warmth of sustenance, leaving him oblivious of the nameless nobody girl who stared and who he duly ignored, to whom he would discover decades later, deliver her whispered adorations in

419

the dusk, in the dark, kneeling in the watery lighthouse, and here he was through the blur of her tears, not in her mind's eye but genuflecting and then catching his knee, pretending it was sore in case anyone saw, sliding with caution into the pew impossible here was the one who had sold her a scam of counterfeit I. O. U.'s — a big bounced check her dad would burn Blake's heart he said, when the fiancé fled, and here, as if the hurt weren't enough, as if the pain came to collect interest, here he was reaching out his hands to hold the baby who was wincing in pain, crying while Minor C's neck veins were widening, bluish, like rivers from a distance, through the scarlet that flushed through his burnt umber face like the Nile at high tide to be heard over the rising wail which ceased as soon as Blake took the child — because of intuition or stupor.

"I've been the whole time outside the door. Didn't want to disrupt, disrespect — do anything that could hurt you more. I heard from your mom you were here," he whispered, and the hot of his breath was oppressive but she stayed, stoical or shocked, betrayed.

"I rushed," his hand covered his chest, all breath for half a minute.

He was dressed for the funeral in a second-hand plaid blue-green shirt smelling of mothballs, a ragged-cuffed blazer as if borrowed from his father almost as an afterthought as he walked out of his house, hair like a mop head full of dirt.

She pulled her veil partly away from her face. "Nonna's," she said, tracing the mantilla whose silken border soothed her more than seemed possible. "She's still alive."

"Beautiful," he said, slowly, then motioned to the blazer's rough cuffs. "Not quite. Half-decent. My father's," then without a trace of irony or vengeance: "He's still with us for all his sins.

"I can hardly see his anymore for mine." His whisper was so faint she had to lean in to hear him. "Forgive me please for all the wrongs the lifetime supply of every single substantial failure I hate I'll fight I'll do anything at all — but especially the *little things* — if you'll let me love you," he stopped.

She could not believe she was spitting these words in whispers — what she wanted to shout. "What in the world it's meaningless, abstractions, okay, empty gesture in reconciliation unless you name specific wrongs. All I gave you, all you had, and that you threw it all away demands an accounting, line by line, not because I'm a bitch but because as the pastor said (did you hear him?) the way down is the way up. A way . . . to justice. Or trust."

He flexed his hand, cracked his knuckles, stretched his fingers as if around a globe. "What. What do you want me, here, to name them. Here?" Bothered and earnest, big-eyed, bobbing up and down with the baby.

She looked around as if in disbelief. "Yes. Yes. Yes. If you're serious. But no not here. No not now. Tomorrow or tomorrow if you're totally serious, seriously showing up and asking for a . . . second life. With me. I can't think straight. We'll have to see."

"I didn't mean to ask anything. I want to be here is all."

Stella's knees wavered and faltered, eyes alighting on the cross without a corpse, determined what she did was not a betrayal: passing the dead man's son like a package to the man who had fled who was rocking the child with care, delicate, scared even, as if he might drop him, Blake, a fragile object for certain but for all that alive, at least, on arrival.

Blake did not object to her condemnatory glare at him as she crumpled, and he did not hesitate, as he turned to mouth *have mercy* to which she responded *on me too* — so she folded her fingers as he cupped the child's head and Jason, lifting his heavy brow like a little barbell above his puffed-in eyes, switched his gaze from Stella to the stranger who held him. As his cries ceased from fear or relief, as Blake, knee-locked, light-headed, off-beat, oblivious, swayed in the front pew for all the faithful and not least the faithless to see, and she covered her eyes with her folded hands as he kept swaying with not only nerves but a will that stilled — as baby squirmed, stretching frantic for his mother — and as her eyes rolled back in a faint she at last saw and accepted the loss of the once indomitable man in the coffin, fists against all, all fists against, and her heart turned to the boy through the door with freshly-grayed hair who swayed sweetly to the chariot swinging, swayed still after the song ended, wanted to be, himself, to be, in whom she could see the lover and father who could be.

The funeral was done. Everyone else had stepped forth from the pews except for Stella, who prayed on the margin of the closing scene. Jason screamed through the shuttered back doors as Blake paced and paced across the hallway planks that seemed to creak in contest with the child whose head sounded as if it might burst, like a bath bubble, upward toward the ceiling. The vigorous shriek brought her peace, faint as it was, and somehow lovely. Peter's closed coffin blocked the door, awaited the hearse and the hollowed-out dirt, the worms, God, writhing against the cold metal, the border of his casket. Blake could touch and taste the burial from his days working cemetery security.

. . .

The sight of the coffin when she went out to exit buoyed her sinking mind back to before, the time when the corpse, cloaked in steel, was still animate, when Peter was running like mad for alderman — a night when he brought her out on campaign. She remembered the way he led a whole block — fifty-some people — down Bond Avenue on a late, sleepy, Sunday night. He rallied the cussing, fussing neighbors — dispirited, like a troop of the dead — to rise against the "tragic accident" — decrying the very term "accident" — "as if there is no intentionality in omission, in negligence, in the recklessness that claims lives daily," decrying too the "dead-on-arrival description of 'tragic death,' it's a soporific, it's a prepared formula like a pharmacy prescription to fool us into feeling, finally — or failing to feel, as it's a pain killer — failing to fail, as if all that goes down goes down in spite of our goodness, as if nothing could have been done to prevent it!" Hearing his tenacious tone she kept her thoughts on tragedy to herself. Like a walking lightning rod waiting to be struck, Peter roused them from their lightless houses, sunken porches, to "cook from the furnace of our wretched race souls that rise up when we'd rather melt down." Throwing his arms and pointing his fingers, twirling and twisting in every direction, he bid them build from the scraps of the accident a makeshift traffic circle, crying out, "We cannot wait for the state to do us justice! Holy Mother State is unseeing the actualities of our existences! We must scrape some semblance of justice from our wreckage, like gleaners looking for silver lining in the gutters, in landfills! If justice means starting with traffic circles made from trash — so be it! Amen?" Little children and elderly men, middle-aged women with stoops in their steps, dragged out the overflowing garbage cans Sanitation had started neglecting when walking the neighborhood was knee-jerk fatal. Even the evening before, after the unknown fool hit Miss Beatrice and ran his wheels at highway speed down the narrow dark night's street, the police had taken an hour to arrive, and by the time the ambulance came the woman who had been walking home from the corner grocer's with a can of cooking oil had become — "how to say it, a rigorous corpse, the commission of omission, the awful emblem of our condition." Peter's soles scraped against a board, a plank sharp-angled into the sky, and he pulled out the nails that threatened to puncture his rubber soles as he ascended, balancing on a crossing of boards, discarded wood and a piece of the hood, a rearview mirror he kicked lightly to the left where it crashed, shattered in the street, though he fast recovered his tentative poise, stealing a smile, showing his teeth.

The neighbors who had gathered tilted their heads as he stared down a Chevy headed straight for him. Half the street lamps blinked. Peter, arms akimbo, did not. The car played chicken but swerved. Staring, as if looking for that young man who'd gone to bed last night for the first time in his life lacking a mother, her as-if-always-there snoring filling the dark room down the hall, lacking the cornmeal chicken she was planning for Sunday brunch after church, lacking her laughter and her temper as she threw (as she was known to) a pot (or two) at his head when he came home after curfew. Stella followed his eyes and found the boy's shadow cast across Miss Beatrice's big porch — the blue boards Peter had helped paint, lit by a security light. Peter climbed the pole the hit-and-run had ricocheted into, the propped-up, decapitated stop sign, the sign the pastor had dragged to the center and squeezed between stuffed green trash cans. Suspended there like a crazed crossing guard, he held his arms out scarecrow fashion, halting traffic with a resigned stare that scared some of the kids to the sidelines, a stare that looked quite close to despair but which she knew was not his blues but rather the strange sleep of his face which hid his will when he steeled it, when he stole inhuman strength as if from nothing.

Satisfied, shaking hands, brushing bits of trash from their bodies, the crowd dissipated into the night. Peter stood there, unmoved, stubborn, staring through the passing cars' headlights beyond his eyes blinking against the stellar light shed from impossible distances that existed, not infinite in fact but feigning a level of measure that defied the mind, the spaces between the cars and the stars, the distance uncrossed by any man, his gaze widened, eerily bold, refusing to blink at what we had made, at what it had come to, the spaces between the stars and the cars, his vision narrowed until the stare she saw there scared her, for it came from someone beyond recognition, a host of fury who fought the world single-handed in the Chicago night, valiant amidst so much violence, yes, but unable to save himself, his crossing-guard arms stretched all the way out as if to say *take me, here I am, take me*, until she risked traffic and ran right to him and pulled at his pant leg, pleading with Peter to please come down. Come down. Come home. He refused to look down.

She had walked, alone, to that place she called home, a stranger in someone else's kitchen, doing dishes with the watered-down detergent, the garish blue neon sinking to the bottom and exploding suds from the scalding water, her fingers scrubbing from the week-old dishes a desperate effort to domesticate the untallied distance that hid her from him. Wringing filthy refuse from the sponge — burnt bread crust forgotten in the toaster, set afire until Peter blew it out, turned into infinitesimal crumbs ocean-cast driftwood that over the decades breaks down, finally, into scattered specks of wet dust — she was not rid of her soaked-up anger. As she watched her furrowed face in the water, a flash of sweat wetted her forehead and she grasped, frantic, the kitchen garbage, throwing up her insides until only bile and then nothing could be retched from her hurting bowels, from miles of convoluted intestines emptied and throbbing all the miles she had walked with him, hurting the soles of her feet, itching and hot, and then a fevered forehead burning her memories until what she'd done was a welcome blur — as if it could not define her future. She let out a sequence of staccato screams, felt the swell of the fledgling baby whose father she sensed could be dead any day. With a wet dishtowel tossed over her shoulder she took the garbage out to the rusted green waste bin like the dutiful spouse she could no longer play.

And the man in the back who now held her baby, would he play or stay when all his cradling, rocking, pacing would not stop the little one's scream, the uncensored ache, please where did it come from, the undying sound she wanted to make as she tried so hard to keep awake?

In the back of the church Blake paced and paced, the narrow narthex emptied of mourners; he crossed the time in figure eights until the baby's crying ceased, stopped his conjoined cycling circles when he found her peering through the walls, through the sharp-tipped lancet window on the door that let out to the hall, she stared across the roseate glass into his blinking, crossing eyes before her life breath fogged the mirror, ashamed, almost, as if, of the smile that showed, but she shoved, anyway, out and through, the heavy door that was hard to move and stood without a single word, waiting for Blake to back away, but the baby raised the sky-blue flap of his outsized sleeve, Blake leaned in, "Shhh," then Jason sighed and stretched and reached, half-awake, for her mouth, for mama, with a clay-brown hand that tickled from her face a full-fledged grin Blake did not dare to mirror, here, where death had been but minutes before, so he looked, shy, at the wall she had crossed, at the dry rooting mouth of the child between them, at the paint-chipped cerulean of the basement ceiling, and her fingers brushed the baby's lips, the little O looking for milk, the open mouth of the man who held him, and she let out an "Ohhh, Ohhh no, Ohhh," followed by a faltering "God," no glass between them any longer.

A shout in the street ricocheted outside, the shatter of thrown bottles breaking: a cheer. "Stop him, stop him!" and she cracked the church door to screams that climbed from some dozen mouths straining "Oh!" and "No!" in unison. "Stop him! Stop him! Crazy. Gone. Complete, headless crazy, *crazy*! No respect for the damned dead." Someone said "Killer!" and pointed accusation in the direction of a held up sign.

From behind the unreadable, washed-out placard came laughter that broke at the end as if choked. Inharmonious moans stirred again, drowned the stranger's sickly laughter and scaled the worn brick tenement walls, honey-colored in the warmth of the sun but dark blue, now, in the afternoon shadow. Pained sounds as from mourning doves, chests puffed out and ready to burst, zig-zagged skyward like the fire escape ladders, suspended stairways that spelled earthbound safety but were populated by ascending climbers. Groans rose with terrible speed, then dropped, suddenly, deadly mute, to the asphalt pocked with potholes and cracks, where the corpse that used to be Peter — face down — had fallen from the overturned casket, faded head yellow like sunflower petals pressed for years in a forgotten book. His limp limbs flung out as if to wave away the culprit. Seven men of varying heights locked stiffened arms around the body, circling, leaning, becoming the border — no definitive chalk outline, no officious crime scene tape. A fly trespassed the human chain, rounded the head of the dead in mad orbit, a pattern of overlapped, perfected ovals, but never alighted or rested there.

Raising his sawed-off picket fence post, the stranger revealed a mouthless face, tight black mask from neck to nose topped by bulging orange goggles, eyes enlarged like a studied insect's preserved in amber for an experiment. Bodies tried to fall to the ground. No room. They rose but kept their heads low. A stray hand yanked back the culprit's hood. The crowd gave a big, baseball game cheer that waved down into a manic boo. His skin was camouflaged thick-pasted green. Shoulders back, clean-cut hair — dark and gelled like a little tidal wave — he stood on tiptoes and broadcast the message, but the wind folded the flapped sides in. Another gust pushed out the rightmost partition. A single word — *Matter* — was all you could see.

Mater misericordiae.

"Call the police," she shot out to Blake. He pointed to a phalanx of uniform blue, far away, at the street's blind end, their shields translucent but scratched — like fly wings.

The stranger swatted and swatted at the crowd, trying to make his way to the body. His placard bent when it hit the necks of the ones who hovered and hung over Peter. They swayed and stayed in locked defiance. When the placard sign bent and broke, dropped, was seized by fingers that ripped in frenzy, the stranger finally started to speak, tried to make his tender voice tough. "Remember this. Remember me. Before you take my life today. I have no guns. No weapons. Just this" — he held the post high before striking the casket, "I'm here to harvest what's rightfully mine," then, when he could not deface the dead, tossed the whitewashed wood aside. "Everything destined to everyone, taken. Hypocrites of the highest kind. Victors as victims of the top pedigree. Give us back what all was looted. Generations. Generations. Make me feel guilty for making you pay what any sane justice would ask any day. As if anyone could know the truth and stay sane. Until they can raise up the stolen bodies, resurrect them, bring them back, we'll have to take some in reparation. Just for safekeeping. Consider it a pledge. An I. O. U. that means a damn thing. Bring everything out here right now, today. Stack it all in a nice little pile, what you all took, here, now. Today. We'll start to tally and balance the takings." What he said next she could not make out but his throaty voice sounded chafed, even burned, as if he had been chewing ashes.

Minor C — his limp disappearing, wide eyes erasing the sag of crow's feet, fingers shaking like a piano player's cramped into jitters after thankless performance, pleasuring the crowd 'til the dawn's early light — put the culprit in a loose chokehold and yelled, trembling, "Help hold this kid! But don't you dare take him, hurt him, kill him, do not you dare! I said help! Help! Put the yoke on me, if need be, my God!" Two or three others took the tall man's feet, tried to fix him in place but failed. Altercations multiplied. "I wish we could talk" — Cedric covered the mouth that bit and licked wildly and spat and screamed — "no doubt you deserve a fair hearing. No doubt I'd say yes to half of your grievances. Who

427

knows, maybe even ninety-nine percent. But that one sliver takes the ring of truth and forges it into a song fit for slaves." The camouflage of the stranger's face, oily with sweat, smudged on C's hands, and they turned an inexplicable maroon. "Still I see in you the same as Adam. Not a separate, alien species. Look at me!" he pulled back the hair and waited for the goggles, now fogged, to clear.

Cedric held the culprit against the church wall. "I don't want to play at citizen's arrest. I got some mourning to do about now. Put the yoke on me, God, what you will." He breathed hard and sighed as if his strength would give way. Somebody screamed "Help!" and C, turning, hit his head on the fire escape step — the lowermost, rusted out, blackened orange rung. "Help!" spread quickly when the crowd saw the gash, the bit of blood on the pastor's forehead. The word got hotter when the ones who said "Help!" did not know why or what they were asking, confusing the officers, still far out-numbered, who were mainly stuck at the far perimeter. A siren, an ambulance heaving ahead slowly, parted gathered bodies with nowhere to go.

"The thing about justice," C went on, "is we don't really want it. Or do we and only *time* — had we but time — ends, interrupts it. We *could* see to it but 'I don't have time.' How much of justice is within human reach but slips 'cause we waste our split seconds on — what? We don't want it. What *do* we want? What we call spending is wasting away. And," — the crowd, all craned necks 'til now, fell back into mumbling, slunk displeasure — "as much as I can condemn, can mock what we spend our days getting and spending too soon, as much as I hate, on the other hand, that hard limit that no one can change — that even when we give *all* we got to bring about dues, we fall far short — as much as I heave, Hercules, against the supposedly set in stone ceiling to see how much it might give, good God, let's thank Him, thank Him, I say, thank Him, we cannot complete God's rectifying wrath. We every one of us ought to be terrified at being held up to absolute justice. But maybe," his cough came like a regret, "that misguided terror is why so many turn away altogether. I'm done," he said, looking lost. "Look at me starting to say what can't be. Saying nothing real loud."

428

A cop broke through a human chain some fifty long feet away and the stranger, the wave of his hair flattened, continued to struggle against the chokehold. He spat when he spoke. You could hear his teeth clack as he yelled loud enough to be heard by the crowd.

"But how can we want it when we don't see what's wrong? The news," his voice, grown nervous, grasped after an argument that seemed to escape him like the zigzagging ladders on all of the buildings. "Stations won't show what's still hidden for fear the people'll have a heart attack."

"I don't," said C, "I don't doubt that!"

"What all was stolen, what all was taken, what all was siphoned, roundabout, from us. By you. By us. By who?" He broke free from the hold but leaned, chest heaving, against the brick before C again made a yoke of his arms. "Peaceful protests," the stranger went on, sinews of saliva spraying from his mouth. "I was there. Killed. I swear it. I was, did. Turned myself in and was told by a head at a desk, I swear it, go in peace. They hide the clips that could make you look ugly. Help you play act the perfect victim. Forget it! Fodder for the truth-tellers, paranoiacs not without reason who cycle that shit on repeat forever and ever, world wide web without end! Lazy easy way out. Escape!"

"We all are tempted to take the path of least resistance, to plod it, lazily, in two directions. Amen I tell you. Black and white answers on too many matters where the truth is — try to chase it — elusive." He twisted his neck and shook his head as the closest cop was kneed on repeat, kicked in the kidney, spat on and hit with the loosened baton from his dismembered belt, pants sagging as they pounded his crotch. Cedric kept the culprit in a hug. The tedium of waiting for a pair of handcuffs bloated what remained of the ingrained patience from the upturned wrinkles of his sweaty face. "The other half of the busted equation? Analyze everything into ambiguity. Always another angle, perspective, point of view that's been left unconsidered. Infinite interpretations, Xeroxed ghosts of the gotdamn truth." The stranger twisted around and stuck his pink tongue out of the mouth hole. "Come here, child. Look at me, son. You're one of mine," and the culprit leaned, like a beaten boxer, into a lanky hug.

"Double-headed sign of the times," C screamed. His voice carried to the far tenement where a woman some seven stories up leaned out and listened from her window ledge, her ear cupped like the tulip petals her elbows crushed as she strained to hear. "Double-headed sign of the times. Drawing margins with permanent markers" — he loosened to let the stranger breathe and quickly tightened his grip again — "where a thin pencil mark would do just fine. Lightly tracing with erasable pencil where we ought to make unchangeable lines. *Make?* As if we could *make* them! Draw out what's already put there, laid out — God — a legible wager." A crack in the sidewalk beneath his heel was green with the growth of rank weeds. He was the one choking the other but you could see he could hardly breathe. "What *we* all took," C continued, wearily. "Whose 'we'? Who's *we?* You really want the judgment — you want it? Of the nations? By God! You want it? You ready to stand before an amphitheater whose seats stretch out into eternity, where all that's thought aloud and in secret and all that's been done, by you, by we, will be weighed for all its eternal worth, the precious and the specious, the good and the vile, sifted to perfection by so many lines of demarcation we could only *start* to see and to say if we squint and lose our vision trying to —"

A brick struck the base of Minor C's neck and he knelt, irate, in unspeakable pain. Elbow out, his palms pressed his spine until he fell and curled, fetal. Another chorus of discordant moans climbed up the buildings and strove to leap beyond their peaks. The towers tightened around the tenements and made the lives they loomed above small, condescending on all of Chicago like the Nephilim of a new age.

At a broken trot a white horse carried a man from the blind alley of the street and he kicked off the Stop sign with that distended from Spanish leather boots. Where police cars and ambulances could not tread the animal entered and arrived, reined back, front hoof held over the gasping culprit. The boots had labyrinthine patterns that arrested the eye and suspended time. You could look all day at the mazes within mazes and never find the destination. The crowd that had sighed at the horse's arrival contorted now as they took in his rider. He was not an officer. He was not an officer. But he wore the officious garb of the police, perched above the compressed bodies with all the indifference of usurped authority that needs to be acted out to persuade. The horse's exhale came out like a laughter.

A little girl in a well-pressed dress — charcoal-colored with a metallic sparkle that reflected whatever light remained after its advent from years away — carefully shredded the stranger's sign into a pile of handmade snowflakes. She shook her head back in big laughter, braids kept in place by frayed rubber bands that looked like gum chewed and chewed forever, worked by somebody else's teeth, the grind of years against the grating day's evil and wound around the child's hair. Her eyes closed as she ripped the words and dodged the hands that reached to hold her. Above her braids electric wires dangled in clumps like varicose veins, meant for ends they no longer served, the High Voltage sign, once orange with warning, bleached so badly it was barely an outline. Lost, hilarious, she climbed a hydrant, balanced on the corroded bolt, threw up the pieces and watched the flakes fly and fall, softly, over the crowd, as her mother ordered "Get the hell down, back, girl, crazy, back! Don't you dare disobey. We're back! Here. *Baby!*" And the girl, with a twirl of her braid, was gone.

Stella and Blake peered out, drew back. She had never seen so much rage in his face and regretted, with something akin to hatred, her instinctual abhorrence of anger. She wanted, for once, the geometries of eyes dead set on something — risking oblivion. "Stupid, right, to try to do something?" Blake had checked, in an earlier frenzy, baby under arm, the other exit, found it sealed from outside. Everything seemed, at once, orchestrated. Conspiracies for minor historians to tell. "Idiotic to play the hero, here," he asked, "Idiot. I'd be. To do something? As if I could when no one else can't?" But he handed her the crying child and shouldered the archaic door wide open. Shaking silhouettes streamed inside. She took hold of Blake's arm, passed back Jason and whispered, "*Back in a minute. No jealousy. See. What's due. I have to. I have to. Watch him.*" Before he could stop her, before he could answer "There is no *have to!*" in fear for her life, she needled through the swift-closing crack and threw herself into the amorphous crowd, a circular confusion of push and pull, people grappling and shoving and shouting, desperate eyes in both directions — quickening closer to, away from the scene.

An officer, young, hardened chest — bench pressed and Kevlar vested — shoulders broad as his shielded forehead, stretched out his arm like a toll blockade as — crack! — a gunshot flicked his visor and another bullet nicked his neck. She pivoted away from the speck of flesh, the cut out excess of overripe peach, bloodied and chewed and left to rot, trampled underfoot by fleeing feet. Her own soles caught on brown-tinted shards of discarded bottles that lined the world's surface like scattered thorns brighter than the snowflakes, dull and wet, now strewn beside them. "I's trying to help you!" he shouted, downed. Something struck her cheek and she ducked. Startled, stuck, she stared, dizzied, wiped off a spat shell of sunflower seed. It stung like hell but drew no red.

The sense of being center in someone's target — the scare stronger than the ache — sent her surging through a line of old ladies whose black lace hats, well-worn but regal, did not veil admiration and anger and an awe restrained by tongues that went tsk when she knelt beside the adamant corpse and curved her arm over the shape, the remains of the man that people still dared to treat like living Peter Clavier. The strong scent of clove that covered his body became a wood smoke fire in her mind, a pyre that could burn through the city, the states, at once against and aligned with the grain.

When, not breathing, she turned up the face — his same sleepy eyes, the likeness, his lips, the mouth still poised to say one last word — her dress swept around him like a past-bloom petal, Empire Blue Butterfly Bush, surrounding a stamen at the dusk of day at the death of autumn when they bring in the flowers, past the frost-windowed walls of the hothouse — to sift and sort, to salvage, and to save the ones that might be, could be, saved.

JOSHUA HREN is founder and editor of Wiseblood Books and co-founder of the MFA at the University of St. Thomas. He regularly publishes essays and poems in such journals as *The Los Angeles Review of Books* and *The Hedgehog Review*, *First Things* and *America*, *Commonweal* and *Public Discourse*. Joshua is the author of nine books, including the short story collections *This Our Exile* and *In the Wine Press*, *Contemplative Realism: A Theological-Aesthetical Manifesto*, and the novel *Infinite Regress*.

www.ingramcontent.com/pod-product-compliance
Lightning Source LLC
Chambersburg PA
CBHW021842010726
47493CB00005B/1513